BEFORE THE BOMBARDMENT

OSBERT SITWELL was born in 1892, the second child and elder son of Sir George and Lady Ida Sitwell of Renishaw Hall in Derbyshire. With his sister Edith and brother Sacheverell he played a prominent part in the literary, artistic, and social life of England in the first half of this century. He was educated at Eton, and after serving in the Great War became a writer. He published over thirty books, successfully attempting nearly every genre—poetry, fiction, travel, criticism, essays, art appreciation, and autobiography. His many friends included both the survivors of Edwardian high society and the most avant-garde writers and painters of his day; he was a knowledge-able patron of ballet, opera, and all the arts, and a world-traveller. He became a baronet on his father's death in 1943, inheriting Renishaw Hall and the castle of Montegufoni in Italy. In his last years he was progressively hampered by Parkinson's Disease, and died at Montegufoni in 1969.

VICTORIA GLENDINNING is the author of *Edith Sitwell: A Unicorn among Lions*, which won the Duff Cooper Award for 1981, as well as biographies of Elizabeth Bowen and, most recently, Vita Sackville-West. She reviews for the *Sunday Times* and other papers, and is at present working on a life of Rebecca West.

OSBERT SITWELL

Before the Bombardment

INTRODUCED BY
VICTORIA GLENDINNING

'Is it Winter the Huntsman
Who gallops through his iron glades,
Cracking his cruel whip
To the gathering shades?'

Oxford   New York

OXFORD UNIVERSITY PRESS

1985

Oxford University Press, Walton Street, Oxford OX2 6DP

Oxford New York Toronto
Delhi Bombay Calcutta Madras Karachi
Kuala Lumpur Singapore Hong Kong Tokyo
Nairobi Dar es Salaam Cape Town
Melbourne Auckland
and associated companies in
Beirut Berlin Ibadan Mexico City Nicosia

Oxford is a trade mark of Oxford University Press

Introduction © Victoria Glendinning 1985

First published 1926 by Duckworth & Co.
First issued, with Victoria Glendinning's introduction,
as an Oxford University Press paperback 1985

British Library Cataloguing in Publication Data
Sitwell, Osbert
Before the bombardment.
I. Title
823'.912[F]   PR6037.I83
ISBN 0–19–281903–8

Printed in Great Britain by
Richard Clay (The Chaucer Press) Ltd.
Bungay, Suffolk

CONTENTS

INTRODUCTION

By VICTORIA GLENDINNING

OSBERT SITWELL was a prolific writer, and of all the books that he wrote *Before the Bombardment* was his own favourite. He left a request that it should be buried with him; he was cremated, and a copy was duly placed in the urn with his ashes, which are buried in a cemetery near Montegufoni, his castle in Tuscany.

He was in his early thirties when he wrote *Before the Bombardment*, and it was his first novel. He had already published books of poems and short stories, but no full-length fiction. This may be one reason for his affection for the book; another and more important one may be that the writing of it, and its success, helped him across a difficult junction in his life. He and his younger brother Sacheverell had formed a close partnership, sharing a house, friends, and frequent trips abroad. Then in autumn 1925 Sacheverell married, and although Osbert liked and accepted his sister-in-law it was obvious that things could not continue quite as before. Osbert himself would never marry. He had close women friends, and *Before the Bombardment* is proof of that fact that he had understanding and sympathy for women, but his physical inclinations were towards his own sex.

The winter following Sacheverell's marriage was spent in

Amalfi. The brothers had been there together before; now Sacheverell's wife Georgia was with them. Also in the party were Peter Quennell, William Walton, and Adrian Stokes, a young art historian to whom Osbert had a growing romantic attachment. It was not a happy winter, and the tensions became painfully apparent. They were staying at the Capuccini, a hotel high on the crags above the Mediterranean. It had formerly been a monastery, and guests slept in the simple white rooms that had been the monks' cells. The writers of the party worked in their cells every morning. Sacheverell was working on an 'autobiographical fantasia', *All Summer in a Day*; Osbert also turned to scenes of his childhood, and took as his setting a hotel above the sea, like the one in which they were staying. But the hotel in the book faces the cold North Sea, on the coast of Yorkshire in England. Oppressed by the feeling that his world was breaking up, he immersed himself in what was to be *Before the Bombardment*.

His novel is also about a social world that was coming to an end. It is a reconstruction of the Scarborough of his youth, still, because of its distance from London, deeply Victorian in most of its attitudes. The three Sitwell children had spent their summers at Renishaw Hall and their winters in Scarborough, where their parents and both sets of grandparents had houses. Like Miss Fansharpe in the novel, their paternal grandmother had founded a Home for 'fallen women', rounding them up off the streets and setting them to work in a laundry which tore the Sitwells' clothes to shreds every week.

The bombardment in question actually took place, when early one morning in December 1914 three cruisers from the German fleet shelled the town. Osbert's parents were there at the time—Sir George sheltered in the cellar with the servants, Lady Ida refused to leave her bed—but Osbert himself was in London, preparing to embark with the Grenadier Guards for the war in France.

Scarborough, which in the novel is called Newborough, was a fashionable as well as a popular spa and resort in Edwardian days, while remaining stoutly provincial. The pomps and vanities of Scarborough Cricket Week make a lively chapter in this novel, and were to be described again by the author in one of his volumes of autobiography, *Left Hand, Right Hand.* His maternal grandfather Lord Londesborough was founder and president of this annual event, with the role played by Lord Ghoolingham in the novel; the Sitwells and their relations belonged to the 'county', a group only glimpsed in ironic parenthesis in this story.

In these sideswipes Osbert Sitwell expresses his contempt and loathing for most of the values and attitudes of his class. The case against blood sports has rarely been more vehemently or wittily put, as from their 'icebound and isolated forts of ignorance, the garrisons of pheasant-coloured country gentlemen, accompanied by their mates, sally forth to slaughter the birds of the air', or to watch 'little red-brown beasts' being torn to pieces. Public schools, organized games, golf and golfers, cricket, cricketing wives, and war-mongers get the same acerbic treatment. So, it must be said, do the rich Jews who with Edward VII's patronage were making their way in society—never named here as Jews but as 'ringent Eastern gentlemen' or 'Wise Men of the East', whose guttural accents had been 'hitherto prudently confined to the purlieus of Aldgate and pawnshops of Whitechapel'.

These sneers are unattractive. But Osbert Sitwell in this book is anatomizing a society that never recovered from the First World War, and stresses its stupidity, arrogance, hypocrisy, and greed in order to throw into relief the poor quality of the lives of the less fortunate—in this case, single women. *Before the Bombardment* is a comedy of manners, its edge sharpened by anger and pity.

Scarborough is a town of boarding-houses and hotels, and in his youth the two most important hotels were the Pavilion—managed by the parents of the actor Charles Laughton—and the Grand, which is the Superb of this novel. In the off-season, no one would stay even at the Superb by choice; in winter the rough sea and cruel east winds make Newborough an unwelcoming place. Miss Collier-Floodgaye and her companion Miss Bramley are the only visitors; they rattle about in the vast cold hotel like frozen peas, resented by the staff, though becoming objects of consuming interest to the semi-invalid genteel elderly of the town, who eke out their declining days and incomes in 'rooms facing south'.

There is a mixture of nostalgia and appalled horror in Osbert Sitwell's recreation of period and character. *Before the Bombardment* is only just a novel; he introduces Miss Collier-Floodgaye and Miss Bramley with what is really an essay on the dynamics of the relationship between a paid companion and her employer. Full of insight and understanding, this is good social history and good psychology; there is memorable writing here about dependence, manipulation, pride, and humiliation; and while the social pressures analysed are of their period, the intimate personal politics are universals. Osbert Sitwell's achievement is to be funny about poor Miss Bramley, and the hopeless pathos of her life, without being condescending.

The novel proceeds in a series of episodic set-pieces: the hotel itself, the winter gardens, the harbour, the cemetery, the market hall, the moors outside the town, the charity ball at the Superb, the church services, the cricket festival—building up into an exposition not only of a town but also of a social structure. Where the book is weakest, it seems to me, is in those chapters where we are introduced to the permanent inhabitants of Newborough, who seem mere revue sketches, or stereotypes—even though two of those who make guest appearances in this way, the desperate Misses Cantrell-Cooksey, are people treated in depth and sympathetically in an earlier short story, 'Low Tide' (in *Triple Fugue*). What narrative line there is depends on the mischievous interventions of these minor characters; and here *Before the Bombardment* becomes less witty than facetious, and rather repetitive; the genre is that of the E. F. Benson novels that Miss Bramley gets out of the library. Fortunately the more sardonic mode prevails in the novel as a whole.

Before the Bombardment is also a poetic novel, in which the imagery consistently contributes to a judgement on humanity that is only made explicit on the last page. The book begins and ends with evocations of the German housemaid's feelings as she rises before dawn to light the fires in the hotel. These passages are both in subject-matter and in manner like prose paraphrases of a poem, 'Aubade', by the author's sister Edith Sitwell. Much of the descriptive writing is modernist in the manner of T. S. Eliot, as can be judged by the harmonious way in which lines from Eliot, used as chapter-headings, mesh with Osbert Sitwell's poetic prose. Notes in music, or colours reflected from stained glass, become clouds of birds or butterflies overhead, in a mode that Osbert Sitwell himself would have called futuristic and which, in today's writers, would be labelled 'magic realism'.

But something odder and more purposeful than this is going on. Although the setting is cold, grey, and unspeakably English, and although the documentation of clothes and personal effects is almost forensic in its precision, the prevailing imagery is exotic. Sometimes the atmosphere is underwater : the sofas and chairs in the empty lounge of the Superb are rocks on the bottom of an aquarium; in the vicarage, the furniture seems like half-living things lurking in the depths of the ocean. Elsewhere it is tropical: London's greenery in fog and gaslight recalls 'a swampy forest in South America'. The Superb is 'an Indian jungle' when 'the overwhelming gold frondage of cornice and capital' is illuminated. The vaulting of the railway station at Ebur (which is York) becomes black foliage in 'the sun slashed jungles in Africa'.

Osbert Sitwell's interest in human behaviour emerges as zoological. The implication is that we have evolved from apes, and that beneath the hypocritical respectability, society is ape-society still. It doesn't worry him very much: 'the only bad ape is the stagnant, incurious ape'. But it makes nonsense of conventional morality. And worse than this, for the moralistic critic in 1926, was the suggestion, in a virtuoso passage, that a devout church-goer such as Miss Collier-Floodgaye, sincerely exalted by incense, music, and colour, was experiencing not a foretaste of Heaven but a sensual race-memory of the beautiful but brutish primeval forest. Dying, she enters not glory but 'silence and darkness'. The promise of rewards in the next world for sufferings endured in this one is just a cruel joke.

It was Osbert Sitwell's betrayal of class, religion, and the whole edifice of 'civilized' social behaviour—perpetrated wittily, even frivolously—that caused the novel to be howled down in some quarters. One Sunday reviewer accused him of spitting on the whole Victorian age; the book was condemned as vulgar; the *Yorkshire Post*, the local paper of his parents and their friends, called it 'merely caddish'. Only Mary Webb in the *Bookman* praised its wit, depth, subtlety, and 'savage irony'. Naturally, under these circumstances, *Before the Bombardment* was a great success; it was reprinted twice within the first three months, and was taken up by an American publisher. Osbert Sitwell's confidence was restored, and his life took off in new directions.

When he died in 1969 there were, before the Will was read, certain expectations and some speculation among his near and dear about the disposition of his property— followed by surprises and some disillusion. One of the things he did was to leave his copyright and the life-interest in his flat in the castle of Montegufoni to his own 'paid companion'—his secretary, nurse, and last friend, Frank Magro. It is characteristically apt that it should be this novel, whose plot, such as it is, turns on the making of wills and the expectation of legacies, that Osbert Sitwell chose to accompany him to the grave.

PREFACE

THE gentle reader is invited to approach this novel as if it were a historical romance, an alas! imperfect but imaginative reconstruction of an epoch, the memory of which is almost obliterated, an inquest into the causes and conditions that preceded and perhaps were partly responsible for its effacement The scene is laid, mainly, in an English seaside town during the opening years of the twentieth century ; and the story is as much concerned with this town as with any of the characters that move through its streets.

To understand how far that period with which we deal has retreated from us, it is only necessary to find a fashion-plate of twenty years ago and match it against a Cretan wall-painting in the Ashmolean museum. The distant, mysterious inhabitants of that lost world are infinitely nearer to us in their clothes, and probably in their outlook, than our own parents.

And then seaside towns are always silted up with the debris of the past century. The predominant note at Newborough, before the bombardment, was one of long settled comfort and confident respectability. The town faced the world with a Credo the grounds of which it refused even to examine. This belief in the inherent rightness and essential righteousness of the prevailing system was, in reality, but a survival of that Swiss Family Robinson attitude toward life which the English had adopted at the outbreak of the nineteenth century and had maintained until its close; and this belief it is, which throws so inexplicable a charm over the whole period. Elsewhere, in the years down which our narrative is laid, it may be that this confident pose was breaking up: but as a wild flower, imagined to be extinct, or an obsolete but unobtrusive wild animal, may yet linger on in a remote Welsh mountain or wide Yorkshire moor, so in this wind-bound, sea-pounded town, the nineteenth century has been allowed to project its heavy shadow across the opening years of the young era. For it is a mistake to think that a century ends everywhere at the same time, however clear may be the transition from one of these artificially made periods to another. Mr. George Moore has described exquisitely how the eighteenth century lay hidden among the lakes and woods of Ireland until the year 1860; and no doubt the enthusiastic amateur of dead epochs can still find the nineteenth century much poorer, rather angry, but none the less sure and respectable, lurking in unobserved corners, in Parliament, in the Church, in a seaside hotel.

AMALFI

CHAPTER I

REVEILLE

" When blood is nipp'd, and ways be foul,
Then nightly sings the staring owl,
    To-who ;
To-whit, to-who, a merry note,
While greasy Joan doth keel the pot."

THE tin tongue rattled on, high up under a dome.
So loudly it clacked and racketed through the silence
of this vast edifice that, surely, it must have pierced
through the layers of cloud, at this season stretched like
blankets, one over another endlessly, and must now
echo through the ultimate blue imbecility beyond.
This cerulean lining, however, was in the winter a thing
utterly incredible ; while the grey blankets above and
beneath yet invited slumber, warm deep slumber.
But on and on it cackled, this idiot tongue, trying to
inform the sleeper of its monotonous and invariable
message, slave to a slave. It seemed fearful of betraying
a trust. Six o'clock, six o'clock, six o'clock, it hammered and ranted.

Through an unconscious cunning born of long
experience, the sleeper was able to transform the brief
moments which this metallic music occupied into the
most lingering period of the entire day. While still fast
asleep, she could calculate precisely the last second of
the alarum, and only when the final syncopic death-
rattle was strangled in the clock's throat, did she, almost
automatically, leave the sandy plains or issue forth from

the aromatic summer pine-forests of her native northern
Germany. Indeed the bell itself usually played some part
in the dream, serving both to lengthen and end it.
Now her withered limbs must lumber out of bed into
the frozen air ; she must switch on the light and tumble
into her tousled, rumpled clothes lying on a chair, and by
a judicious, though not too protracted, application of
brush and sponge arrange the wisps of flaxen, flocculent
hair, the straight pale eyes, the long shapeless nose, the
lump on the forehead above the right-hand almost
invisible eyebrow, into their usual weekday perspective,
imparting to them by this process a cohesion and sense
of focus which they had lacked as she lay there sleeping.
All these attributes which have been described now
centred round a personality, and formed Elisa, the
Prussian housemaid at a hotel in the North of England.
Every morning she must pass through these extraordinary
experiences and mutations which constitute getting-up
and dressing in this part of Britain during the winter
months.

Every morning it grew colder, colder and colder, and
all for fourteen pounds a year ! Ten years of it. She
couldn't go on doing it for ever, really she couldn't,
though it was better than that first place, at the Rectory !
Angrily, dumbly, she shook out her body, turned off the
light, and creaked blunderingly out of the room. Now
she was wading through the familiar stillness, a silence
infringed by a thousand crepuscular crepitations, of
the hotel-corridors. As she moved, these minute,
crackling vibrations were lost in the cascades of sound
which her clumsy feet unloosed to dash up against tiled
walls. Soon it would be light, she supposed ; and,
before dawn came, there were the grates and the fires,

the stoves and the boilers, the floors and the staircase, to do : and, not properly, her work. It was a man's work, but just because she was a foreigner, she must do it. She repeated to herself the names of her hated enemies— the grates, the fires and the stoves, the boilers and the floors and the staircase. The lilt of the words gradually formed in her mind into a Housemaid's Miserere, to be repeated, rather meaninglessly but with a sense of comfort She would feel better by and by. She must light the fires

The flames were first born in a faint blue flicker, and then swiftly growing lusty, purred and coquetted at her from their iron cages. The rhythm of their lithe and feline movements woke the reflections that had been slumbering in their nests, high among the overwhelming gold frondage of cornice and capital, which had been overgrown in a breath by the bronze forest of the darkness. Directly the light was turned off, the forest overgrew all this splendour, as an Indian jungle swallows up a city on the very instant of its desertion. To turn on the light was, similarly, the excavation of a buried town. And now the fire woke all these little reflections up in the branches, making them stir and preen themselves, and peep out of their dark high nests, as a wild creature moving through a forest at night would wake all the young birds, set them quivering and twittering.

At any rate, Elisa said to herself, it would grow warmer now. But no sooner had she thereby attempted to instil life into her starved hands and feet than it became necessary for her to draw aside the heavy plush curtains and open the shutters. With an air of protest she threw these clattering back against the wall ; immediately, the cold twilight poked and scratched at the window-panes with its sharp black claws, then moaned like a hunted animal that craves shelter. Blue frost flowers could be seen expanding and contracting on the glass, and the cruel wind squeezed through every crevice, and conducted a paper-chase high into the grey air of the open plot outside, while within the grates the flames for a moment shrank back, became sensitive plants that closed, opened and closed, their red petals.

Now there were the floors : no peace all day long, not a scrap of it (and the chilblains !). Bad enough in the summer, it was ; but the visitors made it lively (though the other servants—being only " temporaries "—got all the tips, of course) and never even half a day's holiday She might work her fingers right off her hand, she might, without anybody as much as minding. And nasty, too, because she was a foreigner. " Remember you are only a German," the manager had said. " German," indeed, and none the worse for that, she supposed ? And she gave the shutter a real bang, as she thought of it, with the back of her brush ; that would teach them, perhaps ; wake them up. Tea for those Two at eight o'clock. A lot of tea she'd get, she shouldn't wonder. What had they come here for, in the winter ? To give trouble, extra trouble, that was all, with their tea and hot water bottles at all hours. " German," indeed ; and she struck the shutter a second time.

The blow resounded up the stairs, through the empty corridors and rows of vacant rooms. " Good gracious, ' Tibbits,' whatever can that be ? " called out the deep, broken voice of Miss Collier-Floodgaye, timid in spite of its rather masculine tones. And the more experienced Miss Bramley in the patient and effusive voice of a paid companion, answered, " Nothing, dear ! It's quite

all right. It must be Elisa. She should be in, in a few
minutes now, with the tea. How did you sleep, dear ? "
" But it's not light yet, Tibbits," the first speaker pro-
tested. " No, dear, but it's nearly eight o'clock," and
Miss Bramley could be heard chinking the gold chains
of her little watch, as though she were hauling in a cable,
hand over hand.

These two visitors were quite unaware of the intense
nature of the interest, almost amounting to a commotion,
for which their presence in the hotel was responsible.
In these two rooms, and in these alone, were to be found
the rarest of specimens, winter visitors. The other rooms
lay in empty rows all these long months, filled with a
bitter green light such as filters through into an aquarium,
waiting for their next denizens. The other hotels in
Newborough were equally guiltless of visitors : for
English seaside resorts had not yet determined to
inaugurate winter seasons with that wild and continuous
display of Christmas hilarity, paper-caps, and any
quantity of objects in paper, wool or cardboard, to be
thrown at friends. The hotel managers had not yet
grasped the fact that to induce the famous Continental
gaiety—that spirit of Carnival—which must always be
their aim, in English hearts, two things and two things
only were essential—incessant noise and a multitude of
pellets, balls, bullets, rolls of paper and streamers with
which the jovial guests could pelt one another. No, at
the time of which we are writing, guests during the dark
months were an unwanted treasure. In the summer
the town was ready for them, but in the short cold days
it did not welcome nor even solicit them . . . after all,
it was a warm-weather place : and there must be something unusual . . . queer . . . about people who came

to a hotel here in the winter. And the visitors could not have many friends, could they ? or they would be spending Christmas with them ? Then who were they, and why had they no friends ? Newborough was intent on an answer.

CHAPTER II

THE DAWN OF FRIENDSHIP

"Here I am, an old man in a dry month,
Being read to by a boy, waiting for rain."

EVEN when Miss Collier-Floodgaye first came to Newborough, she appeared to be in failing health. Old, old with the strength and dignity of an antlered oak, in the manner of that tree, it seemed that—unless she was uprooted by some sudden fury of a wind—her gradual decline might extend over a considerable period. But her dark figure was only, really, to flit for a few winters across a darkening screen.

Her origin was, undoubtedly, an obscure one, and in her conversation she never referred or gave the most minute clue to it. In the build of her gaunt body, though, in the sweep of her features, in her large bones and stately stature, there lingered, surely, something rustic rather than urban. That deep, bold voice, which was her most marked characteristic, still held, it might be, the dying notes of a harsher, more Doric music. A farmer's daughter, perhaps; but assuredly she was no tradesman's offspring. And then, too, she was lacking altogether in the liveliness of the city.

Her dress was a suitable translation of her. Sombre, with never a touch of colour, it enhanced her personality, adding to it the aged, grape-bloom dignity of a raven. Never intricate, bewildering or bewildered, as was the apparel of so many old ladies in Newborough, it yet

conveyed a certain battered and buffeted pride that was
not to be found in all their laces, shawls, frills and
brooches. Her large hands were knotted and veined,
unexpectedly virile, the counterpart of her voice. The
few gold rings which adorned them were rather unexpected, and she wore no other jewellery. One ring in
particular, remains in the memory, a ring designed to
represent intercoiled snakes, with ruby eyes that flashed
a piercing fire as she moved her bony hand. About this
there was a subtle atmosphere, as if it were the testimony
of an incident in the past, or would be the witness of
some event in the future. Her slow gait, her halting
step, the tapping of the malacca cane which aided it,
all enhanced the difference between Miss Collier-
Floodgaye and the ordinary dweller in hotels, and endowed her a little, even, with the air of the Wicked
Fairy who went unasked to the Christening—not that
any aura of evil emanated from her, but that there was
undoubtedly a quality of strangeness clinging to her ;
which also raised her high above any symptoms of silliness that she might display. The whole effect, her very
physique, the structure of her face, her deep voice,
strong grey hair, and brown eye in which sometimes
gleamed a brown-red light, seemed indicative of the
hovering, somewhere in the air about, lurking behind,
or just out of sight, ahead, of Tragedy. Yet she was
ordinary enough in many ways. Though not so well
informed as numerous invalid ladies of Newborough
with regard to the constant crossing and recrossing
genealogies of the county families, she, too, could spend
happy hours in tracing a lost stitch in one of these
intricately knitted septs.

But, however much interested in them, it was clear

that she had never met a member of these tribes in all her long lifetime. Had she, then, been housekeeper to some rich man who had bequeathed her his fortune ? No, for surely her fate had been more interesting, more cruel, even. She was possessed of a dignity that was inborn and ingrained, while her education was as good as that of any other lady of her period. Was she, perhaps, the natural daughter of a distinguished man ? But this, again, hardly seemed a solution of the problem : for her life appeared to cover only the last fifteen years out of some seventy-four or five

Once I thought I had discovered the secret . . . had she been married, fettered for life to lunatic or criminal ? Might not such a history account for the fear—if fear it was—that was felt in all the things personal to her ? She wore no wedding-ring, but there was not about her any suggestion of spinsterhood. In the end, this theory, too, was discarded ; for it seemed impossible in face of so many contradictory facts to reach any conclusion. She never explained where she had lived as a child, girl, young or middle-aged woman, nor did she ever allude to the part of the country from which she had sprung. Indeed, she had apparently contrived to be born into the world without human agency, fully dressed in black, at the age of approximately sixty years. Her past had thrown no discernible shadows. She had no friends to whom she could refer ; and no adventures which she could relate had befallen her. She wished, it seemed, to be accepted as she was, the creature only of immediate past and present.

In disposition the old lady was, most obviously, kind, generous and amiable. Of this there could be no doubt. Yet in all the long, accumulating treasure of her years, she had so far caught and made fast no friend except Miss Bramley, a paid Companion.

Now of all professions in this world, that of salaried friend is usually the most degrading, pernicious in its effect upon employed and employer : a declaration in common of their spiritual bankruptcy. For a poor woman to be forced to sell her friendship is infinitely more evil than for her to be obliged to sell her body. The prostitution is at the same time more prolonged and more hypocritical. The avowed prostitute declares an infamous trade by her ways and appearance. But paid Companionship is a less obvious, more subtle betrayal of personality ; a rarer, less robust vice of weaker souls : while for an old lady to have to descend into the "Agony" or other columns of the *Times* in order to buy friendship is as repulsive, surely, as the spectacle of an old man purchasing his love in the market-place. It is a vice unexcused by any inflammation of the senses : a form of slavery infinitely guileful, pathetic, and fatal alike to vendor and purchaser. It is a fraud committed by two undischarged and unrepentant spiritual-bankrupts, each intent on the deception of the other. Nor is the excuse of training valid, as it is in cases where Companion and Companioned are related. For example, the plight of martyr-daughter, of patient victim-niece, so frequently to be observed in seaside towns and health resorts generally, may appear, at first glance, to be more tragic than that of the paid Companion, because the former reap no financial benefits, however slight, from their martyrdom. In reality, however, their ultimate reward is more certain. The niece bound to hypochondriac aunt, the daughter chained to invalid mother, is but passing through a severe apprenticeship, for the whole time she is learning the tricks of that intricate and difficult art which herself will one day be called upon to practise. Not the faintest nuance of malice, not the most delicate shade of ill-temper is wasted on her, since these are intended to be skilful weapons for future use in her own hand. Hereditary secrets and possessions are these, passed on from mother to daughter, from daughter to niece, from niece to daughter, for innumerable generations. In a lesser way, the preservation of these secrets, the loyalty which informs the entire body of such a society, is reminiscent of a medieval guild. And further, since daughter and niece are supposed to be free agents, they garner an additional reward in the popularity of an imagined sacrifice (" She has been so good, given her whole life to looking after the old lady "), while the paid Companion is not pitied, because the public knows that she " is paid to put up with it." For those who are not parties to this particular bargain of mother and daughter, aunt and niece, refuse to recognize its existence. How are they, then, to comprehend that the brutal ill-temper of the elder woman, the mild reproach of the younger, the constant and maddening sequence of grumbles from one, the patient and galling brightness of the other, are merely so many essays in technique, like a prima donna's rendering of scales ? They will not understand that a properly constituted and hypochondriac elderly relative takes years to manufacture ; that, like a Damascene blade, before being " turned-out," she must be tempered by fire, plunged into icy water, hammered by iron, submitted to countless tests, innumerable processes, constantly and over a long period of years. Fortunately those who are privy to

the bargain recognize its nature, extent and obligations.
It would, indeed, be a Wicked Aunt (infinitely more
serpentine in evil than the Wicked Uncle of the Babes-
in-the-Wood) who, in breach of unwritten contract,
left away her fortune—for to be as unpleasant as this
it is necessary to have substantial private means—a
very foolish Mother's Right-Hand, who, mistaking the
educational nature of her crucifixion, cast away all the
subtle weapons of her armoury—resignation, meekness,
altruism and abnegation—and packed her trunk. But
each can threaten, as the climax of a series of manœuvres
that have extended over several months, that she will
do so, without endangering her prospects or incurring
the genuine displeasure of the other : for each knows
that such a pretence is merely the most effective, final
and dramatic move in the whole pageant of this tactical
display—the big gun which is held in reserve and can
never in reality be dragged up.

Alas, with a paid victim of alien blood, the relationship between employed and employer is beyond com-
parison more tragic, more devastating in its effect
on both. If the Companion is free at any moment to
give notice of the severance of her friendship at a given
date, the whole basis of illusion (the very thing for
which she is paid—the " goods " in fact) is shattered
beyond repair. It becomes, therefore, an understood,
though undefined and unmentionable clause in the
unwritten contract of such employment that it is to
continue throughout the lifetime of the elder lady :
the agreement can only be terminated by her death.
For the Companion to die first would put her completely
outside the pale : it is a sin which cannot even be
referred to in the presence of old ladies.

Similarly, to give notice would be " not to play the game " : for it might hinder the Companioned one from venting her temper, giving rein to her malice, or indulging fully that other fault, whichever it may be, that has hitherto prevented her from making—or at any rate from keeping—unsalaried friends. For the Companioned one is, actually, paying a person to be her friend, in order that herself may continue unchecked in some particular line of vice so violent that no friend unpaid would tolerate it. That is why she has to pay.

And, in the case of a professional Companion, there is another powerful financial motive besides her ordinary emolument : a hope, never, alas, to be a certainty, of a fortune to reach her as a posthumous gift from the elder lady. Unfortunately the employer seldom feels bound to the strict execution of this part of the unwritten contract, seldom feels morally compelled to carry it out, in the way that mother or aunt would feel it incumbent upon them to provide for their daughters or nieces. For mother and aunt learnt their trade in the same hard school, and hold their very worldly goods on the condition, however undefined, that they enable their hereditary secrets and family tricks to be handed on, like the small blue flame of a sacred lamp in a temple, from one generation to another. The unrelated-companioned does not hold her possessions on such easy terms. She does not belong to so strict or haughty a caste. She must buy herself into the companioned-class. Compared with mother or aunt, she is what the Jewish profiteer who purchases a country seat is to the old landlord from whom he acquires it. She has no traditions, and is bound by no sense of obligation. Further, she knows that the gambling clause of the unwritten con-

tract—that one which relates to her will—often hovers
in the mind of her Companion : and this serves to summon up before the elder lady what she most wishes to
forget—Death !—and accordingly irritates her the more,
lashing her into extremes of sulking and ill-temper.
And then, even at the end of these rather fragrant
moments of surrendering to her ruling vice, the employer
is again reminded, by the restraint and forced
"pleasantries" of her Companion, that the latter dare not
answer her back, or give notice, for fear of an alteration
in her will—Death again ! Thus the jangling skeleton
of the richer lady is for ever dancing between them,
clacking its castanet-like bones with a ghastly grace :
while still alive, her own ghost dogs her and seeks to
envenom still further the relations between employer
and employed.

Miss Collier-Floodgaye's motives, however, for hiring
a friend were rather irregular. No violent temper or
brutal fault marred her character. But owing to events
—of which it was possible for others to feel the existence, though not to conjecture the kind—she was sad
(sombre rather than sad, perhaps) and lonely and rich :
and, though undoubtedly courageous (for courage was
a virtue that could be detected even in her mien) it appeared as though she were a little frightened, alarmed,
it may be, by the accumulation of her years. She did
not wish to be left alone in a silence, a silence in which
the few voices that spoke were those of the dead. It is
doubtful if the old lady was frightened of anything more
tangible than her own memories.

But she yearned for friendship. . . . certainly she
yearned for friendship : and since, through lack of
charm, by a total deficiency in all social qualities, she

was debarred from making a friend in the usual way
(however much she longed and strove to do so), she was
in the end obliged to buy one. When this purchase had
been completed, she hoped, perhaps, by means of one
friend, who would always be in her company, thus
learning to understand and appreciate her, to make
others. Miss Bramley, in fact, was in part decoy, in part
interpreter ; for the old lady needed someone who would
translate and dramatize her for other people.

And it seemed to Miss Collier-Floodgaye that she had
found what she wanted. So unused was she to the ways
of a friend that she was able to accept the over-effusive
manner of her new Companion as the genuine coin of
friendship. She could not test this mintage by experience, discount it by previous disappointments, or in
any way compare the genuine money with the counterfeit.

CHAPTER III

SITUATION VACANT

" Freeze, freeze, thou bitter sky,
That dost not bite so nigh
    As benefits forgot :
Though you the waters warp,
Thy sting is not so sharp
    As friend remember'd not."

MISS TERESA BRAMLEY'S life had been no easy one.
From the beginning she had been given her full share
of difficulties. She was one of the two daughters of
Canon Bramley, of Torquay. Her other important
relative was her father's aunt, Miss Titherley-Bramley,
who for many years lived at Newborough. Both her
father and this aunt were supposed to have private
fortunes.

At the age of twenty-six, Miss Bramley had found
herself alone in the world, for her mother had died
many years ago, and her sister, married to a former
curate of the Canon's, was too busy child-bearing to be
of very much use to anyone. The Canon had been so
distressed at his aunt's death—or rather at the unexpected
fact that her estate had, so to speak, predeceased her—
that he never really recovered from the shock of it,
soon afterwards dying himself. After his own death,
a discovery of a similar sort was made. Miss Titherley-
Bramley had failed to leave any evidence behind her of
her long passage through this world, while the chief
proofs of the Canon's travail here below were Miss

26

Teresa Bramley, Mildred (her married sister) and a few faded photographs.

Miss Teresa Bramley was, therefore, left behind with no assets except her youth, a simple country freshness, rather than prettiness, an indifferent education, a naturally charming voice unassisted by any training or knowledge of music, a disposition at once affectionate, religious and extremely malleable, together with a few more assertive, more tangible certificates of genteel birth and upbringing.

Personal belongings are perhaps among the most pathetic forms of human self-expression. Nelson's pigtail at Greenwich Hospital, the cat that once belonged to Petrarch, and stuffed now, is still to be seen in his house, the giant turtle in the Zoological Gardens which, traditionally, was the pet of Richard III, King Alfred's jewel at the Ashmolean, the tortoise-shell-veneered cane that once aided Beau Brummell in his rather unsteady walk, the crescent-shaped hat which Napoleon wore on his return from Elba—perhaps the most remarkable resurrection of the last thousand years—and now to be seen in the palace of Fontainebleau, all these are infinitely more poignant than the written stories of their illustrious proprietors. It is these relics of vanished affection, vanity or fashion, which portray the men who owned them, summon them up before us much more clearly than the most magic brush or the finest pen. Miss Bramley's personal property (net) and private treasures, after the Canon's affairs had been wound up and his debts paid, comprised :

A gold watch, and fine gold chain, the property of her father.

Two silver-backed hall-marked hair brushes, once the property of her mother.

Three Indian silver boxes of intricate Oriental work-manship.

One Oriental Filigree box in Dutch silver.

One bit of brown bread, dating from the 1870 siege of Paris, made of straw and dust, the whole enclosed in an ornamental metal box, fashioned out of a Prussian shell-case, the gift of her former French Nursery-Governess.

Two Volumes, morocco-bound, of Hackett's " Sermons " (London, 1868) and an edition of " Tom Brown's School-days," unsold at the sale of her late father's effects.

One chasuble, worked and presented to the late Canon by the Lady Workers of Torquay, contained in a wooden casket, handsomely decorated with poker work, a Christmas presentation from the inmates of the Torquay Workhouse and Pauper Lunatic Asylum, in grateful recognition of his services.

Two cut-glass scent bottles, a wedding present to Miss Bramley's parents, from their relative, the late Lord Liddlesfield (a valuable certificate, that one).

A coverlet of floral pattern, embroidered in grass-green, sparrow-green, ochre, salmon pink and rose-pink silks, by herself ; and

A photograph, in a Burmese cedar-wood frame, of the late Miss Titherley-Bramley, sitting in her conservatory, feeding a large dog with one hand, and holding up a permanently-waved chrysanthemum of mammoth size in the other.

Besides these effects, there were her clothes, some of them from her aunt's wardrobe, several photographs of her father, and a miniature, painted from a photo-graph, after her decease, of her mother—a very good likeness, it was said, but Miss Bramley hardly remem-bered her.

Thus equipped, Miss Teresa Bramley was launched on life.

.   .   .   .

Luckily her sister had heard of an opportunity for her, otherwise she really did not know what she would have done. It appeared that an old Miss Fansharpe, who lived in Wales, wanted a Companion. A real piece of good fortune, they thought. This venerable person, directly she saw Miss Bramley, " took a fancy " to her. Miss Fansharpe was a great character, benevolent and fond of good works. Having procured Miss Bramley, she proceeded to persecute, and, at the same time, to train her thoroughly. She acted the part of hierophant into the mysteries of companionship.

As a younger woman, Miss Fansharpe had been most active. For three or four decades she had spent a part of each year in Cardiff, and had then founded, in conjunction with her friend, the Bishop of Llandudaft, a Rescue Home for Women. The Bishop and herself were wont to drive about in a brougham at night through the more crowded streets of the city, and whenever they saw a likely subject, swooped out of the carriage and carried the poor girl off. So great was the respect felt for them and their work that no questions were asked. Once in the Home, escape was impossible. Laundry was the task imposed upon these slaves, who were, except on Sundays, never to be seen again. An imagined fall was sufficient passport to an eternal mangling, in every sense of the word, of gentlemen's shirts. The poor women had their revenge : the sexes were engaged in an undying and sturdy warfare. Perhaps thus, too, Eve obtained her revenge on Adam, by compelling him first to wear clothes, and by then proceeding to wash them herself.

As we have hinted, after their imprisonment the inmates never saw the world except in its Sunday aspect : for every Sabbath, but on that day alone of all the days in the week, they were allowed to go out of the grounds (an asphalt yard) to church. Dressed in dark clothes, which were made specially by the command and beneath the eye of Miss Fansharpe, so as to be as ill-fitting and unbecoming as possible—to lessen the chances of temptation for them—stumping along in heavy boots, with their hair pulled back under plain straw hats, their flashing eyes obscured by blue spectacles, this sad crocodile of kidnapped syrens was to be seen every Sunday, under the stern supervision of a Matron, dragging wearily to Divine Service.

There was, indeed, one incident at the Home that for a time focused interest upon it, and even disturbed local opinion ; but this was soon forgotten in the admiration felt for the personalities and the work of both the Bishop and Miss Fansharpe. The Bishop's daughter, who was so intensely religious as almost to rank as a Saint and Seer, and lived in constant expectation of the Second Coming, was not surprised to notice one night a star so radiantly illuminating that she was able at once to identify it as the Star of Bethlehem. This by itself created something of a stir in the district, but when about the same time, several girls in the Home began to show obvious signs of an approaching maternity, which they were unable to explain by any natural causes, excitement knew no bounds. The one difficulty, the only thing, that puzzled the faithful was how to select from such an unexpected, such an embarrassing plenty.

Alas, soon after, it transpired that the flaming star which had been observed, was no new one but was in fact, our old friend Venus, which owing to some natural and recurrent phenomenon, was in a state of peculiar

effulgence ; while, when the inmates of the Home
were given their rather infrequent baths, it was discovered,
to the dismay of those concerned, that a youth had dressed
up as a female and had then contrived to get himself
carried off by the Bishop and Miss Fansharpe. For
many months this recreant had lived in the Home without
thinking it necessary to divulge his sex or identity.
Indeed, even at the moment of his capture the governing
body had been surprised at the fervour and enthusiasm
with which this girl—for such they had taken him to be
—had sought to be incarcerated in the Home.

A time came, at last, when Miss Fansharpe grew too
old to take any serious part in the management of the
Home, though right down to the time of her death, the
dear old lady still maintained an active and vicious
interest in the vicissitudes of her involuntary wards.
She was now more or less bedridden, and lived all the
year through at her country home, Llandriftlog House.
After so energetic a life, she began to feel rather sad
and lonely, no doubt missing the constant excitement
of her former career. She could not read much now,
and knitting and talking to her Companion were her
sole relaxations. With her Companion, she had already,
in a few weeks, developed a technique, which was little
less than astounding in one who was herself a novice,
hitherto companionless. Indeed if, as some think,
genius consists in an infinite capacity for giving pain,
Miss Fansharpe may be said as an employer to have
possessed genius. As Miss Bramley became better and
better trained, it naturally became increasingly difficult
for Miss Fansharpe to goad her into a scene. Thus,
while the quarry grew ever scarcer, it grew yet more
worthy of an Amazon's skill. A moment was reached

when she found it impossible to trap her Companion
into contradicting her. From that instant, the old lady
altered her tactics, developing an extraordinarily ingenious new method, difficult to convey, except by
illustration. The first thing to do was to tire the Companion out, by fussing, fretting and worrying her, in
the manner of Fabius Cunctator. The old lady would,
therefore begin by saying, " Teresa, I understand
that you wish to go into Llandumfniff. It's a very
good plan, I think. But there are three trains, one
leaving here at 8.47, another at 10.8 and a third at
11.20. Which do you think would suit you best ? "
This point Miss Fansharpe would argue for two or
three hours, Miss Bramley meanwhile warily refusing
to commit herself. It was a strain, though, for the
younger woman, and when Miss Fansharpe felt that she
had thoroughly fatigued her and worn her down, she
would then very subtly proceed to the next tactical
point, by pretending to let slip the information that
personally she favoured the 10.8 train. Utterly exhausted,
Miss Bramley would snatch at the possibility of agreement, for by now, she would have been willing to fall
in with any definite view, however inconvenient to
herself, in order to end the discussion. Miss Fansharpe
knew this, and as soon as Miss Bramley had agreed with
her about it, said very mildly " So it's your opinion
that the 10.8 is the best train of the three ? " Miss
Bramley thinking the whole matter over and finished,
said, " Yes, dear." Then, like an angry lioness, the old
lady would spring furiously on her prey, saying, " But
what makes you think so—I don't agree at all. It's
much the worst of them to *my* mind," and a terrific
onslaught would develop. The miraculous part of this

technique was its economy, for it ensured that one subject would yield sufficient ammunition for several severe battles, and at the same time it contained within itself the whole secret of perpetual motion ; for the identical discussion could be turned inside-out, so as to appear different every time, while the mere mechanical action of turning it would precipitate what seemed to be another cause for war, though in reality it was the same one. So perfectly was worked out every possibility, every theme, that the whole display almost attained to the level of a great musical composition.

It cannot be said, though, that Miss Bramley disliked her patroness. On the contrary, though in awe of the old lady, she became really attached to her. Into the life of Llandriftlog, she entered with zest. She was, in fact, a born Companion. And if there were difficulties, there were many consolations. Very often she was allowed to deputize as Lady Bountiful for the elderly invalid : and she was encouraged and supported in her village activities. She did " a great deal of good " locally.

It was interesting to note how the character of the younger woman became set in the mould of the elder. Perhaps a Companion must, as part of her duties, adopt to a certain extent the personality of the old lady to whom she is administering artificial friendship : perhaps she is obliged to take on little tricks of manner, vocal inflexions, gestures, a smile, habits of speech and thought, for by so doing she bestows upon her patroness a spurious life-after-death, an extra span of a generation or two Thus a Companion becomes the counterfeit offspring of the companioned, an offspring more true in physical traits and mental colouring to her progenitor tnan would have been any children of that lady's own bearing.

At home, in the Rectory, Miss Bramley had been rather " Liberal " in her views : but now her political faith was inexorably Conservative.   And it must be reckoned as a testimony to the altruism of human nature—though it is not so rare a phenomenon as might be imagined—that, from this time forth, the worse Miss Bramley was treated by Fortune, the more ardently she strove to support that very social order out of which she had gained so little, and from which there was now, for her, so little to hope.

In a sense it would not be inaccurate to assert that out of this conversion she did acquire something for herself.   Gradually she transformed it into a kind of asset, a spiritual certificate of gentility, which was added to—and matched beautifully—those other ones already enumerated, while it possessed in addition the merit of being more visible, more audible to the public. If some-one were to call, one could not very well rush upstairs, and snatching a silver-backed hair-brush, return with it to the drawing-room, crying out in the manner of a child, " Look at my silver-backed hair-brush ! "   But from the lumber-room of one's mind, it is always per-missible to take out a political creed, and give it an airing.

Miss Bramley's religious views remained unaltered, and these she was able to share with Miss Fansharpe, a fact that brought great comfort to the younger woman. Indeed she really enjoyed the life at Llandriftlog, though it may be that she was learning " adaptability "—or the art of dissembling her feelings even from herself In order to disarm the old lady, her manner became, at first gradually, then increasingly, effusive. For Miss Fansharpe could be " difficult "—yes " difficult " was the word. One could understand it, Miss Bramley reflected, for how cruel it must be after so active and so *interesting* a life, to be confined almost entirely to your bed ! And she was so philanthropic, too, a dear old creature if one only understood her ways.

Miss Fansharpe, for her part, often seemed eager to make the younger woman confident as to her future, was always seeking fresh methods by which to let her Companion know that she had been " remembered " in her will, that there was a legacy. The transmission of such intelligence is inevitably embarrassing, and the old lady, in her tactful benevolence, even went so far as to organize a slight skirmish with Miss Bramley on some abstract issue, such as the home life of the Prince of Wales (afterward King Edward) or the precise meaning of the word " Primrose," in the context of " Primrose League," in order to hint darkly that disagreement with her views would incur the penalty of an altered will. This, no doubt, was simply the old lady's delicate way of letting her Companion know that there was a legacy in waiting for her.

But Miss Fansharpe's constant anxiety to reassure Miss Bramley about her future had for the Companion another most awkward and perhaps not entirely unforeseen consequence. Tidings of the old lady's new testamentary depositions reached Colonel Fansharpe, her only nephew and heir. How far the percolation of this news was his aunt's intention is a matter that will probably never quite be cleared up. But it did not seem as though she was altogether displeased at the leakage. Indeed, while her nephew and his wife were

in the house, she was always more than usually affectionate
to her Companion.

Formerly Colonel Fansharpe and his wife, Ivy, had
paid visits of barely three or four nights at a time to
their aunt, and these had only taken place about twice
a year. But, with the advent of her Companion, their
visits became more frequent and of longer duration.
During these family parties, Miss Bramley's life was apt
to become harassing. For Colonel Fansharpe did not
like her, and let it be known round about that he regarded
her as a " damned scheming woman "—while he even
went so far as to characterize her singing, which generally
endeared her to all hearts, as " Another of That Woman's
devilish tricks," no doubt regarding it merely as one of
the devices by which she was endeavouring to obtain
and wield the mystic sceptre of " undue influence."
Both Colonel and Mrs. Fansharpe were ever on the
watch. They bitterly resented Miss Bramley's necessary
adoption of their aunt's mannerisms. Ivy, specially,
contrived, though always with an air of courtesy, a
thousand subtle machinations for Miss Bramley's discomfiture, a thousand ways through which she could
allow her dislike and distrust to become apparent, without committing any overt act of war, on account of
which the Companion could have acted, demanding an
explanation or taking the matter before the old lady.
No, there was nothing positive : but Ivy could be seen
counting the silver spoons, or the umbrellas in the hall.
She was so bad at arithmetic, she would explain, and
always practised adding-up whenever there was an opportunity. She would, in the presence of the Companion,
dilate on the iniquities of " scheming " or would very
humbly (and this was the most irritating of her tricks)

ask for Miss Bramley's permission, in front of Miss Fansharpe, to pick a flower in the garden. This little act of courtesy served both to embarrass the Companion and, what was more important, to embroil her with the old lady, who would become senseless from rage if a single one of her proprietary rights was in any way infringed.

It was difficult to escape Miss Fansharpe's anger, almost impossible to cheat her of her prey. Singularly free from prejudice, though only for the duration of an argument, she would, in order to engage her Companion in single combat, change her views, normally so well-defined, with the circular spinning motion of a whirlwind, the direful force of a tornado. Useless was it for Miss Bramley to make any timid attempt to keep pace with the lightning make-up and quick-change artistry of such a virtuoso ; absolutely useless ; far better for her to face the storm, which would then, after a sharp will-altering climax, be followed by a scene of lachrymose and affectionate reconciliation.

In between these sudden squalls, in between these family visits, Miss Bramley's life was often peaceful Moreover, she found it enjoyable. She formed the habit of writing to her married sister twice a week, and the letter reproduced below is one typical of her epistolary gifts in the latter period of her companionship, when she had already somewhat assumed the character of Miss Fansharpe's Second-Self. Indeed, it is a letter such as might almost have been written by that old lady. Her use of underlining and capital letters justifies itself, for by it she was able to produce effects not to be obtained by any other means, to express a meaning not otherwise to be conveyed. It is a literary device, an important ingredient in her style.

LLANDRIFTLOG HOUSE,
LLANDRIFTLOG, N.W.
25 *Feb.*, 1900.

DEAREST MILDRED,

Your charming and serviceable gift of a pigskin pocket-book (most useful for Croquet-engagements in the Summer) was delayed in the post, and only reached me yesterday. For here, we are having a Dear old-fashioned winter, and until yesterday there had been no post for ten days. But the old place looks so Nice and Bright and cheerful, with the snow outside, like a white carpet, rolled up to the dining-room window-sills—just the sort of house that Poor Papa dreamed of. He would indeed have loved it, with its pretty, Quaint Wellingtonias and Scotch firs in the garden—they always look so Picturesque under snow, do they not ? Our only concern is for our dear little feathered friends : but we put out half a Coconut each day. Only this morning a dear little robin came and tapped at my window.

The prospect from the house is, indeed, Wild and Picturesque, but within all is bustle and cheerfulness : and one never feels dull for a moment. Last week, for example (was it *Thursday*, or Friday, I wonder ?—but now, dear, that I have your delightful and serviceable gift, I shall be able to remember more accurately) the Rector was coming to tea, and we had prepared for him, as a special Little luxury, some *Soda* scones (I wonder if you know them ? so good and Economical.) Unfortunately the Severe weather prevented his coming here. I forget if I mentioned him in my Monday—or was it Tuesday—letter ? He is a Newcomer, and his name is the Rev. Bernard Broometoken. A most interesting man, *We* think him ; but, unfortunately, *Afflicted*. It is a truly sad case. Owing, they say, to a shock received when young, he developed General Paralysis combined with St. Vitus's dance, which is said to be most unusual. In spite of it all, he is so gentle and *Unassuming*, and his Views on the Oxford Movement are quite unlike any I have heard expressed, even at the dear old Rectory ; so original and wittily put. As a younger man he worked a great deal among the Romans, for owing to his affliction he was forced to spend the winter at San Remo, where he officiated in the English Church during the winter-months. It must indeed have been interesting work; but he is convinced, as regards the Romish Church, that Reform must come from *Within*. He is obviously a man who thinks for himself, and should go *Far*. He is a widower, and has now no help-meet to support him in his distress, though his five daughters are all nice girls, and devoted to their Dear Father. Yet they are not strong. Ruby, the eldest, is unfortunately deaf, while Rose (and *so* pretty) is, so they say, rather dumb. The other girls are still children. There are only four sons grown up—and these, though Dutiful, are, I fear, a Sad grief to their widowed Father. Desmond and Wilfred are both Afflicted, though very bright, and Percy (Mr. Broometoken's favourite, too, which makes it so *Sad*) has inherited his Father's paralysis but without the facial liveliness and Alert expression that accompany it in his case.

The War, of course, overshadows all our little joys and pleasures, and only our *admiration* of the Dear Queen's Courage keeps us cheerful. The Behaviour of the Radicals (if they are Radicals, and not simply Socialists) in Taking the part of the enemies of their *Country*, in supporting *Bullies* and *Murderers*, when they are at our Very Gate (for that is what It amounts to) is past belief. Have they no religion, no patriotism? Fortunately as far as *We* are in a position to judge here, the Feeling of the Country is so strong that we doubt if they will *ever* get in again. We must Trust Buller, and remember that Right is Might. We may be only a poor little island; They may be a Continent crammed with gold and diamonds : but we have faced worse things than that—and, besides, to whom can they *sell* them? And then, don't you feel, dear, as We do, that we are a People with a Mission? let us pray that we shall not shirk the Task imposed upon Us, and that, should it become necessary in the Best interests of the Natives (as Miss Fansharpe thinks it may) to annex the whole of Africa,

we shall not Flinch or Turn Away.   It is a duty.   We
Cannot leave the Natives alone.

Fortunately Miss Fansharpe keeps wonderfully well
and looks the Sweetest Picture of an Old Lady (I wish
I could send you a " snap ") as she lies in bed with her
White-hair and Lace-cap.   But I am sorry to say she
has been Troubled about one of the girls in the Home.
The Story is a Real Tragedy—a second time, too, it
appears.

Yrs. affecte. sister,

TERESA BRAMLEY.

P.S.—Could you forward me a Copy of the " Absent-
minded Beggar "; and then let me know how much I
owe you for it, dear ? Have you any news of Poor Minnie ?
Many messages of greeting to Harold and the children.

A few days after this letter was dispatched, Miss
Fansharpe passed peacefully away in her sleep at the
ripe age of eighty-seven.

After the funeral in the manner of a bygone age, the
old lady's will was read by her solicitor. It was now
discovered to the intense relish of Colonel and Mrs
Fansharpe that their aunt had not, after all, left an
annuity to her Companion. They did not mind " the
woman being remembered " in the will. That in a way
was only right and just, and dear Aunt Henrietta was
far too noble and sweet a character—they felt—ever to
err except on the side of generosity. Still, they had to
admit, she had shown a strong vein of common-sense,
and had proved herself a Fansharpe through and through.
Of course she had been far too generous—there were
many gifts and mementoes. All her religious books
she left to the Home, and each girl in it was to be provided, free of charge, with a black band round her arm
and a pair of stout walking-boots.

Instead of an annuity, then, Miss Fansharpe had

thanked her Companion for her faithful care, and bequeathed her a seventy-year-old Broadwood Upright Piano (because her Companion was so fond of music), a silver hand-mirror on the back of which were represented in repoussé the faces, sprouting wings instead of whiskers, like so many bloated white-bats, of five angels or cherubs, after a picture by Sir Joshua Reynolds (because it had been a " little Christmas gift " from her Companion) and ten pounds to buy a mourning dress.

Thus Miss Bramley was given another chance, launched on life for a second time, with her possessions slightly augmented.

She was fifteen years older, and, as a Companion, rigidly trained in the best school. She had now formally accepted as her creed the views of an Impoverished Gentlewoman and her voice though a little frayed, was still charming. She was able to add the silver mirror to the other objects of vertu of which she was the fortunate possessor (it went beautifully with the hair-brushes and silver boxes) and besides the mourning-dress, she had plenty of good plain clothes, and serviceable straw hats. And then there were the photographs, of course ! —enough things to make any room look nice.

The upright piano Miss Bramley sold locally for the sum of twenty pounds, in order to escape payment of carriage and storage dues ; and, with her worldly fortune thus increased, left Llandriftlog for London. Colonel Fansharpe, though he still regarded her suspiciously, was civil, even kind, in his manner; but as, during a snowstorm, Miss Bramley drove away from the door, she could see Ivy Fansharpe, in the brilliantly lighted rooms, engaged in a perfect hurricane of counting. One, two, three the umbrellas in the hall ; one, two, three, four, five the best tea-spoons ; one, two, three, four the ornaments on the drawing-room mantelpiece. It was sad leaving the old place and feeling one was not trusted. But one must be resigned to these things. It was the Lord's will . . . and He would provide—at least that was what her dear father had always said . . .

CHAPTER IV

IN ROOMS

" They are rattling breakfast plates in basement kitchens,
And along the trampled edges of the street
I am aware of the damp souls of housemaids
Sprouting despondently at area gates."

LONDON seemed to have become rather overwhelming. It was many years since Miss Bramley had visited it, not since Peregrine's christening, she thought; and then she had only stayed for a few days. It was so noisy, with all those dreadful omnibuses and their swearing coachmen; and then the four-wheelers and hansoms and bicycles made it positively dangerous to cross the street nowadays. Fortunately the police were most kind and attentive, otherwise she really did not know what she would have done !

The room in Ebury Street, which Mildred had found for her, was quite quiet, at any rate. Perhaps a little . . gloomy after Llandriftlog . . . but then one couldn't have everything, could one, and one mustn't grumble, must one ?

The lodgings were kept by a fat, retired butler, with a red nose, and his emaciated, whining wife. She was usually on the doorstep, without a hat on, pressing her fringe down on her forehead with her hand, away from the clutches of the mischievous wind, and deploring the days that were past—days, apparently of an unimagined grandeur, spent as lady's maid in the houses of the

43

great. Consequently she suffered from almost permanent neuralgia, which, again, aided her excruciatingly shrill lamentations. Her husband was not often in the house, but it was always to be understood that he would be back in a minute, back from some sudden and important mission. Miss Bramley's bed-sitting-room, on the third floor, was lined with a dark-red varnished wall-paper, which set off a gilt-framed and very fly-blown mammoth mirror that reflected back again, only more sadly, the wall-paper. On the mantelpiece there was a large, square black marble clock, like the old front of Devonshire House in shape, which was a very infernal machine for ticking and chimed every quarter of an hour; and, on each side of it, stood a vast candelabrum, its limbs hopelessly entangled in a dusty gauze cobweb, the object of which must ever remain a mystery. It looked as if it had been caught unexpectedly by the landlady in a butterfly net during one of her infrequent trips to the country. The window curtains were of fringed green plush, and there was a portière to match. The place was perfect of its kind, even down to the perpetual, rather pleasant smell of roast mutton and baked potatoes, warring with the other, distinctive odour exhaled by the bathroom geyser, a scent composed, in equal quantities, of gas and hot copper. Recurrent trouble with this remarkable but truculent machine was a decided feature of life in the house. A singular contraption, it was the only method of warming the water and imparted an air of caprice and whimsicality to the whole establishment. Sometimes when it was quite obvious to everyone in the house that the gas was full on and escaping very freely, the geyser would refuse for hours even a flicker, however many matches were struck and applied to it ; while, at other moments, it would light unexpectedly, giving a loud and festive pop, as though in sardonic mimicry of a champagne cork being drawn—perhaps a spiteful reference to the retired butler's habits—then proceed to give a spirited imitation of galloping horses, and, finally, within a few seconds, would explode with the report of a bomb, and flood the entire house with boiling water

Of course Miss Bramley was a great deal in her room. Each day she must read the *Times* and *Morning Post*, studying the " Situations Vacant " column, or search the other one headed " Situations Required " to see if her own advertisement had been entered. The worst of it was that putting in a notice became so expensive after a time. There seemed to be nothing, absolutely nothing at the moment. The War, no doubt. Everywhere, she heard the same thing. And, then, much of her time was spent in her room because, you see, she knew so few people in London. Of course Mildred, her sister, was most kind, very kind indeed, and asked her to lunch every Thursday and to cold supper on Sunday evenings. Mildred was now extremely prosperous, for her husband, Canon Hancock, a clergyman who believed in healthy, manly sports, holding that they helped true worship, had invented a contrivance, made of bamboo and watch-springs—like a mouse-trap at the end of a fishing-rod—for the ferreting out of " ping-pong " balls which had fallen under sofas, or bounced themselves on to the tops of cupboards. " Ping-pong " was the game of the moment; every country house, London mansion and suburban villa resounded with its wooden chatter and repartee, so that the clergyman's invention had brought him in a substantial sum. It

had helped him, too, in his career, filling the church
with ping-pong enthusiasts who could hear in his
sermons, even, some echo of the sound of their favourite
and fatuous recreation, and had heightened his fame
among his brother clergy, by singling him out from them
as a modern ecclesiastic ; though some, it may be, were
envious.

There was nothing, Miss Bramley felt, like brains.
Oh, why couldn't *she* invent something ? But what a
wonderful age of inventions we were living in, what with
Harold's " Ping-Pong-Picker "—as it was called—and
that geyser ; and then there were phonographs, too,
with their funny little tubular brown records, smelling
of damp cardboard (Harold had bought one), and
pianolas, and those funny motor-cars (she would be
terrified of riding in one, herself) and everything.
Really one felt quite proud to live in such an age.
Most interesting. And it was nice to see Mildred so
prosperous, though she told Miss Bramley that she was
really no better off than before, because of " the numerous calls on her income." Still, Harold's living was
a good one. They lived just behind Lancaster Gate, in
the Vicarage, which they had made so " pretty and
countrified." But, alas, Mildred was busy, so busy—
too busy, as she told Teresa, to see as much of her as
she would have wished . . but perhaps later . . .
afterwards . . . but they were both extremely kind,
and always asked a great many questions, and were,
undoubtedly, most helpful. Since her prosperity,
Mildred (though Miss Bramley had not analysed the
change in her sister) had developed a beautiful new voice,
especially for the discouragement and intimidation of
the needy—and, as she was inclined to think, needless—

poor, while at the same time the firm certainty of its
tone reassured the nervous rich. It was the voice of a
plump person, a voice clear and cultured, impersonal
yet emphatic—a real Charity Institution voice. By its
aid she could render poor as " poo-ah "—a sound which
contained in itself I know not what of condemnation—
and " dear " as " deahr." Every day, through the
absence of suitable situations, the renewed failure of
Miss Bramley's application, in the columns of the
Times, became more poignant to her. And Mildred
could hear of nothing. It was dreadful . . . where
was it to end ? She could not go on like this for ever
. . ₁ the expense, too ! . . . and then if one slept badly
and was depressed, one was less likely to find a post.
But though Miss Bramley realized this, she could not
help becoming more lost, by day and night, in mathe-
matical calculations based on her bank-book.

. . . .

One morning, after five weeks spent in searching, she
found what she had been seeking, and felt that it was
for her ; " Elderly Gentlewoman of Independent Means,"
she read, " wishes for Refined and Well-Connected
Lady Companion, musical and accomplished." She
applied for the situation at once. A few days later,
Miss Bramley set out, in her best clothes, for the Badminton Hotel, there to interview her future. She did
not wear her mourning dress, for after careful consideration she was afraid it might give a bad impression,
or make the old lady melancholy. When people were
old, they did not like to be reminded of death. One had
to think of these things, for so much depended on them.
She put on a blue dress, therefore, quiet in tone, but

over-inclined to fret and worry in detail, like a Gothic
cathedral ; covered with cobwebby frills and unnecessary
though quite gentle and modest attempts at animation.
However innocuous, these tiny flowerings were irritating
as the minute yet quite distinct scratching of a mouse
in the night.

Alas, she was now no longer the Rector's pretty
daughter. The face was drawn, and rather sallow, and
she had developed, as a defence, too much charm.
There was a little tightening of the muscles round the
mouth, which revealed itself when she was agitated—
a trembling of nerves which were still expectant of
an attack from Miss Fansharpe. As long as Miss
Bramley lived she would carry this indelible memento
of her dead patroness, the only one which it had not been
within the power of that lady to put in or take out of her
will. This tremor she could, with some difficulty,
smother by means of a rather too fixed smile. Though
only a small thing, it might go against her, prejudice the
old lady whom she was to interview, especially if at all
excitable herself. She must cover it up, therefore, and
smile. She must look cheerful and bright : it would
never do to appear timid. Her hands, now rather
shrivelled, were very cold. Nerves again, she supposed.
She treated herself to a final glance in the fly-blown
mirror, gave a slight tug at her " toque," arranged her
veil, and walked downstairs, and out into Ebury Street,
which lay in the afternoon light as brown, smooth
and unpretentious as a canal in a northern industrial
town.

She beckoned to a four-wheeler—it looked less
" fast " than a hansom cab, she thought. In less than
thirty-five minutes she was at the Badminton Hotel,

off Piccadilly, and was being ushered up into a private sitting-room. Miss Collier-Floodgaye received her very kindly. They talked a little about the War: the Boer atrocities were past belief. Only a few days before, a Boer farmer had taken deliberate aim at a band of English soldiers, who were trying to enter his house, had killed two of them . . . on the veldt, too, which somehow made it so much more horrible . . . and then he had made out that they were trying to burn his farm! It was said that several English children had disappeared . . . one had been found, it was rumoured, with its tiny toes cut off . . . foul play, somewhere. What a terrible grief it must be to the Dear Old Queen. But Miss Collier-Floodgaye was more interested in the Princess of Wales. There, she said in her deep voice, was a really beautiful woman. And so young looking. Now Miss Fansharpe had always taught Miss Bramley to regard the Princess as rather "insipid-looking," but she possessed enough sense to see that one must move with the times, and indulged in a warm eulogy of the Princess, ending up with some lines of Tennyson's:

> " Sea-king's daughter from over the sea,
> Saxon and Norman and Dane are we."

she declaimed.

Nor can it be said that when Miss Bramley delivered this encomium, she was insincere: for whatever she said, she meant and felt . . . while she was saying it. Now the old lady asked her to sing, and sitting down at the piano, Miss Bramley sang:

> " She is far from the land
> Where her dear hero sleeps."

Miss Collier-Floodgaye was so pleased with the performance that she had to sing it again. A sweet voice, the old lady thought, without any airs or graces. That was exactly what she liked. So many people became affected directly they tried to sing.

And, in truth, Miss Bramley's singing, of its sort, was at its best that afternoon. The little trill which lay hidden in the upper register of the voice, rose sweetly as a bird into the air, pecking gently at the china vases on the mantelpiece, fluttering softly round the walls and ceilings. Miss Collier-Floodgaye was really moved by it. Tea was brought in, and the Companionship settled.

.   .   .   .   .   .

It was an immense relief : though after living under the martial law of Miss Fansharpe she found Miss Collier-Floodgaye unusual . . . yes, unusual. The elder lady never seemed to want to indulge in a skirmish, never wished to bully, seldom grumbled. It seemed so strange that Miss Bramley wondered at times whether she could go on with it. The Companion's nerves, from habit, would be braced up periodically against the coming of some terrific onslaught . . . and since, now, one never developed, she would be left with a feeling of expectancy, which she was unable to interpret for herself, an intuition of impending disaster. If Miss Collier-Floodgaye had risen to the occasion, and had bullied her thoroughly for half an hour, this feeling would have been dissipated. But such was not the old lady's way. Gradually Miss Bramley became accustomed to the calm tenor of her new life . . . but, still, there was something lacking in her new friend . . . she was not really (Miss Bramley hated to say it, even to herself)

such a lady as Miss Fansharpe . . . had none of the
little ways . . . *you* know . . . not just those little
ways. . . . There was, always, something by which you
could tell, wasn't there . . .? What was it? she
wondered.

From the first moment of meeting her, Miss Bramley
felt that her new friend was failing, but very slowly,
imperceptibly; she might go on for many years yet
with the same mode of life that she was leading now.
Her memory was one of her weakest points. Occasionally she would, for example, refer to events, of which
her Companion could make nothing, in a manner
suggesting that she thought the younger woman shared
her recollections; but she would never be sufficiently
explicit to give Miss Bramley any idea of the actual sort
of circumstance to which she was alluding, and if
questioned, it would then dawn upon her that of course
the Companion knew nothing of such happenings, and
she would refrain from any further mention of it. It
was terrible, too, the way in which the old lady forgot
things! so inconvenient and gave so much trouble.
It was not just inaccuracy, it was real absent-mindedness,
so unlike Miss Fansharpe. Sometimes Miss Collier-
Floodgaye would make an appointment with a lawyer
or dressmaker, forget altogether, and then maintain
that she had kept it! Or again, she would imagine
that she had an engagement, when she had never made
one at all, and then be angry because the lawyer, or
dressmaker, had not been ready to receive her.

The months telescoped themselves into years, were
folded up into packets and put down. London in the
summer months was delightful, with its occasional
ballad-concerts, and concerts every Sunday at the

Queen's Hall. It was so nice to be able to hear a little music, for, though the reign of Miss Fansharpe, being over, had attained that golden varnished glow which accrues to old-master paintings and to past scenes in one's own life, it was useless to pretend that Miss Bramley had been able to enjoy much music at Llandriftlog. But then Miss Fansharpe had not really cared for music, did not approve of it . . . though of course on the whole she had liked Miss Bramley's singing. It had not been a mere caprice, for it appeared that the old lady had possessed her reasons for such a prejudice. She had been, it seems, the confidante of a sad story from a girl in the Home, who was a Lady . . . so Miss Fansharpe had said . . . and had once Trusted a Man Who Played the Piano . . . but things were different nowadays. Miss Collier-Floodgaye was genuinely fond of music, indeed of almost any sound of any sort . . . but then, Miss Bramley was forced to admit if Miss Collier-Floodgaye lacked the strong *moral* tone that had inspired Miss Fansharpe's every action, infused her every word, all the same she was much more " artistic " all round than the dead lady had ever been. Everybody had their faults, the Companion supposed, and one must try to make allowances, mustn't one ?

Nearly every Sunday, too, they went to church together, but often Miss Collier-Floodgaye would walk out before the sermon. This Miss Bramley did not like —it was irreligious and at the same time *conspicuous*. The truth of it was, as the Companion suspected, that the old lady really liked a very High Church service. But Miss Bramley was nothing if not Evangelical and would not give in : she *would not go* to places where they indulged in " Romish frippery."

Life in London was very exciting. On the 17th May, 1900, there arrived once more a solemn moment in our national life. To quote the leading article of a popular newspaper the following day :

Mafeking, after 216 days of siege and starvation and bombardment, is relieved. The last and third of the besieged garrisons has been snatched from the grasp of the Boer commandos, and the British flag has been kept flying over the most sorely tried of the three towns. Deep, indeed, must be the nation's gratitude to the Almighty Dispenser of all fates for this issue ; deep, too, its admiration, regard, and thankfulness for the heroism, constancy and endurance of Colonel Baden-Powell and his memorable band. And in our congratulations, let us not forget the greatest of living English generals, the man who has turned defeat into victory, who has conquered the Free State, and is now marching with inflexible resolution upon the Transvaal. Lord Roberts, our Commander-in-Chief, promised that the relief should come by May 18. He has kept his word.

In this hour of joy, it is the nation's duty to express its thanks to those who have fought and suffered, not by mere acclamation, but by giving practical proof of its sympathy and regard. Let us all recall the work of the heroic women who chose to share the daily toil and torment of our soldiers, who ministered to the sick and wounded and rendered the last sad office to the dying. Let us think of them shunning the refuge of the women's laager and facing the terrors of the constant warfare—and what that has meant is not lightly realized. Let us remember them starving in silence with cheerful faces that they might keep their country's flag flying overhead ; confronting death and a miserable death and preferring any fate rather than surrender.

And of the men who have fought under Colonel Baden-Powell, what shall we say ? Only that they proved themselves worthy to be ranked with the greatest heroes of our race. For all time their fates will be remembered,

their names will be an example, and the defenders of
Mafeking will live in history as men of whom the greatest
Empire in the world will be proud. Throughout the
tragical events of December and January—those melancholy months of war—we can point to them with exulta-
tion. They were an inspiration to us, though they never
knew it, for they, in that far-off isolated town, could
not understand with what anxiety and growing admiration their exploits were followed at home. They were
equal to every emergency ; they committed no faults ;
they were never found wanting. Starving, and dying of
hunger, they met and beat off the last furious onslaught
of the Boers, with what grievous loss we have yet to learn.
Many, too many of the heroic garrison have laid down
their lives, " Dark to the triumph they died to gain,"
they did not repent the sacrifice, they gave gladly their
all, and remembering their devotion we can say in the
sacred words, " It is well," as we sorrow for them.

It goes without saying that when the news arrived,
London burst forth into demonstrations of joy. Cheers
for Colonel Baden-Powell, whose light-heartedness and
resourcefulness have to a special degree won the regard
of our race, and even the grudging admiration of the
Continent ; round the streets flags and demonstrations
were everywhere. The event was an historical one. We
have waited for the news in mingled confidence and apprehension, yet with the inner belief that the God of all
justice was upon our side, and that He would not suffer
defeat and humiliation to be the lot of this heroic band.
We have not been disappointed. The nation, steadfast
through defeat, merciful in victory, may well acclaim the
steadfastness of the defenders of Mafeking.

London, indeed, did burst forth into demonstrations
of joy. A prominent and respected judge ran out of his
house into the streets of the Imperial City sounding his
dinner gong, a vast bronze cylinder of Oriental workman-
ship. This was only one incident in a night filled with
the pageant of Empery. The streets were crowded and

palpitating with singing, cheering and dancing patriots
almost mad with joy at the defeat at long last inflicted
upon our ungenerous, unsportsmanlike and sneaking
foe. Now at length they would realize that it was not
safe to hit someone smaller than yourself. It was
touching, our two ladies thought, to observe the way in
which grown men went wild with delight, sang, danced,
and even fell down in the street from emotion.

Before a year had gone came a moment even more
solemn. There was the alarming illness and then the
death of Queen Victoria . . . this latter perhaps the
most extraordinary event—at least so it seemed at the
time—since her birth.

The funeral procession for which all the foreign
monarchs came over was beautiful. To quote, again,
a celebrated morning paper of the next day :

The attitude of all was in keeping with the occasion.
The city was a city of mourners. Black and the Royal
Purple were everywhere, even the humblest and poorest
made efforts by their dress to show their respect for the
dead. History may have its surprises, but never again
shall we look upon a mourning world. To those who knew
it, the experience will prove inestimable. No one could
attend so august a service as these last solemn rites at
Windsor and remain unchanged. The grandiose simplicity
of our English prayer-book seemed to hush the ambitions
and humble the purpose of all the great ones of the earth
there gathered together. And then the memory pictured
the Queen, whom we so lately saw, and whose death
assembled so many monarchs, and memory lost itself in
wondering respect. To her were consecrated the grandeur
and solemnity of the service ; for her sake the whole world
was disturbed. Kings walked behind her coffin in glad
subordination to her wisdom and nobility. It is true
that the majesty of death always appals us ; death falsely

called the great leveller ennobles those upon whom he
places his icy finger.

The world bowed its knee because it recognized not only
a majestic death, but a majestic life. It mourned the
lady whose public virtues will long remain, let us hope, a
shining example.

Circumstances, too, conspired in the strangest manner
to introduce dramatic effects into these great rites.
The setting of the sun as the Queen's body entered Ports-
mouth Harbour was a coincidence, the dignity of which
was felt by all. It was as though nature joined in the
people's grief.

Alas! Miss Collier-Floodgaye and Miss Bramley
were not able themselves to observe this dramatic
gesture on the part of Nature, but they were able to
enjoy—if enjoy is the right word—the passing of the
funeral procession. The most inspiring figure, the
ladies agreed, was the German Emperor. Of course
he ought never to have sent that telegram to Kruger,
it was disgraceful (what could he have been thinking of?
But then foreigners are so funny in that sort of way . . .
do not see things like English people). You would have
thought that Kruger's appearance (what an unpleasant
face that horrid old man had—the last cartoon of him
in *Punch* wearing a top hat and fur coat, and holding
an umbrella was wonderfully good) would have been
enough for the German Emperor (did the Kaiser read
Punch? they asked themselves). But then, whatever
his faults, he was so quick, clever and changeable—
the artistic temperament that so many foreigners
possessed. Not, of course, that he was a foreigner
entirely, for after all he was the Queen's grandson:
though he did not look a bit English with his funny
twirling moustachios; but the artistic temperament

was a queer thing. They said he was almost a genius—though he had a disease of the ear, a withered arm, and cancer, and could not live long. How wonderfully great men fight against misfortune !

Personally, Miss Collier-Floodgaye wished the Tsar had been there. Such a good-looking man, but not a bit barbaric or Russian in appearance. More, she supposed, like the Duke of York (would he ever come to the throne ? . . . how sad it had been about the Duke of Clarence . . . and poor Princess May engaged to him). Miss Bramley doubted whether the Duke of York *ever would* come to the throne, though she admitted that it was beginning to be credible now that the Prince of Wales was King . . . (not that he was crowned yet). She had never felt that he would be King. (Not clever like the Kaiser.) His subjects adored the Tsar ; Miss Collier-Floodgaye had been told that they called him the Little White Father, but Russians were like that, so loyal and religious. They would go through fire and water for their Tsar. There was no doubt, Miss Collier-Floodgaye affirmed, that they were the People of the Future. Fortunately for him, the Tsar had married the granddaughter of Queen Victoria. She was sure to keep him straight and see that he did not abuse his great power. Nothing much could go wrong while *she* was there to look after him. All the same, Miss Collier-Floodgaye was glad that herself had not got to rule over Russia—and now, as if they had not got enough, they wanted India too. As for Miss Bramley, she confessed that if she had been the Tsarina, she would have been terrified of bombs and those dreadful Nihilists . . . dreadful . . . to go out and never know if you would come back again. Meanwhile, there was the

King Carlos of Portugal riding by, in his white uniform, quite an imposing figure.

.   .   .   .   .   .

The summer passed, and there came round the Coronation, the delayed Coronation of King Edward. What an awful thing appendicitis must be ! It came, so they said, from eating grape pips—not of course that King Edward was in the habit of eating grape pips, but he must, they supposed, have swallowed one by mistake (curious, though, that bullfinches never suffered from it). It was so very odd, though, that no one ever had been ill from appendicitis when Miss Collier-Floodgaye was a young girl. What had happened to our ancestors when they had appendicitis ? However the Coronation, when it came, was magnificent. Such lovely illuminations !

The Badminton Hotel was most comfortable, and all the servants so *obliging*. It was very near everything, too ; near the theatres. They did not go so often to theatres as to concerts, but they went, of course, to see *San Toy*. That was a real success ! And they made a rule of going to see any musical comedy in which Edna May was performing, because she was so sweet and genuine and unaffected, with a lovely voice. They went to see Beerbohm Tree's productions, as well : *Ulysses*, all those wonderful poetic plays by Stephen Phillips. The scene in Hades was most effective, though really almost too overpowering and frightening

But it was difficult to go out much to plays in the winter, unless one went to a matinée, for the old lady suffered severely from bronchial attacks and a kind of asthma. Any foggy night seemed to bring it on ; and London, when one could not get out, was rather lonely : though there were always, of course, interesting people staying in the hotel. But Miss Collier-Floodgaye was too much inclined to talk to anyone she saw, the result of a life that must hitherto have been lonely.

During the first few years, which they spent in London and in short visits to seaside resorts, Miss Bramley had become steadily more attached to the old lady, though with this new feeling of friendship other sensations mingled. But the two ladies got on very well together. Miss Bramley was privileged to call the elder lady " Cecilia," while Miss Collier-Floodgaye called the Companion by her Christian name—or, rather, by a pet variant of it—" Tibbits." Miss Fansharpe would never have done such a thing. She had revelled in the sonority of " Teresa." But there could be no doubt that Miss Collier-Floodgaye was kind, extremely kind. Yet it is doubtful whether this amiability was in the eyes of the Companion altogether a virtue. The truth is that though Miss Bramley liked, indeed loved, her new friend, she looked down upon her for her kindness and affability. Was this because there existed a stratum of intense and unexpected hardness in the character of the younger woman, or because she had been, as a Companion, rigorously trained, fashioned by Miss Fansharpe into a marvellous instrument, for anyone with a temper, possessed of a sensitive technique, to play upon, and therefore despised Miss Collier-Floodgaye for her lack of virtuosity? Contempt, certainly, entered into Miss Bramley's affection for the old lady . . . but, in spite of it, she was grateful to her.

One day, after Miss Bramley had been in her employ some years, Miss Collier-Floodgaye informed her that she intended to see her solicitor, and make a new will— or rather add a codicil to her old one—bequeathing to

her Companion all her property. Often in after years
the old lady was to revert to this fact, as if to assure
the younger woman that she need have no fear of the
future. And Miss Bramley, for her part—though this tale
was one she had heard before, and of the truth of which
she must by this time have begun to entertain suspicions
—was once more inclined to believe it. For Cecilia
was, she had to admit, most kind and considerate . . .
if rather difficult . . . in small ways, of course. And
though she was not aware of it, Miss Bramley had not
until now in her life received much kindness. Thus,
even if contempt mingled with her affection, she was
sincerely attached to the old lady.

This new emotion experienced by Miss Bramley, this
feeling of friendship, was not, however, without its
disadvantages for Miss Collier-Floodgaye : instead of
drawing her out, instead of interpreting her to others,
as the old lady had hoped, the Companion was careful,
as it were, only to let her out of herself when they were
by themselves. For from this novel, disturbing sensation
was being born slowly, painfully, another emotion,
jealousy : and Miss Bramley was frigid in manner to
anyone who displayed a tendency to become intimate
with the old lady. Even upon the casual acquaintance
of a hotel—upon that pathetic over-dressed proportion
of England's surplus middle-aged females, which in the
short span between sunrise and sunset, birth and death,
finds an assurance of eternity in the involute inanities
of a conversation carried on among itself, and thus lives
by taking in its own spiritual washing or, occasionally,
washing its own dirty linen—Miss Bramley turned a
severe and then a threatening eye. Indeed it was the
Companion who had turned instructress and was now

training the Companioned, the Companion who was courageously cross and bad-tempered, fearing no reprisals. In fact, under the genial warmth of Miss Collier-Floodgaye's kindness, the character of the younger woman was suddenly beginning to sprout in new, unexpected, sometimes undesirable ways. It was as though the inexorable system of restraints and restrictions responsible for the gnarled, crouched, crooked growth of a dwarf Japanese tree had suddenly been removed, and long after one had imagined it set for ever in its present mould, the tree had begun to thaw its shape, to draw up and disentangle itself, to sprout and bud and blossom, attempting a growth to which it could never now attain, so that the mere effort which this attempt entailed must spoil the grotesque symmetry imposed upon it, without hope of the compensating gain of that balanced woodland beauty for which it strove.

Many persons must have attributed the manifestations of ill-temper in which Miss Bramley indulged, if her friend tried to make a new acquaintance, to the scheming nature of the Companion—for this is an attribute with which Companions to rich old ladies are invariably, inevitably credited. It was, no doubt, simply presumed that she was fearful of the financial consequences to herself of any new friendship upon which the old lady might embark. But this motive did not account to any great extent—at any rate not during this period of their intimacy—for the Companion's behaviour. A more reasonable, as well as charitable, explanation of it would have been that Miss Bramley was for the first time experiencing jealousy, that primitive symptom and complement of affection. She had never, it is true, treated Miss Fansharpe's friends in this manner ; but then she had never really been fond of Miss Fansharpe. Her mind, however, had been so innocent of friendship that she had not realized it during Miss Fansharpe's lifetime, and, now that the old lady was dead, took her affection for her as established. Herself had accepted all the little tricks of disarmament, the effusive and gushing ways, which she had been forced to develop for her own protection, as the genuine expression of that mysterious thing, friendship. Then, suddenly, the counterfeit coin which she had been taught, been forced, to pass off had become genuine! Alas, so false was it still in appearance that strangers would not, could not, believe in its authenticity.

No, Miss Collier-Floodgaye had earned her affection and contempt. If any feeling at all connected with the old lady's will ever entered Miss Bramley's mind, it was that a fresh codicil, as betokening new allegiances, new affections, would—however slight in themselves were the bequests—be painful as indicating that while Miss Collier-Floodgaye had once been so fond of her— and of her alone—as to name the Companion heir to the entire fortune, the old lady had latterly rated this friendship less highly and had permitted others to share with the Companion the final testamentary proof of it. It may be, again, that Miss Bramley was not even as much occupied as this with the pecuniary side of her friendship. As a Companion she had been rigidly trained, and had probably been taught to consider any surmise about a will, even in her own mind, as taboo— taboo in thought as in conversation. And a discipline such as that which Miss Fansharpe had imposed upon her takes many years of soft indulgence to break down entirely.

.   .   .   .

During the winter in London, Miss Collier-Floodgaye could not get out much, because of her asthma. Consequently she would sit—not in her own private room—but in the public sitting-rooms ; and directly Miss Bramley turned her back, would begin a conversation with some visitor ; would even tell them about her money affairs . . . inclined to be boastful, the Companion remarked. Then, if she did go out, a severe attack of asthma would follow—the fogs, no doubt. It was, therefore, Miss Bramley who conceived the idea of spending a winter at Newborough, Miss Bramley who first suggested it. Very nice people still lived there, she was told, though she had not visited it since, as a child, she had stayed with her aunt, Miss Titherley-Bramley. It had been delightful. And Harold had been compelled to go there, two years ago, in connection with his work for the Ecclesiastical Rest Home (where he had installed a ping-pong table and founded a challenge cup) so he had decided to make a holiday of it, taking Mildred and the children with him. They had liked it very much, very much indeed. And all the Curates in the Home loved the place, they said. After all, if one did not care for Newborough, one need not visit it again, need one, dear ? And then Cecilia liked being " braced," and Newborough was so bracing, whereas Torquay, as Miss Bramley knew, for she had lived there, was inclined to be relaxing.

CHAPTER V

FACING SOUTH

" Un soleil sans chaleur plane au-dessus six mois,
Et les six autres mois la nuit couvre la terre.
C'est un pays plus nu que la terre polaire ;
Ni bêtes, ni ruisseaux, ni verdure, ni bois ! "

AN impression of gaiety during its season must always
be the aim and attraction of a seaside resort. To produce
this effect, Newborough relied even more upon the
crowds that flowered with a brief radiance in street,
avenue, and crescent through the few summer months.
than upon the bold gesture with which it stood, as if
at bay, confronting the elements, or upon the clean,
spreading gold pavements diurnally revealed and
obscured by its burgeoning green tides that under the
warm sun seemed to break into white petals as you
watched them. And if the sea blossomed at these
moments, how much more so did the town ! Though
of no one plan or pattern, it was a natural garden in
which could be exhibited ever-varying human flowers,
flowers beautiful or grotesque : and through these
pleasances, summer flickered for a while with a northern
fervour, with the intensity of an aurora borealis.

Essentially it was the crowds that gave life to the town.
Newborough depended, in fact, for its characteristic air
of vitality as much upon the fluttering mobs that in
the season decked it, as an old tree counts for its adornment upon the yearly birth and unfolding of its buds.
The town resembled an old tree, too, in that while
throughout the winter it feigned death, in reality it was

merely hibernating, gathering to itself fresh strength for the vernal effort that must ensue. As through black and angular branches, the cruel winds soughed and moaned through the empty winter streets, or cracked their steel-tipped whips at the street corners. Only the perpetual thud and hammer of waves at the walls below quickened this corpse of a town with a chafing movement, as if, as a last resort, artificial respiration were being applied to it. In addition, the battering of the sea imparted a sense of continuity, of being in touch with history, and the huge desert of time that lay behind it. All history, which is life ; all life—which meant to this town death —had been brought hither over the backs of these whale-like, jostling, grey waves that still leap and plunge under the cliffs. Celt and Norman, Saxon and Dane, had followed the same troubled and rebellious pathway. Beneath the precipitous, broken wall of the Norman castle, up on its jutting hill, was hidden the foundation of a Roman Camp. Occasionally this Castle had notched the long stick of English history, with the atrocious murder of a royal favourite, with a barbarous slaughter of traitors, by the reception of a hunchback and assassin-king, or finally, by harbouring the Roundheads, who from this retreat carried out their raids for the destruction of the few isolated works of art that blossomed miraculously in this arid district, noticeable as the plants that in the springtime flaunt their shrill, glazed cups among polar wastes. It was always with a tragedy that the stick had been notched. But now History appeared to have sunk into a respectable, genteel old lady with a past into which it were better not to enquire, while the town depended for its present existence—as must all health resorts—not so much upon the death, as upon the continued ill-health or eccentricity of its residents, who would, but for their being thus afflicted, move to live elsewhere. The numerous local doctors had banished as far as possible a sudden or definite death, and had instead, developed their aptitude for inducing in patients a subtle state of suspended animation, which corroded the will and transformed the visitor, as if by magic, into a resident.

Yet the breakers still thundered, foaming at wall and cliff, eating them up ever so slowly. And during the winter this sound communicated to the sensitive a feeling of nervous tension that, in the years of which we are writing, grew steadily more acute. Something was beginning to stir again, to move in the dark winter nights . . . something was being prepared far away behind the curtaining of the grey foam, the black rolling waves, something sudden and disastrous . . . a pompeian fate was surely in store for this placid town ; but what could it be, since no volcano let her feathers droop softly over these northern waters ? It was, in fact, History once again collecting her pack of ghouls for another and more ferocious attack. Death was once more to stretch, in concert with her, his cold, bony fingers over the grey wastes toward this town. With that occurrence we are not properly concerned, but nevertheless our story must be told to the monotonous accompaniment of waves beating like the drums of gathering armies : an accompaniment so tremendously out of scale that its very force adds, as it were, a certain mad interest to the varying trivial and human events which the tale describes.

.   .   .   .   .   .

When these splintering steel rollers thudded at the

town all day, and hammered, muffled by wind all the
night long, as though secretly preparing for it a coffin,
life in the borough became infinitely local. Newborough
reverted to being a small country-town, except for its
greater proportion of idle shops and voracious tradesmen.
The old, the white, and the asthmatic had installed themselves by this time in their upper rooms—which by a
respectable but quite useless convention, for here all
winter winds were equally withering, all prospects
similarly bleak—must face South. Between these
numerous rooms of Southern aspect, however, a never
failing line of communication was formed, and heroically
maintained in the very teeth of the East wind, by an
eager chain of clergymen, nurses, doctors, masseurs and
volunteers for gossip generally. In the manner of the
honey bee, these active workers sipped the gossip of
each flower, which, by a constant flitting and droning
from one blossom to another, they were at the same
time able to fertilize, forcing it to bring forth a new
crop of honey for them the following year. Thus they
were partly responsible for the sweet yield of each new
flower, each new scandal, by which they were to benefit,
and, by passing on to the next flower, would probably
cause to spring up a hundred more seeds that would
again flourish into new and lusty scandals.

The genuine local magnates had either by now
taken shelter in their vast yellow-cardboard mansions
in the fog-bound squares of London—mysterious, almost
invisible mansions whence they conducted their annual
winter harlequinade under the flaring greenery, that
suggested a swampy forest in South America, born of
mingled yellow fog and gas-light, gradually building up,
in the manner of coral insects, a whole mountain of

parcels for the coming festival—or had retired to their frost-bitten seats in the countryside adjacent to Newborough, where, too, they prepared for a riotously expensive and imbecile celebration of Christmas. From these latter icebound and isolated forts of ignorance, the garrisons of pheasant-coloured country gentlemen, accompanied by their mates, sallied forth to slaughter the birds of the air. The respect in which each male of the herd was held altered every day, moved up and down as by a sliding scale, in direct proportion to the massacre he had achieved. At midday, or shortly after, they would pause in their slaughter and would hold a feast in the middle of the shambles and would then again return to their carnage. In the hamlets and small towns which they dominated, the county families continued to preserve the pure tradition of English logic by themselves rearing vast quantities of birds solely in order to kill them later, while at the same time they were busily engaged in collecting subscriptions for the establishment of a " Bird Sanctuary " for " our feathered friends." Or else they would preside one evening over a concert in aid of the " noble work " carried on by the " Society for the Prevention of Cruelty to Animals," and then the next day they would themselves ride out to hunt. More foxes would be chased until they were finally exhausted and could move no more, until the little red-brown beasts would be torn to pieces, like Jezebel, by the expectant dogs, and those young members of the ferocious tribe who were taking part in these rites for the first time would have their cheeks anointed with the blood, yet warm, of the poor furry creature. On the way home, one of the hunters would stop to give a carter in charge for beating his horse.

It is here interesting to turn aside for a moment to
note, and wonder at the fact, that it is always the horse
these people protect. In England deer, foxes, badgers,
otters and hares may be practically eaten alive, the
dogs that worry them munching pieces of flesh that still
quiver with life ; rabbits may be put in sacks, and then
ejected, a few yards from a varied assembly of dogs, to
be bludgeoned with clubs by a mixed herd of male and
female sadists, or they may, with general approbation,
have their blood sucked by human-trained ferrets, who
fasten cruel teeth on their unoffending throats. Pheasants,
grouse, snipe, partridges and nearly any other bird
can be shot at sight. Similarly, the English big-game
hunter abroad seems determined on the extinction of
nearly every animal except the horse. One can understand his wishing to cover his own tracks by attempted
parricide, by wiping out of existence everywhere the man-
ape, the gorilla, orang-outang, and chimpanzee, but
why need he assassinate such wise and graceful creatures
as elephant and giraffe ? But who ever heard of a hunter
out after the heads of the wild horse ? The bull-fight,
too, is taboo to these savages because, in the course of it,
their pet, their darling, the horse may be injured. No
pity is felt for the bull. Yet of all animals the horse,
though occasionally beautiful, is the stupidest, is merely
an obsolete method of locomotion, an animated, strong-
willed and headstrong Stephenson's Rocket. By its
slowness in the town, by its silliness in the country, it
is surely responsible for more deaths in city and countryside than all the elephants and motor-omnibuses of the
world heaped together. Not that anyone wishes to see
the horse, however low it may rank in animal life, mal-
treated or injured, but it is time that the creature was

relegated to private collections or to museums and zoological gardens.

These logicians were, then, in the winter too busily occupied with their multifarious activities in death-dealing to visit the neighbouring towns. Newborough was now given over, except for an occasional shopping raid, to its all-the-year-round inhabitants ; and the departure of the grandees in the early autumn was a signal for certain lesser figures to emerge from their summer hiding-places. Afraid of being overshadowed, these either went away for the summer months or, pretending that they had departed, remained indoors. But directly Lady Ghoolingham left Newborough—for her exit was the maroon which sounded safety to them—they crept out from their several retreats, gradually inflating themselves to a due degree of importance, and at the same time aping in their manner, with much accuracy, the great who had just gone away. This latter trick was a fault in technique, because it at once suggested that mimicry of this kind must have been founded on fairly close study, and that these winter-patricians must in reality have been very near the town all the time to observe so minutely small details of deportment, and to maintain such a successful impersonation. Mrs. Shrubfield, for example, would appear (as when a great actress is taken ill and an understudy plays in her stead) in the leading rôle, that of Lady Ghoolingham. It is true that in looks, in dress, they did not very much resemble each other, but in each case, the part was conceived, was interpreted, in the same way. The plump, pyramidal chest and head—for the neck was not obtruded on one's notice—of Mrs. Shrubfield, the shoulders draped in a black mantle, the face smiling and surmounted in its turn by the double curving smile of a black wig, crowned with a bonnet (which never varied, for it was copied each year on the principle of " The King is dead, long live the King ") was borne along in mimic state by two black horses. On the box sat a coachman and footman, both wearing in cold weather a short black fur cape, which repeated the pyramidal shape within, and imparted to the entire equipage a certain quality of poise, of rhythm as it were.

Occasionally Mrs. Shrubfield's twinkling eye of jet, an optic carefully trained for such detective work, would track down a friend. She would tap the footman on the back with a folded fan, that together with an umbrella, the handle of it carved and painted to imitate a parrot's head, was part of the insignia of her hibernal office ; without them both she was never seen in public. The footman, having received this ritual tap, this accolade, passed it on to the coachman, who, knowing full well its meaning, immediately drew up without making any enquiry of his mistress, for it signified that Mrs. Shrubfield wished to have " a little chat," to " hear all the news." As a matter of fact, she was inclined to give more than she received. No sooner had the carriage drawn up, indeed, than a muffled oracle came forth from the depth of the great pyramid. But owing to veils, frills, and above all to furs, the limpid meaning of the prophetess was somewhat obscured. Always rather out of breath, as if after some tremendous effort, her first action, therefore, would be to disentangle the wolf, fox, skunk, stoat, squirrel—or whatever the dear little animal was—which, presumably indulging in a fit of local colour, aimed at impersonating the English whiting and so, thoughtfully clasping its own tail in its mouth round her billowy throat, now kept her warm. But the little creature was resolute and tenacious as well as kindly. At first it would spin round her neck playfully, chasing its own tail like a puppy. Then trouble would ensue with its teeth, which appeared to be snapping in death rigors. The struggle became titanic, resembling that of Hercules when he wrestled with the lion. Yet even when one first saw Mrs. Shrubfield, one felt that everything in the world was possessed of a purpose that could be explained, that, at the same time, there existed no difficulty that would not yield to a combination of firm courtesy and applied reason. Every roughness could, indeed would, be made smooth. And, sure enough, the minute though rebellious creature, was soon tranquillized, a triumph as much due to diplomacy as to brute force. Beaming with good nature, in spite of her recent encounter with a wild beast, and with a wheezy geniality which was supposed to be not always unaided by artificial stimulants, Mrs. Shrubfield would now proceed to hand out little cosmopolitan clichés in French, German and Italian. Of these lingual accomplishments she was immensely proud, nor even in her most exhilarated moments did such gifts desert her.

This appearance of Mrs. Shrubfield in her winter rôle of Grande Dame was resented to an extraordinary degree by the invalid population, which was nevertheless, by its own edict, powerless to oppose her coup. Others there were, however—Miss Waddington for instance—who, supported silently by the contingent that still bravely faced South in their upper rooms, strove to divide the sceptre with her.

CHAPTER VI

TERMINUS

" I who have sat by Thebes below the wall
And walked among the lowest of the dead."

APART, then, from this local winter-noblesse, of whom
Mrs. Shrubfield was a worthy, if not indisputable leader,
apart from the gossiping tradesmen at their untrodden
doorsteps, there were only to be seen in the streets at
this season well-known figures, whose peculiarities
distinguished them and were, as well, a source of continual, eager discussion. These unfortunates were often
the wrack of some former remote tide of summer visitors,
their wanderings now bounded by poverty and the sea.

There was, for example, Mr. Paul Bradbourne. It
still remains doubtful which of many experiences, some
of them in the end unpleasant for himself, and all of
them tragic in their consequences for others, had finally
deposited him upon this winter strand. But he must, by
this time have reached nearly seventy years of age, and
thirty of these, at least, he had spent here.

A sinister enough figure was this little apple-cheeked
gentleman jockey and former friend of the then Prince
of Wales, as he passed by in his woe-begone, well-cut
checks, sucking an appropriate straw. In his hand he
held a riding-crop, with a long, folded lash, and every
few minutes he would smack with it his beautifully
polished, brown-leather gaiters. Into this empty gesture
he poured an intensity of feeling. It became, as he did

73

it, a symbol of sporting worldliness. Half French by birth—for his mother had been a famous French actress, who, after a complicated career, had married his father, a rakish officer in the Life Guards—he had lived much in Paris as a young man, but had never been back to it since the fall of Napoleon III. Indeed the last sound he had heard was the bull-mouthed bellowing of the guns outside Paris in 1870, for he was cut off from all auditory impressions of the modern world. Only once more in his lifetime was any vibration exterior to Mr. Bradbourne to reach his consciousness.

But this disability did not much inconvenience him, for few people attempted, few wished, speech with this little old man. The truth was that there were unpleasant stories about him . . . rumours sufficiently unpleasant to outweigh in the minds of the townspeople the proven facts of his former friendship with the great. As he went by, the plump, red shopmen, with their bushy, bristling whiskers, eyebrows and moustaches, could be observed pointing him out, whispering, and shaking with loud, lewd laughter, while, on the other hand, the solidly dressed, stately wives of doctors, lawyers and clergymen could be noticed flurrying their young daughters past him, and commanding them not to turn round. If the inquisitive young demanded why they were forbidden to look back at " the funny old gentleman," they were made to feel that by this enquiry they had not only committed a grave impropriety, but had also probably forfeited for their parents the general esteem in which they had hitherto been held. Thus in many a schoolroom a breath of brimstone, an attractive aura of ogreism lingered about this small, rather evil figure. But himself was possessed by no such scruples about

turning round to stare, and as though deafness had sharpened his eyes, out of them darted, like a cobra's tongue,
a forked grey flame, which seemed to flicker lingeringly
round the flaxen pigtails of the young girls now receding
into the perspective.

Paul Bradbourne had been rich in his time, but having
ruined himself as well as many others, must now live on a
small allowance doled out by unwilling relatives. Still,
it had been a great day for them when they had finally
succeeded in landing such an expensive reprobate alive
in a small red coffin at Newborough. This square little
house, with its few windows like over-prominent eyes,
had seldom been entered by anyone except its owner
and his housekeeper, and was a point upon which was
focused an amount of local interest. But for the watchers
nothing ever transpired. Yet out of all the town, only
one or two men from the Club, who excused themselves
by letting it be known that they " liked a good sport,"
were ever sufficiently conquered by their curiosity to
speak to him. These, when they encountered him in
bars by chance, would roar questions at him about past
racing days and dead personalities. If he answered them,
his speech was that of the deaf, hollow and impersonal,
though often he would make no reply—perhaps because
he could not hear, perhaps because he despised them—
merely allowing the grey fire of his eye to scorch their
faces. When, however, he was inclined to talk, his lower
jaw dropped, then opened and shut rapidly, as if on a
hinge, in the abrupt manner and with the jerky rhythm
of a ventriloquist's dummy. Indeed he resembled an
automaton of the Second Empire, so small and neat was
he, his body thin, angularly elegant, as though stuffed
with straw, his movements disconnected and broken.

He perhaps comforted himself that, in as far as his mind could interpret life, he had lived, compressing as much adult experience as possible into a small span. But, in reality, life had ended many decades before death occurred. It was dull enough now that his old friend had ascended the throne. Nevertheless, though bankrupt in all else, body, mind, friends, money and present pleasures, there were yet in his possession things of which it was impossible for any human being—even a relative—to deprive him . . . his memories. These, by allowing no present sound to obtrude upon the sanctity of the past, it is probable that his deafness intensified. He was continually, as he grew older, away from Newborough, in those Paris dance halls, cafés and gambling saloons which had long ceased to exist except in his own mind, continually in places where he had been admired and well-known, a general favourite. Once more he could hear the peculiar leafy rustle made by the silken flounces of the crinolines, as they rippled caressingly past, while patchouli floated to him over the shrill east wind, whose shrieking he could not hear, whose sting he could hardly feel. Once more in his empty conch sounded the langorous lilt, beating up into a furious storm, of the Hungarian band, in their slung jackets and gaudy frogged uniforms. Or, he was back in the fabulous spring days of his youth, when May burnt with a steady green flame now unknown, and, as though the honeyed west wind had lifted suddenly a curtain, every tree was revealed weighed down by blossom, from the formal, pointed flambeaux of the chestnuts to the gold-flecked white foam of the fruit trees, to the hedge of hawthorns that were, at these moments, avenues of white-winged ships in full sail across a green ocean. He was moored in a

punt on the Seine with beautiful companions now dead
at his side, while under them the sleek-maned river-
horses played gently, softly rolling and tumbling. He
must be back soon for a first night at a theatre ; already
the whiskered critics were beginning to gather for their
attack. And to-morrow, there were the races, and, soon,
would sound again in the petrified shell of his ear, the
genial, rather guttural congratulations of the Prince
on a remarkable win

.   .   .

Very different from Mr. Paul Bradbourne were the
two little Misses Finnis—the peripatetic Miss Pansy
and Miss Penelope—daughters of the mid-Victorian
artist of that name, portrayer of so much pensive youth
and beauty wilting amid azalea and almond blossom.
These sisters, so pathetic in their half-hearted gentlehood,
so kind yet so badly made, were queer progeny for that
old laurelled æsthete who had for so long tyrannized
over them. During their father's lifetime, these slaves
had been too busy looking after him, too busy cooking
and tidying, atoning for his extravagances, to have
any spare minutes in which to develop themselves mentally or physically. And now the great man, to whom
it had been their pride to minister, was forgotten by all
save themselves, and they must hurry past on their
short basset-like legs to give some secret piano lesson to
a child of vulgar parentage, to instil in the right-hand
of a rich tradesman's daughter the requisite large
flourish of a lady's handwriting, or on a similar task of
carefully guarded opprobrium. A timid look of recognition smiled from those eyes of faithful, basset brown,
and they bowed tentatively. They blushed as they did
so, a cold heliotrope blush, and the false brown fringe,

with its regular curls, seemed to be creeping downward over their foreheads in an amiable attempt to shelter them from embarrassment. The odious nature of their task was to be read in their kindly, furtive glances. "Nowadays," one sister would remark to the other, "the commoner you are, the more money you have. It's dreadful," and she would give a little frost-bitten laugh. Their own comprehension of the iniquity of their Judas-like dealing made them more fervent in such protestations. For by initiating these children into the mysterious accomplishments of a local lady, by divulging the correct style of handwriting, the secret of scraping through with a water-colour or reaching home safely after a piano piece, they were, they felt, betraying the class to which themselves so tenaciously clung. Their action was equivalent to the disclosure, for sake of money, on the part of a Freemason, of the precious, closely hidden rites of his society. And one day their treachery would leak out (it was sure to do so) and they would be exposed, ruined. What condign punishment, what awful humiliation, would then be inflicted upon them by the genteel but ferocious denizens of square and crescent!

Fortunately, though, in their good nature, the sisters were of the greatest use to the numberless wealthy invalids of the town, who were therefore determined, however well-informed of these lapses, not to notice—nor to relieve the circumstances that occasioned—them. On Miss Pansy and Miss Penelope hurried, in their threadbare blue coats and skirts, iridescent feather boas tied round their short necks, the whole effect crowned with wide-brimmed, dark-blue straw hats.

They bowed, in passing, to Sir Timothy Tidmarshe,

who could be seen walking very rapidly, with an unusual but quite obvious combination of pomposity and intense fright, down St. Peter's Street—Sir Timothy was that proud possession of every seaside town, a marine Baronet. In character he was consequential but amiable, eccentric, and above all, superstitious. Extraordinary events would really overwhelm him occasionally, so that it was no wonder that the poor gentleman was a believer in good and ill fortune. One day after lunch, for instance, he had turned into an auction room, where a sale was in progress—for he liked, he used to say, to see things going on. He happened, an unusual occurrence in any case, to fall asleep with his eyes open, and woke up to find himself the involuntary purchaser of a diamond and ruby tiara, which he had never seen, for £5,000. Further, at the moment, Sir Timothy was singularly innocent of money, but, out of pride, he was obliged to buy, and not to dispute, the wretched bauble, and out of fear to keep it hidden from Lady Tidmarshe for the rest of his life. He did not dare send it to the bank, for they might wish to know why, in the present state of his account, he had purchased such a thing, and, as well, it might give a bad impression of his moral character. Every day he was in terror that the blazing-eyed creature might be discovered. One never knew, even if one locked it up, whether it was secure. And whatever was he to say to Lady Tidmarshe if she found it ? He would have to explain, too, why he had not shown it her before ; so that in a way, every hour that passed without her discovering it, would make the difficulty more acute when the dread day should arrive. She would be sure to credit him with some purpose in his wish for concealment. Why had he hidden it, she would ask ?—women were so jealous. And he would seek reassurance by the consultation of a thousand auguries.

In the end the tiara was only found after the Baronet's death, at the bottom of a locked chest of drawers. Its discovery was the opportunity for much talk and many surmises, and caused great pain to his family, above all to his lady.

Lady Tidmarshe, though in constant care over her own precedence, had but one real anxiety in the world —and one that, luckily, she was able to share with her daughter—how best to " keep up Papa's Position." With this object always in view, she had, perhaps prudently, by a kind of feminine intuition, decided never to be seen in public. Many years before, she had passed this dignified decree of voluntary self-confinement, comparable to the gesture of Pope Pio Nono after the loss of his temporal dominions. If she went out, she might " lower " herself . . . it might not be realized who she was . . . and people were so pushing nowadays . . . but if she remained in an almost Papal seclusion, no one could fail to yield her correct precedence to her. After all nobody could attempt to get into the room in front of her, if herself was already in it . . . moreover, there was more in it than that . . . for if she received no one, then how could anyone get in front of her. . . ? It was much wiser. She consented, however, to receive one or two vassals, such as the Misses Finnis ; but for the rest she remained in her own house, writing constant letters of condolence (for her friends seemed always to be losing their relatives) which she was able to permeate with a wonderful atmosphere of patronage, and sending an occasional bunch of wizened grapes, with a card attached, to an infuriated invalid.

One curious consequence of her decree of invisibility
was that in appearance Lady Tidmarshe had really
become almost invisible, non-existent, a ghost in her
own drawing-room—or rather, by some modification of
the fate that overtook Lot's wife, she seemed to have
been transformed, through sudden shock, into a pillar of
pepper and salt. Her features were not there . . . life
was obviously extinct . . . there was only this colouring,
as of an Aberdeen terrier. Her hair was parted in the
middle, while at the back she wore it in a fossilized flat
coil, in the form of an ammonite. Extremely attached
to dogs, her movements were invariably accompanied
by the faint tintinnabulation of teaspoons and by the
deep roar of dachshunds in full battle—for of all dogs
these have the angriest, most bass voices. Whether it
was this affection of hers which was responsible for her
condescending affability to Miss Pansy and Miss
Penelope is uncertain, but they were, except for relatives,
a tame doctor and a pet freak-curate, almost the only
people whom the august and self-immured lady would
be sure to receive. To these two protegées she would
descant on the past glories and lost beauties of their
" place " in the country (why Sir Timothy had sold this
Paradise, which like Lady Tidmarshe was invisible to
all eyes except those of the family, to settle in Newborough, remains a mystery) in much the same manner
that the old Pope might have painted, for the benefit
of the younger Cardinals, the forfeited grandeurs of
Quirinal and Castel Gandolfo. Miss Pansy and Miss
Penelope were, in fact, the authorized filters through
which these stories of bygone splendour were allowed,
encouraged even, to pass for the nutrition of the Monstrous Regiment resolutely facing South. To see Lady

Tidmarshe, with Miss Tidmarshe, sitting in her silver-tinkling drawing-room, talking to the Misses Finnis, and surrounded by her guardian fleet of dachshunds was to be furnished with an alternative theory to the Origin of Species. This heresy would deduce a basset, instead of a simian, descent for mankind, since human could here be seen blending down into animal by slow, imperceptible stages.

Sir Timothy, when not out walking, lived in his study, a room on the ground floor, lined for luck with Egyptian mummies and scarabs, with black cats (which battled fearfully with the dachshunds upstairs) pieces of rope from which notorious criminals had been suspended, lady-birds, old horse-shoes, fragments of the human pelvis, pentagrams, swastikas, money-spiders, and a perfect meadow of four-leafed clovers. A great part of the year was spent by him in tapping wood and eating mince pies before Christmas, while, when the new moon swung a bright scythe through its golden harvest, the Baronet had to be led blindfolded to the window, for fear of seeing it accidentally through glass.

Meanwhile Miss Tidmarshe—a terrible castigation was in store for anyone who should refer to her as Miss Evelyn Tidmarshe—sat in her room, pondering on her Position, drinking hot, black tea, and then telling the prognostic tea-leaves as though they were a Rosary, for she inherited the proclivities of both parents. Miss Tidmarshe, too, had adopted a Vatican attitude toward the outside world. As she hardly ever appeared, there were many legends, sedulously tended by the Misses Finnis, current about in the town, such as that she was that queer, illusive thing " Very artistic," and possessed of " a positive genius for the guitar." It was not until

she was over fifty years of age, however, that Miss
Tidmarshe, clad in glowing gypsy garments of red and
yellow, a crimson rose behind one ear, but still sporting
a fringe like that of Queen Alexandra, was induced to
leave her room and give a special display for a local
charity upon her favourite instrument.

Poor Sir Timothy lived in abject terror of his daughter,
who was apt to denounce him to her mother for his " want
of natural dignity." But if the poor Baronet was afraid
of Miss Tidmarshe, it was as nothing to the awe in which
he held his sons, a pack as ferocious and plentiful as
Lady Tidmarshe's dachshunds. Paragraphs were wont
to appear in the local paper—written, insinuated the ill-
natured, by no less a person than Miss Tidmarshe, so
that the information might be regarded as coming straight
from the Kennel—to the effect that the " fine old sporting
baronet, Sir Timothy Tidmarshe, and Lady Tidmarshe,
his gracious lady, are at present staying at their marine
residence, where they are entertaining in addition to
Miss Tidmarshe, their six warrior sons." No two members
of this martial brood held commissions in the same
regiment, yet this did not prevent the brothers from
quarrelling horribly among themselves ; for the sextet
appeared to be always on leave and all at the same time,
while now not only the question of personal, but also of
regimental precedence was able to enter into their battles.
The only cause that united them was the harrying of their
father. As regarded himself, Sir Timothy could always
count on their perfect unanimity. They would join up
together, stamp feet, shout, shake fists and demand
money, while, in the background, Lady Tidmarshe and
her daughter would afford them a silent support, en-
wrapping the Baronet in a thick blanket of keenly felt

but unexpressed disapproval. Hence Sir Timothy's nervous way, when out walking, of looking from side to side, for his sons could often be seen in the streets of Newborough, treading in different directions, all with their elbows turned out at right angles, their moustaches turned up imperially, while they perpetually dragged up and shot their shirt-cuffs with a gesture of supreme personal dignity.

Sir Timothy would in the meantime be shuddering swiftly through the streets, praying for the continued obscurity of that tiara, turning his eyes from side to side in the hope of eluding his sons, tapping wood, taking his hat off to chimney-sweeps and piebald ponies, meeting funerals at the correct angle, dashing away after dropped horse-shoes, hurling himself impetuously in the flight of a sea-gull, or improvising a thousand little grotesque feats of balance on kerb and pavement—these acrobatics being part of a private system of omens which he had devised. Alas, soon he was to meet his eldest son, face to face.

.   .   .   .   .   .

Another frequent, favourite street spectacle was Mr. and Mrs. de Flouncey, the dancing instructors. Both of these prophets of Terpsichore were now grey and well stricken in years, but they could not afford to let this be seen. It might ruin them. Nor could they ever afford to be tired. They must always be gay, young and full of high spirits. A little hair still feebly feathered Mr. de Flouncey's head, and of these few flat strands he made the greatest use, dyeing them, then winding them round his bald forehead turban-wise. Mrs. de Flouncey, on the other hand, had come out boldly with a wig, over which was arranged a hair net to give an extra touch of realism.

The teetotum-like gaiety in which this couple was invariably, inevitably involved, had imparted a look of severe strain. This look was covered over with twinkling smiles, rather full of teeth, but indicative of youth and engaging frivolity. Besides, no doubt, they still felt young, for it had always been understood that Mr. de Flouncey's father had been a French Marquis, obliged to fly from his native country after one of those bouts of revolution in which that light-hearted people engage from time to time. Revolution, and French people generally, were not much approved of in Newborough as yet; but still it had to be admitted that the French were different from English people, and this apocryphal ancestry helped Mr. de Flouncey's professional reputation and was, at the same time, felt to explain and excuse his almost painful " joie-de-vivre."

Mr. de Flouncey had champagne-cork eyes, and a moustache ending in waxed rat-tails. Mrs. de Flouncey was gnarled but mouse-like. Since they were always on their way to a party—and, unlike the reader and writer of this story, a party which they were paid to attend—they were continually in evening dress under full daylight. Mr. de Flouncey wore a long brown cover-coat as a shield to this glory, but it was short enough to reveal the end of his evening tail-coat. While this glimpse, combined with the overt grandeur of top-hat and white cotton gloves, allowed those passing to conjecture the existence of a hidden blaze—that radiance of buttonhole, gleaming white shirt front, flushing a deep crimson where a red silk handkerchief was tucked in to the beginning of an equally flashing waistcoat, jewelled studs, heavy gold watch-chain, gold fobs, and many seals that even now, as he moved, could be heard pealing their golden carillons, and that soon, when he danced, would clash and ring out in time to the music. Mrs. de Flouncey wore an antiquated velvet opera-cloak over a pleated turquoise-blue crêpe dress, that suggested in tone and texture the coloured paper covers that are found encircling a pot of ferns or an aspidistra in a lodging-house. Both husband and wife were the stewards, wearing prodigious badges, of every charitable function, every Masonic dance, every entertainment, even, of Primrose League or local Liberal Associations. For, as the Monarchy is above politics, so did their calling place Mr. and Mrs. de Flouncey high above party feeling, while at the same time it bestowed upon them a political immunity unknown to the Royal Family—an immunity which enabled them to take part, without giving offence, in the celebrations of every sept. Moreover, apart from their prestige in the town, this gay couple commanded the esteem of National Dancing circles—that is to say that they attended each annual meeting of the Dance Teachers' Guild or whatever may be the name of that association which is for ever attempting to foist unwanted new dances on the public, and at the same time complaining bitterly if the public adopts a new dance on its own initiative. Syncopated rhythms, which were to alter dancing out of all recognition, had not yet made their appearance in any English ballroom, but when they did arrive, they came unintroduced by the Association, and, indeed, much to its dismay. Alas, the tidal wave of ragtime, gradually rolling toward these shores from the New World, was to overwhelm Mr. and Mrs. de Flouncey, who were by that time too old to do anything but oppose it. Their God was a strange God called " Smooth Rhythm," though in reality their dancing was excessively full of jerks and contortions, each step insisting too strongly on its own individuality, refusing to give and take, disconnected both from predecessor and heir. For this very reason it was most difficult to learn dancing from the de Flounceys, for each step was taught as an object in itself—a conjuring trick—and it was impossible to trace or remember any connection between one of these isolated attitudes and the next. Indeed so little transition had Mr. de Flouncey's genteel rhythms that even when static, in repose, talking to a friend for example, he appeared to be finishing an old step or on the verge of a new one. Every attitude he adopted seemed one suddenly arrested from a figure in the lancers, as though, in the middle of his professional services, he had been afflicted with catalepsy and had retained the graceful pose of that minute, but frozen, made rigid. These sectional slices of the dance were, in truth, but the stock-in-trade of the other more mysterious art which he dispensed professionally—deportment.

Beside being adept at polka, lancers and waltz, the de Flounceys were the repository in which was stored the secret of the correct practice of such forgotten rites as Veleta, Albert Veleta, and Highland Fling.

Alas, the flood of ragtime was approaching. When it reached them, poor Mr. and Mrs. de Flouncey, already old but still bravely struggling, were carried out to sea and on to oblivion ; she sank completely ; but his cork-like eyes could still be seen popping up to the surface occasionally, with a dazed, reproachful look in them. The town was inundated with blue-faced, side-whiskered Tango teachers in their stead—Tango teachers who earned annually twenty times the de Flounceys' total capital, and spent the winter teaching the new elegancies in Nice and Monte Carlo.

·　　·　　·　　·　　·　　·

There were other persons, of course, more noticeable than Mr. Bradbourne, the Tidmarshes, the Misses Finnis or the de Flounceys.   There were the two children of Alderman Worrell, who would ride through the streets every day on their way to the sands.   The boy was about seven, the girl eight, years of age, and they suffered from some rare disease, which made them enormously fat, red and expressionless, as if carrying the aldermanic tradition of their parents to its furthest, fullest conclusion. They seemed overblown cupids as they passed on their ponies, with never a glance or smile.   Equestrian exercise was a necessity for their health, and therefore perhaps pardonable.   Then there were the two Misses Cantrell-Cooksey, now penniless but still painted, and even yet clad in their extraordinary garments.   And, most exotic of all specimens, perhaps, there was the Count de Bolmarano.   A rich, retired local tradesman, he had purchased a papal title, and had adopted a style of his own in clothes, for he always wore a very tight-waisted frock coat with an astrachan collar, and a top hat, under the front brim of which (for he was completely bald) was attached a solitary row of curls, so that, with an exaggeration of courtesy, he doffed not only his hat, but also his hair, to any lady of his acquaintance.   The middle of the road was his chosen path, for in those days there was not yet very much danger from motor-cars ; and down it he would walk with a smile of supreme satisfaction.

All that could be discovered, detected about such persons had long ago become the property of every citizen of Newborough.   Thus the advent of an unknown personage in the winter months would be a happening of the first order, and one not easily accountable.   The news would be repeated and magnified through the empty streets, as the volume of a speech is increased through an amplifier. It would be known straightway in every inhabited house, and, apparently, without human agency There are mountain villages in India, it is related, where the last piece of political information is in the possession of the natives before it has reached the great cities, engirdled as they are with telephone, telegraph and wireless The news is picked up by these sable villagers, these human receivers, as from the very winds. So it must have been, too, in Newborough.

CHAPTER VII

ON THE TRACK

Etonnant voyageurs ! Quelles nobles histoires.
Nous lisons dans vos yeux profonds comme les mers !
Montrez nous les écrins de vos riches mémoires,
Ces bijoux merveilleux, faits d'astres et d'éthers.

IT was, then, into this winter atmosphere that Miss
Collier-Floodgaye and Miss Bramley chose to precipitate
themselves, though it is quite true that at the moment
of doing so they were unconscious of the detailed and
curious attention which their every movement would
incur. But, if there was an arrival in the town at this
season of sufficient standing, wealth or eccentricity to
be noticed at all, the scrutiny, made sharp through long
practice, of a whole army of veterans in ambush would be
focused upon this one poor mortal. The object of this
interest would stroll, all unconscious, down the grey-
brick promenades, the tawny stone terraces ; in the upper
windows there would ensue a surge of white muslin
curtains, that resembled the wash of a tidal wave, but
would recede unnoticed from below. In reality, however,
the stranger might as well be lying, properly set out
upon a glass slide under a microscope, for on this speci-
men would be concentrated the minute and trained
attention of a thousand heads concealed behind blinds,
curtains and glass panes. Dear Old Persons, who had
spent many months, years even, in a bed-ridden condition, would allow themselves to be wrapped in light-pink
woollen shawls and propped up comfortably near the
window, there to enjoy a rare but intense ecstasy of
scientific observation.

There were, of course, at the head of this army of volunteer—if veteran—research workers, recognized experts of long standing. Such were both Mrs Shrub-field and old Miss Waddington. Since her recent masterly handling of the Cantrell-Cooksey scandal, the latter lady, especially, had obtained an unrivalled influence over her followers. But Mrs. Shrubfield, too, had distinguished herself in many a nigh hopeless fray, and opinion in the town had been forced to add a wreath of laurel to that fringe of vine leaves with which it had already crowned her.

Unfortunately, since a certain amount of jealousy between leaders of the same rank, in the same profession —between Field-Marshals for instance—is inevitable, these two ladies did not, at this period, love, however much they might respect, each other. While equally distinguished, equally successful, their methods were different. But in times of grave emergency, old feuds are forgotten in the common cause. When, therefore, the monumental pyramid that constituted the upper half of Mrs. Shrubfield, was observed being borne past in triumph by black horses, and was then seen to relax and unfold on to Miss Waddington's doorstep, excite-ment knew no bounds. It was rightly felt in the town that only some matter of supreme, of almost national, importance could have been responsible for such a sacrifice of pride. Something, in fact, was on hand. The invalid rooms, high up in the air, were a-twitter with expectancy, like so many nests of young sparrows at sight of a succulent meal.

. . . . . .

Old Miss Waddington had been a little better that winter, and was sitting up in her bedroom, by the fire, reading a weekly edition, published every Friday, of the local paper, and hoping to detect a clue to some new mystery. She was studying an account of the Hospital Ball. A tame affair, it sounded—stupid and tiresome of Ella (where can she be, by the by ?) not going to it. The papers never gave one an idea of anything. Probably something had happened, if only one knew. She passed on to a new heading,

" FASHIONABLE BAZAAR

AT

GHOOLINGHAM HOUSE."

That sounded promising, at any rate. What a relief to find something interesting. She read further :

> " With every augury of success a two days' bazaar was opened by the Mayoress (Mrs. W. L. Bamberger) in the ball-room of Ghoolingham House, which has been the scene of so many brilliant local functions. The bazaar is in aid of St. Catherine's Convalescent Home, where extensive sanitary alterations and improvements are rendered necessary for the health and well-being of the patients. A letter was read from the Earl of Ghoolingham, expressing his sorrow, and that of the Countess, his wife, at being unable to be present in person. In an un-ostentatious manner, however, they have once again demonstrated, by their thoughtfulness and liberal-mindedness, how thoroughly they make the anxieties and needs of this Convalescent Home their own.
>
> The ball-room lends itself admirably for the purpose of a bazaar. The stalls are arranged in a circle, with the flower stall and newspaper stall running down the centre. They are decorated alike with white Indian muslin, with bunches of Scotch white heather placed here and there, and a bordering of ivy, the tasteful drapery being supplied by Messrs. Beamish & Sons. The effect is pretty, combining simplicity with neatness. In keeping with the surroundings, the stall-holders wore bunches of white heather, also from Scotland, tied with white satin ribbon. Appended is a list of those engaged at the various stalls.

City of Ebur Stall.—Miss Agger, Miss Gladys Anthracks, Mrs. Binger, Miss Bower, Miss Barbara Bower, Miss Bowyer, Mrs. Bitt, Miss Bite, Mrs. Darcy Doherty and the Misses Doherty, Lady Poole, the Hon. Hylda de Trifling-Sedbury and Miss Sedgewick.

East Riding Fancy Stall.—Mrs. Peddar, the Misses Peach, Miss Pansy Pipp and Miss Hermione Bartlett.

Newspaper Stall.—Mrs. W. L. Bamberger (the Mayoress of Newborough), Miss Beatrice Bamberger and Miss (Bobby) Berry.

Fruit Stall.—Miss Anthracks.

Confectionery Stall.—Lady Dombay, Lady Dinger, the Misses Doodle and Miss Delia Donner

Parcel Stall.—Miss Thornfox.

Flower Stall.—Hon. Mrs. D. Richety-Rudyer, Miss Persephone Rudyer, Lady Racket, Mrs. Rolls, Mrs. Rump and Miss Ruby Rump. . . .''

. . . . . .

Just at that moment Miss Waddington was startled out of the almost subconscious state into which the associations and rhythm of these assorted names had caused her to fall, by the sound of a carriage driving up to the door. A ring at the bell, and then—for by this time the dear old lady was already on the landing outside her bedroom—the name of Mrs. Shrubfield. (What could it portend ? Was it, perhaps, connected with some affair rising out of the second day of the Bazaar ? Could that be it, she wondered ? In any case she realized at once that here was no moment for trifling or standing on one's dignity.) She could hear Mrs. Shrubfield's skunk—or was it fox ?—snapping its teeth briskly in the hall below, and a mingled odour of camphor, wild animals and port wine was wafted up to the watcher at the top of the stairs. Soon a wheezy cosmopolitan geniality made itself felt throughout the house. She must be talking to Ella. In a trice—yes, that is the exact word for it, in a trice—Miss Waddington had thrown another shawl round her shoulders and was walking unaided—a thing she had not done for ten years —down the stairs. Her energy was extraordinary, for emergency called up all her latent powers of leadership. Almost before she could have believed it possible, she was in the drawing-room.

"Ah, Miss Waddington, *Carissima Signorina*," Mrs Shrubfield brought out in her melodious but husky voice, " *Ça va bien?* How are you? *Va Bene, speriamo?* (Why be affected at a moment like this, thought Miss Waddington, can she never be natural, like anyone else ?) " *Gibt es was Neues?* " I felt I must come and see you now that I'm back (where from, I should like to know ? What a mass of affectation !) How fortunate you are never to go away, dear lady. But then, you know what it's like when one has a lot of friends, I expect ? Though I'm quite old now, people still pester me, positively pester me, to go to them. And then, it's so nice to come back to Newborough, though it's altered a lot. The town seems quite empty (and the bottle, I should think, reflected Miss Waddington, port or only hock ?) Hardly anyone in it . . . *mais si, il y a quelques unes qui viennent d'arriver. Es sind neue Gäste zum Superbenhof gekommen.* In fact, *il y a de nouvelles arrivées a l'hôtel. C'est drôle, n'est-ce pas? Molt' interessante.* At the Superb (so that's it, why couldn't she say so before ?) *deux dames qui ne sortent jamais Molta vecchia, l'una.* The other one must be her Companion, I should think. (Miss Waddington had now lost all feelings of anger at her rival's affectations : for one leader can appreciate the qualities of another, without the question of like or dislike entering into such a purely technical matter.) Do you know them, I wonder, *Carissima Signorina?* I've never heard of them before . . . but the elder one does not look to me like a *Nobile Donna*."

.   .   .   .   .   .

For many weeks after this dramatic " rencontre," as Mrs. Shrubfield would have phrased it, the two Marshals were inseparable : a common interest bridged the chasm between them, until in the end a solid friendship was built miraculously on the ever-shifting sands of such a mystery. In future, when Mrs. Shrubfield called, Ella was sent upstairs to read *Punch*; while Miss Waddington, contrary to all her winter regulations, drove out several times to have tea with her new ally, for Mrs. Shrubfield even went so far as to send round her carriage for the old lady. When, therefore, the rank and file of the Monstrous Regiment saw from their upper windows the familiar equipage, with its two black horses, with its two pyramidal figures on the box, bearing along at a stately trot—not the expected greater pyramid of Mrs. Shrubfield, not the two curves of the black wig, and the completing black bonnet above—but the frail, mauve-clad, asthmatic form of Miss Waddington, the aged head thrust forward and nodding as if already on the trail, the eyes, too, slightly bloodshot to complete this conception, it can be imagined how a thrill of wonder mingled with enthusiasm and the blood ran hot again in their ardent veins. Excitement mounted higher. Telephone and front door bell rang continuously and without ceasing. The bees were at work again, flitting from blossom to blossom. Tea became stronger and stronger, nerves ever more taut. . . . Soon the news was out . . . a Miss Collier-Floodgaye, it seemed, and a Companion . . . at least so it was supposed . . . staying at the Superb . . . in the winter too . . . Mr. Spry, the framer, had seen them walking down St.

Peter's Street . . . no doubt about it, he'd seen them himself, actually, and had told Clara . . . you know Clara . ⸝ about it . . . walking down St. Peter's Street . . . walking, too . . . not even as if they kept a carriage .   in the winter, too . . . oh, odd, very odd indeed.

The next step, of course, was to ascertain which doctor attended the two new arrivals. This highly specialized piece of research work was entrusted by Mrs. Shrubfield to Miss Waddington. But, to her dismay, she discovered that neither Dr. Sibmarshe nor his rather pushing young partner, Dr. MacRacket, had yet fathomed the unknown with their stethoscopes. It was too bad of them ; *she'd* say " Ninety-nine " to *them*, when she saw them. After all, it was their business to get new patients . . . what made it so extraordinary, too, was that Miss Waddington knew that the Management of the Superb always recommended one of these two doctors to their guests .   . fortunately there were other links and other methods. The matter could not be allowed to rest where it was.

John, the hall-porter at the Superb, of twenty years' standing, was a local figure of the first magnitude, and in direct communication with a countless number of invalid rooms, which moreover—however much he might despise them in his heart—he must, for the sake of pecuniary advantage, conciliate

In the first careless rapture of two new arrivals, several old ladies who had confined themselves to their beds, winter after winter, were injudicious enough to clamber into their bath-chairs, and allow themselves to be trundled round—as though in the death-embrace of an overturned giant blackbeetle—to the Superb. On arrival they would, rather wearily, ask John if there

were any letters for them, a transparent manœuvre.
They would then seek to engage him in a talk, which
beginning with a general application would swoop
mercilessly to a particular instance. The use of such
tactics was incorrect and injudicious. These old ladies,
however enthusiastic in the cause, had proved themselves mere amateurs, and John, contemptuous of their
technique, would divulge nothing. Even Lady Tidmarshe, to whom the news must have penetrated through
the two little Misses Finnis, went so far as to send her
maid to John with a bunch of the famous withered and
mildewed grapes, which looked as if they had spent the
previous night in her parrot's cage, and ask him to come
and see her one day. John, however, was determined
to let nothing escape him yet awhile, though he saw
a moment when information would reach a premium,
and therefore collected assiduously what there was of it.
In order to find out further details about the two visitors,
he refrained from bullying Elisa (the " German Sausage,"
as he had wittily christened her) and even sought to
pacify and please her. But she came of a warrior nation,
and would have none of it.

Miss Waddington's subtle expertness was in a category
altogether different from the bungling attempts we have
described. Deliriously, day and night, she knitted a
red woollen comforter, " nice and warm for the winter,"
as a gift for John's youngest son. The moment came when
the scarf was finished, and she was able to send for the
child's mother to receive it. By this method, every
detail (alas! there were but few) was soon in her possession, and could be served out as a treat, after any
slight skirmish, to her attendant niece.

She rang the bell. " Emily, I am out except to Mrs
Shrubfield. I must have a talk with Miss Ella; please

send her up to me." A sound of feverish, but mousy, footsteps on the stairs, and Ella rustled into the room, anxious, but still striving to look bright. What could she have done now, or was Aunt Hester preparing for something, an asthmatic tornado or a hurricane cold ? " Yes, Aunt Hester, did you want me ? I hope you're all right, dear ? Do you want another shawl or anything ? " But at this instant the old lady exuded amiability.

" No, dear, it's only that I should like a little chat . . . a Miss Collier-Floodgaye . . . yes . . . rich and elderly . . . oh, the name sounds all right, dear, of course it does. But then it would, wouldn't it ? Oh, that you may depend upon. . . . All the same, I don't know it. Of course there's Canon Floodgay at St. Saviour's, and though very High Church—indeed almost more than that—he came originally of good family . . . at least, so they say. But then why, dear child, need he be so theatrical . . . Anthems and Rubrics and things. And that awful picture ! . . . *in* the church, actually . . . and not in the least bit *like* Our Lord ! At any rate, it's not *my* idea of Him. With eyes like that, oh no, dear ! I wouldn't trust the Canon, not for an instant . . . what with all those Rubrics and Anthems and things . . . it would never surprise me if, in the end, it was discovered that he went in for incense. What did I say, dear ? Yes, incense. Never surprise me. And they say that he gives Mrs. Floodgay a lot of anxiety. But, in any case, he is Floodgay, not Collier-Floodgaye ; and Mrs. Floodgay, you'll remember, dear, happened to drop in to tea here yesterday. Absolutely no relation, she said to me. None whatsoever. Alone in the world we are, she said, with the Canon and Cécile. Pretty, bright little thing, she ought to know if anyone did,

oughtn't she? I really like that little woman . . .
besides, they spell it without an " e " . . . but a Miss
Collier-Floodgaye is, without doubt, staying at the
Superb (don't fidget, dear!) with . . . (andante) . . .
(and then allegro) her Companion. (There, that will
give you something to think about for a change, fidgeting
like that, the old lady thought to herself, and brought it
out suddenly, sharply, like a smack. That will surprise
you!) Oh yes, she must be a rich woman, Leeds, very
likely; I shouldn't wonder if that was it . . . rich, of
that there can be no doubt. Always dresses in black—
a stiff knee, too; and walks with a stick . . . and walks
with a stick, always walks with a stick. Louise Shrubfield saw her, herself. (" Of course," I said to her,
" the stick may only be her *affectation*, I do so like
people to be *natural*.") A mystery somewhere . . .
dressed all in black, oh odd, very odd, very odd and
queer, indeed . . dressed all in black, with a stiff knee
. . . and a *stick* . . . you know. And I've heard, too,
that she's short-sighted . . I told Louise Shrubfield ...
I said to her, ' They say she's blind . . . in the best
sense, of course. . . .' She didn't like that, I can tell
you, Ella. But really she had been so affected . . . still,
there's a lot of good in her . . . and so well-informed. . . .
What was I saying? Oh yes, dresses all in black, with
a stiff knee and a stick, and short-sighted Lives in
London in the summer, so they say. In a hotel, so I hear
. . . yes, a hotel . . . oh odd, very odd, indeed! A
Companion . . . and a stiff knee . . . dresses in black,
and always leans on a walking-stick. Oh, so odd. The
Companion sings beautifully, so they say, with real
expression (that's what I like. That's what I like,
expression). Not so much what she sings, they say, as
the way she sings it . . . and what makes it prettier

still, plays by ear ! Quite natural, with a sweet little voice and no training. She sings, you know, that song by the Italian . . . you don't, dear ? . . . of course you do ! . . . you know, this one (and here the niece was treated to wheezy, wintry variations on Tosti's ' Good-bye '). Very pretty, with a lilt to it. A lilt to it and much feeling ! I often wonder, dear, why you don't sing. It's such a help to girls, I think . . . a Miss Bramley, the Companion . . . and seems to know more of the *World* . . . a niece, it is supposed, of old Miss *Titherley*-Bramley, who lived for years in the large-white-house-next-but-one-to-where-Mrs.-Sibmarshe's-mother-lived-before-her-daughters-married. But surely you can recognize it from that, can't you ? (I never liked that house . . . something about it. . . .) She was very *musical*, too, and always drove about in a Victoria followed by two Dalmatians . . . of course you do, dear . . . spotted dogs. And piebald horses, too, now that I come to think of it, for I remember Sir Timothy Tidmarshe always waiting there in the morning to see it, and take his hat off . . . piebald horses and died, oh years ago ! before you were born. She left very little money behind her. I recall it quite well, for everybody was surprised ; because, after all, she'd had a house and garden, a carriage, and Dalmatians and everything . . . which niece can it be ? That's the point . . . there were two, if I remember. . . . Oh ? Is it Mrs. Shrubfield ? I'll see her at once then. Certainly. Ella, you had better run away and write letters. Don't argue, dear. How am I to know ' Who to ' ? "

CHAPTER VIII

THE NEW REIGN

' It is only this last century that the crack appeared,
That the mark came on the ceiling, and the plaster broke,
That we came to knock the idols down,
And quickly put up others ;
Like burglars at a shrine
Who take the God, and leave a copy . . .''

MISS BRAMLEY found Newborough more altered than she had expected ; it seemed larger and richer. There was a new sea wall, and a magnificent public rose-garden, with a few roses still in bloom . . . in bloom, actually, in November. It made her feel quite as if she was abroad—or rather what she imagined it must feel like to be abroad. There was a subtle difference in the atmosphere of the place, though it seemed very empty.

The truth was, had she realized it, that the golden sun of Edwardian prosperity was mounting elsewhere to its meridian, and affecting life even here. Manners were changing under its genial warmth, which caressed, under certain conditions, the unjust no less than the just, and heartily embraced the " lesser tribes without the law," as long as they were not also without money.

At the Court all were young, it was understood (and, indeed, after Queen Victoria, nearly anyone was young) and all were gay. If the Court was not really as young as it looked, at any rate it only looked half its age. Queen Alexandra, it was said, might pass for twenty-

eight. There appeared now to be no border line
between twenty-five and seventy-five, and, in one of the
phrases of the day, "anyone who was anyone" was
somewhere between those ages. The words "delicious,"
"heavenly," and "divine" and "too, too weird" were
to be heard for the first time on the pouting, jutting lips
of the middle-classes, while the ringent Eastern gentlemen from Brighton and Bombay, Bagdad and Berlin,
who now made their first, rather clumsy though genial,
bows, at any European Court, skipped like young rams
and bounded—above all, bounded—like young leopards.
Finance had begun to come into its own—and everybody
else's—attended by the caressing scents of henna and
bath-salts, and to the appropriate accompaniment of
Puccini's music, with its inevitable suggestion of constant
hot water and every modern convenience. For the first
time, strange accents, lisping in authoritative numbers,
were making themselves heard within the precincts
of the House of Lords : lisps and spluttering guttural
sounds which had been hitherto prudently confined to
the purlieus of Aldgate and pawnshops of Whitechapel.
A rodent-like scuffling and scampering could be heard
everywhere in London, as our guests gnawed their way
through into the West End. For, to this Golden Age,
there was, fittingly enough, a golden key—Comfort !
It was known that King Edward "liked to be comfortable " ; and the Wise Men of the East had grasped
the fact that it was their mission to make him so. Every
Havana-rolled tobacco leaf, which they offered him,
might be returned to them, they hoped, transformed
by the Royal Hand into a strawberry leaf   Since the
days of Napoleon III, who inundated his country with
"Syrian," "Armenian," and "Egyptian" Barons, the

Race had known nothing like it, and there was a general rush to contribute to the " Barty Funds."

After all, there was nothing wrong in comfort, was there ? Hoarse, glutinous and wheezing laughter at the primness and hard angles of the Victorian reign was to be heard resounding through the newly-built hotels now blossoming in London. Carpets were woven so thickly as to entrap the feet, arm-chairs were upholstered as for the harbouring of a hippopotamus.

But the welcome extravagance of the New Order was still ever so faintly reflected in these northern waters, for Newborough was, as always, rather behind the times, catching up a little self-consciously and with a loud panting. Even now, even here, however, certain modifications of life were visible, though the town had been as yet affected more indirectly than directly. A frothy sea of lace was receding for the first time for sixty years from the wanton legs of chair and table. The mantelshelf with all its fringed apparatus of red flannel globules and stalactites was delivered up to the lumber-room, while the chimneypiece beneath was now allowed once more to proclaim an unashamed nudity. The mansions of the richer and younger section of Newborough were beginning to be filled with soft mauve and green cushions. The apoplectic flush was beginning to die away from the walls of the dining-room, in which meals grew ever shorter and better. Every day the arm-chairs could almost be seen growing, like the Empire, larger and softer. The furnishing shops, which here, by some strange rules, always combined their decorating proclivities with the business of undertaking, now declared in their windows boldly flowering chintzes. With the advent of the motor-car, colour, banished by the Age of Steam, again inherited the land. For the steam engine had for half a century usurped the throne : a funnel, and not the effigy of Queen Victoria, should have been the minted token of her reign. In the next decade, with the artful help of the Borough Engineer, many changes would be effected in Newborough. Through his over-exertion, the entire town would be swept out of sight beneath a pink, an awful, avalanche of Dorothy Perkins roses. Everywhere " pergolas," supposedly Italian in design, and cement-edged ponds of goldfish, were to supplant the herring-patterned red roofs and huddled houses of the fishermen—houses that had preserved to an extraordinary degree the Rowland-sonian quality of the English eighteenth century—or were to drive out the wistful elegiac elegance of rustic summer-house, reeded pool and weeping willow which had hitherto been the feature of English public gardens. The character, prim or primitive, of the town was to wilt beneath a fallacious sub-tropical exoticism. Palm trees, however unwilling, were to be forced, at the point of the spade, to oust such trees as beech and sycamore, and were then to be coerced into unfolding their withered leaves on to the icy northern air ; cactuses, too, were to be made to exhibit in public the suicidal tendencies brought out in them by the East wind. Finally, there was an absolute epidemic of Japanese rock-gardens.

On the other hand, the habit of life among the majority of local old ladies, doctors, and clergymen, was to remain unaffected for a long time. The upper rooms facing south in square, crescent and terrace remained unaltered and apparently unalterable, ever bathed in the sunset glow of Victorianism. Within the limited space of her sick-room, each invalid preserved inviolate a fragment of the Victorian reign, though each portion varied in epoch. Miss Waddington's bedroom, for example, might have been an actual bit broken off the Golden Jubilee ; while the widow of the Anglo-Indian Colonel, who lived next door, still inhabited a room that belonged quite as plainly to the now legendary periods of Indian Mutiny and Crimean War.

Alas, as the brief Edwardian reign deepened into an apoplectic flush, the richer and younger part of the local life was being drawn more and more to London. The old, comfortable doctrine—comfortable, because it endowed each believer in it with a small holding of duty which he must cultivate, while the absolute necessity of his doing so prevented him from ever feeling any regrets—that it was necessary to do one's duty in that state of life to which it had pleased the Devil to call one, was breaking down for ever. Whereas in Victorian days if a man disliked living at Newborough he felt it all the more a compelling duty to remain there, or as he would have put it, to "reside" there, the young men acknowledged in similar circumstances, no such obligation. They just left, without any regret or remorse. The large bow-windowed stone houses were becoming derelict, and wailing for bygone gentility was loud in every room that faced south. For, even if members of the younger generation visited the town in the summer, they seldom were possessed of stoicism sufficient to enable them there to pass the winter. Thus interest was focused more intently upon those who, in unconscious mutiny against their period, came for the winter to this borealic borough. Besides, it was so " quiet " in the dead months.

But, even if Newborough was a little quiet in the winter, Miss Bramley did not dislike it on that account.

Llandriftlog had been quiet, too : she was used to it.
There was such a good piano in the drawing-room, and,
as the hotel was empty, she could practise as much
as she liked.   Really it was like being in one's own
house !   Now, though, she almost wished she had not
sold the other piano.   She could quite well have had it
put in her room.   But you see, everything had been so
uncertain that it had seemed better at the time to sell. . . .
Still, the one in the drawing-room was really good, and
that was a comfort.   And, too, it was tuned regularly ;
for Mrs. de Flouncey used to play it for her husband's
dancing classes every Thursday . . . (she seemed a nice
woman, obliging, full of information, and fond of music)
You could always tell a Broadwood piano anywhere . . .
the " timbre," she supposed.   Unusual, too, to find one
in a hotel, at any rate one in as good condition.   But
there it was, the hotel was superior to most other hotels.

The hotel was, certainly, unlike other hotels ; but it is
useless to pretend that the eastern wave of luxury,
which was now spending itself in London, had as yet
broken over the interior of this, one of the first built
hotels in England.   Encaustic tiles make it echo, red
flock papers make it dark.   The rooms are too large,
too well designed.   With floating palm trees and ferns
in them, they have, more than ever, the air of an empty
aquarium waiting for new, half-human, half-marine
specimens until even the round ottomans in the centre
of the floor become so many closed-up red anemones
on the tank bottom, the sofas and chairs loose rocks.
Move these, and from under will crawl sideways some
crustacean and armoured spinster, or a purple-faced
monster of an old oceanic Colonel.   When, however, the
observer looks more closely, the greenery is too arid to

justify such imagery ; the leaves of palm and aspidistra are hard and withered, scratch the wall at any draught. Indeed the palm trees lumbering up in the corners of the rooms are so tall, their outspread fingers so bony, that they resemble rather the reconstructed extinct monsters at a Natural History Museum than anything in an aquarium.

The three tiers of galleries, out of which open the rows of bedrooms, close round the hall and about the staircase. Opposite the foot of this, across the hall—or " lounge " as it had recently, in a fit of euphemism, been rechristened by the Management, is an oval-shaped ballroom ablaze with Saxe-Coburg cupids and gilt leafage ; for though when this hotel was growing up into the air the Consort already rested in his Mausoleum, the influence of his solid but fantastic taste is everywhere manifest.

Alas, apart from the ottomans and rock-like sofas, most of the chairs and tables in the lounge and elsewhere are too flimsy, too temporary for their setting. In a fever of modernity, the Management had spirited away much of the heavy, original furniture and had mingled with what was left a host of wicker chairs and tables. When, in the winter, these wicker chairs are empty, unprotected by the provincial visitors' overlapping flaps of flesh, their unworthiness is very obvious. Emptiness being a fruitful source of ghosts, the creaking and moaning of vacant wicker haunts lounge and sitting-room with impressions of the ample bodies of vanished summer visitors. Through these vast dark rooms and passages, empty yet expectant as a dusty stage unused for many years, move the figures, diminutive in scale compared with their background, of Miss Collier-Floodgaye, Miss Bramley, Elisa, the housemaid, John the hall porter, and a few shadowy supers. No one else moved through these dim, silent places at such a season.

Still, Miss Bramley comforted herself that the hotel being empty in the winter was a decided advantage: for Cecilia would not be able to make friends with strangers. Now Miss Fansharpe would never have *dreamt* of making friends with people she did not know. Never! But then one must realize that Cecilia was . . . well, "different." Differently brought up, that must account for it; and then, of course, everyone had their faults.

As Miss Collier-Floodgaye grew older, she had seemed to Miss Bramley to become more and more vague, more and more liable to confide in strangers . . . a confidence very unexpected, since she never trusted to anyone, not even to her Companion, the details of the early and middle periods of her life. And she was becoming so boastful, that was the worst of it . . . boastful, not at all ladylike; proud of her money with the pride of one unused to it. She would even talk to strangers about stocks and shares . . . to *strangers* . . . stocks and shares . . . you know . . . not quite the sort of thing to do. No . . . could one even imagine Miss Fansharpe doing such a thing? . . . and then, from whispered and intricate discussions of the life led by the Royal Family (personally Miss Bramley could still "not see much" in Queen Alexandra's face) Miss Collier-Floodgaye would pass on to discuss with "total strangers" —and a "total stranger," it must be understood, was worse, infinitely worse, than an ordinary stranger, a sort of super-Ishmael, disconnected *in toto* from the rest of humanity—the lives of those fashionable persons to

whom, Miss Bramley in her own mind was positive,
Cecilia had never once spoken and whom she had
probably never even seen. Of course, the old lady was
so forgetful that it was just within the bounds of credi-
bility that she had met them, and was, except at moments
when their names were recalled to her, oblivious of the
fact   Or it might be that at such instants she genuinely imagined, and, for the duration of the talk actually
believed, that she was acquainted with these illustrious
immortals of the illustrated weekly journals. It was, in
fact, impossible to arrive at any sure conclusion in the
matter . . . but, anyhow . . . to strangers, to *total*
strangers . . . very sad and deplorable.

At Newborough in the winter, however, there were
apparently but few persons to whom Miss Collier-
Floodgaye could impart these hypothetical encounters.
Yet the tragedy of it, if only the old lady had realized,
was that there were so many hundred invalids all round
her, literally pining away from curiosity and lack of
gossip. A thousand pairs of eyes, all facing south, were
fixed on this singular couple; yet no one had got into
communication with them, for there were certain rules
that had to be observed in this, as in all other sports.
Yet even Miss Waddington and Mrs. Shrubfield were
puzzled as to the best method of prosecuting their
campaign. It was not the moment, for example, to
call . . . or to write . . . no, not yet : *dopo*, *peut-être*

Despite the seeming difficulty of finding a confidante,
Miss Collier-Floodgaye had achieved one. Miss Bramley,
to her disgust, actually found her gossiping one day to
the German housemaid. Really too bad, and not at all
the thing to do. However perhaps for once, Miss Bramley
said to herself rather maliciously (for Miss Bramley's

character, now unchecked, was altering) Cecilia had
found someone to believe her. It was possible. Of course
what the old lady really needed was a hobby; the
Companion felt sure of it. Everyone ought to have a
hobby (invisible blinkers to shut off human frailties
such as illness and death—frailties which are always
just round the corner). Yes, a hobby. Miss Bramley's
father had always said that " there was nothing that
took a woman out of herself like Rescue Work " .
how true ! . . . look at Miss Fansharpe . . . but then
perhaps Cecilia was too old for it now . . though, in
a sense, it was a pursuit for the elderly. Or else she
ought to read more. And it was so easy to get books ;
a splendid lending library close by, and another small
one on the West Cliff. E. F. Benson, Robert Hichens,
Marie Corelli, Hall Caine (Miss Collier-Floodgaye had
been so fond of Marie Corelli's books—but she seemed
to be getting " so bitter " now), and everything one
could need . . . you know, really nice books . . .
exciting too. And sometimes one could get the latest
novel the very day it came out, which made a great
difference. Much more interesting and *so* much cheaper
than buying it. In fact, in the winter one could get almost
any book one wanted. Poetry, too, if one cared for it.
Certainly Cecilia ought to read more. But she was very
nervous, and poetry seemed to make her worse—she
ought not to read detective stories either—something light
and cheerful was what she must get. Luckily Newborough was supposed to be good for the nerves, though
at the same time bracing, ever so bracing.

CHAPTER IX

CANNON AND ANCHOR
"Theirs not to reason why,
Theirs but to do, and die."

IT was only necessary to observe Miss Collier-Flood-gaye's ascetic style and sombre mien for an instant to know that, however correct had been Miss Waddington's identification of Miss Bramley as niece of that lamented lady of musical and Dalmatian memory, her diagnosis of Leeds in the case of Miss Collier-Floodgaye was at fault. But then, in spite of every effort compatible with dignity, Miss Waddington had not yet been able to cast a practised eye over her. It is impossible for a doctor to attribute symptoms to their right cause, if himself has not examined the patient. Yet Miss Waddington did not like to " hang about " too much in front of the hotel, in her bath chair : it looked unsporting, rather like taking a shot at a sitting pheasant. It might even, by lowering their estimate of the capacity and " fair play " sense of their leader, impair the *moral* of the storm troops under her command. Therefore, though she could often borrow Mrs. Shrubfield's carriage, or even go for a drive with her in a direction expertly appraised as likely to yield good sport, though she could pass the hotel door once or even twice in the day, she could not wait about in front of it. And so far in her raids she had always drawn blank. If only she had been able to see

Miss Collier-Floodgaye and her Companion leaving the hotel, she would no doubt have reached a much surer conclusion as to the new-comer's origin

For that old lady's tall, rather rugged frame no more suitable setting could have been devised than the appropriately austere background offered by the Superb Hotel. The building imparted to the scene a touch of grandeur. It uprose from the town, dominating the entire prospect, in the manner of Landseer's "Monarch of the Glen," its four domes, instead of antlers, towering up into the glowering winter sky. Icy little currents of air battered at it in vain throughout the dark months. Against the whole pack of hunting winds, that snarled and howled so hungrily, it stood at bay : for the giant building was at this season the natural foe and destined prey of every element.

One of the first hotels, as opposed to inns, attempted in England, it was built at a time when the housing of large numbers of paying guests under one roof was everywhere a new conception—so new, so startling, even, that the idea of providing comfort for them need not enter at all into the calculations of its creators. It was only necessary, then, to build a hotel large enough to house a great number of guests, for the daring novelty of the thing to fill the place, and keep it full. Space, and richness of gilding were, as we have seen, the objects desired within ; so, an impression of size and grandeur had been the exterior effects aimed at, and, in a sense, achieved. This hotel looked as though it had been built for the internment of grim, rich but still respectable manufacturers from the industrial cities. It lacked altogether that Louis Quinze atmosphere of the cosmopolitan caravansaries that now spring up everywhere, even in ruined England, for the pleasure of fraudulent international financiers, and in order to flatter them with a feeling of security. For that purpose, too, each hotel of the sort must be indistinguishable from another ; thus in London, Buenos Ayres, Cairo, Tokyo and Montreal, they are all the same.

The Superb Hotel, on the other hand, offers no comfort, spiritual, mental or bodily, but it is impossible to challenge its possession of a certain quality of stern, grandiose beauty. For the echoes of good building were still faintly ringing in the upper air when this hotel was created, nearly seventy years ago. Ruskin's arid but exotic teachings had not yet destroyed the old tradition. The Superb is obviously the work of an architect, as opposed to that of a commercial builder or latter-day luxury expert of the great hotel companies. It stands there, its two vast façades capable of holding out against the four winds, a rock composed of yellow brick in an undeniably rare tint, decorated with surface patterns in other bricks of equally unusual red and purple, crowned with a high slate roof and four barrel-like domes, the colour of cinders. No building could crown an important position more satisfactorily. Even the porch, in shape so akin to the fashionable bonnet of the period, even the mid-Victorian masks and statues that leer down so slyly— monocled satyrs in top hats and crinolined caryatides— possess an indisputable atmosphere. When it was built no other social system was deemed possible, and so it was intended like the Great Pyramid to stand through all eternity, but an eternity that was to differ in no respect from the present. Later generations may perhaps wonder at it as the Romans of the Dark Ages marvelled at the Colosseum, explaining it away as the creation of wizards and strange gods. Like that enormous building, it may, too, become the quarry out of which the houses of a future Renaissance will be constructed. There is, in its erection, no trace of small economies, no sign of plaster being used to eke out the brick and stone, the tiles and marbles. It is built on no foundation of sand : on the contrary, the roots of it are dug far into the solid rock beneath, while the sea façade stretches down boldly toward the crouching but rebellious ocean, thus doubling on that side its already cyclopean stature. Here it ends in a vast asphalt terrace, each corner of which is marked by the flourish of an almost feudal barbican. Upon this monstrous hub the entire system of the town's summer life revolves. Bath chairs, cabs, funiculars, tramways, shops, public gardens, promenades, crescents, terraces, the sands, the sea even, flutter round it as coloured ribbons whirl round an electric fan. In the winter, the prospect, while it lacks such gaiety, gains a compensating air of proud desolation, and of great forces temporarily held in check; it compels such respect as all men must feel before some mighty machinery, mill or furnace, at rest.

On the entrance side out of which flowers that enchanting but preposterous porch, the Superb Hotel surveys an open space, and confronts across it the incarnadined countenance of the Gentlemen's Club, in the bow window of which an enormous telescope, resembling a huge piece of artillery, appears to be aiming at it, though in reality trained on the sea. In the middle of this perpetual conflict is a circular green-baize garden, a no man's land, necklaced by a single string of black cabs. Even in December and January the cabs still wait there, expectant of altogether legendary visitors, while from the green-painted cab-stand, the emerald clasp to the necklace, issues a cheerful odour of mingled oats and beer, food for horses and men. The baize circle is protected by iron railings, and by a hedge of scraggy, transparent shrubs, while in the centre of it, deposited in state, on this green cushion, lie those twin symbols of our civilization, the very regalia of the Modern World, a Cannon and an Anchor. These two symbols govern the world by turns, force and faith, War and Peace, and at the time of which we are writing, it was the Cannon rather than the Anchor which attracted the attention of the curious. Now, perhaps, the Anchor is the curiosity, of more interest to the passers-by.

The Cannon was Crimean, and at it, in those far-away days, peered curiously the children, on whom in a few years its brood was to batten. No sooner had these children, gazing at it so intently, swinging and clamber-ing on the railings, become grown men than they would be exported as fodder for this senseless god, who was to have his greatest temple in the grey wastes just across the ocean that they can hear sighing, singing or roaring below. And they will die, (so they will think,) in defence of that other ancient symbol, the Anchor. Faith will drive them on. At present, however, these heads, as they look at the Crimean Cannon, are full of romantic ideas, encouraged by the empty wind of Tennyson's poetry, which they have been taught to recite in the schoolroom, poems in which are inculcated the doctrines of cringing, war-mongering and general stupidity. "Theirs not to reason why," indeed! They pay little enough attention to the Anchor. But this imposing Anchor, like other symbols, is not quite what it seems.

Appropriately enough it was once the anchor of a celebrated smuggler, patriot and believer in private enter-
prise ; so that, all the time, the Cannon and the Anchor
were really in league. One was no more deceptive than
the other.

CHAPTER X
TREATS

"What do you see, Shadow, in the water's glass;
What see you, Shadow, in the shadows that pass?"

THE two friends did not in the least feel the oppression of their surroundings. Though all Newborough soon knew them by sight, they were during their first winter acquainted with no one in the town. But neither of them felt the deprivation. Indeed this period of halcyon quiet, far removed from any material worries, and without disturbance of any kind, was probably the happiest period of Miss Bramley's adult life. The practice of her singing gave her great pleasure, and about this time she learnt several new songs. It may have been symptomatic that these were the "Indian Love Lyrics" of Amy Woodford Finden and Laurence Hope. The waves of Edwardian exoticism were perhaps beginning to break over her, to demoralize her. Certainly, Miss Fansharpe would never have encouraged her to sing them. But though she felt, somehow, that she would never learn to interpret them with the ease and understanding with which she was able to render Frank Lambert's songs, she could not conceal from herself that there was something very moving about them . . . something weird, queer and oriental. She would love to go to the East, really she would, with all its "Jams," jewels and jungles.

Nor were the "Indian Love Lyrics" the only signs of a progressive metamorphosis in Miss Bramley. The

dwarf tree was sloughing its old shape, was growing and
loosening to an alarming extent, now that the rules,
which had governed its growth, were relaxed. This
change was due, partly to Miss Collier-Floodgaye's
assumption of equality with her Companion, and partly
to that new sense of worldly security which supported
Miss Bramley. With Miss Fansharpe, the Companion,
however much deceived by the hints and promises of that
old lady, had never felt secure. She had been constantly
aware that she lived on the edge of that periodically
active volcano, Miss Fansharpe's temper. In fact, it had
been a life of perpetual tight-rope walking—she realized
that now. And only those who have walked on a tight-rope
can ever know the ecstasy of walking on solid ground.

Accordingly, in this ecstasy, she was transformed.
If not less religious, she had at any rate become more
mundane, fonder of the pleasures of that life which she had
hitherto been taught to regard as a " miserable span."
Mildred, for one, began to detect a new note in her sister's
letters, and confided in Harold that their tone had become less spiritual. She prayed that Teresa might not de-
teriorate—or, as she said, in her new voice, " deteaheah-
riate." One could " nevah" tell. Only the elect, the very
elect, could remain unspoilt by prosperity. It was a test.

Even (and this was most unexpected), even Miss
Bramley's Evangelical views began to soften . . . she
rather liked a little colour now . . . and, by a judicious
compromise, the old lady and her Companion could now
go to the same church (St. Peter's), Miss Collier-
Floodgaye sacrificing her incense on condition that
Miss Bramley swallowed the anthem.

Really, they were very happy. Newborough was
rather cold in the winter, but fortunately neither of them

minded the cold. Miss Collier-Floodgaye, old as she was, could face the most bitter weather without ill effect. It must have been the fogs in London, they were sure, which had given the old lady her asthma (this affliction was always referred to as a personal belonging—" my asthma," " her asthma," " my friend's asthma "). The best of it was, the Companion would remark, there was never a day, scarcely, when it was not possible to go out. That, they argued (for neither of them had ever left England) was what was so splendid about the English climate. Life was regular, consisting in a varied monotony. If the afternoon was " fine," which did not so much indicate blue sky as the actual absence or aftermath of snow, sleet or rain, the two ladies, very warmly clad and veiled, would usually promenade slowly up and down the long hotel terrace. The extent of this asphalt stretch even whittled down Miss Collier-Floodgaye's large frame, till she and her Companion dwindled to two flies walking on a window pane. Up and down they paced, with a slightly broken rhythm, due to the old lady's stiff knee and consequent use of a cane as lever. The terrace was very broad : the wall at its border high enough to prevent them seeing the foreground of the ocean. To keep this in view, they must expose themselves to winds that swept down upon the edge, and whistled round the corner barbicans. Standing by the wall they could, of course, watch the grey backs of the waves, in their whale-like tumblings and splashings, clumsily colliding with cement walls, and sending over them every few seconds an angry spout of white foam to ascend a hundred feet in the air. But usually they kept close to the shelter of the towering hotel, and from it could see nothing save an infinite expanse of grey cloud and grey atmosphere,

endless grey backs jostling themselves into an impenetrable distance of spray and vapour. When they reached
the end of the terrace, looking toward the Castle that
rode its hill as a man rides a horse, they could see the
red-tiled roofs of the fishermen's cottages sweeping down
in ribbed patterns to the level of the grey monsters
below. As they turned slowly round, a salt wind would
circle down on them like a hawk, and tear their faces,
even through their thick veils, with unexpectedly ferocious
beak. Sometimes from the open sea would descend a
wind, strong enough to pummel the breath out of them,
and impede their movements, as though it were trying
to bind their limbs, even as they walked, with thongs of
ice. Too cold to stay out for long, one lady would remark
to the other : besides, it was beginning to get dark,
already. And they would then turn back into the cavernous obscurity of the hotel. Still, they supposed, the sea
air was—must be—very good for them. So refreshing,
you know. Then, too, their bedrooms did not face the
sea, because of the wind at night : no, their rooms looked
out on the Cannon and Anchor. Much more homely
and quiet. Still, you see, it was necessary for them to
get out, in order to have a little real sea air.

Very gloomy the hotel seemed as they walked back into
it. Soon, though, Miss Bramley's voice could be heard
cooing, trilling in and out, rustling among the solid gold
flowers, the leaves and branches of the upper air. The
drawing-room was so high and dark that it could have
swallowed up a whole flight of such bird-like voices.
Softly-sung demoded songs would flutter round the
fountains of clear but meaningless notes which were
their accompaniment, till the whole effect was one of a
moonlit mid-Victorian aviary with running fountains,

ferns and palms, with the pallid sheen of water dripping through the darkness, and a flash of exotic brightness from the captive birds as they flew past. The singing rose and fell, caressing with dragging feathers the unfathomable height of the room, fluttering and struggling round in the twilight.

Now the singer would pass on to other, newer songs, and would evoke a penny-bazaar orientalism. Under cover of the darkness, too, she could safely attempt those little professional tricks and grimaces of which she had observed the use at ballad-concerts, but which she had so far lacked the courage to bring out in open daylight. The effects were carried out with brio, but the voice was wearing, perhaps, a trifle thin.

Miss Collier-Floodgaye loved these half-hours of music, and it was a great source of joy to her Companion to feel that her gifts were appreciated. The old lady would lie there, with her feet up, on a sofa, listening, silent and stiff as a felled tree. As the room grew yet darker, the singing became bolder and more pure : the birds were transformed into nightingales, and cascades of silver notes tumbled transparently down from the dark branches in which they were cradled. But now tea was brought in, and the last song died away in a golden glow. The waiter turned on every light, and each leaf of the richly orna-mented frieze and cornice weltered in a stiff, stifling glory.

The two friends did not often go out in the morning, for Miss Collier-Floodgaye took great pleasure in late rising—a habit which made the Companion wonder if she had not at some time been under the necessity of getting up early every day. But, of course, they had their special " treats "—and every now and then it would occur to Miss Collier-Floodgaye that there was *some-*

thing about the morning air which was to be sought in vain at all other hours. She was sure it must be good for one. Then she would dress, and soon they would set off, very slowly, for the Winter Gardens.

This pleasure resort was inappropriately named, for between October and May hardly anyone entered it. It was a large stretch of cliff tortured into terrace, garden and thicket, and breaking out toward its base into an eruption of buildings. For a short time in the summer it blazed with bands, flowers and people, until the general effect from the sea was of a hillside entirely covered with moving, mingling confetti. But now, during these short grey days and long black nights, it was entirely given over to the uneasy, shivering ghosts of the summer. It was the dusty, discarded chrysalis of a butterfly— infinitely used-up and empty. About all places of this kind, which close for the winter, there is an indescribable air of desolation : indeed, the knowledge that they will open again in the spring adds to the sense of calamity, rather than detracts from it. This identical feeling of " closed for the winter " will be experienced by a visitor new to the streets and houses of Pompeii. That town, too, is an empty chrysalis, a summer resort hermetically sealed by a volcano for a winter that has already lasted nineteen centuries. The untidiness of it presupposes that it will shortly be reopened. The trivialities of that distant moment have not been swept away : bread is still left about in the ovens, wine still in the amphoras in the public bars ; the plaster and stucco show their cheapness more surely. Only a touch of paint here and there is needed. But if we thought that Pompeii would shortly be put to rights and peopled again, how infinitely more dreary it would seem.

So it was at the Winter Gardens ; except that here the North added a quality of devastation all its own, for in the winter, the whole place was given over to be sacked and raped by the elements. Those bluff rivals, the Gods of Sea and Wind, took it for their own from humanity, used it as a neutral ground on which they could meet in joust and tourney, as once the Kings of France and England disputed on the Field of the Cloth of Gold. Here Æolus and Poseidon wrestled all the winter long, boisterously unexhausted.

All the gates but one were closed. Over this it was obvious that the two competing Gods, realizing that the townspeople had a right of way through their tournament-ground during the summer, had reached a compromise with mankind ; for they had installed in the lodge as custodian a being that belonged in equal proportion to sea, air and earth ; part fish, part bird, part human. This fierce old white-whiskered crustacean, with a long beak, and prominent eyes that were, however, veiled by age and rage, resided in a minute barnacle of a lodge which had been attached to the bare rock. Miss Bramley, who always dreaded this moment in an otherwise delightful morning, gently touched the glass slide through which glared the ferocious guardian, and proffered, as the price of two tickets, a tremulous shilling. Unmollified by the little woman's terror, the crustacean thrust out a hard-shelled claw, clutched the shilling, meanwhile grinding his mandibles with rage, and then swiftly assuming his bird personality, tapped the bit of silver eagerly with his beak. He was always suspicious of winter visitors (what did they want here in the *winter* ?) and it was his considered opinion that their object was to pass off on to him false coin. This one appeared to be good, though, so he quickly threw out two pink tickets at the ladies and whirled the turnstile, which he controlled from the interior of his lodge, with a clacking sound that was an excellent imitation of the cry of a corn-crake. Startled by this, the visitors were caught in his remorseless iron whirlpool, and deposited, safe but flurried, on an enormous terrace. The crustacean, smiling and obviously congratulating himself on the success of his manœuvre, then relapsed into his warm shell.

The long stone raft where the old lady and her Companion were now walking, was castellated at its edge as the waves, upon which it appeared to be floating. Further on, under the shelter of the cliff, rose a huge group of buildings, theatre, concert-hall, and café, while on the near side of it lay a thinly arcaded row of shops, all closed for the winter. Though the windows were unshuttered, the doors were clamped and bolted, and on them had already formed little crusts of salt and deposits of rust. The windows still displayed open boxes of cigarettes, first spoiled by the sun, and now left here to be nibbled by brown damp, or glass jars full of sweets oozing metallic colours, coalescing into dreadful liquid rainbows. The florist's shop, full of empty but rattling glass vases was, perhaps, most ghastly of all. The light-transmitting, bulging shapes were at first altogether invisible until their vibration called attention to this or that transparent vacuous form hovering in the air, in the same way that only the movement of a translucent jelly fish, which has assumed for its own protection the look of the surrounding sea, betrays its vague form floating in the ocean. And then behind these sinister spectres, and apparently as a tribute to them, could be perceived crosses and wreaths of damp, but still dusty,

everlasting flowers. Next to the florist was the wide
window of the chief hairdresser in the town ; here again
the door only was shuttered while imprisoned behind
their glass walls several coquettishly mildewed wax
ladies were coyly grimacing. One or two of these were
cut off prematurely, like the effigy of the Sovereign on
coin or postage-stamp, but others did not forbid a glimpse
of alluring rotundities, for the full figures of the last
century were still in vogue. It seemed as though these
ladies had been the victims, several years previously,
of that strange fate so often predicted for children by
their nurses : they must, surely, have been rehearsing
these pouts and dimples, when suddenly the wind had
changed, and they had remained ever since caught fast
in the arch posture of the moment. Wax figures, perhaps
because they are moulded and set in the very breath
of an instant, age more rapidly, more obviously, than
anything in the world. It is as possible to put a date to
them as it is to a fashion plate. And it added to the mad
indecency of the spectacle, that these abandoned females,
by their style of hairdressing and of such drapery as
they possessed beside the natural shelter of their tresses,
had obviously been thus disporting themselves in the
window for several years. One of these figures, at the
time of transmutation, had evidently just been about to
start for a fancy dress ball ; for she exposed a head of
white powdered hair, and with a gracefully curved little
finger indicated the position of a crescent-shaped black
patch, placed there for the further emphasis of a dimple.
This delicious gesture was wasted on empty air. It was
dreadful to think of the poor silly remaining there all
the winter, while the ogre-mouthed winds howled round
her, and the sea thrust out at her its threatening white

claws. But, here, at last was her justification, for Miss Collier-Floodgaye was delighted with her, so pretty, she thought the arrangement, and fanciful. Indeed, both ladies paused, examining everything in the window, curls, old-fashioned ringlets, " transformations " and fringes. It is odd to note that, though they hardly ever looked in a shop window in London, here they could seldom resist cataloguing with their eyes every object in every shop window they passed. Nor did the fact that these shops were closed for the winter at all deprive them of their pleasure. As they walked slowly along, they could see, through the arches of the colonnades, the waves leaping at the walls, and could hear the thud they made landing safely on the terrace. Now the shops were nearly finished ; there was only the book-shop to come, full of novels with damp-stained backs, and a few old papers, lying about, and the gigantic show case of the photographer—or, as he preferred to be called, a " Camera-Portraitist." Out of this glass sheet, local beauties leered briskly into the gloom : for these were the days of the " Odol Smile " and mouths gleamed white and curving as the new moon. So great was the dental enthusiasm of the public, that had some fortunate belle been endowed with a double row of teeth, she would have been admired proportionately. No such originality, however, was here displayed, but still every tooth could be counted by enthusiastic lovers of beauty. Usually the photographs had a plain sepia background, but in others still survived those enchanting two-dimensional properties of the photographic studio, oak-tree and rustic bench, caverns, torrents, turrets, garden vases, bits of Venice, snow sledges or Gothic ruins, while one lady even went so far as to hold a book on her lap. Rather affected, Miss Bramley thought, and tried to read the title. To Miss Collier-Floodgaye these photographs were of particular interest, for she was a great admirer of youth and beauty. They moved on again. Now they passed the bar, the huge panels of its many doors filled in with small squares of coloured glass which served both to obscure somewhat, from without, the interior scene of riotous jollity, and, at the same time, to enhance, from within, the brightness of a prospect which to those gathered there, was already, on its own, assuming an increasingly vivid and lively tint. From this vast, now empty, gilded saloon was still wafted an odour of whisky, port and bad cigars, but instead of the roguish gold-toothed laughter of barmaids, there only issued forth in these winter months the sound of the salt-lipped winds rattling eager fingers among the empty bottles that still littered the shelves.

Miss Collier-Floodgaye and Miss Bramley moved on to the empty terrace, toward the band-stand, which now harboured no music save that of Æolus, trumpeting his victorious calls, perpetually blaring out till every trembling piece of iron and wood danced to his triumph. Above, as far as the eye could see, stretched path and terrace. On slanting surfaces of green grass could be seen huge stars, ovals or circles of brown earth, which seemed the freshly-dug, fantastic graves of the strange monsters that must have inherited this extraordinary, this dead world, but were, in reality, merely the beds destined for next year's flowers. In the hollows of the cliff-sides were bosquets, now bare of leaves, through which the Wind God wildly hunted a fallen twig, leaf, or torn envelope. The trees were thin, frightened ; they shrank back before so much violence. A lone

tower, near by, lifted up its head three storeys into the
grey air. This furnished a possible clue to the whole
scene ; otherwise the widespread desolation, this parade
of life brought suddenly to a standstill, was inexplicable.
This tower, then, must have been the haunt of a wise,
white-bearded astronomer, who, climbing up, high above
this pleasure city, one evening—one evening when all
the air breathed flowers, when the blossoms on the
ground died away in the darkness only to come trembling
out again with a new fervour in the deep blue pastures
above—was appalled to read by the arrangement of them,
the impendence over this strange terraced and green-
sheltered town of an unavoidable doom. He had been
able to warn the people in time for them to evade this
disaster, but in the haste of their flight, they had only
just had a moment in which to bolt their shop doors,
and then to scuttle away as fast as they could. Only
the two little figures below had remained, had survived.
And even these were now hurrying off as fast as the limp of
the elder one would allow them. But they had enjoyed their
walk very much. So interesting, it had been, and gave one
an idea of what Newborough must be like in the summer.

.   .   .   .   .   .

On other, rarer, mornings—for this was a test by
which the old lady could prove to herself how well she
was feeling—she would pay a visit to the market, or to
the harbour, at this season the only centres of activity
in the town. The harbour cried a deep-toned masculine
to the market's shrill but emphatic feminine. To compare
them would be to measure a portrait of an Admiral by
Holbein against one of Rubens' profuse females.

If the quays had not been so difficult to walk on,
Miss Collier-Floodgaye would have taken a promenade

there much more often, for both she and Miss Bramley
loved the harbour and its business. But the long jetties
were unevenly paved, slippery with fishy remnants, scaly
as a whale's back : further, they were lumbered with
boxes of salt for herring-curing, barrels of sail-coloured
kippers, and mounds of white-stomached fish, over which
haggled—and sometimes swore—old women, whose
heads were enveloped in grey woollen shawls, whose
hands were like claws from their constant handling and
cutting-open of fish. As they ripped apart their silvery
victims, throwing on one side their entrails, a host of
sea-gulls would descend on them, fighting and uttering
their ferocious cries. The wind, too, had the cruel beak
of a gull (cruellest of all bird-masks) and tore savagely
at the tarpaulin faces of the fish-wives, banged and
buffeted the sails and rigging of the ships at the quay-
side. The air was pungent with salt, tar, sea-weed,
kippers and coarse tobacco. The fishermen and sailors,
in their blue jerseys, many of them with rough red beards
and a gold ear-ring, lurched jauntily along the piers,
or lingered nonchalantly at the points where a jetty met
the foreshore. Unlike the prosperous tradesmen on the
cliffs above, these men never deigned to notice strangers.
They called to each other, and talked among themselves :
but they had seen so many things in their voyages that
had a thousand howdahed elephants and a volcano
sprung up at the harbour side, they would not have
allowed themselves to indulge a landsman's curiosity.
Thus Miss Collier-Floodgaye and Miss Bramley escaped
their attention altogether. The deep voices of the men
barked out amid hammering and clanging, the whole
merging into a din that was the equivalent in sound to
the harsh odour of the air, while even the albatross

wings of the waves, as they struggled over the walls, beating at them with their white feathers, could not for long muffle this uproar.

The market, though situate in another universe of sight and sound from the harbour, was not far from it in actual space. It was possible for the old lady, even though she was lame, to visit both in the same morning. But it was a pity to cram into one day all the pleasures of life : besides, it was better to visit each of these places at an early hour, when the scenes were more typical. The market was open every day, but Wednesday was the real market day, the best day on which to go.

The market hall was a handsome stone building with a high glass roof, that multiplied every sound beneath it. Here rusticity, as opposed to the cosmopolitanism of the sailors, ran riot. Under the hard light, which fell through the roof as through a slab of ice, a stranger would be speedily detected, and gimleted through and through by the keen steel eyes of the countryside.

The stalls were arranged in four or five rows, running back to back down the length of this rectangular building. And hither, once every week, came the country women, from distant moor, hill or dale. To reach in good time this stone temple it was necessary for them to leave their farmsteads at four or five o'clock on a bleak, black morning, jogging along the frozen ruts of the road in carts that, like cornucopiæ, overflowed with the stored autumn riches of the countryside. For many a dark mile they jolted on, until the grey light began to creep up, and, leaden though it was, sufficed to kindle the inflammable red lanterns of hip and haw, and a hundred other berries that now glowed warmly among the cobweb-tangled and rimy twigs of hedge and thicket. The flat lines of the stone walls alternated with these hedges, and repeated the rhythm given out by the flat-topped hills, which cut off an interminable perspective of grey thawing. But before this greyness of the North, which sheds a light that never favours unduly even the most sparkling object, but distributes impartially its realistic effects over things dull and brilliant, had done justice to everything it touched, the carts were already being unpiled outside the market. All this accumulated wealth was now poured into one vast receptacle, and there ensued an ordered profusion infinitely more impressive than the tumbled riches of the carts. There were countless pyramids of russet apples, and blushing apples, polished till their shining red convexities reflected, though distorting these expressionless discs in a thousand different ways, the similar high-coloured circles that formed the faces of the country women. The apples filled the air with a sweet, anæsthetic odour that mingled with the stale, butterfly suggestion of cabbage leaves, the warm sleepy smell of onions, and the scent of damp mould, immediately calling up in the mind the rotund tunes chased in vain by brass bands at a flower show. But added to these exhalations were others strange to such functions. There was the Southern sharp smell of tangerines, imported here from who knows what Southern palm-crested coast, and the woodland freshness of nuts, which lay in shallow baskets, in all their primitive simplicity of shielding green leaves. There were whole hillocks of pears that repeated in their shape the pattern of an Indian shawl, or the map of South America, bands of earthy potatoes, wide baskets of onions gleaming in purple and gold, and piles of severed cauliflower-heads peeping piteously out of their high green collars. Near by, cream, butter and cheeses of many sorts, exposed their various pearly or silken surfaces, and there were baskets full of the neat, prim faces of eggs. Honeycombs, in which the fabulous industry of the worker-bees had stored, not only the distilled scent of those vast tracts of heather that sweep away from the town, but also every memory they possessed of summer days, were here for sale. Then there were flowers, baskets of late camphor-scented chrysanthemums that resembled huge spiders, or early, ill-advised spring-blossoms, hyacinths like blue or pink flames, or daffodils with their nodding canary heads pressed close together. Bulbs could also be purchased, or flowers already budding, and brought here in their native mould. Shallow baskets, lying on the ground, were full of pink or red double daisies, nestling on tufts of green, and still rooted in the earth from which they had grown, so that they resembled a fragment torn out of the foreground of a picture by Botticelli. Here surely, on these geometrical, curling leaves and button-like flowers, the growth of which permits the bare earth to show between, a green though smiling beauty should have pressed down a pallid, rhythmic foot. At one stall, snowdrops sourly tinkled their ice-veined sledge bells, while a few very domesticated primula plants were on the point of donning their print dresses for the spring. To add to this prospect of legendary plants, there were fowls alive and dead. Cocks and hens (as distinctively Chinese or Japanese as peacocks, that carry on their heads the proud emerald diadem of their Shah, are Persian) imparted a fantastic oriental grace to this English solidity, gilding the air with the rococo flames of their combs. There were top-heavy, knock-kneed ducks and verdigris-beaked turkeys, most of them dead, and hanging from rails, with disembowelled hares, their noses fast in a child's tin pail. The rabbits, though, were alive hunching their fluffy arcs in wooden hutches, pressing back their furry ears, casting piteous looks from eyes placed in their profiles according to the conventions of Egyptian art. The scene had that quality of exuberant abundance, that blend of trailing flowers into dripping blood, that merging of feathery beauty into red, mangled flesh, that is only to be found in Flemish or Dutch still lives; in, for example, one of those enormous canvases by Snyders, formerly the adornment of so many dining-rooms in English country houses. Above this miraculous profusion darted, like shrill birds, the beaked voices of the country women, their bodies swaddled in layer after layer of winter clothing, till they looked ungainly as Esquimaux, waddling to show something to a customer, while all the time their intense greed for money was masked by faces red and smooth as those of dolls.

Besides these perishable treasures that have been described, there were more permanent objects for sale at counters round the walls of the market, steel knives and babies' rattles, china dishes and terra-cotta pots. The two ladies would buy artificial flowers because they looked so natural: for here it was possible for Miss Collier-Floodgaye and Miss Bramley to buy objects they did not in the least require, or really wish for, at half the price which they would have to pay elsewhere for objects they actually needed. Unable to resist such a feminine bargain, our two ladies would return to the hotel—being compelled, incidentally, to take an expensive cab on the way owing to the weight of their parcels—laden with a truly marvellous miscellany of purchases, all of which would shortly, owing to their uselessness, descend, like manna, in a grateful shower upon Elisa. To her they brought inestimable solace, though she never really had time to look at them.

After one of these infrequent morning excursions, Miss Collier-Floodgaye would rest all the afternoon, while Miss Bramley would practise her new songs below in the drawing-room. But these excitements were not the only ones. On certain afternoons, instead of "taking a turn" on the terrace they would walk through the streets, at this time of year often wrapped all day long in a plausible twilight. From time to time they would stop to gaze at some effort in window-dressing, some winter panorama, in which a cardboard Father Christmas, in a red dressing-gown with a white beard and his arms full of crackers, perspired lamentably over a gas-lit, mica snow-field. Newborough shops were so up-to-date, Miss Collier-Floodgaye thought. It was really wonderful how they "*got*" all the latest ideas. The two ladies moved slowly on through streets where countless pairs of eyes watched them, where countless tongues prepared a report. Perhaps they would finish their small promenade by circling round one of the crescents. Within a few seconds the news of their approach would spread, as though by magic. Pale and until now listless forms would be rapidly propped up and cushioned like idols in cotton wool, to survey this interesting—no, more than interesting, historic—perambulation. The excitement seethed and foamed through the upper rooms. It was infectious and could penetrate any wall, sweep from room to room, from window to window, like the Black Death. Breaking out mildly in one upper chamber, that faced South, this plague could send its germs right through the walls of the next house, which was empty, and attack an old lady lying in bed two doors away. In a moment, frail and infirm as she was, this fresh victim would be at the window, and the virulent epidemic would have imparted its infection to old Miss Waddington, at the end of the Crescent. At last, she beheld them. . . . Goodness Gracious, so that was the woman! And Ella had said they were " quite ordinary." One simply couldn't trust the girl, that was what it amounted to. Could she never get anything right ? So Louisa Shrubfield had been right all the time. She had said, over and over again, in that affected way of hers, a *limp* and a malacca cane . . . something more than just *queer*, it seemed to Miss Waddington.

All round the Crescent pale old eyes sparkled with a delicious fire ; while cheeks, hot as those of feverish children, were pressed close to the transparent ice of the window-panes. Queer . . . very queer, and not the sort of people, evidently, upon whom one could call. A limp, you see. Besides, if one called—that is, if one was well enough to call—one would know everything, and then there would be no excitement. It would be as though a trout fisher were to catch the trout in the middle of tickling it. It would never do. Better, perhaps, wait to see what Miss Waddington decided.

Meanwhile the two friends were walking unconcernedly below. Miss Collier-Floodgaye noticed nothing unusual about the upper windows ; while Miss Bramley, if for a moment she detected a gleaming eye, would preen herself, smooth out her little flounces, frills and lace edgings, and imagine a kind voice, in a fire-lit room, saying " There goes that *attractive* niece of dear old Miss Titherley-Bramley. It's easy to see that *she's* well-bred. And such a lovely voice, she has, so they say . ."

But, best of all treats, was that one heralded by Miss Collier-Floodgaye's announcement, early in the morning, that what she needed was a "breath of fresh air" or "a blow"—though one might have imagined that the icy stiletto of the winter wind, stabbing through every crack, crevice and keyhole, would have sufficed to give her the necessary fillip. They would lunch rather early, at twelve forty-five, and at about two o'clock would set out in a closed cab drawn by two horses, and drive up on to the moors that begin about five miles away from Newborough, and stretch away to Flitpool, and beyond Flitpool toward the ultimate icebergs of Thule. When the two ladies had driven some ten miles, they would fade slowly into this strange prospect of undulating slopes and low table-lands—so flat-topped and wide-based that it seemed as though they were mountains, the top of which had been sliced off with a knife, perhaps because their Creator wished for a section, in order to test His handiwork—which repeated themselves for ever into swathing after swathing of grey mist. In spite of the uncertain and hazy tracts into which this distance emptied itself, it was never-theless one of enormous width and remote possibilities. However misty, the very mist, and the lines that could just be distinguished through it, proclaimed wide areas. The monotony of its colour, which was in the winter an invariable black alternating with brown, endowed this landscape with a rhythm elsewhere to be sought in vain. In its reserve and apparent coldness, in its occasional, well-hidden flashes of genius (as when a green oasis of woods and bubbling streams is wedged in a gulf between two of these angular hills) and in the distant voice of the lonely grey sea, leaping at high brown cliffs, this prospect at once declared itself much more truly the heart of

England than are the lush lanes of Devonshire, or the dreary imitation deserts of the downs. The wavering but flat lines were unbroken, save for the glacial stones of vast dimensions, which crouched like petrified, extinct monsters in the mists, or where they were fractured by a hill, so sudden in its rise that it seemed to have been scooped out of an adjacent hollow with a spoon, for convex and concave precisely corresponded. Again there might be a group of three or four burial mounds in the foreground, to repeat the same rhythm in a minor key. In shape they echoed exactly the flat-topped tables, and seemed in no whit more artificial. If these were the tombs of kings, then yonder hill must be the tomb of a God. These melancholy, monochromatic wastes by the sea were, indeed, studded with many such burial mounds—tombs of early kings, kings of unknown race—so that at one time they must have harboured a population much more numerous than that which they sheltered at present. Who they were, these early leaders, has never been discovered. Once in a while a local antiquary would disinter a huge gold necklace, or even a high crown of gold. The moors were still littered with their sharp flint implements. But these personal belongings and weapons helped rather to deepen, than to solve, the mystery. Gold crowns and delicate jewellery do not tally with such savage and inefficient instruments of death. For what dim and decaying race, for what lurking and now extinct animals, had these weapons been devised? Some enemy must, surely, have been skulking in these wide areas of land, in which comparative invisibility is so easy. It was impossible to answer these questions. No doubt the kings had come from over the ocean, across that pathway, which was so perilous to this land. They lay at rest now, in their enduring mounds, and once each year the earth that covers them would blaze out in the kingly mourning colour. Countless royal palls of this description have they witnessed, these deep-socketed eyes over which project such jutting ridges of bone. Once every year the entire earth, from sea to horizon, would be washed away beneath a flood of purple. Then, for a few weeks, the landscape was transformed, all the values of mound and tableland altered out of recognition. But now it was again brown and bare, and the only sounds that bit into the intense quiet, which lurked just under the roaring wind, were the dead-world cries, such music as will survive after mankind has perished, of the sea-gulls as they swerved in on the wind. Few houses could be seen, and from these issued the aromatic smell of burning peat, while above them a blue ribbon of smoke was being whirled and knotted, and then dispersed, into the air. The square grey houses, which broke this monotony so seldom, were blind and dumb : not an echo rose from them. And, as a final touch to this stretch of desolation, there stood a few black, leafless trees, frozen into impossible attitudes by the wind from the sea ; trees that stretched their arms toward the grey sky and brown land, while the weight of their bodies was thrown forward, toward them, as if in flight. It seemed as though these grotesque, primeval shapes had once been giants, giants racing in terror from the oncoming rush of the ocean, which could still be seen behind them, dashing and hurling itself at the rocks ; but the fury of the salt wind had been too much even for their strength, and they had been petrified into these monstrosities, still in the very action of their terror-stricken flight, but now able only to creak and groan like ghosts upon an empty wind.

Into this prospect the figure of Miss Collier-Floodgaye fitted with a singular consistency ; she showed in stature, dress, countenance, the same gaunt and rugged characteristics. Out of some such background as this, she must surely have first emerged. But now she and her Companion must turn back ; they must not walk too far from the cab, for fear of being lost. One might easily lose one's way, they thought. Newborough was out of sight, and there was only to be seen this vast expanse of grey and brown, and, on the other side, the great whale-backs of the jostling waves, from here turned by the magic of distance into a cloud of grey-backed birds that fluffed and unfurled their wings with a flash of whiteness. And if the way was lost, one could shout for ever without any answer being borne back, except the scratching rustle of wind through dead heather. So they drove on toward the warm and glassy town, its lights already sprinkling the sea-shore for miles round with a dusting of stars. It was dark by the time they entered the town, and the interiors of the outlying houses stood out brightly, fern in foreground, piano and figure behind. They passed the forge, diabolically flaming, and filled with hammering black figures. Now they were in the shopping streets, full of people. And here they were at the hotel, already ! Really it took no time, getting back. But what a delightful afternoon ! The old lady declared she felt quite a different person.

But the hotel looked dark and sombre. In a few minutes, though, tea would be ready, and after that Miss Bramley would sing once more. Or perhaps both ladies would smoke a cigarette ; for Miss Bramley—another symptom—had lately adopted this habit, though it would have made Miss Fansharpe's bones rattle like castanets in her grave, had she known. But then many ladies at the Court smoke now, and one must realize that Queen Victoria's reign was over. Miss Collier-Floodgaye, indeed, had smoked for several years ; a cigarette, perhaps, being for her too the symbol of deliverance from some unknown subjugation. In any case, it suited her large, rather masculine frame and her temperament which, though nervous, was not fussy.

Then, quite soon, the two ladies must dress for dinner. Dinner was at 7.30, and a rather formal affair, alone in an enormous dining-room, partitioned off by screens, over which the winter winds played a continual game of hide-and-seek. There were several other tables, all laid as if a host of visitors were expected, for, even thus divided, the room was vast. Each table had a lamp, with a red, railway-carriage shade on it, which cast a hectic glow upon the faces of our two heroines, and made their shawls and scarves look even warmer than they were. The meal was conducted to the accompaniment of a long menu in French, which translated itself into the most faded, woebegone English dishes. A little wine ; for wine, Dr. MacRacket (he had now, by means of Miss Waddington's entente with the hall-porter's wife over the red comforter, been installed as Miss Collier-Floodgaye's medical adviser) had assured them, acted as " a tonic on the system, but only if taken in moderation " ; but no coffee, of course, for coffee keeps one awake. This negation, this absence of coffee brought dinner to a conclusion, and the ritual end of the performance was always the same. Miss Collier-Floodgaye would enquire, " Have we done ? " and to this Miss

Bramley would intone back, " Shall we come ? " The
two ladies would then rise from the table, and go up to
the empty drawing-room, where they would smoke
another cigarette, Miss Collier-Floodgaye would indulge
in a solitary game of patience (" Miss Milligan " was
the best, she thought) or play double-patience—or
even " piquet," with her Companion. Miss Collier-
Floodgaye loved cards. She wished she could pay bridge.
It must be such an exciting game. King Edward, they
said, revelled in it. She wondered whether Queen
Alexandra played or not ? There was no knowing. She
was told that quite a number of bridge-parties took
place in the town (to whom, Miss Bramley wondered,
had she been talking now ? So infra dig.). Quite a lot.
Even the wives of certain clergymen played, so they
said. Miss Bramley was not sure that this was right :
ought clergymen's wives to be quite so worldly ? But
Miss Collier-Floodgaye saw no harm in it, not nowadays.
Things used to be different, of course.

After a game or two the ladies would mount up in
the lift to their rooms on the first floor. Elisa, the German
housemaid, came to see if they wanted anything. At this
time of night, she was usually in a better mood. Yes,
she had filled their hot-water bottles ; as hot as they
could be : there had been a wreck, just round the corner
of Jaspar Bay, the lifeboat had put out, but had been
forced to come in again, and the washing would be back
on Friday evening without fail.

As Miss Bramley got into bed, she thought what a nice
day it had been. Cecilia was inconsiderate in some ways,
but she was really fond of her. Somehow everything
seemed more cheerful now than at Llandriftlog. In fact,
Miss Bramley was happy.

CHAPTER XI

BEHIND THE LINES

" We, too, have spun our Sunday round
Of Church and Beef, and, after-sleep
In houses where obtrudes no sound
But breathing, regular and deep,
Till Sabbath sentiment, well fed,
Demands a visit to the Dead."

MISS COLLIER-FLOODGAYE and Miss Bramley were
delighted to be back in Newborough. They felt tired,
" *run down*," you know—after their summer in London.
Then they had moved to Folkestone for August and
September, but the change had done them little good.
The place wasn't bracing, in the way that Newborough
was bracing, and it had been so crowded and noisy, full
of common *trippers*. They supposed all seaside towns
were like that in the season. What a pity it was that such
nice places should be spoilt.

But the winter at Newborough was very different,
and Miss Bramley was sure that the quiet helped to
rest Cecilia's mind. One must not forget that Cecilia
was an old lady, and ought not to see too many people
at her age. Her vagueness had grown to an alarming
extent. All the same, tired or not tired, the moment
Miss Bramley turned her back, the old lady would get
into conversation with strangers, *total* strangers. Really
if Miss Bramley had not been there herself to see it,
she would never have believed it possible—such extraordinary people—and telling them everything . . .
money again, too. All Miss Bramley hoped, was that

the old lady would not meet bad companions at New-borough. But how could she, as they knew no one? And fancy preferring conversation with people of that sort to hearing the Indian Love Lyrics!

At any rate the old lady pretended to be pleased at being back. They were thankful to find themselves in their old rooms again. The servants were so civil and accommodating, and gave the two ladies quite a welcome. Miss Bramley had grown fond of Elisa (of course she was a German and many people did not like Germans) but she did her work well (it was wonderful how the Germans worked, she had been told. That, they said, was why they had shot ahead so rapidly) and was quick, and didn't answer back. Only on Sundays was she at all disobliging—put out by her walk in the Cemetery, no doubt.

For every Sunday, in the winter, the Slave of the Alarum Clock was given an afternoon off. If the afternoon was fine—and in the North it must be admitted that autumnal Sunday afternoons have a habit of cold blueness—she would walk in the Cemetery. For this half-religious, half-mundane joy, Elisa wore a special heliotrope-coloured plush dress, with a high collar, which she had brought with her from her native land twenty years before, and a large black hat. She also carried a parasol, which, since she only used it at the most once a week, she had never been able to break in, never quite had time to tame, and consequently carried when she walked, at a great distance from herself, as though it were a dangerous wild animal being led along at arm's length on a chain. Her features, hair and complexion, all were arranged in a special Sunday perspective, so that, as by a sundial, one could by looking at them, even if waking out of sleep, tell the exact hour of the exact afternoon. Unfortunately this ceremonial visit to the Dead had the same effect upon Elisa that Sunday church-going produces upon old ladies. The emotion roused in her by the beauty of the scene, and that state of eventual bliss for which the scene stood sponsor, exacerbated her temper, which was as yet but mortal. Hot-water-bottles that night would be cold as ice, beds the next morning would be dexterously given a semi-apple-pie quality—just not bad enough for visitors to be unable to complain to the director—and rattling and banging would resound through room and corridor.

The scene in the Cemetery on a fine afternoon afforded Elisa great pleasure. It was so pretty and animated, full of nurses of the well-to-do, who sauntered piously along, pushing perambulators, and exchanging with one another the latest scandals. Then there were poorer families, the mother on the left, the father on the right, and a chain of children between them, holding hands. These parties were more silent. But all of them were in their best clothes. The men wore bowler hats, and had given their moustaches an additional heavenward twirl for the Sabbath.

Beautifully kept it was, too, with a magnificent flourish of chrysanthemums and china asters. The geraniums were over now, the gardener said ; but all the same, with falling golden leaves, and weeping willows still dripping their seaweed-like tresses over white marble angels, the place was at its best. It was touching to see how every Sunday, week after week, relatives would visit this or that grave to place a wreath on it. One woman, the Sexton confided to Elisa, had been up here every Sunday for thirty-three years, always with a nice bit of fern, a marguerite daisy, or a geranium. Some of the tombs were beautiful : vases and broken columns, weeping angels, Gothic lettering with a border of ivy in carved stone, vases, crosses and obelisks in Aberdeen granite—which the Sexton said, when one took everything together, one thing with another, probably made a better show for the money laid out than anything else—pretty colour, a beautiful polish (real finish that one couldn't mistake) and would last for ever. Real granite it was. In fact he often said to his wife, " Maria," he said, " if I should go first, nothing elaborate. Just a simple bit of Aberdeen," so that you could see that he meant it.

This place brought Elisa more closely into touch with the English people than anything else in the town. They were a difficult race to understand ; but they had the same feeling for a cemetery that the Germans have— that one could say for them . . . the actual funerals might be better in Germany . . . better arranged, more orderly . . . but the cemeteries here were beauti-ful. This almost reminded her of the one at Potsdam. . . .

A few weeks before the return of Miss Collier-Flood-gaye and her Companion to Newborough, Elisa had been walking, alone as usual, in the Cemetery. She had just paused to note the detail of a rather pretty grave, when such a nice woman came up and spoke to her, commenting on the tidiness of the tomb. It appeared that Miss Thompson (for such was the stranger's name) was parlourmaid to an old Miss Waddington, who lived in Ghoolingham Crescent. Elisa was much flattered ; for though rigid in etiquette, and not, as a rule, caring to speak to anyone without an introduction, she could see at once that Miss Thompson was a nice, respectable woman ; and then, usually, those in " private service," those with old ladies like this Miss Waddington, were so stuck-up, gave themselves such airs, would not speak to hotel servants, despised them all. Though she had lived here many years now, Elisa had no friends in the town, except the Sexton, and him she knew merely in his professional capacity, as, for example, an amateur of Egyptian sculpture, who attends regularly the lectures of a celebrated Professor of Egyptology, is, perhaps, acquainted with that luminary. The relationship was merely one of master and pupil. It was a change to be taken a little notice of, Elisa reflected. Besides, Miss Thompson knew all about her, had seen her in the Cemetery for years. She even asked the hotel servant to tea one day. They would have shrimps, for a treat, she said, and Elisa must tell her all about Germany. Was the hotel full now, she asked? Who was staying in it? Was the funny old lady who had been there last year—with a Companion—coming back again? Oh! she was, was she, in another month's time? And then Miss Thompson had to go back to get tea ready. For her mistress was expecting a friend to tea, she said, a Mrs. Shrubfield.

" Rummy thing," said the Sexton to Elisa, " I've known Miss Thompson for years, and never known her take a fancy to anyone like that before. Stuck up, as a rule," he said, " haughty like." Elisa was still more impressed and flattered.

.   .   .   .   .

Elisa was pleased to see the two ladies. It was a Tuesday, and her Sunday evening temper had spun its course: she was able to sling a pallid smile of welcome across her features. Indeed, the return of Miss Collier-Floodgaye and Miss Bramley to Newborough was (though these ladies were not aware of it) an important event in the life of the town. The summer armistice was at an end. Mrs. Shrubfield had marched in triumph

back to Newborough and, even now, she and Miss
Waddington were perfecting their plans for a new offen-
sive. Everything augured well—the battalions, in
their rooms of Southern aspect, refreshed by rest,
plentiful rations, and constant cups of hot tea, were
enthusiastic and ready to rush on. As we have seen,
contact with the enemy had already been established
by Miss Waddington's scout. Further, it was rumoured
in the town—though this may have been only an hallucin-
ation born of excitement—that the invisible Lady
Tidmarshe had taken on human form for a while again,
and had been seen, hovering, like the Angel of Mons,
at the head of the troops, spurring them on to victory ;
that she had volunteered to lend the prestige of her
precedence to the two Marshals, and to aid them with
advice, that was the fruit of an experience, which,
though now superannuated, had in its time been considerable. Probably all these rumours were unfounded.
Even the two Misses Finnis could not be certain. Lady
Tidmarshe did not mention the matter to them, and they
hardly liked to ask. Sir Timothy seemed more nervous
than usual, and Miss Tidmarshe could be heard practising
on the banjo, in her bedroom, a new march of Sousa's.

In any case, if such supernatural aid had been afforded
them, the two leaders made no confession of it. Instead,
they were putting the finishing touches to a scheme, the
very simplicity of which was to take one's breath away, and
prove more surely than anything else the genius which made
them worthy of the great trust reposed in them. For some
weeks both Mrs. Shrubfield and Miss Waddington had
assiduously flattered and fawned upon Mrs. Haddocriss,
wife of Archdeacon Haddocriss ; and, in connection with
rumours cited above, it may not have been entirely
without significance that during the same period a foot-

man in the Tidmarshe livery was most certainly observed
leaving a bunch of blue, mildewed grapes—a bunch that
appeared to have made its escape from the fruit department and to have passed several happy nights at the
greengrocer's, and, through a pardonable error, to have
become entangled at last among the vegetables, spending
joyous hours of play with cabbage and cauliflower. This
Message from Beyond the Barrier was cradled in a green
wicker basket.

Mrs. Haddocriss was a grim lady, with a long back-
bone, and long teeth that would never quite meet in the
middle, but upon every separate one of which was
written a Scottish grit and determination. Her eye
was cold, blue and charitable. In all the town her
chief aversion was to Mrs. Floodgay, the wife of a cleric
who rivalled her husband in influence. Now it suited
Miss Waddington and Mrs. Shrubfield—indeed it was
necessary to them—that Mrs. Haddocriss and Mrs.
Floodgay should be friends. With Mrs. Floodgay the
two leaders had anticipated—and in fact had met with—
no resistance to their plan, for they had always regarded
her as their spy, their scout, their creature. But upon
Mrs. Haddocriss they had been forced to lavish infinite
time and care, tact and patience before they could cajole
her into the requisite mood of amiability. Now, however, everything had been satisfactorily arranged, and
the delicate plant of such a friendship began to expand
and sprout its shrill green growth in the warm, fire-lit
room of Miss Waddington.

Mrs. Haddocriss had called upon Miss Collier-
Floodgaye just before that lady had left for London at
the end of the spring. It had been part of her duty
to do so, as Miss Collier-Floodgaye and Miss Bramley
were regular attendants at her husband's church. An

introduction to the old lady by Mrs. Haddocriss could scarcely, then, be regarded even by the most exacting critic, as an infringement of the rules of sport or warfare. The two Marshals were determined, therefore, that when a suitable occasion presented itself, Mrs. Haddocriss should introduce Mrs. Floodgay to Miss Collier-Floodgaye, the basis of this introduction being the similarity of their names, the omission of the " e." Once this presentation had been effected, the two ladies could dispense with the services of the grim and troublesome Mrs. Haddocriss, for they had little doubt but that Mrs Floodgay would soon gain the confidence of Miss Collier-Floodgaye. The latter was, they had heard, of a more talkative disposition than one would have expected, and Mrs. Floodgay was a " dear, insinuating little person." Thus, through their advance guard, they would be able in the most natural manner to meet Miss Collier-Floodgaye whenever it might be convenient for them to do so ; and, in the meantime, the safety of their lines of communication would be guaranteed. They would be in receipt of the latest intelligence during all the winter, without the least danger of hitch or leakage.

Everything, of course, depended on the trustworthiness and loyalty to their cause of Mrs. Floodgay. But insubordination on the part of their agent had never even occurred to them as a possibility ; while it was incredible that such a willing slave could wish to foster ambitions of her own.

The only question, therefore, that remained to be decided was, which moment to choose for the introduction. Mrs. Haddocriss had promised to do her share. After church, on Sunday, was perhaps the most favourable opportunity.

CHAPTER XII

NORTHERN CARNIVAL

> " Timotheus placed on high
> Amid the tuneful quire,
> With flying fingers touched the lyre :
> The trembling notes ascend the sky,
>   And heav'nly joys inspire.
> The song began from Jove."

THE monotony of winter life at the Hotel was not un-broken. Occasionally there would be a lapse into start-ling gaiety, a hunt ball, a hospital ball, a ball, even, in aid of the Life-Boat. During their first winter at the Superb, Miss Collier-Floodgaye and Miss Bramley had taken no part in such subscriptive pleasures. But now the elder lady began to complain that her life here was dull, and also that the sound of these festivities wafted up to her room, kept her awake at night, so that she might just as well be sitting up. Miss Bramley thought it wiser to let her watch the scene. It was better to give way, or she might wish to spend the next winter in London, and begin her promiscuous con-versations all over again. With Miss Bramley beside her at these balls, she could not get into much mischief.

What imparted an interest to such affairs was the participation in them of the " County." (It was, per-haps, her gradual apprehension of this fact which prompted Miss Collier-Floodgaye's desire to be present at them.) The county, with its three " Ridings," was the largest and richest in Great Britain, and still main-tained a social life—infinitely more impenetrable than that in London—of its own—a social life that suggested the seventeenth century, but a seventeenth century suffering from arrested mental development, elephantiasis and consumption, overgrown yet undeveloped, hectic yet weakly. Newborough was usually ignored by the County, which preferred to remain blue-nosed and frost-bitten in its country houses, or immured in the grey, cloistral recesses of the bleak northern capital. But a charity fund of any kind offered a chance to assert its social prestige, and accordingly it would be gracious, and sweep down in hordes on the Hotel. Otherwise it only consented to recognize Newborough during the annual cricket festival, when it would descend, haughty beneath panama hats and fringed parasols.

For one of these dances, the Hotel would suddenly, and for one night, be full of County families. Doors would slam continuously, and the vast, antediluvian lifts would become huge, gilded cages from which rose without ceasing, a senseless but never-ending exchange of chatter and banter; up and down the cage would hum, with the sound of an organ in a church; the folding iron doors would rattle back and slam again, and hoarse laughter and giggling would fill the corridors. The young people were enjoying themselves. Pale cohorts of young ladies, their dresses as much a part of the northern capital as the stone is part of its dismal Minster, would wanly entice a swarm of encrimsoned young hunting squires. The high ceilings would give shelter to whole flights of shrill giggles, or would double the deep roll of bucolic laughter—laughter at jokes which harked back in pattern, and even in substance, to many a dead century; while, released for a moment from the hereditary duties of chaperonage, immense dowagers would, among themselves, give rein to a conversation so frank, full-blooded and scandalous that even an army mess-room would have shrunk back, surprised. In this society there was no faint breath of modern, smart æstheticism. In London, it is true, the fashionable world was beginning to take an interest in such things as furniture, house decoration, and the theatre ; but to these people, though their houses were full of treasures, of furniture and pictures, accumulated by their more cultured ancestors, though an occasional wall-paper by William Morris may have sneaked, unnoticed, on to their walls, the possibility of such interest was inconceivable. To such a pitch had a century of modern public-school education, with its organized games, its petrified system of teaching and lack of all reality, reduced a once mentally vigorous and capable class. Other things, too, had affected the " County." Though its ranks were closely guarded, the snakes had long ago entered this Eden. There was now a counterfeit, as well as a genuine, " County " ; and between the two were many gradations. The rich, loud, floridly handsome daughters of manufacturers from the fog-bound industrial cities or of ship-owners from the murky ports, had penetrated into the " County," and to a certain extent permeated its spirit. They had adopted its standards, though adding a new and blatant vulgarity to its tone, while their brothers were, this being due again to the equalizing and democratic tendencies of the public schools, indistinguishable from the genuine article in dullness, and only inferior to them, perhaps, in looks. The women, indeed, of this new, wealthy community were soon to leave the county behind, socially, in the broader world of the cosmopolitan capitals, for they had more energy than the ordinary young girl of the now devitalized county families. To those of them who could remember a more humble beginning, or who were, at any rate, aware of one, their present existence must have appeared as a perpetual masquerade, and since pretence is always invigorating, this had endowed them with endurance and joy in life. To the same cause is to be attributed the increased vitality of the Jews, now that they have been allowed to discard their medieval uniform, to adopt European dress and ape European manners. Their life is one round of pretence, of pretending to be Europeans, Christians, Englishmen English Gentlemen, Peers, and Viceroys. The ghetto has been stamped flat, and has become the scene of a permanent carnival for its former inhabitants. Thus, too, these mercantile young ladies were provided with a never-ending scope for dressing-up. This gave them their strong hold on life, though, at the same time, it removed them even further than the genuine section of the County from any sense of reality.

These febrile and frenetic attempts at gaiety on the part of a society so distinct from the life of Newborough, though so near it in actual geographical space that its materialization in the ball-room was almost as if the shades, that some believe to walk among us perpetually, were for an evening's pleasure endowed with visible substance, produced a quite extraordinary effect upon the townspeople. Individuals, who could ill afford it, who were wont at other times to deny themselves the most reasonable pleasures from motives of economy, would at once subscribe to such dances, entering into these spendthrift amusements with great enjoyment and without the faintest sense of remorse. Even the Monstrous Regiment would send delegates to these functions—delegates carefully picked for the proven reliability of their evidence—in order to be informed, as soon as possible, of the latest happenings, of who was there, and how clothed. Nor, even, did the clergy, and most certainly not their wives, perceive any reason why they should abstain from such innocent diversions. For days beforehand, excitement would be mounting, ever mounting ; Miss Collier-Floodgaye and Miss Bramley would confess to each other, not without pleasure, that the hotel was " quite noisy." Borne in on this spring-tide of joyous expectation, old ladies, each one in a hooded bath-chair (for already it would have started raining) that resembled a nautilus which had run up its sail, would be cast up on the very steps of the Superb. These old persons would demand from John the most precise information, who had booked rooms, which rooms and how much the guests would be charged for them ? If the old ladies were debarred by ill-health from themselves taking part in such re- searches, a niece or companion would timidly act as proxy for them. Meanwhile aproned workmen would be carrying ladders that caught in every cornice and chandelier, would be clumsily opening and shutting doors, or treading in heavily-nailed boots over tiled floors. Soon the aspidistras and withered plants in lounge, ball-room and dining-room, were to be aug- mented by whole oases of tall palm trees from the chief local nursery garden. The platform, on which the band was to play, the gilt decoration of the ball-room, would become unrecognizable beneath the binding green chains and cobwebs of smilax, damply clinging as the hair of mermaids, while the five-pointed red tinsel flames of numerous poinsettias would crackle round the edge

of the ball-room like so many young bonfires. Then
(it was still raining) a tongue of scarlet carpet would loll
out of the slobbering porch of the Superb, and an
awning would pitch its striped tent across the pavement
outside. All these details would be as well known, and
known as soon, to the invalid population as to Miss
Collier-Floodgaye and her Companion, who could
survey the operations from their centre.

When night—the night upon which so many varied
hopes were fixed—fell like a leaden pall over the streets
and squares of Newborough, even then the preparations
for the festivity were not yet complete. But by eight
o'clock the last workman had folded up his apron, put
on his cap, and departed. The detail, dead and dusty,
of the hotel interior was very conspicuous under a dazzling
illumination, and was further emphasized by the flowers
and evergreens, until it seemed as though the face of a
dead man peered through the floral tributes at a lying-in-
state. But this intense, morbid vacancy, stillness and
stiffness only constituted the blackest hour before the dawn.
Soon the ball-room doors would be thrown wide open.

Already a rain-drenched crowd of women, among
whom were sprinkled a few young men in mackintoshes,
jostled round the striped awning outside the hotel.
Such was—or, rather, could be—the courage of the
invalids, facing South, that many of them, who did not
run to a niece or Companion, had, in order that they
might be in receipt of an immediate and accurate description of revel and revellers, dispensed with their
maids (and with the fear of burglary which this sacrifice
entailed) and had sent them to wait outside the Superb.
They were to return, as soon as the last guest had arrived,
and there was to be no dawdling.

First the cabs began to lumber up, vast black leather, rumbling vehicles. Then would follow the carriages, among them Mrs. Shrubfield's, bearing in it that lady's temporarily captive cousin, a skilled reporter. A few dapper motor-cars would draw up, with an exquisitely smooth, bedside manner, for these were the property of the more daring and up-to-date doctors of the town. All these vehicles would eject a torrent of black-coated men, and an indistinguishable mass of ladies, whose heads and shoulders were swathed in sunset clouds of rose-pink and light-blue tulle. At nine o'clock, rather late—for they had been due at 8.30—but fresh from the railway train and Leeds (there was a strong local superstition that a band from Leeds was the best band) the musicians would enter the ball-room. Each would unpack his instrument, inspect it carefully, rap it with his bow or finger, and then on his own account begin to play on it a particular refrain, while these four or five popular tunes, coincident, but refusing to mingle, imparted an air of quite insane gaiety to the crowd gradually accumulating outside in the hall. The obdurate and vacuous strains, in which was repeated unconsciously the motif of " County " and townspeople, and in which, further, were implicit so many obsolete geometrical problems, in which one straight line unbendingly refuses to meet another, ascended into the upper air. But these subtle and haunting suggestions of possible social difficulties in the future quite failed to induce any idea at all in the minds of that legion of girls, daughters of local doctors and clergymen, which was beginning to assemble in the hall and overflow into the " lounge."

The future revellers gathered together, then, in a silence that apart from this uncanny, polyphonic music, was only broken by an occasional, quite inadvertent titter, which, gathering force, speed and substance as it ascended, served to embarrass increasingly its owner and effectively aided the silence. Another giggle would escape by stealth, and the same process would be repeated. Each giglot, as the sly laugh sped from her, was pledged to everlasting silence. There would be much pulling on, tugging, and smoothing out of white kid gloves. Each girl held a programme of the dance, printed in silver on a pale blue card, by the rosy pencil attached to it with a blue silken string. These swung and creaked ominously in the wind at each opening or shutting of the door, and, to those ladies whose dance lists were still unfilled, must have seemed so many corpses dangling on a gallows. Dancing would begin with a waltz, but until almost punctually an hour late, at nine-thirty, the " County " burst in, chattering, and pretending to be alone on its own property, the abandon of the occasion was but fitfully felt. Now, however, with the entry of these various too pale or too rubicund persons, the gaiety would start in earnest. The problem originally announced by the musicians, when each started a separate refrain, could be seen taking on actuality, though in a different form, for these two universes of " County " and seaside town would pass and dance through each other, would thus mingle momentarily but never become entangled or intertwined. Each dancing couple was a unit, a planet belonging to one of the two universes, which could move through the other one, but would yet never be of it.

The two friends sat on chairs against the wall opposite to the band, and, among the fluffily dressed dancers and chaperones, Miss Collier-Floodgaye struck a dignified discord by the sobriety, rich but sombre, of her appearance. Up in the gallery, over the huge doors they could detect Elisa's pale face and sandy hair. In her pleasure at the scene below, all her grievances had been forgotten, and a broad peasant smile was rearranging her features. What she liked best were the waltzes ! And indeed most of the dances were of this species, though after every cluster of three or four consecutive ones, there was inserted, for the sake of variety, an obsolete polka—pathetic moment when, in a sudden spasm of Polish verve, the doctors' wives danced openly with their husbands (though they knew " it was not the thing to do ") and bounced, flounced, hopped and skipped round the room to these almost incomprehensibly jerky rhythms of their youth. Then after about every eighth dance, would come the lancers, effete descendant of the quadrille. The " County " arranged its own sets, and the elder ladies, sporting diamond stars or a tiara, would hurl their weight into these steps with a truly admirable zest, to clownish cries of " I do love to see the young people enjoying themselves." As a matter of accuracy, the younger section of the " County " was bored and disgusted by such displays of rustic grace, which, it felt, must rather damage the elect in the eyes of the townspeople. and had determined to reserve its romping for a later and more justifiable occasion.

Whatever the lancers may have been in its youth, it was now a most singular spectacle. In its accompanying music could already be detected an incipient death rattle, while the persons dancing it suddenly assumed the air of so many performing animals, for the rhythm of each step was precisely that of a poodle, with a stick in its mouth, crowned with a top hat, attempting to walk on its hind legs, or of a chestnut horse that had been taught to walk in time to the music of the. *Haute Ecole*. Miss Collier-Floodgaye never took part in the lancers, though it was a dance in which many old persons joined ; she thought it a pretty sight, but, all the same, she preferred to watch a waltz, for, as she observed to her Companion, she considered a waltz the very poetry of motion.

In those days it was still a matter of inherited belief that the waltz was indispensable. There was, as yet, no sign of that syncopated rhythm which was in so short a time to conquer and drag captive the whole of the dancing world, and, incidentally, in its triumph to destroy the De Flounceys. If, indeed, any portent of the approaching Negro Conquest of Europe was there to be remarked, it was to be sought less in the music than in the dancing of the younger people. In one or two instances, their steps may have constituted the first-found footprint of Black Man Friday on the Newborough sands. Generally speaking, however, the dancing ranged from the frenzied hopping of Dr. Sibmarshe (one of the early pupils of the De Flounceys) through the Viennese languor of Mrs. Sibmarshe, on to the more gliding yet broken rhythms of a few rather emancipated county families.

Now would come supper, an orgy of quails and champagne—held in the provinces to be the two symbols of metropolitan luxury—enhanced by vivid ices and angry jellies of an indescribably lost-world quality. These were further reinforced by the symbol of England's gastronomic empery, " trifle " or " tipsy-cake," a confection composed of bits of old sponge cake that had been out all night on bad port wine, and intensified by the

presence of a pretentious custard which, with good
fortune, might pass itself off as cream that had taken
the wrong turning.   The tables groaned under the weight
of a hundred deleterious foods prepared by the professional poisoner of the catering firm employed, while
the chairs groaned under the weight of the hundred superb
dowagers who courageously devoured these concoctions
The tables at which sat the county families called loudly
to each other across the red glow of the dining-room,
now freed from its partitions and fully illuminated,
while the town tables were either abashed or else defiantly
lively.   Ensued more dancing and frequent suppers.
Hunting noises became incipient, and then epidemic ;
while, finally (and this was, at once, for everyone the
climax of the ball, and for many young persons their
opportunity of venting a special rowdiness, which they
had been saving up all through the evening and had
wisely refused to squander on the lancers) there came
the " Gallop."   In this romp, it was necessary for all
those taking part—and, indeed, expected of them—to
behave as roughly, and to shout as loudly, as possible.
Young and old joined in together.   The weight of the
elder section of the " County " enabled it to be rougher
and louder than any other, but there was considerable
rivalry.   A public-school atmosphere ran riot.   The
band, refreshed by champagne, played louder and louder,
faster and faster ; they halloo'd and hooted with laughter.
But the laughter of the dancers, and above all, the
hunting noises, rose high above the efforts of the band.
Hair became crooked and more crooked, dresses were
torn, diamond stars were awry.   Feet trod on trains,
and there were rending noises, perspiration flowed
copiously, breathing grew louder and more stertorous,

there was much heaving and palpitation, and enjoyment grew more rapturous and more general. The sound of all this throbbing pulsation (for everyone felt sure, now, that the dance had been a success) rose up and up in the air, and thundered through the hall and corridors outside, the clamour increased in volume by its rolling through the empty corridors. Up and up it reached, above the three tiers of rooms, to where, under her dome, Elisa now lay asleep, though soon to be woken by the brazen voice of her slave. It stirred her, as she lay there, and she turned to wonder at the great roaring in the pine forest.

Such was the scene upon which the two friends gazed with sympathy; for they stayed till the very end; they had enjoyed it so much. And it had been just as they were going out to supper that Mrs. Haddocriss had stepped up to Miss Collier-Floodgaye, and had said to her, " I want you to know Mrs. Floodgay and her daughter. You ought to know one another for you must be related, the name is such a rare one. They spell it without an " e " of course. But you must be relatives, really you must."

CHAPTER XIII

NO BIGGER THAN A MAN'S HAND

Shadow, Shadow,
Here you come,
More swiftly running than a river's flow.

FROM the first moment of meeting them, Miss Collier-Floodgaye felt an inclination of friendship toward both mother and daughter ; while they, for their part, were most attentive and kind to the old lady. Not for an instant did they deny the suggested kinship—indeed they welcomed the connection. And Miss Collier-Floodgaye was enchanted to acknowledge such charming relatives. During the last few years she had begun to comprehend fully what a deprivation to her was the lack of a family circle. She had tried to fill the void with Miss Bramley, but though fond of her Companion, indeed much attached to her, the friendship between them, she felt, could never be quite the same thing as that subsisting between relatives. It might be deeper, their friendship, but it could never be so *easy* as a family one. It may have been Miss Collier-Floodgaye's lack of relatives that enabled her to hold this opinion. At any rate, she felt that kin gave friendship a fair start, a place from which it was easy to kick-off. Besides, she had so great a need of affection, and of people to whom she could talk, that one friend was not sufficient for her. Her hope had been that Miss Bramley would act as her impresario, that through her Companion she would gain more easily the confidence of others.

But this hope had been frustrated by her Companion's firmness, by the very intensity of Miss Bramley's feeling for her, which made any other friendship attempted a cause for apprehension, a thing to be checked at all cost. With relatives, however, this jealousy on Miss Bramley's part became at once indefensible. Who but those that possess relatives have the right to be suspicious of them ?

Then, too, Miss Collier-Floodgaye had often lamented that the name must die with her. It was dreadful. And now, suddenly, she had found a family that would hand on the banner of her personality. Truly it was a remarkable coincidence, and they must be cousins, for not only were their surnames the same—practically the same—but the daughter's Christian name was Cécile, a variant of her own Cecilia. How very strange ! It quite cheered her to find this confirmation of their kinship. It entranced her to discover a family related to her own—a ready-made family circle. She accepted the theory that the Floodgays were cousins of hers without any desire to test unduly the evidence for such a suggestion.

The only drawback to this impromptu and advantageous arrangement was the behaviour of Miss Bramley. " Tibbits," Miss Collier-Floodgaye noticed, was becoming cross and dictatorial—yes, dictatorial. Still, she was a good soul. Yet the old lady was forced to confess that her Companion lacked the *fascination* of her new friends. And, really, it was too bad of " Tibbits " to have been so off-hand   rude, almost . . with them.

It must be owned that Miss Bramley's manner to the Floodgays was rather abrupt.   She did not like them

She had distrusted them at first sight.   And how could anyone approve of their way with the old lady ?   It was too familiar.   After all, it was their first meeting, the very first time they had met her.   " Cécile " and "Aunt Cecilia " indeed !   Why, Miss Bramley had never allowed anyone except her family, Miss Fansharpe and Miss Collier-Floodgaye to call her Teresa.   Never— no one had ever suggested it : not even *suggested* it ! Then, too, she had heard Canon Floodgay preach . . . and, well it might be old-fashioned of her, but she liked a Clergyman TO BE a Clergyman (you know, like the dear old Rector at Llandriftlog . . . how he had got on ! . . . Dean of Malta now.   She had always felt that he was cut out for a distinguished career—in fact, she might be wrong, but, in a cleric, she preferred Affliction to Affectation) . . . to be a Clergyman.   To sum it up, the *Canon* was *Theatrical*.   Yes, that was the word : more like the stage than the pulpit !

It was curious that as soon as Miss Bramley saw the Floodgays she realized that they constituted a threat to her intimacy with the old lady.   And this intimacy she valued much more than she knew.   All her old prejudices, which dated from her upbringing, or from her captivity at Llandriftlog, came rushing back to her. The dwarf tree drew in its shoots and uneasy, belated blossomings, and relapsed into its previous harsh but definite shape.   She became again Low Church and Puritanical ; the only one of the new characteristics which remained with her was an outspoken severity. She was no longer timid.

Miss Bramley was therefore very frigid, very formal, in response to Mrs. Floodgay's overtures.   When the Canon's wife remarked on the similarity of the names

Cécile and Cecilia, pretending to see in it more than a mere coincidence, Miss Bramley replied firmly, " It certainly is *very* queer . . . but as a matter of fact my friend has no relatives living. Isn't that so, Cecilia dear ? You have often told me."

Thus Miss Bramley, at her first meeting with them, was unwise enough to make her association with the Floodgays a rather difficult one ; for her answer had made them feel that she regarded them as pushing. Cecilia had looked very uncomfortable, too: but then she should not encourage such people. What Miss Bramley liked—and she should tell Cecilia so—was RESERVE.

The next day the Floodgays called on them and Mrs. Floodgay invited her newly discovered relative to play bridge the following afternoon at St. Saviour's Rectory. Miss Bramley intervened at once, and before the old lady could reply, said, with great resolution, " Miss Collier-Floodgaye must not tire herself at her age ; and, in any case, she has never played bridge, and does not know how to play it." Mrs. Floodgay countered gaily, by offering to teach her, remarking that it was never too late to learn, while, to Miss Bramley's consternation, the old lady accepted the offer ! It really was " unlike her." She could not be quite herself, Miss Bramley felt, to-day. So undignified. Could one imagine Miss Fansharpe doing such a thing ? It was not that Miss Bramley minded Cecilia going—oh, no ! it was not that—but it was her conviction that the wives of clergymen ought not to gamble. Surely it was their duty to Set an Example ? . . . yes, Mrs. Floodgay ought to endeavour to set an example. That was it. She should not spend her time playing bridge : which was bad enough in itself : while it was even rumoured that she gambled. Low points, indeed. And without examining the testimony for this charge, Miss Bramley assumed, for her purposes, that it was true. She was sure it was true. " Low points " were written in every line of Mrs. Floodgay's face. Low points, indeed! Even low points accorded ill with High Church principles, she should imagine. Quite unpacified by her epigram, Miss Bramley proceeded to lash herself into a fury. Not very polite, she should have thought, to ask Miss Collier-Floodgaye to a party, and to omit inviting her friend, in that way. No, not the sort of thing a *Lady* would care to do. The matter could not rest where it was. Cecilia must not be made the prey of such people. No. Enquiries must be set afoot. There was something unusual . . . odd . . . almost (she hated to use the word) . . . DOUBTFUL about them. She wouldn't trust either Mrs. Floodgay or her daughter for an instant. She couldn't say why, but there it was. Write to Mildred as soon as possible : that was the best thing to do. Oh, the Archdeacon would be sure to know . . . bound to know something . . . very likely he would know the Floodgays . . . might have met them at a clerical garden party. Why, she even remembered Harold saying one day, "As in every branch of life, I fear it must be admitted that there are all sorts in the Church. Yes, all sorts." She would write to Mildred at once then . . . besides she must, in any case, answer that last letter, now that she had heard from the Dean about Peregrine.

THE SUPERB HOTEL, NEWBOROUGH,
Nov. 29th, 1907.

MY DEAR MILDRED,

I am so pleased to have been of some little use to you in the matter of Malta. The Dean (who, you will re-

member, is my old friend, Dr. Broometoken) is delighted
to have Peregrine as organist. But it appears that
Rooms are at present difficult to find in the island. He has
taken a lot of trouble, and, alas, these little things are
made more difficult for him by his afflictions, which are,
I am sorry to hear, increasing in severity. The *St. Vitus*,
especially, causes him now the greatest agitation. Peregrine should, therefore, certainly write to thank him
personally. After much looking about, the *dear* Old
Dean has hit upon two rooms, from which the Boy can
choose. One is to be rented at twenty-five shillings a
week from Two *unmarried* Ladies (Church of England)
with a superb view (He writes) over the harbour and a
new geyser; while the other apartment, at a shilling
a week less, is kept by a Roman Catholic Couple, and
has a *light* Continental breakfast thrown in. It is for
Peregrine to choose. The Dean prefers *Not* to make
the choice himself.

Now, dear Sister, I must ask your good offices in return.
We attended the Hospital Ball here two nights ago, and
There met a Mrs. Floodgay, the wife of Canon Floodgay.
Could you ascertain for me what is thought of them?
In these days one has to be careful whom one knows;
she struck me as . . . I do not like to say it . . .
but . . . *fast*! Perhaps Harold could find out from
his Bishop? Far be it from me to cast the first stone;
but she plays *Bridge*. They say, gambles, even, for
low points, while he is very High Church. There was
Trouble, I think, over a Tabernacle, while I have heard
him accused of incense, or even worse. Do let me know
what you hear.

For the rest, we have been full of our little Trivial
pleasures, Sales of Work and Concerts. Have you, by the
way, heard any of Guy d'Hardelot's music? They say
it is a Woman. I have tried over some of the songs
lately, and though rather unusual, I must admit they
struck me as full of *Melody*. I love melody, don't you,
dear?—in music, of course, I mean. Have you heard
further from Poor Minnie?

Yr. Affecte. sister,

TERESA BRAMLEY.

P.S.—The name is FLOODGAY (at St. Saviour's). You won't forget, will you, dear? The weather continues cold but bright.

A reply reached Miss Bramley two days later, but unfortunately it contained very little definite information :

THE RECTORY,
LANCASTER GATE,
LONDON, W.
Nov. 30th, 1907.

MY DEAR TERESA,

Your letter was most welcome. Harold and I are indeed grateful to you for your enquiries at Malta. It is, as you must conjecture, a sad grief for us. But what can a Parent do? It is not for us to question His ways. Besides, there appears to be a strain of music in the family. It is no use looking back.

It is the opinion of both Harold and myself that Peregrine should choose the room kept by the two Church of England ladies, though personally we regret the installation of the geyser. After what has happened, we feel that at all costs, Peregrine must avoid the canker of luxury.

Harold has been in communication with the Bishop about Canon Floodgay. It appears that he has the reputation of being eccentric and Theatrical. If he should hear more, I will let you know at once.

I am shocked to hear about Mrs. Floodgay. There appears to be a general Loosening in Modern Life. What queer times we live in, when a clean, healthy-minded game like " Ping-Pong " is driven out by a card-game of Oriental or even as some think of Negro origin (I often wonder to myself whether, if Peregrine had kept up his " Ping-Pong," as his Father advised, this would ever have happened). As for gambling, you will no doubt remember what our Dear Old Father wrote in his New Year Message for 1884, in the Parish Magazine. I was looking it up only last week. Even to-day it reads so true, like a Clarion Call. In case you have forgotten it, let me recall it to you. " The prevalence of Gambling, which—with the exception of one vice . . . (I allude to *Drink*, though not when taken in Moderation) is the meanest of human vices, is most distressing." How clear the Message ! People have lost the art of writing like that now, I think.

I heard from Australia a few days ago, and am glad to be able to give you good news of Poor Minnie. She is at last to be married, to a Mr. Eldred. The engagement, it seems, has been a distressingly long one : but it appears that he is a Delightful man, a Professor in Queenstown University, and a direct descendant of Ethelred the Unready. What a comfort to know that she will be provided for.

Do you still keep up your Croquet, I wonder ? If so, I should like to send you for Christmas another little pig-skin pocket-book for your engagements. I designed the cover myself. Poppies and lilies. Some little time ago I took up Artistic leather work, and have had *Quite* a success with my Blotters. Besides, it is a most engrossing occupation. There is nothing like a hobby, is there ? It takes the mind off things like nothing else.

Yr. affecte. sister,

MILDRED HANCOCK.

P.S.—How fortunate you are to miss the fogs."

Alas ! Archdeacon Hancock was never able to find out more about the Floodgays.

CHAPTER XIV

THE FLOODGAYS

Said King Pompey, the Emperor's ape,
Shuddering black in his temporal cape
Of dust : " The dust is everything,
The heart to love, and the voice to sing."

IT must not be assumed that Mrs. Floodgay was a
" schemer." She was not. But she was devoted to
the interests of her daughter, and had heard all about
Miss Collier-Floodgaye's circumstances from Miss
Waddington and Mrs. Shrubfield.

And the clergyman's wife, in the manner of the whole
race of mothers, had developed a vision, a glorious vision
of Cécile happily married, and in enjoyment of a comfortable, even ample, income bequeathed her under
romantic circumstances, by a lately discovered elderly
relative, the end of whose life Cécile had helped to
brighten. Nor must it be assumed from this that Mrs.
Floodgay was a doting mother. She was, on the contrary,
sharp with Cécile, only too ready to find fault. But, in
spite of this, she wanted to see her daughter comfortably
potted-out from the parent plant.

And then . . . the poor old lady's life must be *so*
lonely. Especially, as Mrs. Floodgay remarked to
Cécile, with a woman like Miss Bramley, who does not
seem very agreeable or kind to her, does she ? Dreadful,
really, to have no relatives and to be dependent on a
Paid Companion. And far too kind, probably, ever
to turn her away. For her own part, Mrs. Floodgay

would feel quite uneasy, left alone with a Paid Companion . ... really frightened, you know, for terrible as it might seem, those things do occur sometimes, don't they?

With a touch of asperity, rather unusual in her, outside her own family circle, Mrs. Floodgay reflected on " that Class of Woman," which was invariably, she understood, " scheming " and never to be trusted. No really Nice Woman would become a Paid Companion, would she? And even if her father had been in the Church, it signified very little. Anybody seemed to get into the Church nowadays. Evidently Miss Bramley wanted the poor old woman to lead a regular *hermit's* life, seeing no one, going nowhere. But Mrs. Floodgay meant to bring a touch of cheerfulness into this drab existence. Canon's wife uppermost for the moment, she resolved to do her duty, " Come what may." For, after all, it was one's duty, wasn't it, to be kind . . to try to succour and be helpful . . . ? It would be an awful thing to feel deserted in one's old age. Awful. And that was precisely why Mrs. Floodgay had offered to teach the old lady how to play bridge.

The next afternoon saw Miss Collier-Floodgaye at St. Saviour's Rectory, learning the game. There could be no gainsaying the charm and attraction of her new relatives. Such an interesting family, and so full of life. Cécile, in particular, was a darling, pretty, bright and attentive. Young people rarely had such beautiful manners nowadays. And her hair! Mrs. Floodgay told the old lady, in confidence, that Cécile's hair was so long that when it was let down, she could sit, stand, or if necessary even jump on it. A girl like that would get on anywhere. Her hair was more than—what was it?—a crowning mercy? . . .

no, a crowning glory. It was positively a career. Like
one of those old Italian pictures, she was, exactly, with
her masses of auburn hair and large hazel eyes. Such
a pretty laugh she had, too ; vivacious, in fact ! (Here
Miss Bramley, tired already of eulogies, interrupted
to say that she knew that type, animated and with auburn
hair . . . Miss Fansharpe's Home had been full of them.)
And Mrs. Floodgay—May Floodgay—was so attractive,
a sweet little woman and so artistic. Very lively, with
a great sense of humour ; almost roguish, indeed—not
a bit like a clergyman's wife. Why, one could even
comment on other clergymen's wives, in front of her ;
she wouldn't be in the least bit offended. Yet she
never spoke ill of anyone. Never. The only time that
Miss Collier-Floodgaye ever heard her even approach
such a thing, was when she solemnly warned the old lady
against two women, a Miss Waddington and a friend of
hers, who were, it appeared dangerous—but that was
entirely in the old lady's interest—after all she knew
so few people, and naturally May did not want her to
make friends who might be harmful to her. And then
how kind it was of May—for of course since they were
related, they had at once come down to Christian name
terms—to teach an old lady to play bridge. So kind.
Willing to take so much trouble. Miss Collier-Floodgaye
had always wanted to learn the game, always : and she
picked it up quite easily ; it seemed to come to her
naturally, she thought—though it needed a lot of
playing . . . you know . . . brains, not like other games.

.   .   .   .   .

Miss Collier-Floodgaye would never cease from such
pæans, while Miss Bramley's dissent, whether expressed
by silence or in the spoken word, only drove her to

further orgies of enthusiasm, and to a closer friendship with the clergyman's family. She began to frequent the Rectory. Her position there, as a theoretical cousin, gave her a much needed background, filled in the gaps and hollows of her life, added heights and depths to the prevailing flat surface of her existence. It was so pleasant to share their life with them. Aunt Cecilia, Cécile called her. It made her feel thoroughly at home.

Now in her estimate of Cécile, the old lady was not mistaken. The daughter seemed to contradict in her own person all the theories of heredity.

At first one might have supposed that the fact that her character appeared so faultless was merely the result of a cunning foreshortening and false-perspective, of her being shown in relief against the background of her parents (for, with persons or animals of the same species, it is always the youngest who seems—and nearly always is, in actuality—the nicest), or, again, that the example of her family had served to her as a conscious warning. But it was not so. There was in the child an essential soundness, probably transmitted to her from a distant generation, over the heads of her parents. All her affection, all her energy, which expressed itself physically in the colour of her hair, was accumulating within her, in the same way that energy is stored within a battery, to be expended one day upon friends, and more especially upon husband and children ; for had her parents only realized it, Cécile was by her nature bound to marry. But at present she was young, young with that combined grace and clumsiness which belongs to a period of volcanic growth. She stood, as it were, almost hidden by the growing, waving sentiments that she had sown,

in the same way that the figure of a man can be swallowed
up in a field of luxuriant August corn, lost to sight in
waving, golden intricacies, the green shoots of which
himself had nurtured. That torment of constant
watching and nagging which, if inflicted upon a daughter
by a mother, is often informed by a truly diabolic
intuition—an intuition, indeed, often so penetrating
that it enables the parent to perceive clearly the existence
of predilections so secret and suppressed that they are
unknown to the child herself—Cécile endured with a
feminine fortitude, with that peculiar bravery of women,
whose instinct is ever to return pleasure for pain. Not
for a moment would she permit herself to realize that
there was in her heart for her parents anything but
affection, and over them she threw the enveloping cloak
of her own charity.   But that, thus, she gave more than
she received, rendered her peculiarly liable to gusts of
affection, made her touchingly responsive to the kindness
of Miss Collier-Floodgaye. And there soon grew up
between them, even under the threatening shadow of
Miss Bramley, a silent but genuine friendship.   Nothing
that Cécile's parents could do to make it appear sham,
shallow or false could in any way alter its quality : while,
on the other hand, Miss Collier-Floodgaye's consciousness of its sincerity helped Cécile's parents to deceive
the old lady more easily. When Miss Bramley, for
example, tried to demonstrate to her friend the falsity
of Mrs. Floodgay, the old lady's sure knowledge of
Cécile's character strengthened her conviction of the
corresponding sincerity of the mother. Instinctively
Cécile, for her part, felt that Miss Bramley distrusted
her ; which made her in return dislike Miss Bramley,
accept her parents' view of the Companion's " scheming "

nature, and become the champion of the very couple that oppressed her.

And then the Canon, Miss Collier-Floodgaye pondered, what a fascinating man ! Amusing and witty, yet, with it all, a man-of-the-world (it was such a comfort to find a clergyman who was a man of the world). You know, didn't disapprove of everything. Original too. A great career in front of him, Miss Collier-Floodgaye should imagine, for he was still quite young . . . young for a clergyman, that was. A Bishop one day, probably. Of course some people abused him, and said he ought to have been an actor : but that was only their jealousy, and, besides, he was so high-spirited. You could not expect him to behave like other clergymen. Of course the others did not care for him, because *his* church was always full to overflowing, not a pew empty in the whole church. Directly he mounted the pulpit, he could do exactly what he liked with his congregation : *anything* he liked . . . occasionally he may have been unwise— but, then, he was so original. He should not, she supposed, have attacked other of his " clergy-brethren " from the rostrum, actually : and, no doubt, he ought not, strictly speaking, to have imitated them. She could quite see that. Still, he was only human, like other people, and he was such a wonderful mimic ! What a humorous, clean-cut, clerical face he had, too, with its accentuated, incised lines, running from nostril to mouth, from mouth to chin. The eyes were light grey, with fair eyebrows and eyelashes (it was untrue to say, as his enemies said, that he had none) and his head was crowned with a mass of curling auburn hair, which had receded a little from the forehead. In his dalmatics, he looked most impressive : might have been made for them. And the church was so pretty; there could be no doubt of that. Miss Collier-Floodgaye even went so far in her enthusiasm for the Canon as to admire the representation of our Lord, which had been the cause of so much dissension in the flock.

It had long been felt by his brother ecclesiastics that Canon Floodgay's congregation would not " put up with his tricks for ever." It was cheap to behave like that. It might be true, as some said on his behalf, that the church was always full when he preached : but it was not, was it, with his own parishioners ? Any priest, they opined, could attract such a congregation, as long as he did not object to making himself conspicuous or extraordinary. But a church was a holy edifice, and not a music-hall. Personally speaking, his brethren had a great aversion from self-advertisement, from tricks and trumpery of all sorts.

When, therefore, Canon Floodgay imported " the Thing," and hung it up in the church (actually hung it up *in* the *church !*) his brethren were not surprised at the results. No ; the vergers were Wise and not Foolish Vergers. After all, it was for them, and for the Church-Wardens, to guard the good name of their church, was it not ? And so tawdry and bizarre.

Eventually, however, to the disappointment of some fellow-clerics and the fury of others, the affair was compromised, and the picture nailed up, outside in the porch. Yet, fancy ! for the money he had spent on the object, he might have built another lych-gate ! It was true that there was one there already, but one could not have too many, could one ?

The whole business had created a very unfortunate impression. The Canon's thumbnail sketches of his confrères, delivered from the pulpit, became ever more biting and incisive, while as a consequence, his church became each Sunday more crowded. The whole of the winter population of the West Cliff trundled across the bridge to St. Saviour's, decked out against the cold in every species of fur and feather. Every window that faced South sent its own contingent, while Mrs. Shrubfield and Miss Waddington, in close concert over other matters, drove there together. The wraith of Lady Tidmarshe was said to have been seen depositing her representatives, the Misses Finnis, at the lych-gate. The Canon's impersonations became still more life-like, still more frequent. The congregation seethed with excitement, and there were occasional bursts of involuntary applause. The St. Saviour's Parish Magazine, in which the gifts of Canon Floodgay were finding a new and withering outlet, was in general demand, and could be sold at a premium. This continued success still further envenomed the other clerics of the town. Bishops began to interfere—or, as was said, to intervene— and it was hinted that the Canon was anxious now to find a new living, and one that would give him more scope for his undoubted talents. Foreign Missions, his brother clergy thought, might offer him that larger field for activities for which a man of his energy must be looking. Life in New Guinea would be so interesting, they felt, to a *clever* man, and must hold so many opportunities for doing good . . . but Mrs. Floodgay decided that there was much more good to be done at home . . . there was so much bitterness, and such a want of charity in the town, that it was better to stay there and try to smooth things out and to brighten the lives of the inhabitants of Newborough. The Canon agreed with his wife.

CHAPTER XV

CHURCH-INTERIOR

" While the Seraphs recline
On divans divine
In a smooth seventh heaven of polished pitch-pine."

So the Canon remained where he was, and Miss Collier-Floodgaye, for one, thoroughly enjoyed the services. At first Miss Bramley accompanied her to one or two services there, for she wished to ascertain the real state of affairs. But soon the Companion intimated that in future, if the old lady would consent to it, she should attend divine service at St. Thomas's, where no frippery was allowed to distract the attention of the flock from true worship. Further, she insinuated that, with regard to St. Saviour's, she preferred going to a theatre for that sort of entertainment. In fact, there was a time and place for everything. Miss Collier-Floodgaye was forced, therefore, to go to church by herself every Sunday—an act which any other old lady with a paid Companion would have considered as a breach of unwritten contract, and one that would entail for the younger lady the most severe reproofs and reproaches, the direst penalties. But Miss Collier-Floodgaye was generous, and understood. Her Companion, she knew, was upset. Indeed " Tibbits " was becoming quite irritable and unlike herself. She would never now do anything she was asked to do . . . wouldn't go to St. Saviour's, wouldn't visit the Vicarage, wouldn't sing

for the Floodgays—not even for their Parish Sales
of Work! And she was so fond of singing at
Sales of Work, too, as a rule. It was most annoying.
Still, poor thing, it was only her affection for her
friend that made her like that. So much, the old lady
realized.

Now that the Companion was relapsing more and more
into her former severity of outline, she found the service
at St. Peter's too high for her taste, and assisted at worship at St. Thomas's, which was evangelical enough for
even the most rabid hater of ritual. But Miss Collier-
Floodgaye, for her part, hardly missed the presence of
Miss Bramley in church as much as the Companion
imagined. Up till now religion had meant little to the
old lady : she had always been rather inclined, as we
have seen, to evade regular church-going, to cough and
walk out before the Sermon, or to " feel a cold coming
on," and decide that it was wiser to remain indoors.
But now for the first time, she suddenly felt the call of
worship, through a ritual that was rich enough to capture
her sombre yet emotional spirit. Never before had she
been able to combine the pleasures of the World with
the consolations of Spiritual Life. She was as much
moved by the Canon's rantings, roarings, and distraught
air as she was diverted by his lightning, quick-change
impersonations. The anthems, too, were indisputably
the best in the town—nothing better in London (probably
that came of having an *artistic* wife, Miss Collier-
Floodgaye thought) and the Organist was a real musician,
gave recitals, and played the March from *Lohengrin*,
so weird . . . (*Peer Gynt*, too) while the voices of the
choristers were beautiful in the extreme. There was
nothing so touching as a boy's voice, nothing ; and

during the singing of those strange mid-Victorian anthems, the English reply to Grand Opera—in which the great figures of Biblical history are made to masquerade before us in antimacassars instead of fig leaves, in top hat and frock coat, in bonnet and crinoline instead of their native Hebrew dress, while the cairngorm takes the place of the Urim and Thummin—little sensual thrills of religious ecstasy passed through her gaunt and aged frame, electrifying it, making it seem young once more.

The atmosphere of the church was personal. The stained glass windows, with their series of " Modern Saints," such as Florence Nightingale, Father Damien, and General Gordon—the last of whom was figured pursuing the heathen Chinee in the sacred cause of opium, with no weapon in his hand but a cane, while round his head was an irregular halo of thick white and green glass that successfully, but quite unintentionally, communicated the idea to the initiated of a nimbus of broken whisky bottles—were most pretty and uncommon. The presence in this array of Father Damien, a Catholic, served further, to emphasize the Canon's breadth of outlook. Then there was a painted pulpit, very unusual in an English church, while between Bodley-Gothic arches were hung large, pre-Raphaelite-tainted Stations of the Cross. The incense, the singing, the scarlet garments of the choir, the continuous bowing, and turning to the right and left, which was here the procedure, all produced for Miss Collier-Floodgaye a superb impression of worship. Indeed so much did all this pageantry move the old lady that it was to the next Sunday morning service that she now looked forward as to the crowning pleasure of the week.

Every Sunday she would sit in her special pew, listening intently, and following with her eyes the dancing of the multi-coloured lights from the windows. As outside the winter clouds scudded like white ships across the sour blue of the Northern sky, these effects were shut off abruptly, or turned on again as suddenly. In the church, the warmth, the incense, the droning music, and fantastic dresses of the assembled, all closed in together to form a tropical haven. Large butterflies of green or purple light, fire-flies of blue or vermilion, hovered and trembled in the air, or fluttered listlessly over the faces and apparel of the congregation. Strange feather boas undulated through this jewelled obscurity, boas like the pythons that would exist in a forest created by the Futurists, so bright and iridescent their hues, or coiled themselves round the scraggy necks of elderly spinsters, while nearly every fur, which, when truly tenanted, had ever rustled through equatorial jungles or crackled over the uncharted ice of Polar seas, was represented in this exotic flock. Through this forest, over these bright flowers, the inquisitive butterflies roamed and loitered tremulously, while the hum and whirl of the organ supplied an appropriate, rather waspish music. The warm shrilling of these radiant insects rose and fell as they shimmered over the cold stone walls, or leapt gaily toward the pointed dimness of the roof. Occasionally, even, one of these little winged creatures would alight on her sombre dress, or pause for an instant on her gnarled and twisted hands; then, in response, the ruby eyes of her ring would flash back a venomous fire at it. Now, again, the butterflies would dance over the wall and above the pulpit, and the voices of the choir-boys, cherubs' voices they seemed, would laughingly pursue them with their golden nets, right up into the lingering Gothic twilight of the arches. Then the light would change and become menacing, as outside a cloud obscured with its white patch the weak eye of that aged Cyclops, the winter sun. In the church, though, the darkness that ensued was hot and ominous as that which heralded an equatorial storm, and the organ rolled out its thunder, while all the creatures of dazzling wing, humming-birds, moths and fire-flies sought safety somewhere high up under the shelter of the wooden beams, waiting their time to dart out again and hover impertinently over the array of orchidaceous blossoms below.

It was strange to think that her Companion should refuse to share this new, this intense pleasure. But very different were the services which Miss Bramley attended so regularly at St. Thomas's. Outside that edifice was no array of cabs or carriages : no social ostentation or mundane love of colour was here allowed to mock the holy nature of the Sabbath. The congregation, many of whom were over eighty, was usually dressed in silks of black and grey, which rustled and crinkled with a quiet but assertive dignity. Indeed even a brown dress was regarded as " rather loud." On the other hand, a certain elaboration was felt to be fitting, and any amount of ornaments, as long as they were not too large or " flashy," could be worn. Bits of lace, bits of jewellery, bits of ribbon, but all able only to call attention to themselves by their quantity, plastered the fronts of these churchgoers. The men were more sallow, fewer, and less military than those at St. Saviour's ; if they ever feasted, it would be tea and not whisky that passed their blue and rather bumpy lips. The ladies, who, as we have said, were elderly, were encased in caskets of whale-bone; many a leviathan must have spouted and wallowed in death agony to prop up these sagging and withered forms. Umbrellas were innumerable, hats flat and feathery. The church itself was simple, a few plain panels of pitch pine, a daring but controlled outbreak of German fumed oak, and for the rest, plain grey Gothic stone : nothing more, no, nothing more—except that there were two carved oak brackets which displayed the numbers of the hymns, and that a large brass fowl, of pious expression, supported a huge Bible from which the lessons were read. The lessons for the day were indicated, the only touch of colour, by a wide, red silk marker with a heavy gold fringe.

But it must not be assumed from the presence of the hymn-registering brackets referred to above, that there was music in the church. There was not. This was no place for *recitals* or anything of that sort, no concert room or stage for theatrical display. The music, plain and churchwarden-Gothic as the church itself, or as the lady who was responsible for it, was contributed by Dr. Limpsby's eldest daughter (Dr. Limpsby was the vicar of the parish) assisted by an aunt. There were no anthems, but the flock joined with sibilant fervour in the hymns. Though the whole service breathed Christian devotion, there was no " show." The flock remained resolutely looking to the North during the Creed, without bowing or turning, or paying attention to idols. Little did the weather outside affect the colour of the church interior, where plain glass, with a greenish tinge in it, interposed what appeared to be a never-ending curtain of rain between mankind and the certainty of the Wrath to Come. " Peace, perfect Peace, in this Dark

World of Sin," was the keynote alike of the building and
of the service that it housed. But the peace, however
impermanent, was genteel and refined. The " Romans "
were the danger !

When church was over, Miss Bramley would return
home in that resolutely righteous bad temper that marks
the true churchgoer—a temper that was certain to come
into conflict later with all the ghoulish furies that
possessed Elisa after her weekly visit to the Cemetery.
No wonder, then, that Miss Collier-Floodgaye tended to
avoid the Superb Hotel on Sundays.

For latterly a habit had sprung up that implied a new
intimacy between the old lady and Canon Floodgay's
family. As Miss Bramley no longer accompanied her
to church, Miss Collier-Floodgaye would go back with
them to luncheon, on such Sundays as the Canon was
not away preaching in other towns. This recurrent
invitation gave her the greatest pleasure ; for not only
was she devoted to her theoretical relatives, but it added
to her sense of prestige to be seen walking back with
them to the Vicarage—was equivalent to being seen
having supper with a celebrated actress after a triumphant first night. And, however fatigued the Canon
might be by his histrionic exertions, luncheon was
invariably gay and charming. Such wonderful spirits.
And the family welcomed the presence of the old lady,
for their little difficulties (and there were several of
them) were, in honour of their new relative, suppressed.
This censorship made the meal much pleasanter for
themselves as well as for Miss Collier-Floodgaye, and
this increased their liking for her. They felt instinctively,
that life was less worrying when she was present. " She
makes things go," the Canon would pronounce

Previously, it must be owned, Sunday luncheon had been a rather depressing, even intimidating, affair. Cécile had formerly regarded it as the most unpleasant feature of each week. The development of the meal was stereotyped, as well as perilous. Her father would be tired and irritable, and this state of exhaustion would supply Mrs. Floodgay with just the opportunity she needed for working off her own nervous irritability. If the special little darts and goads, manufactured for this very occasion during the week to which the Sunday luncheon put a pictorial finish—those little darts and goads with which she opened her attack—failed, in their objective or effectiveness, this redoubtable little toreador of a woman would revert to her weapon, the Canon's supposed fondness for his maidservants. This had been the cause and instrument of a thousand combats. In her most pathetic and unguarded moments, Mrs. Floodgay was wont to confide these suspicions to her friends, and they had consequently been picked clean—or rather, dirty—like so many bones, in every invalid room in Newborough. (Poor little woman, so bright and pretty! So often one failed to see the tragedy for the brave and smiling manner that covered it.) The Canon would rise to his defence in a towering temper, while, at the same time, he referred to the unfortunate maids, against whom his wife was hurling these insinuations, as his "handmaidens." This would drive Mrs. Floodgay into further frenzies : she would deliver a furious on-slaught upon "irreligious and unseemly affectations." The Canon would now take up the attack, and would accuse his wife of extravagance—a charge of which she was as innocent as was her husband of the accusation which she had just brought against him, for she had been

forced all her life to practise the most strict economy.
Mrs. Floodgay would countercharge her husband with
meanness, and, just at the moment when each of them
had reached the climax of their ill-temper, they would
combine to turn on Cécile. A social failure, that was what
she was ! With whom, they would like to know, had she
danced two nights before, except with that awkward
spotty son of Dr. Sibmarshe, and with the elderly mental-
case who was boarded out with Dr. MacRacket every
winter ? *Not much* of a success. For what, her father
wondered, had her parents given her so good an education,
even at the cost of pinching themselves (here to emphasize
their point, they both pinched her, and tugged at her
blouse). For what had they sent her to be " finished off "
in Paris—for the spotty son of Dr. Sibmarshe, and for
the elderly mental-case, boarded out every winter with
Dr. MacRacket, did she suppose ? But it would always
be the same, as long as she stood there, by the ball-
room door, looking self-conscious and pulling her gloves
on and off. She made nothing of herself—that was it.
She ought to show off her accomplishments, play the
piano occasionally, or do a scarf-dance, like the one she
learnt in Paris. And then why didn't she do her hair
differently ? What was the use of having so much of it,
if she did nothing with it ? And with that, both parents
would descend upon her, tweaking and pulling her hair
in different directions.

Happily, however, during the winter months these evi-
dences of family feeling were for Miss Collier-Floodgaye's
sake hidden away : while Mrs. Floodgay even conquered
temporarily her passion for confiding in others her
stories of the Canon's apocryphal infidelities. . . stories
which might easily have been detrimental to his career.

CHAPTER XVI

AVIS !   AVIS !   AVIS !

" O for a beaker full of the warm South,
   Full of the true, the blushful Hippocrene,
      With beaded bubbles winking at the brim,
      And purple-stained mouth."

THINGS had not gone well lately with the two Marshals
of the invalid army. In the defection of Mrs. Floodgay
to the enemy, they had sustained a blow as unexpected
as it was deadly, and one that might easily endanger their
joint command. That such an instrument of their own
making should turn against them, was an occurrence
that had never even suggested itself to them, veterans
though they were and accustomed to the calamitous
changes of fortune. Even before this piece of treachery
had overwhelmed them, they had felt the necessity
of spectacular triumph in order to infuse the troops,
who had followed them faithfully for a whole winter
without being rewarded by any great victory, with a
renewed confidence in their powers of leadership.
Accordingly, they had laid their plans and had baited
the trap with infinite care and patience. For weeks
they had been forced to expend untold tact, flattery and
charm upon that forbidding fortress, Mrs. Haddocriss.
For several consecutive Sundays, moreover, Miss Waddington had been obliged to dispense with the services
of Thompson, her parlourmaid, in order to gain a
strategic point ; while her niece, Ella, had been commanded to spend endless afternoons waiting outside

the Superb Hotel in the snow, or running through the
wet with a message to Mrs. Haddocriss. Every detail
had been thought out, every device made use of, when
suddenly, just as they had achieved their first signal
triumph in the introduction of Miss Collier-Floodgaye
to Mrs. Floodgay, the fruits of victory had been snatched
away from them by the hand of a traitor, and then,
worse still, proffered back to them in the form of Dead
Sea Fruit. For not only had Mrs. Floodgay deserted
to the foe in front of all the troops, but she had then
warned Miss Collier-Floodgaye against Miss Waddington and Mrs. Shrubfield, filling her with prejudice
against them, without any suitable fate, such as the
earth opening to swallow her up, overwhelming
her.

It was not the way of such veterans to mitigate the
bitterness of their defeat by an attempt to belittle the
extent of it. They had been dealt a crushing blow, one
that had already immensely damaged their prestige,
and the example of which might easily serve as an
encouragement to further mutinies. And not a single
grape from Lady Tidmarshe for a fortnight! They
realized to the full their humiliation. Moreover they
felt that in certain ways themselves were to blame for
this result of their labours. This was the second winter
of their waiting on the Superb Mystery, yet they were
no nearer to any knowledge of its essential constituent
facts. They had observed the symptoms, but were still
unable to diagnose the disease. Perhaps, they felt, they
ought to have pursued a more simple tactical system
. . . ought to have called on Miss Collier-Floodgaye
in the ordinary manner : but, then, that would have
been unsporting, equivalent to taming the fox before

hunting it (for deer, only, may be tamed before being
hunted). They ought never, of course they ought not,
to have trusted Mrs. Floodgay, that monster of their
own creation, who was now poisoning the mind of their
quarry against them. But they had felt so sure of her,
because they had made her. Who, indeed, had taken
any notice of her at all until they had " taken her up " ?
And now the impious creature had turned upon her
creators, in the same way that the other monster called
into being by Frankenstein had turned upon him. It
was dreadful ! But the fiend should not go unscathed
through Newborough. Already they had ignored her,
cut her in public : but if she thought that this was the
most dire punishment which her disaffection would
bring down upon her, she was mistaken. Oh, yes, they
knew a few little secrets . . . perhaps she had forgotten
her lachrymose confidences, horrid, whining little thing.
Perhaps she had forgotten telling them of her doubts and
fears about the Canon and his maidservants. . . . Well,
she should *see* . . . what if the Bishop—the Bishop who
was already not over-approving of incense and taber-
nacles, should hear of these little peccadilloes too ?
What, then ? . . . the penalty, if not death, would at
least be *deportation !* Somehow they felt that a woman
who was so " artistic," always prattling nonsense about
Burne-Jones and Watts, would not feel quite at home as
the wife of a missionary among the Headhunters of
Borneo. But that was what it would come to, if they
had anything to do with it. Just a little note to the
Bishop, just a friendly little chat, that was all that was
necessary. . . .

Both ladies felt that they must once more openly
assert their leadership, frankly display those qualities

which entitled them to it. But, just as they were relaying
their plans, rebuilding their stately façade, and in constant
communication with the Superb Hotel through Thompson
and Elisa, another overwhelming disaster put them out
of action. Mrs. Shrubfield fell ill !

Not only was this a serious matter in itself—for
Miss Waddington realized that the Superb Affair had
now assumed such proportions that no solitary expert,
however keenly burnt the flame of her genius, could
deal with it—but the amount of ill-natured and scandalous
gossip which this illness involved must of necessity
damage still further in the eyes of the troops the prestige
of the two great figures who led them. It was no use
being cross, Miss Waddington felt, with Louise. She
could not help it . . . there had been stories of the same
kind before . . it was better not to believe, not to
notice, and never to refer to it, otherwise their relationship in the future might be difficult. But she should not
have allowed *such* a thing to occur at *such* a moment
 . . however Miss Waddington would see Dr. Mac-
Racket and impress upon him in person how essential
it was that the truth should be kept a secret from others,
while at the same time she endeavoured to cajole him
into confiding in herself the exact nature of the events
that had taken place. When Louise was better, Miss
Waddington supposed it would be wiser to know nothing,
pretend to think it an ordinary attack of influenza.
But Mrs. Floodgay should be made to pay for this too.
It was as much her doing as if she had struck Louise
down with her own hand.

The entire truth of the matter will probably never be
known to the outside world, but the probability is that
it follows somewhat in the lines of the very definite

rumour which was current in the town. For some time, doubtless as a result of the prolonged mental stress which the campaign had imposed upon her, and in her grief at the desperate outcome of it, Mrs. Shrubfield had been in a queer state of health. Periods of profound and useless depression alternated swiftly with fits so unnecessary and almost delirious hilarity, induced, of the lady insinuated, "by one of those deleterious 'toniques' which the doctor will order me." Perhaps the complaint was infectious, for the same symptoms, combined with a certain unsteadiness and discoloration of the face, were to be observed in both her coachman and footman; Miss Waddington peeping from her window, had herself caught sight of this presumably plague-stricken trio, crying and laughing as they rolled from side to side, for the pyramids had assumed mobility and were quaking like jellies. Soon afterward, Miss Waddington heard the front door bell ring, and this was followed by a rollicking hoot of raucous laughter, and then Thompson appeared, looking very disconcerted and put out, and bearing an empty bottle on a silver salver. To the neck of it was attached a label on which was written "with love et meilleurs sentiments, to Hester Waddington from Louise" while, within, as though a message from a drowning man, was a piece of paper, on which was scrawled, "*Acqua, per piacere !*" It was, no doubt, a touching tribute, a gift in the same spirit as that which prompts a cat to place the corpse of a mouse on its master's doormat; but none the less irritating for that! Luckily Ella was out, and Miss Waddington commanded Thompson to tell no one of the afternoon's happenings, But, nevertheless, this gift was somewhat of a shock to the old lady.

Meanwhile, Mrs. Shrubfield's condition showed no improvement, and she had to be put to bed. Her restlessness increased to a point where her attendant relatives found it necessary to call in Dr. MacRacket. The physician entered her bedroom, and placed his top-hat on a table by the wide-open window, for it was one of those warm, rainy afternoons that occasionally intervene between wind and snow in the northern winters. The rooks could be heard cawing outside, and the air was sweet and mild. The branches of the trees, level with the window, seemed to hold in their outlines a fulness that already promised vernal budding. A shaft of wan sunlight rested on the hat, which stood like a funnel lined with white smoke on the table, palely illumined its white satin lining that enfolded a flesh-pink stethoscope as an open shell protects and sets off its fragile but roseate inhabitant. To the doctor this delicate contrivance was a symbol, the scientific equivalent of a Marshal's baton. All of a sudden—it is stated—Mrs. Shrubfield soared up from her bed, seized the top-hat and hurled it and its content out into space, to fall three storeys, while in the same instant, she tore off every lingering fragment of clothing, and announced publicly, with great sonority, and in the four chief international languages, her conviction that " Nobody loves Me." She then complained that the room was moving and sat down on the window-ledge. Thus, it will be seen that never, in deepest depression or highest exhilaration, did the lingual gifts of this accomplished lady desert her.

At first the doctor was nonplussed. He should no doubt have remembered the notices posted up in foreign sleeping-cars, and have countered by replying,

IL EST DANGEREUX DE SE PENCHER EN DEHORS.

NICHT HINAUSLEHNEN.

E VIETATO SPORGERSI.

DO NOT LEAN OUT OF THE WINDOW WHILE THE TRAIN IS IN MOTION.

Instead, he said to her severely, " Mrs. Shrubfield, unless you consent to remain *indoors*, I must refuse to attend you in future." Even so, however, some minutes had passed before he could finally persuade his unruly, if unfortunate, patient to come away from her window-sill.

CHAPTER XVII

LADIES OF THE OLD SCHOOL

"In various talks th' instructive hours they pass,
Who gave a ball, or paid the visit last ;
One speaks the glory of the British Queen,
And one describes a charming Indian screen ;
A third interprets notions, looks and eyes ;
At every word a reputation dies."

By her one casual introduction at the Hospital Ball, Mrs.
Haddocriss had profoundly affected the lives of five people,
in not one of whom was she really at all interested More
especially had she been the instrument of transforming
the lives of Miss Collier-Floodgaye and her Companion.

Miss Bramley had grown used, since she first came to
live with the old lady, to a new liberty of action and
utterance. She now expressed herself in conversation
more freely than ever before. Previous habit to a certain
extent prevailed against it, or controlled its method,
but, nevertheless—though still effusive in manner, even
when annoyed and irritable—she had become accustomed
to making a more complete revelation of her feelings and
opinions than had been possible in her life up till now.
Indeed she was so foolish as to allow her irritability to
get entangled with her effusiveness and to dilute her
charm. The result, a poignant mingling of the pat and
the scratch, made the carrying on of a conversation with
her at this period of her companionship rather similar
to undergoing the process of vaccination.

To Miss Fansharpe, Miss Bramley would never have
ventured to suggest a preference, never have dared to

admit a dislike : nor for an instant would the Companion have presumed to comment on any friend of that lamented lady. But with Miss Collier-Floodgaye, even now that Miss Bramley's character was in many directions drawing in its new shoots and relapsing into its old growth, the Companion had not surrendered her newly acquired privilege of free speech. After all, she had to do everything for the old lady, and it was annoying, was it not, when a friend to whom one was devoted made a spectacle—yes, she regretted having to say it —but a spectacle of herself ? Running after people of that sort (for nearly every day Miss Collier-Floodgaye would meet her new relatives, and if a day passed without her seeing them, would fret and become quite haggard). Undignified-and-all-that. She wasn't young enough, either, to sit there puffing at a cigarette and playing bridge all night long Not that there was any harm in smoking a cigarette now and then . . . even for an old lady. But she was obviously in failing health, and ought not to neglect herself . . . becoming so absent-minded, too . . . of course there was nothing actually the matter with her except age . . . she ought to get out more into the open air, and lead a quieter life. And Miss Bramley sighed, though she did not know why. For now there were no more of those delightful drives up on to the moors, no more of those enjoyable walks through the Market or Winter Gardens. What use was there in the doctor coming to see her every day if she would not do what he told her ? He could only impress upon her that she ought not to overtire herself. Really . . . she was obstinate and pig-headed . . . yes, positively pig-headed . . . and Miss Bramley's voice, as she practised a new song alone in the immense and over-gilded drawing-room, took on a new quality of pathos.

On the few occasions when she was obliged to visit the Floodgays everything was most awkward. All this "Aunt Cecilia" business got on her nerves: "Aunt Cecilia" this, "Aunt Cecilia" that, and "Aunt Cecilia" the other, or "Cécile, run upstairs and get your Aunt Cecilia's muff." And, to see a person of whom one was fond, playing the wrong cards continually, talking about people she didn't know, and being so boastful! "Duchess of Devonshire," indeed! Now Miss Fansharpe, no doubt, had had her faults, but she could never have behaved like that . . . never. And then, though Cecilia could leave her money to whom she chose (that was her own affair) she must *not* talk about it in front of people who were almost strangers. It was not a thing a lady could do. Actually in Miss Bramley's own presence, Cecilia had announced that she intended to leave a part of her fortune to the Floodgays. Not a thing a lady could do. "Naturally" (in front of her, remember!) "I have made Tibbits" (she ought to say "Miss Bramley" in the presence of people of that sort) "my heir. But I shall remember your kindness to me as well. It has made such a difference." Well, she was quite right there: it *had* made a difference. Oh, yes: Mrs. Floodgay may have thought that Miss Bramley had not seen her turn round at this, to count the people in the room and see if the old lady's promise had been properly witnessed by other "schemers" (and there were plenty of them) on whom they could rely. But fortunately nothing escapes some people . . . a fine Canon's wife!

Another time Miss Bramley heard her friend saying with quite a lot of people in the room, "Cécile dear

child, when you are going to be married, come to me :
you must let your old aunt provide your dowry " : and,
as she patted the young girl, the snake-ring flashed its
blood-shot eye at the Companion. Of course Mrs.
Floodgay sat there, with a fond maternal look fixed
on Cécile. But Miss Bramley, though she did not feel
in the least sorry for the girl, could see the threatening
glint in it, the uneasy suspicion that her fool of a daughter
might not " play up." And the Canon, in Miss Bramley's
opinion, was as bad as any of them.

Cecilia seemed to be getting her will on her mind.
She was for ever mentioning it. She was always imploring her Companion to remind her that she must see her
lawyer. " I am getting old now, Tibbits," she would
say : " and I ought to get things into order. There are
various little mementoes to arrange . . . of course the
main will is all right, I think ; but I ought to see him.
Do jog my memory. It's not as good as it used to be."
(" Then you shouldn't waste your time and strength
playing bridge, dear") " Do remind me to send for him."

Really, Miss Bramley felt, it was no affair of hers.
She disapproved of the whole business. Certainly
Cecilia had a perfect right to dispose of her own fortune
—everyone realized that ; but, knowing her Companion's
opinion of these new friends, it was inconsiderate of
Cecilia to keep on mentioning her will in this way.
It could only mean that she was going to alter it, and
leave them something. Most inconsiderate. It was not
that she minded : but they did not deserve it. Why,
she had hardly known them for more than a few days !
And they were killing her (that was what it amounted
to) with all these bridge-parties and tea-parties. A thoroughly bad influence. Directly the old lady could be

kept away from them, even for a day or two, she was different (except that she fretted), more like herself. More like her *old* self. That was it, exactly. To sum the whole matter up Mrs. Floodgay was an intriguing kind of woman, a regular " schemer."

One was fortunate, perhaps, in having other interests. And a scale took wing from her rather wry mouth into the gloomy air above, fluttering soft wings against the solid gold leaves and flowers of the cornice. Luckily there were so many interesting new songs coming out just now. " Less than the Dust," for example ; and its pseudo-oriental strains echoed dismally through the vacant grandeur. Probably Cecilia wouldn't be back till nearly seven. It was too bad. Even Elisa had noticed the difference in her. So tired and forgetful, and much more lame, she thought. And Elisa did not notice things easily. She had heard all about Mrs. Floodgay, it appeared, from some parlour-maid who was a friend of hers. A dangerous, scheming sort of woman, the parlour-maid had said. But Cecilia seemed to be infatuated, absolutely infatuated, with the whole family.

Toward the end of the winter, though, Miss Bramley made some delightful acquaintances of her own : such charming, kindly, old-fashioned creatures. One evening a note (what beautiful writing) arrived by hand, from an old Miss Waddington.

" Dear Miss Bramley," the letter ran, " I understand that you are a niece of my old friend, Miss Titherley-Bramley, and so take the liberty of writing to you. I remember her so well, with her Dalmatians and black-and-white horses : and it would give me the greatest pleasure to make the acquaintance of her dear niece. Could you, perhaps, manage to *peep* in to tea on Thursday ? If you could come rather early, at four o'clock or even at three-forty-five, we could have a quiet chat about old times. I fear my niece, Ella, will be out, but I have invited another old friend of your dear Aunt's to meet you— a Mrs. Shrubfield. She has been far from well lately— —influenza and a carriage accident, or something of that sort—so you must forgive her if her manner is at all emotional. She has suffered dreadfully, and is given occasionally to short fits of crying or laughing. I trust, however, that by Thursday, she will have grown stronger, and in any case you are sure to find her a most cultivated, accomplished and agreeable companion, and as a rule, cheerful, even cheery in her conversation. If you can come, it will give Mrs. Shrubfield great pleasure to send her Victoria round for you to the hotel. But please do not mention her illness to her, as she is quite unaware of these seizures, and the knowledge of them would, I have no doubt, cause her intense distress. I fear you will find us rather quiet and old-fashioned. I must warn you that *neither* of *us* play *Bridge*. I hope you won't mind ?

And now, dear Miss Bramley, may I ask a little favour ? I hear that you have inherited a full share of your family's love of music. They say that you accompany yourself beautifully, and it would be such a kindness if you would sing for a little to an elderly invalid, who is obliged, alas ! to live very much cut-off from the world.

Sincerely yours,
HESTER WADDINGTON."

A charming letter, and so well-worded. So kind, too, and friendly to offer to send round a carriage. Real old-world courtesy. Miss Collier-Floodgaye was going out on the afternoon named to a bridge-party at St. Saviour's Vicarage. Miss Bramley, therefore, decided to accept the invitation. After all, one must think of oneself *a little*. . . .

Tea was most enjoyable, really delightful. Both the old ladies—for Mrs. Shrubfield was fortunately well enough to be there—appeared to be interested in her (because

of her Aunt, she supposed) and overwhelmed her with
questions ; Miss Waddington, dear old person, seemed
very frail, she thought. Mrs. Shrubfield, too, was charming and remarkably well-informed, talked every language
as well as if it were her own. It was all the nicer of
Mrs. Shrubfield to come, as she never *touched* tea herself.
It didn't agree with her. The doctor had told her she
ought never to let it pass her lips. *Jamais de la vie*,
he had said. So that she was here merely in order to
meet Miss Bramley, and do honour to an Aunt's Niece.
Both ladies knew all about Cecilia, too, but informed
Miss Bramley that they did not see much of Mrs. Floodgay . . . no . . . peculiar . . . yes . . . yes . . . odd,
almost . . . and so materially-minded, didn't she think
so ? . . . of course they ought not to say so to Miss
Bramley, for they knew she was a great friend of Mrs.
Floodgay's. But it was difficult not to say what they
felt, for it seemed to them already as if they had known
her since she was a child : and after all she was so young :
and when one was young one must be warned . . . and
you see, well they did not quite know how to put it,
but the Canon had an odd reputation . . . (all the maids
left, it was said) and Miss Bramley ought not to be left
alone in the room with him. Not for a moment. It wasn't
safe. They only told her this because they knew she was
always at the Vicarage . . . what ? not always there ?
Not a great friend of Mrs. Floodgay's ? How extraordinary ! Now wasn't that like people ! Fancy ! . . .
perhaps then the Floodgays were friends of Miss Collier-
Floodgaye's, was that it ? In spite of the similarity of
their names, though, they couldn't be related. Oh no,
oh dear no ! For Mrs. Floodgay, though Miss Waddington seldom saw her, had happened to call one day

before . . . yes, she was sure it was *before* . . . she had *met* Miss Collier-Floodgaye, and had definitely denied any such connection . . . it was out of the question, she had said. Yes, Miss Waddington supposed she must have asked her if they were related . . she could not remember why. But she recalled quite distinctly Mrs. Floodgay's answer. " No relation, absolutely no relation at all, and you can say I said so." So it was odd, wasn't it, that the girl, that queer girl with the carroty hair, should now call the old lady "Aunt Cecilia." Yes. As a matter of fact, Miss Waddington was sorry for the Mother. Herself was not in the least superstitious, but you know what girls are, and Ella (dear, dear, she's out now !) was always up to some mischief (once a tomboy, always a tomboy)—well, she had gone to the crystal-gazer—Madame de Kalbe— who lived on the way down to the valley and sold jet jewellery. In order to put her off the real scent, Ella had given her part of Mrs. Floodgay's broken bootlace, or something, which she had found on the stairs. Mme. de Kalbe " went off " at once into a trance, and what she saw was so dreadful that Miss Waddington hardly liked to tell Miss Bramley. At first, she had seen a clergyman having a quarrel with a Bishop, then she had begun to scream and struggle, and had apparently seen a missionary, his wife, and a daughter (with *red* hair !) being killed and eaten by cannibals . . somewhere in Borneo or New Guinea—or perhaps, both ! And, you see, one can't escape one's fate, can one ? It was terrible. But, of course, one mustn't let the rumour get about. Oh, you'll promise, won't you, never to tell anyone ? It might upset them. Such a dreadful end for materially-minded people.

Having allowed these important facts to slip out, just like that, the two old ladies asked Miss Bramley to sing. It would be delicious. Do, oh, do ! How difficult it must be to accompany oneself. *Clara Butt* could not do it. It needs a real musician, doesn't it ? Oh, please do sing that lovely . . . what is it . . . " Have you forgotten love so soon, that night of June, that night of June ? " . . . no, no. " Could you remember love so soon ? " no, that's not quite it . . . " Have you forgot that night of June, that Juny night, that nighty June ? —no, " that night so soon ? " wasn't that it ?

Fortunately Miss Bramley knew the song to which they referred. She prepared to sit down at the piano, first pushing back from it a little Indian embroidered cover, encrusted with minute bits of circular mirror that winked, opening and shutting diamond eyes, like so many devils. Upon this diabolic drapery wavered, for the hard pieces of looking-glass formed an uneven, unsteady surface, several silver vases, and a round, bulging sky-blue pot, dented here and there into unseemly dimples, and breaking into an edge of blue foam at the top, from which sprang a surprised green fern shaped like a question-mark. This fern was soft and crinkly as a green paper ostrich feather, and crawling all over with black insect-like seeds. Then there were photographs in silver frames—amongst them a signed one of Lady Ghoolingham in Coronation robes, balancing her coronet as a sea-lion balances a ball on the tip of its nose, and at the same time (a domestic touch, this) clasping an Aberdeen terrier to her ample ermine. The gift of this photograph to Miss Waddington had been the result of a sudden political panic, for it had been sent round everywhere in a frantic, final effort to

secure the representation of the borough for a rather
unpopular, though quite imbecile, Tory candidate.

The notes flickered up into the warm orange air,
and struck little rattling vibrations out of every orna-
ment on the piano, or beyond on the small, littered tables
that impeded movement, so that one waded rather than
walked through the room. Now every object spoke and
danced with its own accent : and the marble clock on
the mantelpiece punctuated this sub-human chatter with
a suggestion of mockery, hooting out the time in a clear,
owlish voice. All these voices could be detected through
the tones of the singer, tones which, though they veiled
them, yet called them into being, as they flitted hither
and thither, caressing the ears of the two elder ladies
as if they were not notes, but titillating items of gossip.

Mrs. Shrubfield was so entranced with the performance that she asked Miss Bramley to sing a German
song, and, overcome equally by the music and by her
own familiarity with the words, conducted, more or less,
with one foot, and joined in the chorus with the other.
This established even more of an atmosphere between
her and the singer. Miss Bramley left the house, quite
bewitched by her two new friends, and promising that
she would often return to sing for them. It was rather
nice to have one's music appreciated. She had hardly
sung at all lately. Cecilia never asked her to sing, now
that she spent all her time in Mrs. Floodgay's drawing-
room, or " Salon," as she thought it. Well, if what the
fortune-teller had said was true, Mrs. Floodgay would
have some funny-looking savages in her salon soon.
What a relief it was to find two people who were clever
without being affected or grasping, and so kind !

.   .   .   .   .   .

The truth of the matter was that the two Marshals had been in despair at the continual set-backs—to call them nothing more serious—inflicted upon them. As soon as she was better, Mrs. Shrubfield had agreed with Miss Waddington that something had to be—must be —done to retrieve both their reputations for leadership and their prestige generally. A letter to Miss Bramley was almost the only solution : for it was imperative to use that technique in which they excelled, and which was the residue left over from an infinite experience of this sort of affair, and, again, it was absolutely necessary to make use of that technique in an ostentatious manner, so that the rebellious ranks should observe, wonder at and applaud. Now this letter was a fine tactical man- œuvre, for, sent at a moment when they judged, and rightly, that Miss Bramley was lonely, depressed and jealous, it placed them at once in her confidence by its assertion of long-standing family friendship, and gained them that trust at the very moment, when, owing to the sense of neglect under which she was smarting, she was most likely to confide : while, better still, their invitation to an early tea, coupled with the friendly offer of an open conveyance, served to parade their captive in broad daylight before the ranks, who lined the terraces, squares and crescents, infirm but at attention. Thus, too, the Emperors of Rome once dragged conquered monarchs through the streets of the Imperial City, after a victorious campaign, so that every citizen should be able to estimate for herself the martial prowess of his ruler. Mrs. Shrub- field and Miss Waddington had, however, with the added humanity of a later age, placed their captive inside, and not behind, their triumphal chariot.

    .   .   .   .   .

That night, alone at dinner with Miss Collier-Flood-gaye, in the enormous red, cruciform dining-room (or, as the head-waiter called it, under special directions from the Management, " Sally Mangey ") Miss Bramley imparted her information : the Floodgays had themselves denied the relationship which they now claimed. But her news was of no avail. " You don't like them, ' Tibbits '—that's all it is "—the old lady replied. She was always like that now, wouldn't hear anything against them. She must be infatuated—no, more than that, hypnotized by them.

And, indeed, the old lady loved the Floodgays, for among them she had discovered that which for so long she had tried to find—an interpreter : through the clergyman's wife she was enabled to enter upon other friendships, from which, through lack of social qualities she would otherwise have been debarred. For the cleverness of Mrs. Floodgay was that of an impresario. She could present and interpret, explain and draw out. " I love my friends to make friends with one another," she was in the habit of saying. And once taught, Miss Collier-Floodgaye became a pupil of promise. Though an opsimath in friendship, she reflected credit upon her teachers.

Now this gift of interpretation was one with which Miss Bramley had never been endowed : or perhaps the correct explanation of her lack of it was that as a Companion she was merely an instrument that had been fashioned by a more forcible will and personality for its own more perfect self-expression. To Miss Fansharpe she had been a nearly perfect Companion. But Miss Collier-Floodgaye, though her will, too, was much stronger than that of Miss Bramley, needed more than a recording instrument for her own personality : she needed an interpretative machine. She was afflicted with something in her character equivalent to a stammer in speech—something which prevented a simple, natural expression of herself, and had to be cajoled, and aided tactfully : moreover her native kindliness allowed the jealous disposition of her Companion to intervene, like an impenetrable fog, between herself and any new persons whom she might meet, and toward whom she might feel an inclination of friendship. But now the old lady was beginning to weave, with the aid of Mrs. Floodgay, a life of her own and independent of Miss Bramley's : though, for all that, without her Companion to look after her, she would not have been able to carry it on. She was old now, and far from well.

.   .   .   .   .   .

Of course when Miss Bramley met the Floodgays, she had to be polite . . . polite, but not cordial. Once or twice, even, she was forced, more or less forced, to sing before them. But they were far from being the appreciative audience that one might have expected from all Cecilia's chatter of their being " so artistic." Instead of talking about her singing, and gathering round her, as round a jockey who has just won a race, when she had finished, they discussed instead the possibility of a flying visit from Melba to the " Winter Gardens " during the coming summer. Every seat was already booked up, they said. . . . After all, she had never set up to be a Melba : but it isn't so much the voice or song, as the way you sing it. There was such a thing as expression, wasn't there : and such a thing as gratitude, as for that ?

Really Cecilia's behaviour was scarcely fair. Though

Miss Bramley had consented, much against her better judgment, she must say, to sing at St. Saviour's Vicarage, yet the old lady would never do anything in return, for her. She refused to visit either Miss Waddington or Mrs. Shrubfield. Put against them by that scheming-Canon's-wife, no doubt. After all, one could hardly treat a Waddington quite like that, could one ? (Meanwhile Miss Waddington and Mrs. Shrubfield were absolutely held-up. Here was the train laid, and everything prepared : and the rude old woman would not come. Really they were beginning to wish they had never set eyes on her—or, rather, heard of her. But *they* could *see* through it. Mrs. Floodgay should pay for it, bitterly, in the utmost ends of the earth.) Miss Bramley reflected that the whole truth was that now Miss Collier-Floodgaye really had no time in which to do anything, for every spare moment she spent with her " new relations." (Relations, indeed !) Infatuated and hypnotized, that was what it was !

And these continual, eternal bridge-parties were so bad for her : of course they were. A strain, impossible for so old a lady to bear for long. She hardly ever got out for a walk now : and her lameness and stiffness were consequently increasing. She would, for example, drive round to St. Saviour's Vicarage in order to get there as quickly as possible. And Miss Bramley would not in the least have objected to going with her as far as the door, so that the old lady might get the benefit of walking in the fresh air. But no, she must always drive round there in a closed cab. And her conversation at dinner, after her return from these parties, was not the same as it used to be . . . vague . . . that was the word for it. It consisted, almost entirely, of talk about these bridge-parties, what Mrs. Floodgay had been doing, whom she had met there, or what the Canon had said, and irritating little stories illustrative of Cécile's affectionate nature.   Her nerves were becoming affected, too.   She had always been rather nervous, but now it was terrible : at night she was for ever turning on the light, or crying out.

The old lady adored these games of bridge.   She would be drawn in a large, black cab through the empty black streets of the winter, where nested the scorpions of the East wind.   These would be roused by the jolting of her cumbrous vehicle, and would sting her through every crevice.   Then she would arrive, and hurry up the stairs, much more rapidly than many persons half her age and lacking her infirmities, for she loved the Floodgays.

CHAPTER XVIII

THE SALON

" The skilful nymph reviews her force with care ;
Let spades be Trumps ! she said, and Trumps they were."

OF course, the Floodgays were not rich, but the house
was quite charming, and the drawing-room unique—
unlike any other drawing-room in Newborough.   Simple
it was, and rather empty, perhaps, and with incandescent
gas greenly illuminating, instead of electric light.   But
that was always the way in a Vicarage : besides, it
looked just like electric light, for the globes were turned
downward in a last, but still hopeful, effort at dissimula-
tion—for in our age (at once a symbol and a symptom of
it) gas pretends to be electric light, while electric light
is made to become atavistic, must pretend that it is a
candle.   Under this green, dim, yet pretentious light,
objects could be seen palely loitering, as though they
were those things half-animal and half-vegetable, which
lurk so faintly in the depths of the ocean.   The walls
of the room were also green, softly and sadly green
with a suggestion of moss in a country churchyard.
This colour scheme had been decided on by Mrs. Floodgay, partly from the praiseworthy maternal desire " to
make the most of Cécile's hair," and partly because it
appeared to be the most suitable background for the
display of her collection of framed engravings after
Watts and Burne-Jones.   Prominent among these, was
that well-known representation of a rather dizzy lady,

sitting blindfolded but still under the spell of an acute nausea, upon a spinning globe, while at the same time, like a true, free-born Englishwoman, she maintains a "stiff upper lip," and resolutely insists upon finishing the piece which she is playing upon a harp with broken strings. This strangely moving, allegorical scene is entitled "Hope."

The curtains of the drawing-room were green, too, and for colour the hostess relied solely upon flowers. Always, even in the winter, a few daffodils—"daffies," as Mrs. Floodgay called them in her pretty, sprightly way—added distinction to the room. What Miss Collier-Floodgaye especially appreciated about May was this—that she was so lively and artistic, without being in the least "stuck-up," or forcing her knowledge upon you : could talk just like anyone else when she wished to. But merely by placing one daffodil, though— or a chrysanthemum—in an earthenware jug or copper vase, she could get more effect out of it than any other woman in Newborough could obtain out of a whole box of flowers from the South of France—that was the advantage of being really "artistic." Again, being original, as well as artistic and economical, she would now and then place some autumn foliage, red rose-berries and blue, frost-bitten bramble in a large vase that stood in the corner of the room. Or she would make a most effective use of "honesty"—those withered white branches on which crackle a number of round skeleton disks, that seem the ghostly, minute and deformed progeny of battledore and tennis-racquet—and "cape-gooseberries" ("winter cherries" they are called some-times) which consist of a number of rusty orange lan-terns, that kindly obscure a shrivelled red berry, like a dying flame, within. These preserved flowers constitute an eternal denial of the possibility of spring, while, if they are moved, they sound out a weird and creaking music, exhale an asphyxiating dust.

Then, too, Miss Collier-Floodgaye admired the manner in which the Canon and his wife had kept up with things. May could always be depended upon to know what was going on, unlike so many other clergymen's wives ; and was " mondaine " (worldly was too harsh an adjective) as well as artistic, and so bright and alive.

Her drawing-room was more than a drawing-room. It was a meeting-place, you know, a Salon—not that she looked down in the slightest on those who were not so well informed, whose tastes were dissimilar or not so advanced ; but that she managed to combine so many different sorts of people—who could not have got on with one another elsewhere. On the days when there were bridge-parties, the drawing-room looked so delightful, so different from other rooms, with its three or four green-topped tables set out, with shaded candles on them ; while all the more interesting people in the town were sure to be there, even if they only played for counters. Miss Collier-Floodgaye did not agree with the view that clergymen's wives ought not to gamble (after all, one must move with the times), but, in any case, it was a very different matter if Mrs. Floodgay's partner carried her . . . otherwise (one knew what people were) there would probably be a lot of unpleasant gossip . . . complaints, even, to the Bishop.

Mr. J. St. Rollo Ramsden was undoubtedly the most cultured caryatid of all those that uplifted Mrs. Flood-

gay's salon. His dome-like brow formed a perfect
support for such a ceiling. Short, fattish, with a pointed,
rather blond, beard, it was his conviction that he looked
like a picture of a cavalier by Vandyke, whereas he
really more resembled a study of a dwarf in court dress
by Velasquez. For he was always smartly garbed,
with a pear-shaped pearl pin in his exquisitely knotted
tie ; and in his buttonhole there generally melted an
ice-cream-pink and frilled carnation. Further he had
all the over-importance of the undersized. He was
usually to be seen moving his plump white hands, of
which he was very proud, in explanatory but civilized
gestures, or moving up and down on his finger a substantial signet ring, then the hall-mark of a University
education. Though in his late middle-age, he still preserved the fresh complexion of one who has never been
contradicted—for he was owner and headmaster of a
flourishing private school on the West Cliff—and was
famed for his lively reminiscences of Horace, Ovid,
the elder Pitt, Labouchere, and Mr. Joseph Chamber-
lain. By the other inmates of the Salon, not so well
grounded, not so well acquainted with famous names,
it was supposed that Mr. St. Rollo Ramsden and these
great men had all been boys together ; that the schoolmaster, though younger than many of them (than
Colonel Spofforth for example) was by some inexplicable
fatality the sole survivor from a Golden Age of history
in which, still under the ægis of Queen Victoria, had
flourished people as diverse as Napoleon and Catullus,
Galileo, Julius Cæsar, and Dr. Arnold. Colonel
Spofforth, the Mutiny-veteran frequenter of the Salon,
was wont to say of him, with that economy of vocabulary
that ever distinguishes the military man, "An enter-

taining fella and one damnably-well-in-the-know,
doncherno. I don't know half the things that little
fella knows, and yet I'm twice the age of the little fella,
doncherno."

As befitted a man-of-the-world, Mr. St. Rollo Ramsden's interest was excited by a number of matters,
matters political, religious, theatrical, sporting and artistic. In addition to the names mentioned above, he was
captivated by such persons and things as Virgil, Joan
of Arc (he always called her Jeanne d'Arc), Pompeii,
Polar Expeditions, Queen Elizabeth, St. Francis of
Assisi, Romney, St. Jerome, Henry Irving, the German
Emperor, the Japanese, Cricket Averages, the Bishop
of London, *Punch*, Ellen Terry, Rudyard Kipling (how
he understood boys . . . those *delicious* " Jungle
Stories "), Gilbert-and-Sullivan, the Royal Academy,
school songs, Cleopatra and the Navy League. On
these, and many other subjects, he was a perfect mine of
useless information.

His school on the West Cliff consisted of sixty boys
between the ages of nine and thirteen, all wearing round
red caps decorated with an indecipherable gothic
monogram in yellow wool, and writing carefully censored
letters home every Sunday, and was conducted on the
most modern lines. Nearly every week there was a
lantern lecture on Flora in New Guinea, Wild Life in
Tierra del Fuego, the Scenery of the Holy Land (this
was delivered at pleasantly regular intervals by an old
bearded clergyman like a white gorilla, with no roof to
his mouth, and was a source of endless delight to the boys),
on The Survival of Folk Dancing at Barnsley and Rother-
ham (with, in addition to the slides, illustrative steps and
music supplied by two of the several daughters of another

clergyman) and—and this was the most important of all—the Work of the Navy League. So great was Mr St. Rollo Ramsden's enthusiasm for this latter object that the boys were forced to subscribe their pitiful pence to it, while such phrases as the "All Red Route," "the British Raj," and the "Police Force of the World" were seldom off his cherry-plump lips.

The school (St. Jerome's) had undoubtedly enriched him, and among his justifiable extravagances was a white-haired mother of over eighty (who in spite of her age, was very vigorous, interfered with the matrons, heard the boys their collects every Thursday, had as a young girl once shaken hands with Lord Beaconsfield at a garden party, and was the owner of a very creditable collection of old Debretts and Burke's *Landed Gentry*), stamps, which helped to widen the mind, he said, geographically speaking, and the cultivation of mammoth inward-growing chrysanthemums. He boasted, too, special suits of clothes and appropriate liveries for golf, cricket, football, hockey, shooting, riding (but not hunting), bridge, winter-sports and the Town Council : while, in addition, he possessed several evening suits, and dinner jackets, a purple, silk-faced and frogged smoking-coat, a number of pipes in a rack, and a quantity of spats, studs, sticks, umbrellas, boot-trees, tie-pins and shooting-sticks. The latter were a great joy to him, for they imparted a subtle man-of-the-world, sporting touch. Horticulturally speaking, he made a good show of red geraniums, giant calceolarias, and sweet-peas, as well as the chrysanthemums which were his especial pride. At the moment that we meet him, he was showing a natural tendency toward rock-gardens ; and all sorts of horrible, hairy little plants, with almost invisible flowers attached to them, were peeping out from under boulders which were very rightly attempting to crush them : but, like the Early Christians, they flourished under oppression.   Summed up, in fact, the schoolmaster was a courteous and cultivated English Gentleman, regrettably respectful to those above, painfully considerate in manner to those below him in station.

The unexpected facets of this protean personality were, perhaps, those gallant and religious.   He was a great lady's man, for ever placing compliments, full-blown as his favourite blossoms, at the feet of old ladies : this, he did partly out of a genuine admiration for them, partly out of Christian courtesy, a wish to assure them that their charms survived, that they were still captivating and desirable.

At one time Mrs. Shrubfield and Mr. St. Rollo Ramsden had been great friends.   The schoolmaster was as apt in classical allusion as was the old lady versed in French " esprit " and German " stimmung."   At that period to hear Mrs. Shrubfield dealing out French, German and Italian phrases with a scintillating coquetry while, in swift return, Mr. St. Rollo Ramsden went snap with a tag from Horace, or boldly declared no trumps with a line of Homer's, was to sip for the moment the best of both worlds, classic and modern.   It was a battle of the wits, but a battle that betokened great affection. Indeed, it was more than suspected that the schoolmaster wished to share lawfully the considerable spoils of the monumental pyramid.   Alas, it was not to be : mischief was made, and the friendship rapidly 'cooled down. Some people aver that when he went to call on her one day he found her black wig crowned too unsymmetrically with vine leaves, while her views on love proved to be too classical, even for such an enthusiast as himself. He thought of the boys' mothers . . . of the rollicking welcome which Mrs. Shrubfield might accord them . . . and fled.

As for the theological side of his character, he was not content with reading the lessons every Sunday in a challenging voice, but was prone to fits of religious emotion, liable to Solitary Vigils in the School Chapel. Moreover, on one occasion a Vision was vouchsafed him. As we have stated, he had made quite a fortune out of his school ; but it must be admitted that, in spite of this, the boys were not well-fed. A diet of stale, mildewed and musty bread, margarine, navy-blue beef from Australia, and equally patriotic mutton from New Zealand, suet-and-treacle, suet-and-jam, suet-and-currants, suet-and-dripping, is never very exhilarating or—as for that—very healthy. Well, it appears that one evening he was communing alone in the Chapel on his knees, like a Christian Knight of old, when there was a sudden flash, as of a waterfall, and the figure of Our Lord stood for an instant before Mr. St. Rollo Ramsden, and spake the words " FEED MY LAMBS." Then the glorious image faded out as rapidly as it had substantiated. In a mood of repentant ecstasy, the Headmaster confessed what had happened standing up before his pupils the same evening. " Boys," he said—or rather "Boës " —for he was an adept at elocution—" there is not one of us who does not sometimes commit an error. I have a personal explanation to make to you. A wonderful experience has been maene this afternoon. . . ."

The narration of his adventure naturally interested his pupils, who were henceforth dragooned by the Matrons into eating, or filling their pockets with, twice

the amount of suet that had nauseated them hitherto.
Boys are notoriously irreverent, and one or two confided
to their fellows that in their opinion it would have been
more considerate on the part of the Holy Presence
if from His mouth had issued the mystic words, " Quality
before Quantity," or if in fact He had come boldly forward and told the Headmaster to give them eatable food,
and not so much of it.

For the rest, Mr. St. Rollo Ramsden was an accomplished versifier. His poems on such subjects as the
Diamond Jubilee .

> " Lady, on thy diamond throne,
> As each year succeeds another,
> May a humble subject own,
> We come nearer, each to other,
> Empress, Queen, and Royal Mother? "

and on the Coronation of King Edward, had been
published in various journals. He was, in addition, a
polished orator, and was seldom able to resist the chance
of an appearance on any platform, however much he
might disagree with the principles enunciated from it.
This gave him a great reputation for courtesy and
impartiality, and made him in constant request as a
chairman. In the bouts of oratory to which he fell
victim, his hands came in very useful. His elocution
was perfectly studied ; his periods were as beautifully
rounded and groomed as his own person. His perora-
tions were magnificent, and decorated with a thousand
little blossoms culled from Virgil, Horace, Byron and
Tennyson. In Newborough it was felt that he was an
orator left over from another age, and to reproduce
one of the Headmaster's favourite quotations, that " Take

him all in all, we shall not look upon his like again " :
but, at the same time, it must be owned that it was one
of the favourite, if more perilous, diversions of his pupils,
to climb up the fire-escape to his window, and watch
Mr. St. Rollo Ramsden, wearing the right clothes,
practising his speech with appropriate gestures, in front
of a large *console* mirror.

Colonel Spofforth was, perhaps, next in importance
of the male caryatids that upheld the Salon, where it
was understood that one would never take him for eighty-
five. He was quite different from Mr. St. Rollo Ramsden
but interesting and entertaining. His tale of Lucknow,
of " tying the Dagos to the guns, and then firing them
off, by Gad," was by now almost historical, while
many of his later stories, such as that of, " The other day
I tried to speak to the Missus on the Telephone, by Jove.
Waited half an hour. Ha-ha. Dammit if anything
happens. Get-up and go to the telephone again: have
lunch : ha-ha. Go back to the telephone. Still no
reply. Queer thing, I said, that—and confound it if
I didn't find I'd been asking for the wrong number
the whole time," were both historically and hysterically
interesting to those who had been denied the privilege
of hearing them before.

The female caryatids varied in their attractions.
There was Mrs. Hunterly, known to her enemies as the
Fighting Temeraire, because of the vast hats, like the
sails and rigging of a ship, which she invariably wore,
and because of the tenacious and savage disposition
which she evinced across a bridge-table. Tall, angular,
and word-clipping, a military rather than a nautical
simile should have been found for her. An intimidating
red-brown fire flashed from her fine, direct eyes, and she

had the hard, open-air complexion of one who stays in England all the summer for winter-sports. Her drawing-room was also a card resort, full of spidery Chippendale chairs, like bicycle wheels, and of bric-à-brac, which had crawled all over the walls and was now starting on its conquest of the ceiling. All these objects were set off by a yellow wall-paper, which was supposed to be an artistic touch of great daring.

Then there was Mrs. Masterton, who boasted as many breasts as Diana of the Ephesians, all encased in parma-violet silk, and masses of white hair piled up prodigiously upon the top of her head (" Just like a French Marquise," Mrs. Floodgay used to say of her), while a touch of more than usual distinction was sometimes added to these gatherings by the presence of Mrs. Wilfred Too-many.

Mrs. Toomany, a thin, arid little woman, resembled a grilled bone. She wore a false curling fringe over her forehead, and false pearl drop-earrings, and had acquired an unrivalled social prestige in Newborough by her profession of friend to the fashionable dissolute. Herself debarred from immorality by appearance and inherited habit of mind, she had very cleverly made a special line in titled drunkards and divorcees (this, it must be remembered, at a time when they were a much rarer article than now), and of any people, rich or of good family, who were so dissolute and boring withal that no one else would have anything to do with them. She was the chief apostle of " *Tout comprendre, c'est tout pardonner,*" and was for ever munching this motto with unction, and oozing a rather odious sympathy. That, from the point of view of her profession, she showed genius is undoubted : for many of the people whom she pursued, captured, and upon whom she was now in constant attendance, were snobs, in spite, or perhaps because, of their having lost caste ; and Mrs. Toomany was not elegant either in appearance or manner : yet once caught they never tried to escape her : while her real gifts were still more demonstrated by the fact that she could now be trusted to anticipate a scandal, to become intimate with the perpetrators of one, long before it had become a fact in time or space. Thus she was able to travel in scandal as along a fourth dimension : able at a glance to detect its presence with equal ease whether lurking in the past, present or future : for it, she had the trained snout that a pig develops for truffle-hunting : more, she was an infallible indicator of future corruption, an instrument so delicately poised that the faintest heralding symptom of moral decay was at once revealed to her. She was ever at pains to champion the tediously disreputable, and the atmosphere of sympathetic understanding which she exhaled was positively suffocating. She would stay with these friends of hers for months, and then, in the intervals of her gilded scavengering, would relapse into the obscurity of her mother's residence on the West Cliff. Her mother was intensely proud of her daughter.

Mrs. Terringham-Jones, the wife of the rich piano manufacturer, was often to be seen in the Salon, too. Unfortunately, her husband was a Radical. But Arthur (the Canon) was not at all narrow-minded Whether one liked it or not, he said, one must recognize that a Liberal Government was in power, and might remain in office for years. It was never wise for a clergyman to quarrel with supporters of the Government. So, in spite of her principles and those of her other friends.

Mrs. Floodgay defended and protected the wealthy lady, and was in many ways useful to her.

Occasionally there were sudden squalls over the bridge-table ; but, however severe, Mrs. Hunterly would always be seen under full sail, bearing and dealing out in return the most tremendous buffetings. All the ladies present would push their chairs back from the table, stand up and shout. Then Mr. St. Rollo Ramsden would smile playfully, and put in a neat, swift, apt, classical allusion ; Colonel Spofforth would remark that Hyderabad in '57 was nothing to it, by Jove ; and the Canon would first peep slyly round the corner of the door, and then enter the room, smiling indulgently, and rubbing his hands together, " Ladies, ladies, I implore you ! " he would say.

CHAPTER XIX

A LITTLE VISIT

> " Ever let the Fancy roam :
> Pleasure never is at home."

IN the spring instead of going to London, as was her custom, the old lady tried to stay on at Newborough. But Miss Bramley was resolute on this point, and contrived with the aid of Dr. MacRacket to put an end to her manœuvres. It would never do for her to remain at the Superb, tiring herself out all the year round. Obviously she would break up soon, if she were allowed to do that sort of thing, do just as she liked.

As Miss Bramley had suspected, Miss Collier-Floodgaye was on the verge of an illness, and directly she reached London, she fell ill. It was not until the actual strain she had imposed upon herself had ceased, that she felt the full weight of it. Fortunately, she recovered fairly quickly ; but, during the whole time, insisted on writing to her new friends, though she had been told that she must not read, nor write letters. And, what was far worse for her, she imported the Floodgays, mother and daughter, to London for a whole week. Miss Bramley supposed that one ought to have been thankful that the Canon did not come too. He was quite capable of it, she thought.

The visit was most awkward and difficult. It began in this way. Mrs. Floodgay actually had the effrontery to write to the old lady, deploring the length of time that must elapse before herself and " dear Cécile " would see her again. She went on to say that " London must be so interesting, and bright just now. It is many years since we have stayed there." Of course the old lady was delighted (naturally) and telegraphed at once to ask them to stay. If Mrs. Floodgay had not written in that manner, Miss Collier-Floodgaye would never have thought of it. Practically, they had invited themselves ! A fine pair ! Oh, if only they had had to deal with Miss Fansharpe, what an invitation they'd have got. But they could do anything they liked with Cecilia, that was what it amounted to.

Then, when they arrived, they behaved so oddly. At first they made an attempt to be friendly with Miss Bramley, to " get round her." But she had no intention of being deceived by people of that sort ; nor could she approve of the way in which they tried to drag out from her any details she might know of Miss Collier-Floodgaye's early life. " I am sure you must know more than I do, since you are related to her," the Companion had replied with a rustling dignity. Quite unabashed, Mrs. Floodgay even went so far as to ask nibbling little questions about the old lady's income ! It was done quietly and subtly : but was most unpleasant, all the same. No, Miss Bramley felt that she could never like them after that . . . never. It was useless for her to try. She could never get on, she knew she could not, with " scheming " women—you know, regular " schemers," always on the look-out for something. And in her opinion the girl was as bad as any of them.

Then, behind the Companion's back, they extorted new dresses out of the old lady : chose their frocks and hats themselves, and left her to pay. And, good gracious, what frocks and hats ! Hardly the things for the wife and daughter of a clergyman. Miss Bramley could not *imagine* what *her* father would have done had he caught Mildred or herself wearing one of them. But the Floodgays actually had the audacity to exhibit them in the Lounge. She had actually seen them sitting, in that green-latticed room, with palms in every corner of it, under picture-hats! There they were now, in fact! Did you ever know such a thing? Really, she must write to Miss Waddington about it. How she wished now that she had learnt to draw. . . .

It was too much for Miss Bramley, and she went upstairs to write letters. Indeed, during the visit of the Floodgays she spent a great part of the day in her rather box-like bedroom, reading the *Morning Telegraph*, or examining her belongings. First she read about Keir Hardie. The brute wore a red tie in the House of Commons, and had refused to go to the Royal Garden Party at Windsor Castle after Ascot. Then she passed on to the scheme for self-government in South Africa. She agreed with the letter (to which the Editor drew attention) signed "Angry Governess," demanding whether we were to " sacrifice the first-fruits of a hard-earned victory " in order to " hob-nob with scoundrels and traitors to their country." Too bad: this was what came of having the Radicals in power. She felt quite thankful that (and here the muscle round her mouth twitched convulsively) dear old Miss Fansharpe had not lived to see the day. She had, sweet old lady, been such a patriot. It would have broken her heart. Now she paused in her political reflections, in order to turn round and examine the silver hand-mirror, with the five bat-like cupids' heads blistering out from it. A nice legacy—or rather, memento that (for she had never felt any ill-will toward her benefactress) and one that was typical of her, because so thoughtful. She remembered that it had been given to her, you see, by her Companion. And now all the details of its original purchase came back to Miss Bramley. She had bought it in Llandumfniff at the chief jeweller's. " You won't find another one like it," he had said, " Uncommon, artistic, and very good value for the money." Miss Fansharpe had been so pleased with it. Well, it certainly was a nice thing. But there was no denying that Miss Bramley had, she congratulated herself, quite a lot of nice things. How pretty the scent-bottles were (she ought to get some eau-de-Cologne or something— lavender water, perhaps—to put in them) and how dainty the filigree boxes ! The Indian ones were the daintiest, she thought. One day she must try to find a silver-backed tortoise-shell comb to go with the other objects. It oughtn't really to be difficult to find. What a difference it made having one's things round one. And thank goodness ! there was the bedspread. She had been afraid that she had lost it. Of course the housemaid must have moved it : that would be it. But really she must try to look after her things more. Where, for example, had she put that bit of Franco-Prussian bread (apparently during the siege they had, actually, to eat rats ! How extraordinary having a war in Europe, like that !) ? It must be with the chasuble in the large black box, naturally that was where it would be. Quite a historic relic now ! How the bread brought it all back—the French Governess, whom her father always referred to as " Mamzelle," with her upright bearing, her " taissez-vous's " and her shudders at the mention of a German, the Sunday

services with dear Mamma (but how faint her image)
playing the organ, and the three-night visit from Lord
Liddlesfield when the cook let her eat candied cherries
and they had chocolate cake for tea and tea sometimes
under the cedar in the lawn—for it was always summer
unless it snowed, no rain or dull days—and Mildred
falling into the green pond in her new dress with the
red sash and being made to go to bed and the old curate
with the stammer who always brought her a packet of
chocolates.   And then poor Mamma disappeared, they
were told that she had gone on a long journey, were
dressed in black, and sent for a visit of several months
to Aunt Georgie (Miss Titherley-Bramley) at Newborough, donkey-rides on the sands, she remembered,
and hokey-pokey on the foreshore and being ill afterwards, and one day a Dalmatian snapped at her for
nothing and she was beaten ! . . . well, it was a long
time ago now.   Still, she must find that bit of bread
which was the talisman to that far-away, eternal summer.
And Miss Bramley spent a blissful afternoon, oblivious
of the Floodgays, in rummaging through her large
shiny black box.

.   .   .   .   .   .

It cannot be said that, for her part, May Floodgay
cared much for Miss Bramley, though she and Cécile
had at first made tentative attempts at cordiality.   But
Mrs. Floodgay believed, somehow, in *first* impressions.
One so often found out afterwards that one's *first*
impressions had been right, she confessed to Cécile
in front of the enormous canvases by Watts in the Tate
Gallery (there was a *spiritually*-minded man for you,
all spirit and mists and hazes and visions and dreams

and auburn hair and goodness! and yet not sensuous
. . . if one might use the word, like Burne-Jones) and
hers had been that Miss Bramley was . . . well, "a
schemer." She didn't, she couldn't, like the woman.
Cécile, to whom Miss Bramley was horrid, agreed that
the Companion was "funny," so jealous, and would
never leave one alone with Aunt Cecilia for an instant,
unless she was in "one of her moods," and then she
wouldn't come down at all. Surely if one was a Paid
Companion, said Mrs. Floodgay, one ought not to pick
and choose like that . . . and always in correspondence
with that detestable old Miss Waddington . . . oh yes,
at one time she *had* been taken in by her . . . quite
taken in—but she was a wicked, dangerous old woman,
who spread dreadful stories about darling Daddy (for
Mrs. Floodgay was in saintly vein to-day). But something terrible always happened to people of that sort.
However, to go back to Miss Bramley, surely it was
wrong of her to refuse to come down. If it were Mrs.
Floodgay, she would *force* her to come down. She would
go up to the woman's bedroom, and say to her, "There
are two alternatives. Either come down or pack up."
That was how she would put it. People ought not to
give way to temper. And, after all, they had come all
this distance to see Aunt Cecilia, hadn't they? She
might as well be kept under lock and key as be looked
after by Miss Bramley. It was extraordinary that the
old lady had put up with it for so long. Mrs. Floodgay
wouldn't, not if it were her, not for a moment! . . .
too, too absurd, really laughable : for there could not
be anything wrong, could there in trying to "brighten"
the life of an elderly lady, and one, at that, who was a
relative . . . of course she was a relative, or why should

she say so ? (Don't be silly, Cécile.)   In any case, as
the Canon said, it was not for us to question His ways.
Perhaps it was His way of Providing ?   Who knows ?
" He moves in a mysterious way " as the dear old hymn
said. (Oh, look at that foot ! How like Watts to think
of it.)   What was there, *could* there be, wrong in it ?
But then materially-minded people were like that.   Oh
yes, that was materially-minded-people-all-over.   No,
Mrs. Floodgay could never get accustomed to that sort
of atmosphere . . . full of plans and scheming.

Never mind, Cécile : Aunt Cecilia was taking them
to see " Monsieur Beaucaire " that evening ; and the
child had never seen Lewis Waller before. She had missed
him when he came to Newborough (German Measles).
So there was something to look forward to : but she
ought, perhaps, to lie down before dinner. They were
both longing to see it . . . but, all the same, it would
be quite nice to get back to Newborough. . . .

Miss Bramley was certain that their visit had harmed
Miss Collier-Floodgaye, made her worse. Her vagueness was increasing. It was quite dreadful, her forget-
fulness. Even now, after all her fretting and worrying,
she had not seen her lawyer, either in Newborough or in
London. Well, her Companion was certainly not going
to remind her. It would only make her own memory
worse if she became dependent, in this way, on the
memory of another. As it was, Miss Bramley was always
having to put her in mind of things. She must learn
to remember things for herself.

.   .   .   .   .   .

As the summer wore on, the old lady appeared to
improve somewhat in health. It was easy to under-

stand why : Miss Bramley knew *quite* well why it was.
It was simple enough—she had not been tiring herself so much, and had not been bothered by other people.
Yet not for one moment would Miss Collier-Floodgaye
consider her Companion's suggestion that the winter
should be spent at Torquay instead of Newborough.
No, she was longing, evidently, to get back again to
that life for which she was so eminently unsuited.
Indeed, when Torquay was first proposed, Cecilia became
quite angry : one of the few occasions in all these six
or seven years that Miss Bramley had seen her get cross.
In fact, far from any thought of giving up her winters
at Newborough, the old lady insisted on going there at
the beginning of September, two months earlier than
usual, so as to take Cécile to the Cricket Festival. It
was most inconvenient, the hotel would be full, and
Miss Bramley did not even know whether they would
be able to have their usual rooms. At her age, too . .
but then she was so dreadfully obstinate, like a child,
and nothing could be done with her in such moods.

The Companion had dreaded the long train journey,
but the old lady stood it remarkably well. She would
not go into the restaurant car, because of her lameness
and the jolting, so they made quite a picnic in their
carriage. Each had a " station-luncheon-basket " (now
extinct) with two hard-boiled eggs, the whites of which
had turned black out of perversity, an Eton-blue leg of
chicken which tasted of tunnels, a " luncheon-roll,"
with butter, and cheese fresh from the mouse-trap, and
one hard, shiny Cézannesque apple : and, after it, the
waiter brought them some coffee from the restaurant
car.

Soon they had to change carriages at the northern

capital. Ebur Station was grimly fortified, with a hundred round loop-holes of grey sky, and two gigantic arches to support them. The old lady, leaning on the arm of her Companion, limped slowly along the interminable platforms, up-and-down under the shadow of the smoky branches thrown out by the avenues of trains and funnels. Ghastly shrieks and whistlings, melancholy hootings, sounded out continually, the voices, perhaps of some grim, grimy race of harpies, who chatter unmolested up in that black foliage, unseen as the brobdingnagian eagles which are said to hover above the tops of the dense, sun-slashed jungles in Africa. No attention was paid to these supernatural cries by the bustling porters, banging luggage, by the fussing women, accompanied by their maids, or by the self-important gentlemen, who, all smiles, were now leaving Ebur after some committee-meeting which, though no one else was aware of its existence, it had long been their settled conviction, was of national, almost European, importance.

. . . . . .

After all, they were fortunate enough to find themselves in their old rooms at the Superb, with Elisa, more faded and flaxen than ever, to wait upon them. Even Miss Bramley, who had begun to hate Newborough, was pleased at first to find herself there again, and John, the hall porter, though he had much to do, exuded a special first-night geniality. The hotel was very full, and yet more guests were expected for the Cricket Festival. The whole place seemed different, crowded as it now was: and a band was playing in the hall; Germans, she supposed. The weather was held, authoritatively, to be "promising." What a blessing for the town, the manager said to them, if they could have a spell of fine weather. It was, undoubtedly, promising.

At nine o'clock, though, the Floodgays called. It really was too bad of them to come so late, after the old lady had been tired-out by the journey, and keep her up talking like that. Miss Bramley left them, went upstairs, and banged her bedroom door, so that it resounded high above the chatter of the guests.

CHAPTER XX

ST. MARTIN'S SUMMER

" . . . We look
Across shrill meadows—but to find
The cricket-bat defeats the book,
Matter triumphant over mind."

THERE is much of truth contained in the cynical saying, attributed to the Duke of Wellington, that the Battle of Waterloo was won upon the playing-fields of Eton. The very same quality of heroism which intelligent boys prove in the course of learning to endure the spectacle of school-matches, in the process of becoming accustomed to ennui, does one day undoubtedly help them in the battlefield, does teach them to undergo unflinchingly the greater boredom of watching and participating in a larger, more evil, and quite as unnecessary stupidity A boy who learns to like cricket will learn to like anything : while, if forced when very young to play it against his better judgment, he will mind nothing so much in adult life. Indeed, after being at an English private and public school, the remainder of life, however hard, seems a holiday : and even the War came to many a boy leaving school as a relief rather than a catastrophe.

Other games, it may be, have their advantages over cricket. Football, for example, has one which is inestimable—that, at the worst, it can only last for an hour and a half as against the ennui of the full three days which a cricket match may entail : while, too, an expert though unwilling player, can, with the aid of the leather strips and lumps thoughtfully provided on the soles

232

and heels of boots sacred for this waste of time, mete out severe punishment to those chiefly responsible for the game, probably without being detected, or, if discovered, without being held guilty of anything more heinous than an exaggerated enthusiasm. Golf, again, acts in the same way as does a grouse-moor—interns all those addicted to it. A golf course outside a big town serves an excellent purpose in that it segregates, as though in a concentration camp, all the idle and idiot well-to-do, while the over-exertion of the game itself causes them to die some ten or fifteen years earlier than they would by nature, thus acting as a sort of fifteen per cent. life-tax on stupidity. While alive, it not only removes them for the whole day from the sight of those who have work to do, or leisure which they know how to spend profitably, but causes them to don voluntarily a baggy and chequered uniform, which proclaims them for what they are, at half a mile or so off, and thus enables the sane man to escape them. Similarly, a grouse-moor, like a magic carpet, whisks away its devotees to one of the bleakest, most misty and appropriate places in the northern hemisphere, and there imprisons them, to the sound of bagpipes, throughout their most dangerous months.

But cricket has its own peculiar merits as a training school for manhood. It is the very cumulative strain of boredom which this game imposes that constitutes its superiority. Any game, too, which, by laying down fixed rules, teaches boys not to think for themselves, will be of help to them in their mature years ; while, should these years coincide with a period of war, the lesson will be of inestimable value. Curiously enough, though schoolmasters inculcate the doctrine that an inter-school match is a thing of vital importance to the schools taking part in it, that defeat to a team is equivalent to the loss of a battle by an army, yet certain rules are laid down ; and the boy, who, believing these protestations of his teachers, sought genuinely to help his side by the invention and use of some ingenious mechanism, by the breaking of some old rule, or establishment of some new one, would quickly be disillusioned, called to order by the umpire, lowered in the esteem of his comrades, and perhaps afterwards disgraced publicly. Had Nelson, for example, won a cricket match instead of the Battle of Copenhagen, by regarding the umpire through a telescope applied to his blind eye, how much would his fame have suffered. But, fortunately for the English, Nelson was never at school—or if, as some say, he was, quickly ran away from it—for there can be no doubt, we fear, that his action was hardly " playing the game." Things have progressed since then, for no General (we do not speak of Admirals, for they have a tradition of eccentricity : and it may be here worth while to enquire to what extent the superiority of the officers of the English fleet over the officers of the English army is due to the fact that they do not go to public schools) on any side during either the Boer, or Late Great Bore, Wars even thought of winning a battle. No, the behaviour of all parties was correct and decorous in the extreme. In the end, the European War was won by *never* winning a battle, by vast mutual slaughter, and intolerable ennui. The only relief is that, owing to their inefficiency and slowness, it is unnecessary and almost impossible to remember the names of the " leaders," except as a warning.

It is at cricket, then, that the schoolboy first learns

the oft-repeated, dreary lesson that all men must march in time with the pace of the slowest among them. Thus the intelligent boy is made father to the stupid man.

At Newborough, however, the watching of cricket was no mere training. It was the fulfilment of an ancient savage rite. To the local young girl, whether of town or County (for the County participated in these observances) going to the Cricket Festival was equivalent to taking part in the initiation-rites that herald adult life to the young male in certain African tribes. It was the event of the year, for the aged and experienced as much as for the tiro. And Miss Collier-Floodgaye was determined—and Mrs. Floodgay had been determined that Miss Collier-Floodgaye should be determined—that herself should initiate Cécile into these semi-sexual mysteries.

The green, flat lawn was hemmed in by tall, flat inquisitive houses ; yellow, angular houses which rolled hundreds of blood-shot eyes back at the sun when it glanced at them. This circular ground was further surrounded by a wall of yellow brick peculiar to cricket-rings, and this wall was lined on the inside with square wooden pens for the townspeople. In certain spots these stands had a line of deck-chairs in front of them ; seats, these, for the local patricians. At two points, only, was this circular symmetry broken, where rose the Cricket Pavilion, part Swiss chalet, part Neolithic-Lake-Dwelling, above which in fine weather floated a silken banner of blue sea, and opposite, where swelled the canvas Tabernacle of Lord and Lady Ghoolingham. Between these two cynosures there was a continual show of intimacy and interfluctuation, which would be described by critics, if such a thing were to be observed in literary

circles, as " an orgy of mutual admiration." From the
Pavilion issued forth for their imbecile sham-battle
the strangely armoured demigods of professional cricket
—demigods, covered, as though they were soft-shelled
crustaceans, with soft, white armour, pipe-clayed brass-
lets, gauntlets, greaves, vambraces, cod-pieces, and
crowned, perhaps as a mark of their arrested mental
development, with those round caps that usually cling
to the heads of schoolboys—while within the Tabernacle
opposite moved figures yet more august and gigantic,
the vast forms of the Gods themselves, who preside over,
though they do not take part in, this ceremony of
initiation, this scene—who were, indeed, originally
responsible, for the founding of this modern, more
humane Stonehenge, where the mind is sacrificed alive
instead of the body. Even the County stood in awe of
these figures that moved so dimly. And it is symbolic
that though the home of the demigods was as it seemed
permanent and immovable, that of the Gods was temporary and mutable.

Behind and rather at the side of the Tabernacle
crouched a smaller and deprecating tent, that of the
local President. For though the festival was in reality
entirely under the sway of the almost fabulous Lord and
Lady Ghoolingham, yet, in order to impart the necessary
appearance of democratic independence and good-
fellowship (jolly-good-sportsman-and-all-that-and-not-a-
bit-stuck-up-either) they encouraged the election of a
president from the town. But no one paid much attention to him, except at the luncheon interval, and he was
left to worry out for himself those questions of local
precedence with which he was perpetually concerned
It was upon the other tent that the eyes of the town-

noblesse were fixed, fastened in a state of snobbery so ecstatic that the gazers were, after a time, mesmerized, rendered almost semi-conscious.

Usually the Festival consisted of three matches ; the first was an inter-county match, the second an international match, and then, at the end, took place that delightful old English institution titled " Gentlemen *v.* Players." By long custom certain days were more fashionable than others, and it was the second day of the first match which Miss Collier-Floodgaye had chosen for the initiation of Cécile. Miss Bramley had refused her friend's invitation to go with her, so there were just the three of them, May Floodgay, Cécile, and the old lady. They had very good deck-chairs ; could see everything. And . . they were near the Tent. What a lot of panama-hats there were, already, though the game had not even begun ! Evidently the Ghoolinghams could not have arrived yet (the deck-chairs remained intent on one another, ignored the hoarse, paper-unwrapping crowds in their pens : pretended not to see the caps for the panama hats). All the same one could not help noticing the bananas. A horrid smell, on a hot day, like pine-apple drops. Miss Collier-Floodgaye wished people wouldn't sell so common a fruit as bananas, to her mind it spoilt everything : but Cécile liked it, thought it part of the fun, the crowd, the shouting, the paper, the bananas and everything.

Suddenly the occupants of the deck-chairs were struck dumb, paralysed though still able to move their eyes as if not looking, for—heralded by a particularly hoarse voice shouting " Good old Ghooly "—the Gods and Goddesses were descending on to the stage. They walked slowly toward the Tent, talking to each other, smiling a little too graciously, or if unsure whether they knew those persons they were at present passing, smiled in such a way that it would not commit them if they were unacquainted, might be taken as an apology, implying " I am so sorry, was that your foot ? " or " did I tread on your dress ? " while, on the other hand, if they were acquainted, the curve of the mouth, though vague, was so sympathetic, they felt, that not even old friends would feel unrecognized or wounded. It was very hard to recognize everyone ; and by this method nobody would be offended.

What a shame to go on shouting " Bananas," in that way at such a moment, reflected Miss Collier-Floodgaye : " two a penny " indeed. That must be the Duchess of Dunston over there, with the pretty young face and white hair. A sweet face, she called it. White hair always suited a young face, she didn't know why. And that swarthy-looking woman in bright yellow must be Violet Catling, the famous beauty, who was so " smart " —and fast, they said, and bad-tempered. How daring to wear a colour like that, one could not help admiring her for it, could one ? (why couldn't they stop shouting bananas ?) So swarthy, she looked, like a common gypsy. Fine eyes, though. How " society " must be altering, that she could go about as she did ; though the Queen would not receive her, they said. But the Queen was kind and broad-minded ; if it had been Queen Victoria . . . ! Lord Ghoolingham looked such a real sportsman and she—she was, well not handsome exactly, but regal-looking, you know.

The informal procession was now entering the Tabernacle, which swiftly swallowed up its own, so that the figures of the Immortals could be but dimly seen within, moving through the heart of the purple heat and darkness.

Soon the Neolithic chalet began to evacuate its tenants, spherical forms in white : for cricketers were already beginning to get old and fat. " The youngsters were not shaping as they should," it was said, " Was golf the cause, or what was it ? "

At first the game was very silent, except for the drawing-room conversation of bat and ball ; this wooden small-talk would proceed for some time, and then, suddenly, one of the talkers would snub the other, and away would run the fat white mice over the flat green baize. The banana-vendor was silent (why couldn't she have kept quiet before ?) and weird women-enthusiasts, possibly the wives of the cricketers—epicene, tweed-clad figures, crowned with large straw-hats, wearing sensible-brown-shoes with flapping and fantastic leather tongues lolling out of them, and, exhibiting, tucked into their coats, men's ties, blazoned in dreadful stripes that held for them some hidden significance—leant forward, watching with a flushed and strained inanity, or occasion·ally allowed it to be seen by a smile, glance, or exclamation, that they had duly followed some esoteric subtlety of form or style. The men were even less emotional They sat there rigidly, smoking, occasionally tapping their pipes as a woodpecker taps its beak, against the wooden rail in front of them. One wondered if this was their way of communicating with their mates, some form of expression superseded in mankind by speech. But their round, clear eyes held in them no meaning that they could possibly wish to convey to anyone. Now and again there might be a flutter of excitement at some peculiarly imbecile sally, such as when a batsman allowed himself to be caught out, or the umpire decreed, in another case, the mystic " l.b.w."   Even the wooden contingent in the deck-chairs would then vibrate for a moment while in the stands behind them there would be a seething of hats and handkerchiefs ; but these outbursts were rare.

It was fine, really fine, and the air danced over the hot ground. The dry chatter of bat and ball, the humming of sun and grass, the fluttering of aerial forms (for the air could be seen dancing and shrilling over the green spaces) and above the roof of the pavilion the glittering of the northern sea, which threw golden rings of light into the air from each wave crest, as jugglers throw rings into the air on a stage ; all were soothing and cheering, Miss Collier-Floodgaye thought : good for the nerves. How warm, quiet, yet droning, it was.   Gradually for the old woman the green expanse and its railings melted, and changed shape, but into another scene of the same sort. She was now far away, back—before the days of her untethering prosperity—back at other cricket matches, for her father had been Captain of the Eleven in a large, northern village. Hot days had then lulled her, while old ramose trees fanned her with their green feathers. Captain of the Eleven, and much looked up to, he had been. But people must never know : very respected locally, of course ; but timber-merchants always are looked up to, she did not quite know why. Then her father had died, and soon there were no relations. Her brother had been found shot, shot through the head. And she had been so fond of him. How could he have done it ? He had never even mentioned the thought of such a thing ; but he had always been strange, like her mother, dead so long ago, strange and full of fancies. People were for ever following him, he said.

Wherever he moved in the countryside, there was a stirring after him, and branches rustled slowly, slyly, and he could feel faces peering at him through fluttering branches : and there were footfalls, he had said, footfalls on the stairs, and sombre figures grimacing at him in dark corners. But she could understand it, for though she was not like her mother—in fact the very image of her father—yet when she had been very young, or when she was unwell, she, too, was afraid of whispering leaves and crouching shadows. There he was found, lying face down, half buried in bracken, with a shot through his head. " Temporarily Insane," they had found him ; but she could not judge him so. Yet it was a cruel thing for him to leave her like that, to all the talk of the village, and the loneliness in the middle of all this talk was unimaginable. She could not even go to church without being stared at. She had realized that unless she were prepared for a similar end, she must get away from the talk, and from people who reminded her, whose very kindness reminded her, of the past. And she was rich now, so she could get away. After all she had no relations left, except some very distant cousins. She did not dislike them : indeed they were too kind, but she had felt then that she must get away, leave the place, forget everything and become ordinary. She had sold all her property, kept nothing in her possession that could recall the past—except, only, that snake-ring with the ruby eyes, which her brother had been wearing at the time of his death—that brother she had loved so dearly. The ring was unlike others, and it was typical of him to have worn it, for his taste was personal. In fact she supposed, he had been " artistic."

Yes, she had felt then that she must leave the place,

and become ordinary : for that was her chance of safety. Even at that time she had been no longer young, and when you were old it was easier to forget : indeed, she forgot easily, now, forgot everything. And when she moved, how lonely she had been, worse than ever before and getting older. Now, though, she was better : tired, it was true, ever so tired : but she was in the light and the heat and with friends. There must be nothing queer about her, however, or they would not like her, and she would be left lonely again. The humming of sun and grass, the cicada sounds of bat and ball were soothing, while the occasional waves of applause were calming as waves rolling over you. How quiet and warm it was. Gradually the green field melted away, and she was lying in a gently-rocking boat, sailing away from a dark, huge forest of dead timber, in which sombre shadows moved, sailing away, away into the light over the blue waves.

" Cécile, your Aunt Cecilia is asleep, I'm afraid," said Mrs. Floodgay tartly, and, by her phrasing of the sentence, immediately threw the onus of hypothetical relationship to a public-snorer upon her daughter. It would never do, with Lady Ghoolingham near by. If there was a thing Mrs. Floodgay hated, it was to see someone nodding like that, asleep in daylight, the sudden totter and fall of the head, and then the somnolent efforts at deportment, irritated her. Cécile must nudge her aunt ; that was all that could be done. Nudge her and say—yes, it was better to say—" Did you see that stroke, Aunt Cecilia ? " On reflection, perhaps better not say "stroke." It might alarm an old lady waking up. Instead, try saying, " Did you see that hit, Aunt Cecilia ? " No, not like that, so that everyone could see, but softly,

quietly. Really she must know by this time how to do
a thing of that sort. One couldn't be made to look
ridiculous. What man would ever think of proposing
to a girl-who-did-not-know-how-to-nudge-an-aunt-who
happened-to-have-fallen-asleep-and - say- " Look-at-that-
hit-Aunt-Cecilia," she should like to know ? After all—
men weren't all fools, were they ? . . . that was better
now. But of course there was that horrid old Mrs.
Shrubfield watching. (She would be ! Usually at this
time of year she was pretending to be away. Horrid old
mischief-maker, like a large blackbeetle, in her sequined
garments. All Mrs. Floodgay hoped was that she wouldn't
make a scene after the luncheon interval. It was shocking
to see a *woman* in that state.)

Indeed Mrs. Shrubfield could be heard wheezing
internationally into the distance. " *Eccola ! Regardez
ça, liebchen*," she was saying to Ella, Miss Waddington's
niece who was serving as aide-de-camp.

Of course she'd seen it all. Fortunately, however,
the old lady was awake again now. But, naturally Mrs.
Shrubfield would make a story of it : that went without
saying.

" Yes, dear, it will be luncheon soon," and Mrs.
Floodgay was again smiling and twittering sweetly.
She put the old lady in mind of a pretty bird, so soft and
kind : a robin or a chaffinch or something. And Cécile
looked ever so charming with her white filmy dress, and
soft hat trimmed with red poppies : not too fashionable
for a young girl, or too " showy." (How clever the
French were—even when they settled in an English
town—and neat with their fingers). Her hair looked
quite lovely to-day. What a business it must be brushing
it ! The old lady would dearly love to see Cécile married

—to a nice man. She was extremely attached to the
girl and would like to know that she was happily settled.
There must be one condition, however. The husband
would have to call himself Floodgaye—or, it might be
better if he adopted Floodgay-Collier-Floodgaye. It
sounded well and the name *could* not be allowed to
die. Well, she ought to marry soon, with hair like that.
And Miss Collier-Floodgaye felt delighted with herself,
her relatives, and, above all, pleased that she had bought
Cécile that dress. But she was tired, very tired.

Now came the luncheon interval. The deck-chairs
ejected their tenants, who walked about the corner of
the ground in front of the Tabernacle, greeting one
another. Mingled in this mysterious moment, Gods,
demigods and mortals. The heat waved its banners
just above the grass and sent streamers curling into the
air, winding round the legs of the promenaders like
serpents. Miss Collier-Floodgaye lent on the arm of the
young girl, and slowly limped up and down through the
crowd. So that was it ! The yellow dress that the famous
Miss Violet Catling was wearing, was one of those new
" Directoire " gowns she had read about. More daring,
much more daring, than she had supposed. Bright
yellow and slit up to the knee. What would people put
on next, she wondered . . . and a large picture hat.

Generally speaking, the Goddesses were wearing white,
mauve, or yellow ; for these were the fashionable colours
of the year. The Gods were tall, ox-eyed, pink and
moustached as prawns. Lord and Lady Ghoolingham
were talking to the cricketers and to their wives. Why,
Lady Ghoolingham was asking herself, why because one
is married to a famous cricketer, why, because one is a
woman who wears tweeds, brown leather shoes, and a

striped tie, need one shout like that to show one is
happy and at one's ease ?

The part of the crowd which belonged to the town
and its neighbourhood was self-conscious, for this was
a great day—London, as well as local, papers had installed their reporters here for the occasion ; moreover,
Illustrated Society Papers, as well as ordinary London
papers, had despatched their representatives to this
famous field.

Mrs. Floodgay stopped every now and then to speak
to a friend, to lots of friends. Mrs. Sibmarshe whispered
to her confidentially. Mr. St. Rollo Ramsden, his beard
freshly-trimmed, wearing a gorgeous uniform appropriate
to the occasion, and carrying a shooting-stick, so that
he could sit down whenever the spirit seized him, was
here ; for he loved Newborough so much, he said, that
he could never make up his mind to leave it, even during
the holidays. His brown shoes were perfection, having
the exact requisite shade of mahogany, not too new,
nor too far disintegrated, while in his tie he wore a small
ruby and diamond cricket-bat. Did Mrs. Floodgay
remember, he wondered, what Ovid had written, when
he was living in exile, near the Black Sea ? . . . rather
a jolly little thing, he thought. . . . Mrs. Floodgay
could see that dreadful, little deaf old man, Mr. Bradbourne, skulking in the opposite corner. No doubt
he was in one of the common stands, so as to avoid
seeing any old friend who might know him. He would
come to a bad end, she felt sure, an old horror. Then
there were the Terringham-Joneses ; and really Colonel
Spofforth was a marvellous old man, over eighty-five,
now, and walking about like quite a young man, though
strongly reminded by the day of Lucknow in '56

" There we sat, by Jove, in the Club," he said, " absolutely unable to move, doncherno.   Punkah-wallah,
black chap, doncherno, suddenly dropped the punkah
and ran away, you know. ' Where's that damned nigger ?'
I cried. What, what. Just then the . . ." Mrs. Toomany,
more arid than ever, and dressed in a tone of charred
ember which suggested that the grilled bone had now
been burnt quite black, was engaged in her professional
researches. But this sort of truffle-hunting was fatiguing,
and her promenade had been on the whole, a disappointment.   Violet Catling " shaped well," she thought, the
German Prince had a " sympathetic " face, and Lady
Carrie Conyers showed distinct promise, she felt.   Still
she would not care to prognosticate. Everybody seemed
so dull and respectable : there was hardly a person she
knew. Then Mrs. Floodgay spoke to the two little Misses
Finnis, sent there as delegates, she supposed, by someone :
probably that old woman with white hair and prominent
teeth who lived on the West Cliff—half-mad, they said,
always playing with a doll, but rich and very inquisitive :
must know everything that was going on.   Or perhaps
Lady Tidmarshe had sent them.   Miss Pansy Finnis was
wearing the same blue serge dress, in which we met her
in the winter some three years before, the skirt stretched
over the hips and short legs, assuming the shape of a
thimble, but her hat had broken into a pathetic summer
trimming of blue cornflowers.   Miss Penelope, shorter
still, was sporting a rather gay cast-off dress which she
had been given by that queenly woman, Mrs. Terringham-Jones. It was a nobly embroidered affair, and above
all this richesse showed a badly nourished face, in which
were to be detected a hundred shades of blue and purple,
the weals inflicted by genteel poverty. The sisters were

deprecating, sad and amiable to a degree. They smiled and laughed, but their eyes were always rolling round uneasily as though in search of some crust, for almost to that level had they by now been reduced. People did not appear to want piano lessons, or writing lessons, or anything now. The commoner you were, the more money you had.

All that the young people cared about now were these "cinemas" or whatever you call them. It made one feel quite ill to see the sort of people who listened to the Band in the Winter Gardens. You never saw such *frights*. Really it was quite a treat, Mrs. Floodgay, to come here and see such a nice-looking lot of people. It reminded one of the old days, when everybody came to New-borough . . . but Mrs. Floodgay was eyeing the crowd, for she was never sure that she liked Miss Pansy; a crafty look, she had: perhaps more "shifty" than crafty . . . At this precise moment, Mrs. Floodgay caught sight of that mystic figure, who only materialized here once every year, that apparition who heralded the gathering of the Great World, known as the "Passing-Pageant Boy." This Boy, who had long been a grown man, was the representative of the famous illustrated journal. He had intended (he once confided to Mrs Sibmarshe) to "go in" for the Church, but had felt instead the call of the World. He was thirty-five years of age, and took himself most seriously, still wearing, however, an Eton collar and jacket, in order, as he said "to further his literary career." To match his collar, eyebrows and mouth were all turned down, while the nose receded from the rest of his features with a great look of surprise at the triumph it had achieved in this little act of mutiny.

Mrs. Floodgay greeted him and fell into a reverie. She could see it all. "Among those noticed by our representative was Mrs. Floodgay, wife of the celebrated North Country Canon, looking very piquante in a veiled charmeuse of the new tone in mauve ; with her, and she has inherited a full share of her mother's looks, was her attractive daughter, Miss Cécile Floodgay. The latter was wearing such a pretty hat, trimmed with red poppies à la Parisienne." Or, better still, it might be one of those social false-perspectives, in which she and her daughter might figure, "Snapped at the Newborough Cricket Festival. Reading from left to right, Mrs. Floodgay, Miss Cécile Floodgay and friend. Behind can be seen, marked with a cross, the Duchess of Dunston and Lady Carrie Conyers."

It would help Cécile. It would be in all the papers, London and local. Up and down paced the throng expectantly, and Mrs. Floodgay was not the only day-dreamer among them.

The Ghoolinghams were within the Tabernacle, entertaining the demigods to luncheon. The party enjoyed itself immensely and exchanged comments on local dresses and manners. The President was also giving a luncheon party, in the cringing tent huddled up behind the Tabernacle. To this celebration Mrs. Floodgay had been invited to bring her daughter and her friend.

It was very hot, and such a fight took place to get the slab of tepid, scaly salmon, edged by warm cucumber. The whole tent perspired over the hot and trampled grass. Hired waiters with mutton-chop whiskers, and red-noses, quaking with age, handed a trembling plate here and there, with faces streaming. The guests, too, were swollen and purple with the heat. It was hot, oh so hot; and Miss Collier-Floodgaye began to lose herself again. This time she was walking in a green maze, under a burning sun. She could not find her way out of it, anywhere :—and then, suddenly, everything stopped—

They had to lead her out, and drive her back to the hotel. Miss Bramley, fortunately, was in. Oh, no; she was not a bit surprised; the old lady should not be allowed to do such things, which, naturally, were too much of a strain for anyone of her age. Real friends (for Miss Bramley felt that for once she could say what she felt) would not encourage her to take them to tiring functions. No . . . it might only be a fainting-fit, of course. She seemed better now.

CHAPTER XXI

WINTER

The tree's small corinths
Were hard as jacinths,
For it is winter and cold winds sigh . . .
No nightingale
In her farthingale
Of bunchèd leaves lets her singing die.

HOWEVER, Miss Bramley thought it better to send for
Dr. MacRacket. He hurried down to the hotel in the
brougham, drawn by two Velasquez horses, to which
he still remained faithful, and sped up in the lift with
that portentous look of important preoccupation, which
was one of his professional assets. With him he bore
the assorted insignia of his calling : top hat, two
stethoscopes (one shaped like a small wooden trumpet,
while the other was a replica of that pink meteor which
we saw hurtling to its doom in the street below), and a
black shiny bag full of instruments. These he placed
on the table as though they were so many fetishes,
accompanying his movements with varying degrees of
ceremonial. He now apologized to the two ladies in
case he had kept them waiting. The truth was, turning
to Miss Bramley, that he had been called in to see a
friend of hers, Mrs. Shrubfield. Nothing serious,
fortunately : only she was very excitable, and seemed
to have been upset by the cricket festival, or the luncheon,
or something of that sort. Oh, yes, very cultured and
sympathetic. Then he applied one of the stethoscopes
to his patient : fastened his ear to the trumpet end,

and commanded her to echo after him the mystic spell
" 99." He then, as doctors sometimes do, lapsed
strangely into common sense, and told Miss Collier-
Floodgaye plainly that she ought not to exert herself
at her age, ought not to go out so much among people,
ought not to lead so furiously exhausting a life. On the
other hand she should go out more in the fresh air, a
little walk every day, not far enough to tire herself,
or a drive up on to the moors. That was the thing :
if, of course, the weather permitted. Naturally he did
not want her to walk through the rain. If she followed
his advice, she would soon be well. But she must stay
in bed a few days, in order to rest.

When Miss Collier-Floodgaye got up again, she found
that summer and autumn had both spent themselves
in a thunderstorm, and that winter reigned cruelly in
their stead. Needless to say, she was determined to
neglect the Doctor's orders ; or perhaps she had already
forgotten them. For she was, Miss Bramley noticed,
much more absent-minded and visibly more infirm,
but still so obstinate that one could do nothing with her.
She refused to walk, refused to exercise her knee, would
not go out for drives.

Moreover the Floodgays were the first to observe
the change in her. No longer did they ask her to play
bridge at their parties, for her game was too erratic.
They pretended (oh ! Miss Bramley could see through
it !) to be solicitous about the old lady's health, afraid
that large parties would fatigue her, and would only
persuade her to play when there would be few people
present. This altered attitude on the part of her " relatives," though they disguised it as much as they could,
tended to retard rather than to aid Miss Collier-Flood-

gaye's recovery, for it fretted her continually. Nor was
it any less tiring for her, because Mrs. Floodgay, since
she had stopped asking her so much to the Vicarage,
was now, in order to disguise this falling off in hospitality,
always " looking-in " with Cécile about luncheon-time,
" dropping-in " to tea, and, indeed, positively pestering
the old lady. And it was not so much playing bridge
as seeing people which tired her. And she always
returned from the Vicarage over-tired, even if there had
been no one there except the family.

Her obstinacy was as great as ever, perhaps greater,
Miss Bramley thought. When, for example, there was
a ball at the Superb, she would buy tickets for it, make
Cécile and her mother dine with her on the night in
question, and, as often as not, would sit up till two in
the morning. Nothing that anyone could say would
dissuade her from doing this, though it was a habit
that no one of her age could form with impunity. It
was *too* bad of the Floodgays allowing her to do it, of
course ; but just what one would expect of them. It
was useless, the Companion realized, for her to speak
to them directly about it : but she insinuated, and
allowed her feelings to appear in her manner. It was
very obvious that such festivities absolutely exhausted
the old lady, and it was Miss Bramley's belief that
the Canon's family could see it too.

.   .   .   .

This winter Miss Bramley saw as much as possible
of Mrs. Shrubfield and Miss Waddington. Their
friendship was a great solace to her. The two Marshals
of the Monstrous Regiment were, indeed, most gracious
and through them the latest news was sifted, passing

through their perfected mechanism to nourish many a frail old form facing South. Alas, owing to the duration and rigour of the military operations, one or two of the veterans had fallen out of the ranks, and had been buried with full military honours. But the two leaders were determined " to see it through," resolute as ever in their determination to prosecute the campaign with every resource at their disposal, and to bring it to a victorious conclusion. Miss Waddington had suppressed with the utmost vigour her asthmatic tendencies. The doctor was delighted with the progress she had made, and it was obvious that she was now capable of an endurance and effort which would have been impossible to her a few winters previously. " Isn't Aunt Hester wonderful ? " her niece would quaver weakly. While, however much in her own house Mrs. Shrubfield might indulge her leanings toward rollicking jollity or lachrymose despair, yet she never allowed these alternating moods of optimism and pessimism to be witnessed by the rank and file, never came to the battlefield except with an undimmed eye and an unclouded judgment. After the Cricket Festival, it is true, she had been unwell for some days, for the spectacular success which she had achieved by actually being the witness of the fainting— or as she considered it, the seizure—of Miss Collier-Floodgaye, and of the consequent, obvious discomfiture of that odious little Mrs. Floodgay, when she had seen fixed upon her the Marshal's acute and sparkling eye, had unduly excited Mrs. Shrubfield. Miss Waddington, for one, was not inclined to blame her for it. It was all the fault of that stupid girl, Ella. Why had the silly creature supposed that Miss Waddington had sent her there with Mrs. Shrubfield ? Was it neces-

sary to explain everything to her in black-and-white?
(Black-and-White, indeed, had been the cause of the
trouble.)   Could she really have supposed at her age
that it was a treat, organized specially for her, and
that Mrs. Shrubfield was acting as her chaperone?
Really it made one despair of the Girls-of-To-day.   A
curious feature of the friendship between these ladies
was, that though Mrs. Shrubfield was nearly always
present at tea with Miss Waddington, Mrs. Shrubfield
never asked her back in return.   She never drank tea,
she said, it was bad for the nerves : and her nerves,
Carissima, were not what they had been.   Ah, *La Vita*,
c'est difficile ; not all beer and skittles . . . as the servants say.

But by Miss Waddington, Miss Bramley was constantly
invited to tea.   Indeed an unusual amount of entertaining, for so quiet a house, took place both above and
below stairs ; for Elisa, too, was a favourite and indulged
guest beneath, and, so great the impression she had made
on Miss Thompson, that she was several times allowed to
see Miss Waddington for a few minutes.   For these
occasions Miss Waddington would usually relapse into
bed, and would give a remarkable impersonation of a dear,
but rather weak-minded old lady, entirely ruled by her
parlourmaid.   Miss Thompson, however, had warned
the simple Elisa with great solemnity *never* to speak
of these visits to Miss Bramley, who might be jealous :
for Miss Waddington, she added, received the Companion so differently.   Elisa was delighted by these
signs of being held in an especial esteem, an esteem to
which she was not accustomed, and kept her silence,
though she answered any questions that the delicate
old lady tremolo'd at her with the greatest readiness,

and all the accuracy which was possible. It had been Miss Thompson's friendship with Elisa, indeed, that had enabled Mrs. Shrubfield to bring off her coup in the cricket ground.

Miss Bramley, though she was aware of Elisa's friendship with Miss Waddington's parlourmaid, was ignorant of its extent and fervour : nor was she even informed of her friend's rather unbecoming condescension to the housemaid. It would have pained her, for she was so fond of Miss Waddington and of Mrs. Shrubfield : and they made a great show of intimacy with her. They laid more and more stress upon their former friendship with her aunt, until, to listen to them, one would have imagined that the two ladies had never for an instant been separated from the owner of the Dalmatians, and that the mere name of Bramley acted as *open sesame* to their affections. It was really touching, the Companion thought, to notice the subtle ways in which they were always trying to help her. It was obvious that they would go through fire-and-water for her. What an advantage it was to belong to a *family*, a well-known family (that was where Cecilia lost so much. That was what was lacking). Just because of her aunt they were for ever trying to make things easier for her. They never lost interest in her. For example, they never allowed an opportunity to pass of advising her—in the nicest way possible, of course— to end the intimacy between Miss Collier-Floodgaye and the Canon's family. Nothing but ill would come of it, they averred. After all . . . one had heard stories, Mrs. Floodgay herself was responsible for the information. Even the housemaids, she had said : no woman it appeared was safe : and then you could not get away from it, incense was incense ; and bridge-parties, whether Mrs. Floodgay gambled or not (they would not discuss that : that was not the point) were bridge-parties. No good would come of it, that was certain. And last time that Ella had been to Mme. de Kalbe—you know, the Clairvoyante—the forecast had been worse. Even the cannibals were not safe now, it appeared . . . though, of course, they would eat them in the end. But think of the scandal, and of the poor Bishop responsible for sending them there. Mme. de Kalbe had fainted, so great was the shock. Of course, one could not believe everything that fortune-tellers told one ; but still it was queer : described them exactly, Ella had said.

Incidentally, Miss Waddington did not often encourage Ella to be present at these intimate tea-parties. It was the old lady's opinion that " there was no one like Ella for getting in the way." And Miss Bramley did not " take to " the niece : the reason being, though she was not aware of it, that she harboured a great distrust toward unpaid, hereditary Companions. She resented them. They did not know their business, and were, to her unconscious mind, taking the bread out of the mouths of other girls. She felt, then, the contempt and hatred of the professional in any branch of art for the amateur. She did not realize that to be a niece is as much a profession as any other. But as we have said before this is never realized by anyone outside the bargain of mother and daughter, aunt and niece

No, the two Marshals kept Miss Bramley to themselves, and discussed with her the best methods of breaking Mrs. Floodgay's influence over her supposed relative. They renewed their offers of personal assistance : if necessary, either of them was willing herself to interview Miss Collier-Floodgaye and inform her of the sort of people into whose hands she had fallen (after all, it was the Canon's own wife who had told them the stories !). But since Cecilia was so pig-headed, and refused to call on them, or receive them, what was to be done ? The worst of it was that Miss Bramley could not tell them this, for it sounded so rude and might cause offence : so she had to invent excuses for Cecilia. But the two leaders did not need to be told. They could see, they knew, the evil influence at work. That was why that nasty, carroty-haired girl looked so sly . . . but just let her wait. . . .

Miss Bramley's frequent meetings with her two friends, the gay little familiar tea-parties, even their appreciation of her singing, failed to comfort her. For she was a Paid Companion and expected to be treated as one, not to be given this endless liberty in which she had nothing particular to do. She would not probably have minded being bullied, being played-with and tormented as by Miss Fansharpe . . . but for the company of unpaid and amateur Companions to be preferred, openly preferred, to that of the professional, salaried graduate in the art of friendship, constitutes an insult of the deadliest order, though not recognized as such by the rest of the world ; and one that is utterly degrading to the Companion, must in the end entirely destroy her self-respect. Really, it almost made Miss Bramley hate her employer : all the more, because she was genuinely attached to her. And she did not hate her the whole time ; when she was ill, she was as fond of her as ever. Now people insist on treating love and hatred as though they were totally unconnected, instead of being symptoms of the same disease, in the same way that alternating subnormal temperature and high fever may be tokens of an identical illness.   Indeed, love and hatred, apart from those that are the result of purely physical attractions, are nearly always based on an excessive understanding of one person by another, who is therefore rendered peculiarly sensitive to the kindness or unkindness that their conduct implies.   And Miss Bramley possessed a real intuition into Miss Collier-Floodgaye's character.   Naturally the Companion would never even admit to herself that at moments she hated the old lady, for it would have seemed a thing utterly inconceivable—or inadmissible, which was to her the same thing.   Love and hatred were manifestations of a passion that had entered so little into Miss Bramley's life, that she was very far from comprehending them. If anyone had suggested to her that she hated Cecilia, hated her for one moment even, she would have been profoundly shocked, deeply indignant ; but at times, she did undoubtedly feel, beneath the upper layers of her consciousness, a desire to get even with the old lady and, beyond that, to wreak a fit revenge upon the Floodgays.   Apart from these emotions, she was sorry for Cecilia, often very sorry for her.   But the old lady's continual if clumsy consideration for her, and wish not to injure her feelings, only aggravated the Companion further, only made the slighting of her worse and to herself more obvious.

Miss Bramley felt, instinctively, for she had never reasoned it out, that her life was now hollow, deceptive as a hollow tree.   Cecilia never asked her, as she used, to accompany her on any outings.   Gone were those halcyon days of only two years before, when the winter

sun was always rosily shining, pecking at one's face
warmly as a robin nestling (really Miss Bramley thought,
the climate seemed to have changed. So much colder,
the sea and wind always roaring), when they had such
delightful walks in the Winter-Gardens; no longer
did they spend delicious hours " poking about " in the
market, or strolling through the peat-scented moors,
inhaling the acute air. Cecilia hardly ever asked her to
sing, except sometimes, when she was dull, not going
out after dinner to the Vicarage: then of course, she
could be made use of. Not that she minded that,
but simply a PAID Companion, that was what she had
become (alas, in reality, it was exactly what she was not,
and what she wished to be). . . . All these unnecessary
people. Before Cecilia had met them, how different
she had been: and Miss Bramley sighed bitterly, and
if her eyes had been used to tears, these would have
flowed and have comforted her. As it was, the best
thing to do was to order a nice cup of hot tea. But if
she ever rang the bell, Elisa would be sure to grumble.
It was not that the housemaid did not like her; it was
a matter of principle. But what, Miss Bramley reflected,
was the use of hanging up a printed notice, with " Ring
once for the waiter; twice for the chambermaid " on it,
if Elisa insisted on answering if you rang once? It
was scarcely fair: and then the maid would look sulky
for the rest of the day; while since, besides Miss Waddington and Mrs. Shrubfield, she was practically the only
person to whom Miss Bramley could talk, this was very
annoying and awkward. And Miss Bramley had been
told, Germans were so willing as a rule. . . .

Really Cecilia ought *not* to be out to-day. Besides
it was rather hard to have to sit by oneself in a hotel

on a day like this. One could practise one's songs, of course ; but then every artist likes to have an audience. The drawing-room was too large and dark to be in by oneself for long : and dismal, looking over so rough and threatening an ocean. The sound of sea and wind rushing and jostling rose up too sharply at the large windows. It quite got on one's nerves. For, far down below, the waves were hollowing out every kind of crevice, vault, cave, coffin and cavern, every place imaginable in which to secrete bleaching bones, every form of tube and hollow instrument, upon which the wind could play an accompanying and awful music. The prospect was full of the aerial commotion caused by all this labour, full of white foam, the steam given off by this titanic and terrible machinery. The vast, grey, undulating backs rolled sideways against cement walls, rocks, cliffs and precipices, acting as inspired and living hammers. These monsters pushed and heaved against each other, and then with an added force rammed at the obstacles interposed between themselves and human-ity, meeting them with an unimaginable dull and forceful thudding, while, in the very act of clashing with them, they uplifted feline white claws by which to grab hold of the hated, hard objects obstructing them. Still dully roaring, they clambered up with unexpectedly lithe and sinuous movement. For a moment they clung tenac-iously, held their own ; then, unable at present to lift up the whole, enormous weight of their bodies, fell back gurgling and snarling to recruit themselves for another leaping attack.

All this sound and movement made Miss Bramley nervous and irritable, made it impossible for her to sing, or concentrate upon anything but Cecilia's behaviour.

Nor was she a person who could, by natural charm, manufacture her injured feelings into a fresh claim on the affection of the offender. On the contrary, trials and sorrows of this sort merely served to harden the shell of her, making her disagreeable, sourly disagreeable through her mask of effusive sweetness.

Thus it was only by degrees that Miss Collier-Floodgaye, through her ineffective, rather masculine perceptions, realized these slow accumulations of jealousy. In vain she would try to soothe her Companion, saying " Tibbits, if I did not care for you more than for any of my other friends (other friends, indeed !) is it likely that I should make you my heir ? I am only leaving small sums of money or mementoes, such as my little bits of jewellery, to other people : but, meanwhile, do remind me to send for my lawyer."

This gradual sensing on the part of the old lady, of the fact that her Companion was suffering, followed by clumsy attempts to placate and reassure her, only embittered Miss Bramley the more. Really she could not see why she should remind Cecilia about a lawyer, simply in order that the old lady might make a fool of herself by leaving things to people like the Floodgays : after all, if the old lady would only learn to behave sensibly, would stop running after High Church Clergymen and their families, she would be able to remember things for herself. And if people encouraged her to ruin her health and wear out her memory, it was only fitting that they should learn by experience that such conduct would not pay in the end. But Miss Collier-Floodgaye continued : " You must jog my memory about the lawyer." " Don't forget to remind me to see my solicitor" : these and like phrases were often addressed to Miss

Bramley. At other times she would pet and pat her Companion. But no display of affection could now convince Miss Bramley. She possessed insight into her friend's character, as well as jealousy : and, in spite of her annoyance, was genuinely concerned about her. There could be little doubt that the old lady was growing weaker, more absent-minded and weaker, every day : while the very vigour of the effort which she made to disguise this growing vagueness from the Floodgays, only aided and facilitated the disintegration. Miss Bramley realized the state of her friend's health, and fretted over it : was, indeed, perhaps the only person, except Elisa, who grasped fully the seriousness of it, for the Floodgays and the frequenters of their Salon saw merely an old lady who was growing older—they did not understand the steep angle of the decline.

Elisa in a dumb, flaxen way (though the flax was now being transformed by the passage of years into white cotton) had become attached to the old lady, and to the considerable donations which her presence in the hotel during the winter months signified. Not that for a moment the housemaid stopped grumbling (for what was the use of a little money and a half-day off if one was treated like a brute beast and had no one to walk out with, or to keep one company, nobody to talk to except Miss Thompson and the Sexton ?), but, at the same time, she was willing in the intervals of her lamentations to take counsel with Miss Bramley about the old lady, to aid her with the indirect advice of Miss Thompson, who, in her turn, was but a mask for Miss Waddington, and to try to think out what could be done.

Miss Collier-Floodgaye slept so badly now that, her Companion decided, after consultation with Elisa, to move into the same bedroom as the old lady ; nor did she encounter from her any of the objections to this plan which she had expected ; which in a way made things no better, for it amounted to a tacit admission by the old lady of the gravity of her sufferings. All these mutterings in the darkness, these sighings and turnings were, it seemed to the Companion, the tokens of a fatal return to childhood. Occasionally the old woman's deep voice would toll out sentences, fragments of conversation, though penetrated by no meaning which the Companion could distinguish : yet in these emotional phrases were recurrent the same words, the same names. This muffled crying-out, these appeals to persons unknown to her, persons who had probably passed long ago into oblivion, except in the memory of this lonely, old woman, this hovering of an enfeebled mind upon scenes enacted so long ago, made the Companion excessively uneasy. Her sleep was soon invaded by the same microbe of restlessness, and she would lie there for hours listening. For in this dwelling upon days that were past, there was something deeply disturbing, as though one were to hear an old harp, lying dusty and untouched in a lumber-room, suddenly give out again its golden and liquid music. It was terrible, Miss Bramley felt, to see someone, of whom, in spite of everything, one was fond, sliding down the few final years in the space of so many days.

But Dr. MacRacket, cheerful and sensible, did not take an alarmist view of Miss Collier-Floodgaye's health : he insisted that she was, as he phrased it, " sound in heart and limb." The change in her was temporary, she would grow stronger again. " Leave it to me, Miss Bramley. Don't fret. Everything will come right," he would prophesy in his buoyant way. And, in any case, in a seaside town where many old ladies and gentlemen remain in complete dispossession of their faculties until well on into their tenth decade, the doctor was not inclined to treat the question of mind or memory too gravely. After all, her eyesight was as good as ever . . . and with a little regular exercise : and she should try " Plasmon " biscuits—they are wonderful : and then look at old Mr. Woodly-Cateham on the West Cliff, ninety-two and every tooth in his head—or Mrs. Kinderbull, look at her for example ! Oh, no, no, no. It would be all right, quite all right, he assured her.

The optimism of Doctor MacRacket did not persuade Miss Bramley to alter her view of the situation. She was very uneasy : and the most difficult feature of it was that while Miss Collier-Floodgaye's health had grown obviously worse, while her mind was loosening every day, her resolution of character, her obstinacy, in fact, remained unaltered, and, apparently, unalterable. She still insisted on driving round to St. Saviour's Vicarage every day : insisted on going to Mrs. Floodgay's bridge-parties, when she was invited, insisted above all, on attending Morning Service every Sunday, whatever atrocities the weather might perpetrate, and on further tiring herself by lunching with the Floodgays after it. Any battle entered upon with the old lady on these habits of hers, merely succeeded in making her angry, thus injuring her health, without affecting her determination to do as she wanted.

While her character remained otherwise unaffected, her religious fervour was growing. It is probable that Miss Collier-Floodgaye was never now so happy as when she was in church. The music droned right through her, bringing exquisite sensations to her tired nerves : the lights danced round her with a joyous rhythm, the incense brought back to her the sunlit gardens of her youth. She was strangely moved, her sombre spirit was calmed and cheered : while the prestige of the Floodgays was still further enhanced, for it was through them that she had learnt to appreciate this final and most abiding pleasure.

After many weeks, Miss Bramley contrived to wring out of her one concession. Ground down by perpetual fret, Miss Collier-Floodgaye promised that she would walk for half an hour, every " fine " day, round the plot of grass in front of the hotel. This place was the most sheltered from the wind.

CHAPTER XXII

PROMENADE

" Shuffle and hurry, idle feet and slow,
    Grim fall and merry fall, so ugly all !
  Why do you hurry ?   Where is there to go ?
  Why are you shouting ?   Who is there to call ? "

EVERY afternoon at three-thirty down the steps of the
hotel, out from under the bonnet-like porch, would issue
forth well-armoured against the cold, grey air, Miss
Collier-Floodgaye and Miss Bramley. The elder lady
would lean heavily on a stick, and be buttressed upon the
other side by the wispy figure of her Companion. Thin
as ever, Miss Bramley had now allowed her dress to cut
clean away from Rectory conventions. It showed an
intensified tendency to break into small waves of lace,
diminutive eddies and whirls of jewellery, which suited
ill so sallow, defined yet meagre an appearance. Her
fixed smile, invented originally to overspread the little
nervous tic, the contraction of the muscles round the
mouth, that must be considered as the memorial which
Miss Fansharpe had erected to herself during her own
life-time—a memorial, too, on which it had been necessary for that dear old person to spend incessant care and
infinite time—had become habitual, though it was now
contradicted by a pained yet defiant expression in the
eyes.

Miss Collier-Floodgaye, however, admitted of no
relaxation in her dress. She was sombre, gaunt and
outlined as ever. So bony had she become, indeed,
that just as Bernini shows us Daphne on the very verge

of being transformed into a green luxuriance, so the old lady appeared to have been arrested at the exact moment of sprouting into antlers at every extremity. Daphne's hands, Daphne's feet seem to have been caught on the point of budding into delicious little curls of spring foliage; thus, too, Miss Collier-Floodgaye's extremities always suggested that they were about to unfold creakingly into similar ramifications of horn. It may be that the bones were already wishing to assert independence, plotting to be rid of the flesh, impatient to start on their long and solitary vigil.

The two contrasted figures would painfully emerge out of the hotel, disentangling themselves slowly from the clustered and overwhelming detail. Their procedure was always the same, fixed by formal, invariable rule. First they would pause for an instant at the bottom of the steps ; then, looking carefully round, they would lumber across the road, past the comfortable-smelling cab-shelter, past the cabmen—who were standing about in extinct green liveries decorated with tarnished brass buttons, and battered, rakish top-hats, stamping their feet to keep them warm, thrashing their arms across their bodies, and blowing long trails of dragon-breath upon the air—greeting these amiably as they went by. The Companion would now scrape a clumsy key in its rusty lock, and they would pass through the angry-sounding gate into this green heart of the town. Heavily they would revolve round it, on an asphalt path, the black and white marking of which always revived in Miss Bramley's subconscious mind an impression of her aunt's Dalmatians and thus made her think, though herself could not imagine why, of Miss Titherley-Bramley. As they circled laboriously, two winter-vistas would be revealed to them, for the whole space in front of the hotel resolved itself into a long, narrow rectangle, of which the vast bulk of the hotel, looming up over them, formed one of the wide lines. The other, opposite, was taken up by a row of houses, its chief feature the purple flushed façade of the " Gentlemen's Club," from which seemed to rise a stertorous palpitation, a sound of hurrying and harrying. The small sides of the rectangle were formed by the vistas framed in between these two lines of building. One prospect disclosed a side canal of shiny, blue-grey road, on which, in the foreground, floated two weighty islets, supporting lamp-posts, and further embellished by the presence of numerous vestigial guardians, absurd little phallic pillars of polished Aberdeen granite. These, by their present uselessness, yet serve, as do so many relics, for testimony to past glories ; evoked the roaring 'sixties, the stentorian 'seventies, when " Champagne Charlie " was the folk-song of the decade, when Newborough had been a centre of the social world, when lamp-post climbing was con-sidered a suitable midnight diversion for any self-respecting young masher, and when the municipal authorities had striven to guard these highly decorative lamp-posts, which were their particular darlings, by hemming them in with appropriate stumbling-blocks. That, at least, seems the reasonable explanation. But now such glories were past, and the only purpose for which these little pillars could suffice, was that over them the loitering errand-boy could practise perpetually his favourite game of leap-frog, to the neglect of basket and patron.

Beyond this broad canal, with its pair of heavy, for-malized rafts, showed an Italian-Comedy perspective of three streets, full of shops and hurrying little figures, or women pushing perambulators, and pausing to gaze in at the windows with feminine rapacity. Toward the end of their walk, the ladies would see the arch-magician of the town in black coat and bowler hat, walking straight down one pavement of the middle perspective and back along the other, touching the lamps with a long wand, whereupon in each glass flickered a green flame.

The narrow side of the rectangle disclosed distant grey cliffs and hammering sea. The old battle between static and dynamic was once more to be seen clearly in action : while as if to sum up that ancient, fierce feud, in the centre of the circle round which the two ladies revolved, were the twin symbols, Cannon and Anchor. Down below the rolling, wallowing monsters were lashing the cliffs. Sometimes the immense creatures would be crowned with sparkling diadems of foam as they flailed the rocks ; or, again, they were washed roaring on to the beach, there to dissolve into an instantaneous death, as in the atmosphere of this world would a creature from another planet be, before you could see it, disrupted utterly. In a moment these bellowing giants had been transformed into a receding avalanche of snow that would slowly sizzle backward over the pebbles, to be reorganized into various other oncoming bodies.

On the backs of the cliffs across the ravine, above this ceaseless game of thrust and parry, the white houses of the West Cliff, rubbed by the last, frayed edges of winter sunshine, could be seen gleaming and golden as the gorgeous howdahs that elephants carry at a durbar.

Round and round the green circle the two ladies would walk, eyed from the porch by John, the hall-porter, round those symbols, Crimean Cannon and Pirate Anchor. From the houses on the other side, too, a close watch would be kept on them by the representatives of Miss Waddington and Mrs. Shrubfield. Even opera-glasses, even a telescope, were not unknown as the instruments of this intense scrutiny.

The old lady's spirits seemed very low, and she hardly spoke to Miss Bramley at all during their walk.

CHAPTER XXIII

TEA

' On shining altars of Japan they raise
The silver lamp, and fiery spirits blaze ;
From silver spouts the grateful liquors glide,
And China's earth receives the smoking tyde."

INSTEAD of resting after this exercise, the old lady
would insist, more often than not, on lumbering round
in a cab to have tea with the Floodgays. There was no
stopping her when she was in these moods : but it
infuriated Miss Bramley because really it was difficult
to have much patience with a friend who continued
obstinately to wear herself out for such people. Look at
Miss Waddington ! Now, there was a case in point.
She must be older than Cecilia, much older : but she
was too sensible, too well-brought-up (perhaps that was
it) to fatigue herself running after comparative strangers
(in a sense, a comparative stranger was regarded by
Miss Bramley as being even more of a double-dyed
stranger than a total stranger, for in addition to the
Ishmael-quality common to both, there was, somehow
or other, in the word " comparative " an implication of
dubiety) and ought to last many years longer, dear old
lady.

It was at this hour, deserted after her walk, that the
Companion, unless invited to tea by Miss Waddington,
felt more solitary than at any other time in the day :
for tea was the only ritual to which she did not present
a protestant attitude. Tea, to Miss Bramley, meant
infinitely more than a mere beverage : it was a synonym

271

for an hour of sprightly conversation and agreeable camaraderie: while to be forced for ever to have tea by herself was to her the very proof of being outcast from the worlds of fire-lit rooms and friendship.

Thus one afternoon the desolate Miss Bramley was sitting alone in the " lounge," trying to steel her will before ringing the bell to order a lonely, an early tea. She could not make her mind up to it. Seated, as she was, in that echoing, shadowy room, her mind wandered down the long avenue of pleasant trees that lay behind her, a diminishing perspective of summer fêtes-champêtres or of brightly-lit interiors, with the flickering cockscombs of the flames mirroring themselves in china cups and china bowls, while the clear silver music of spoon clinking against cup mingled with the refined hum of well-bred voices, not too loud, nor too deprecatingly soft. Even those first teas at the Rectory at home, under the scented shade of the cedar, the seed of which had been brought from Lebanon by some fervent former incumbent, had been charming and gay: after Mildred's marriage, herself had been allowed to pour out the tea and preside. The curates had always helped to make things " go," and it had been so pretty, with the beds of flowers and evergreens. Then, best of all, followed the drawing-room at Llandriftlog, with its hissing, silver kettle straddling prodigiously over a flame, a flame so hallowed that it was never allowed to be annihilated by such rude processes as blowing from puffed-out cheeks. As, formerly, in various countries, the criminal of illustrious birth was, when at last the dreadful hour of earthly expiation struck, suspended from a silken cord, lest the common hangman's hempen rope should sully his nobility, thus here too, when the time came for the sacred flame to be quenched, a special implement, shaped like a trumpet and wrought of silver, was provided for its stately extinction. Down this, which seemed the pipe of some fairy music inaudible to the grosser senses of mankind, Miss Bramley had been allowed to practise: on it, indeed, at one time, she had attained to a considerable degree of virtuosity, so that when people were present she would be sent for, from her corner, to perform. "Where is Teresa?" Miss Fansharpe used to demand, "Ask her to come here and blow it out for us." There had been so many little touches of that sort about Miss Fansharpe's teas, bowls of hot water, over the steam of which were balanced plates of scones—those special, little " soda " scones which had been provided for the enticement and delectation of Dr. Brometoken, and all sorts of small cakes and biscuits, things unusual, and refined and " out-of-the-common." After she had left Llandriftlog there had been some nice teas at Mildred's, often with a Fuller's walnut-cake, while the thin, tinkling treble of teaspoons harmonized with the distant, more manly music of " ping-pong." And there had been many enjoyable teas at the Badminton, very lively, in the " Palm Lounge," with little tartlets filled with tinned cherries, very French and prettily made, and people going in and out. Lately, too, had come all those delightful intimate tea-parties at Miss Waddington's. How she wished she was going there to-day; but she did not like to call there too often, unless definitely invited: for Miss Waddington asked her constantly, and she did not wish to appear " pushing " . . . why even the teas which Cecilia and herself used to have in the drawing-room—before the old lady had met the Floodgays—had been pleasurable. The tea was good, and there had been

tea-cakes : and, until it was ready, she usually asked
Miss Bramley to sing. She remembered it all so well,
because it was before tea one day that she had sung
for the first time, " Because God made Thee Mine,"
and Cecilia had made her repeat it twice, she had liked
it so much . . . and here . . . now . . . she was alone
in an empty room, for Cecilia (it was no use pretending
to oneself that it was not so) *preferred* to sit there at
St. Saviour's Vicarage, boasting of her money, boasting,
like a badly-brought-up child, of her money, and being
humbugged—for that was what it came to—by that sly,
simpering girl with the red hair, and by her disagreeable,
scheming, and " *fast* " mother.

As Miss Bramley pondered on these past scenes, and
compared them with the present, which she was still
unable to face, for to-day, really, she could hardly bear
to order her solitary tea, a page-boy came in, bearing
on a salver a card, the alternate corners of which were
turned up and down. On this she read the name of Mrs.
Shrubfield, while written below, in a rather shaky hand,
was " *Ma chérie*, would you care to come for a drive,
pour passer le temps, with your ' *molta vecchia* ' friend ?
Then we might have tea somewhere ?—L.S."

How odd her coming round like this, for she never
called at the hotel as a rule ; because she did not know
Miss Collier-Floodgaye, Miss Bramley imagined. But
how thoughtful and kind of the old lady to " look her
up " like this. " Tell Mrs. Shrubfield that Miss Bramley
will be delighted " she said to the page, and hurried
upstairs to get her things on. Soon she was ready, and
going down the steps toward the carriage. The hood of
the Victoria was up, for it was a cold, dank evening and
Mrs. Shrubfield leant out with a true, if rather unsteady,

old-world courtesy, to receive her young friend, for such
she invariably termed her. Thus framed, between hood
and box, the pyramid presented an imposing spectacle.
So great was Mrs. Shrubfield's pleasure at seeing Miss
Bramley, that from her eye it was obvious that she was
suspended half-way between tears and laughter. The
jet of it was softened by a pendent tear. Miss Bramley
got in, and they drove off at a considerable pace. Mrs.
Shrubfield had come out, she said, because she had not
been feeling very well, and had thought that a drive might
do her good. It had struck her suddenly, why not call
at the Superb for that little *darling*, Miss Bramley, and
take her for an outing. She was not feeling at all well,
shaken you know, and very tired, very tired indeed
Her speech was sibilant and indistinct, Miss Bramley
noticed : from weakness, no doubt. Mrs. Shrubfield
was inclined to attribute this unfortunate state of
feebleness in which she found herself partly to those
dreadful " tonics," (" Never take tonichs, they're absho-
lutely fatal," she said. " Tonichsh only make you tired,
O SHO tired ") and partly to the fact that she had
foolishly indulged in a claw of lobster for lunch. Lobster
always had that effect on her. Curious. It was silly of
her to take it. And (hélas !) she was getting old :
washn't whatch she ush'be." A little air was the thing,
she had said to herself : and the coachman (had been
with her years) had wanted little-air too, you know,
lill'air : not feeling quite the thing, he had said to her.
Perhaps he had eaten lobster too (and here Mrs. Shrubfield in sudden, spasmodic recovery, laughed loud and
long). No doubt that was it : lobshter, you know what
seaside towns are !

He seemed a very fast driver, Miss Bramley thought.

And the carriage rocked so. She did not like to say anything, but she could not help wondering whether the motion of the carriage was not connected with Mrs. Shrubfield being unwell. However, in spite of feeling tired, she was so genial and pleasant. Even now, though, she complained of not getting enough air : notwithstanding the fact that the carriage appeared to be positively whizzing through square and crescent (they must be very good horses to go like that, but Miss Bramley could not see quite in which direction they were going, as the hood was up)—and would send her guardian wild-beast spinning like a roulette-ball round her neck in the effort to disentangle tooth from toe, and so gain more ventilation. The horses drew up, all at once, with such a jar that the footman nearly fell off the box (he was not feeling well either, apparently. Miss Bramley began to feel quite worried about them. She hoped so much that they had not *all* been poisoned) and there they were . . . at Miss Waddington's. What a surprise, for Mrs. Shrubfield had never mentioned where they were going for tea. Indeed she seemed somewhat startled too, at first—she had not expected to be there shoshun, she said. She got out, saying " Here we are," with her usual dignity of bearing ; and it was just tea-time. So much nicer than sitting in the Superb with no one to talk to. They rang the bell (Mrs. Shrubfield did it herself, and waved the footman away : but it was difficult to find the bell at once in the dark. Where wash-it ?) several times, but for some time nobody answered it. Then Ella came running to the door. " I am so sorry to have kept you waiting, but I've only just come in. I can't imagine where Thompson is. But of course Aunt Hester will see both of you—she is never out to you. Let me straighten your

bonnet, dear (to Mrs. Shrubfield). There, that's better ! "
And she led them upstairs. Ella threw open the door ;
there sat Miss Waddington, and with her, to Miss
Bramley's intense astonishment, were (and actually
sitting down) Thompson the parlourmaid and . . .
Elisa ! . . .

For a moment, Miss Bramley felt that she was going
to faint, it seemed so unreal and dreamlike. Surely it
was not quite the thing for a Waddington to do, to have
servants to tea in that familiar manner ? What could
she want with Elisa ? And it was so queer that Elisa
should never have mentioned it. Why, Miss Bramley
was almost sure that the German maid had told her she
was going to tea with the Sexton at the Cemetery. It
was extraordinary. . . .

But the effect of the scene that greeted Miss Bramley
was as nothing compared with the result of that lady's
entry upon Miss Waddington, whose fragile old face
(just like a piece of carved ivory, Miss Bramley used to
think) was now suffused with colour, contorted with
varying emotions. The master-eye was swift as ever in
diagnosis : she took in the situation at a glance. Louise
was having another of her " bouts " evidently, and it
was all that fool-of-a-girl again. But this time, it was
too much. Obviously it was not safe to leave the creature
by herself for a moment. The idiot should pack up
to-night, and leave to-morrow morning : and Miss
Waddington would alter her will as soon as the lawyer
could get down to see her.

Meanwhile it was difficult to know what to say.
Fortunately Thompson could be relied upon. By this
time she had already dragged Elisa, still pallidly greeting
Miss Bramley, out of the room. Mrs. Shrubfield was

sobered by her consciousness of the enormity for which
she was responsible, and remained for the moment silent
but gasping, as if having come to the surface after a
dip into ice-cold water. Miss Waddington could therefore concentrate on the two most important points—how
best to disguise from Miss Bramley the actual nature
of Mrs. Shrubfield's illness, and how best to account
to the Companion for the visit upon which she had
intruded. It would never do to leave it unexplained.
That would only make her think of it the more.

Miss Waddington was determined to restore order.
The first thing to do was to look pleasant again, as if
nothing had happened. The only drawback was that
then Ella might think her aunt was pleased with her.
Never mind, the fool would quickly be undeceived after
the departure of the guests.

Oh, Miss Waddington was so pleased to see them.
What a delicious, unexpected visit ! And some fresh tea
was coming up in a minute. Thompson was just getting
it. " Louise, dear," she said to Mrs. Shrubfield, " you
must break your rules for once, and have tea. It will
freshen you up. You look depressed." Indeed, a startled,
tearful expression was fixed in the eyes of that lady.
Thompson, relapsed into the perfect parlour-maid,
brought in the tea, and the hostess began to explain.

How curious to think that Elisa was the maid who
looked after Miss Bramley. What a strange coincidence
(here Mrs. Shrubfield, seeing that she must help, with
a supreme effort, overcame her feelings and remarked
in a voice, which harboured a fat tear of remorse,
" Doesn't it only show how small the world is ! "—too
tired to talk for herself, she wisely acted the part of
Greek chorus). Really, it was extraordinary (" the sort

of thing one reads about," Mrs. Shrubfield added) extraordinary—why, Miss Waddington had known the girl for
years—she was interested in Mission Work ("nothing like
Misshun Work," Mrs. Shrubfield thought, but Miss
Waddington flashed a glance that signalled silence on her)
of all sorts, and especially in its endeavours in some of the
bigger German cities. One of her German friends had
written to her, asking her to " keep an eye " on the girl.
And Miss Waddington felt one could not do enough for
foreigners in a strange land. They must feel so alone,
so deserted (dear old thing, Miss Bramley thought, how
charitable she was !) so she often asked the poor thing
to tea, just to show her that one person regarded her as
a human being like herself : and, she had found it
better (" mush better ") to have Thompson there too.
It put the foreigner more at her ease ; but Miss Waddington had always told Elisa not to mention her, for she
hated these little actions of hers to get about. If these
little actions one did were once to become public property,
one would be prevented from doing any more ; because
people would say (here the tragic chorus, unable to
repress itself further, joined in with, " You know what
people are ") that one did them simply to gain applause
(sweet old lady, that was just like her ! the Companion
reflected). And Miss Waddington had to admit that
she thought the girl was really grateful to her and
understood (" Oh, yesh, she undershtood "). Why the
very fact that she had never mentioned her to Miss
Bramley, went to prove it. A good girl, in her way.
" But, perhaps, my dear," she concluded, to Miss Bramley, " Perhaps you had better not say anything to her
about it. It may embarrass her. Promise me, dear."

Really Miss Waddington was a wonderful old lady.

Her consideration for others continually came as a surprise to one, Miss Bramley reflected. Mrs. Shrubfield seemed very quiet; she hoped so much that she was feeling better. As a matter of fact, by an intense effort of will, Miss Waddington was still holding the unusually jovial lady in check. Her expression had changed; admiration now mingled in it with repentance. But, if still rather overcome, she meant to atone to some little extent for her misdemeanours.

Miss Bramley had to return to the Superb in order to dress for dinner. She rose to go. Miss Waddington commanded Mrs. Shrubfield not to move. "You're too tired, dear. Stay where you are for the present. Deah Teresa (this was the first time she had called Miss Bramley by her Christian name) will understand "— by which she really meant that under the circumstances she hoped Miss Bramley would *not* understand.

Now was Mrs. Shrubfield's moment of triumph. She must do something that would show her normal, sober grasp of foreign languages, and, by installing her still more surely in the Companion's favour, would blind that lady to all little oddities of manner. She did not get up. Instead, she enunciated clearly, but not without effort, " Teresa, *Liebchen*, may I ' tutoyer ' you, as well ? " Miss Bramley walked out into the dark night, where wind and sea could be heard in their perpetual tourney, more than ever enchanted with her two friends. Dear old ladies! And she looked up at the lighted windows with a gust of emotion.

Up there in the fire-gilded room an affecting scene was taking place. The knowledge that through her failing she had nearly brought their plans to naught, hurled away with her own hand the Cup of Victory,

the intensity of the exertion she had made, on realizing
this, to retrieve the position, and to support her fellow-
leader, had been too much for Mrs. Shrubfield. The tears
which she had long held back were flowing. Indeed
this was the only time in their acquaintance that Mrs.
Shrubfield ever mentioned " it " to Miss Waddington.
" Forgive me, Hester," she choked, " if I have been at
all foolish. But I have been so tired out by the whole
affair, that I simply had to take something to keep my
strength up. And, you see, if one's not used to it . . .
I wish I'd never seen that horrid lame, old woman :
and that little beast Mrs. Floodgay is blackening our
characters everywhere. It'll be the death of me." So
moved was she at this instant, that for perhaps the only
time in her life, her lingual gifts deserted her " It will
be the death of me," she repeated, " I have a good mind
to leave Newborough for ever, and find a little ' *ventre-
a-terre* ' in London."

CHAPTER XXIV

THE POOL

" Sleep is a reconciling,
A rest that peace begets ;
Doth not the sun rise smiling
When fair at even he sets ?
Rest you, then, rest, sad eyes
Melt not in weeping
While she lies sleeping."

MISS BRAMLEY had begun to shrink from the long black nights. She was sure that her friend's health was worse, but this the doctor would not admit. The Companion dreaded the sighs, the strugglings, of the old woman in her sleep. These turnings and groanings must have communicated to her their infection, for she was not, in this sense, inherently at all nervous : but now she was filled with apprehension, startled by any sound, however obvious its explanation. It was disturbing to lie there listening, in the lulls that occasionally intervened between the bellowing of the gales outside, to the broken murmuring and deep susurration of the old lady in her sleep. It was not natural. With whom was she conversing in the dark, wintry recesses of her mind ; what was it she feared, the image of something that had occurred at her life's beginning, or the shadow of that which was yet to come to pass—the only sure event that was still left before her, an event of which she would only be able to trace the prognostic shadow, never to grasp the reality by which it was projected ? There were times, indeed, when Miss Bramley felt that she could not go on like this, could not stand it any longer. The days, burdened by loneliness, the nights with their load of fear, were becoming unsupportable. How she wished that she had a little money put away, a little money of her *own*, so that she could live somewhere quietly, near Mildred. Why she might even go out to Malta for a winter, to see Peregrine; the Broometokens would be there. It would be nice to see them again. Of course, though, even if she were suddenly to find herself rich, she could never leave Cecilia, trying as she was, in her present state. Still, there were times . . .

Life revolved regularly enough. Tea and bridge; church and luncheon on Sunday; the walk in the afternoon: tea and bridge again; dinners, complaints of failing memory, and troubled nights that opened out like a telescope.

As for Cecilia's memory, Miss Bramley was determined to aid it no longer. It was bad for her, taught her to depend too much on others. Certainly she was not going to remind the old lady about seeing the lawyer. Surely, as she was always asking to be reminded, she could remember to do it for herself? But that was Cecilia all over. She could always call things to mind, when it was useless, too early or too late. And she only wanted to see the solicitor in order " to make things easier " for the Floodgays (the Companion could hear in her own mind, at this moment the girl saying " Aunt Cecilia," in her silly, ingratiating manner). Well, Miss Bramley was resolved not to interfere, one side or the other. It was no concern of hers : but she was not going out of her way to favour the plans of a scheming woman like Mrs. Floodgay. No, if Cecilia wished to do that sort of thing, she must remember it for herself. Miss

Bramley was willing to do anything else for her, but not that.

If Miss Collier-Floodgaye showed a tendency in any direction, it was toward tiring herself still further. She was inclined to sit up later now, and would seize on any plea for postponing the hour of attempted slumber. Dinner in the hotel was at 7.30, and when the old lady had first come to Newborough, she had been in the habit of retiring to rest at ten. But this winter, even if there was no excuse for sitting up, even if she was alone with her Companion—with whom, now that her aged mind was always and entirely occupied with the Floodgays, she found conversation difficult—in a vast room that stood dark, empty and deserted, it was usually well past eleven o'clock before Miss Bramley could persuade her to go to bed. The Companion considered that a long night, restful or unrestful, was necessary to the health of anyone, especially if that person were old and failing ; but Miss Collier-Floodgaye was content with little sleep, for, with a surer judgment, she perhaps realized that just as bed is the most common scaffold for men's execution, so slumber is the most venomous foe of the elderly. Indeed it is very noticeable that the old favour late hours and early rising, usually attributing this to the fact that they require less sleep than the young. But, in all probability, it is that they are aware, without thinking it out, that directly the controlling will slumbers, old age can seize on the body, attempting to assassinate it as it lies there helpless. How often do we hear of fortunate people who died in their sleep ; a peaceful end, it is said ! Yet who is to know the agony of terror which may have engulfed them in their last moments of dreaming, and which, since they never woke from it, was to them the reality? The hideous nightmare from which we awake is yet sufficient to impregnate the whole day that follows with the blue-black poisonous tint of nightshade, though we know it to be but a fantasy spun out by the unconscious mind, that lumber-room of acquired and inherited memories. But to those that die under the spell of such a storm of horror, the dream is the actuality. They die writhing under the tortures of the Inquisition, stabbed by a murderer, falling down a precipice, or entangled in some catastrophe so involved, in the grip of a fear so intense, that the waking mind cannot conceive it, as truly as if these experiences had befallen them in fact. Perhaps Miss Collier-Floodgaye knew that the night was waiting to catch her, to swallow her up for ever.

The old lady seemed bent, however, on fatiguing herself in every possible way. She was resolute on participating in any gaiety, or attempt at gaiety, that was being planned. This may have been the result of an effort to prove to herself that she was still young, or it may have been due to a belief that so long as she behaved in a normal manner, not refraining from ordinary pleasures, no such unique or final a thing as death could overcome her. Thus, too, Bess of Hardwick is stated to have believed that she would never die while she continued to have new houses built for her, for building had been her life's interest. And, in truth, it was not until there came a hard frost which prevented the laying of bricks, that the venerable lady passed away.

As all else in Miss Collier-Floodgaye weakened, her religious fervour increased. Once, or even twice, a week she would now attend Morning Service at St. Saviour's on a week day, while she never failed to be in her pew

every Sunday : and it tired her as much as anything,
for she allowed it to draw so much vitality away from
her. But the flowers (how well May arranged them !)
the warmth, the colour, the incense, the crowd, the music,
all mingled in an atmosphere that was exciting to her.
The coloured lights would flicker hither and thither,
the colours would change, shift, graduate, in tone as the
organ sounded out, rose up majestically toward the roof
that redoubled the volume of it, till her senses were
caught in all these combining strands that joined together,
almost invisibly, the silken intricacies of a spiritual
cobweb that entangled her reason. The voices of the
singing boys became the actual, welcoming roulades of
the angels, while the rolling thunder of the accompanying
music was transformed into the authentic, awe-inspiring
accents of the Supreme Being. Her spirit was excessively
troubled. Heaven and Hell took on a new and compre-
hensible significance. Heaven was a ritual and emotive
affair, compounded of colour and music, such as this
service, but transcendent and eternal, Hell a black,
never-ending night of fear and torture.

. . . . . .

Shortly before Christmas there was a ball in aid of
the Life-Boat. It was a local festivity. The County
refused to take any part in it, for they could not spare
a moment from the varying massacres of the season.
But though this abstention may have detracted from
the social interest, it is not so certain that it did not
promote the gaiety, of the occasion. The townspeople
displayed an abandon, the secret of which, having been
instilled in most of them as children by Mr. de Flouncey,
whose *joie-de-vivre*, as we have seen, was derived from

a long line of hypothetic French noblemen, could be regarded as Continental by adoption.

Of course Miss Collier-Floodgaye had taken tickets for Cécile and her mother, and, long before the dance had started, was waiting for them in the hall. An inappropriate enough figure she looked, among the accumulating crowd of revellers, all at present silent, pulling on and off their gloves but looking as pleasant as tense expectation would allow.

Miss Bramley had refused to attend this function. She could not express how much she disapproved of the whole proceeding. If Cecilia was determined to shatter what little health remained to her, she, at any rate, refused to take any responsibility in the matter. She was not going to tell Mrs. Floodgay what she thought of it, for that would be undignified, " playing into their hands " ; instead she would allow her outraged feelings to be reflected in her manner, which she had contrived as a mirror for them. But Miss Bramley was really worried about her friend. When she had left her standing in the hall, her anger had evaporated, leaving only a residue of intense concern. The Companion, therefore, made up her mind to watch the dance from the gallery for a while. There she found Elisa, so immersed in the scene of revelry below that she had lost her gift of loquacious lamentation, and had relapsed into that other self, the dumb, flaxen automaton.

Looking down, Miss Bramley could see the girl, dressed in green, (that hair, again) of course pulling at her glove, swinging her programme from its attached pencil. And there, sitting against the wall, were Cecilia and Mrs. Floodgay. The music throbbed out, drumming round the ceiling like a swarm of bees. The couples began to revolve, as though a bed of multicoloured flowers had determined to arrange itself in new patterns. One or two tired and fading blossoms drooped at the side, pushed against the border by the more vigorous flowers.

Cecilia looked absolutely worn out, Miss Bramley thought, so weary and sombre. It was ridiculous for her to pretend that she enjoyed it. She ought not to be sitting there, tiring herself by talking through all that noise. Nothing could be worse for her. Mrs. Floodgay, evidently, was not even listening to her stories. She just sat there, tapping a white shoe in time, more or less, to the music, and piercing her daughter with a reproachfully bright and benignant eye. Not a clumsy movement, not an awkward word on Cécile's part was lost upon Mrs. Floodgay (but she should not speak to the child about it while Aunt Cecilia was there. She should wait till afterward).

Miss Bramley felt angry again. It disgusted her to see her friend sitting there, talking, talking, talking. It was no use fretting—she was obviously determined to stay there all night. Miss Bramley could see that. Really she must be very strong after all. Supper at her age ! The truth of it was that she must have a wonderful constitution, and it was silly of one to worry oneself about her.

Not until past two o'clock did Miss Collier-Floodgaye come upstairs to bed. Miss Bramley had been waiting for her many an hour, for, in spite of her decision not to worry, she had been unable to obtain a moment's rest, gnawed as she was by the iron tooth of jealousy, torn by the steel claws of anxiety. There she lay, listening for the ascending, comforting chant of the lift. Many times it disappointed her. It seemed to her that she had never known it used so much, even during the biggest dances, at this time of night. And after each of its chantings, she hoped to hear the well-known footfall, accompanied by the tapping stick. So often did the lift deceive her by its cheerfulness that, by the time the footstep was heard, she had reached the stage, so well-known to expectant lovers, where, when she heard the long-awaited step, herself refused to believe in its authenticity. At last the door opened; the light was switched on, and the old lady entered.

Miss Bramley was intensely relieved; for, she did not know why, but she understood now that, under the superficial feelings of annoyance and irritation, she had been really alarmed about her friend all the evening. Well, it taught one not to be anxious, for Cecilia seemed perfectly all right. Another time, she should just go to sleep, without fretting. At the same time, Miss Bramley could not help feeling that people who behave in a manner contrary to all sane laws, ought to be made to suffer for it. After all, if herself stayed up to supper, though only half the old lady's age, she would not feel any the better for it. But, in spite of her appearance of "failing," the old lady seemed to be able to do anything she liked with impunity. And, before going to bed, she began about the lawyer again. "Would Tibbits remind her in the morning?" "If you did not tire yourself like this, dear, you would have no need to ask me to remind you," the Companion retorted, quite overcome by her irritation.

But in the night, the old lady appeared to be frightened. The faintest sound in the darkness (and any dark room is full of those inexplicable little rustlings and crepi-

tations of which what we call silence is composed)
would startle her. As soon as Miss Bramley had obtained
a moment's sleep, the old lady would wake her up.
"What's that? Do you hear it?" she would cry.
After all, there was nothing to be afraid of: and if she
behaved like other people of her age, she would not
be visited by such dumb and eyeless terrors.

At last Miss Bramley was permitted to lose herself in a
real stretch of slumber. In the fantastic place and period
where she found herself, Mrs. Floodgay had somehow
or other become Companion to Miss Fansharpe, and
the Colonel—Colonel Fansharpe of whom Miss Bramley
had not thought for many years—had come on a long
visit to his aunt. And Cécile had been engaged as a
housemaid, but Miss Fansharpe did not trust her and
wished to have her placed in her Home, while, at the
same time, she was busily occupied in playing her old
game of cat-and-mouse with Mrs. Floodgay. And dear
old Dr. Broometoken was there, and they were all going
out to Malta to stay with him. Then Dr. Broometoken
said how delightful it would be to bathe . . . yes,
bathe . . . and as they plunged into the embracing
ocean, it became a still-water pool overhung by long
green branches. She was nearly at the bottom of a deep,
calm pool, filled with wan water-flowers and coral
rocks, when a sound, an ever so faint sound, called her
up through the various layers of consciousness. She was
swimming up and up, through the green waters to the
dim daylight at the top of the pond. Would she come
to the surface in time, for someone was drowning?
She could hear the strangled gurgling of the sinking
body. She must hurry to rescue it. Daylight filtered
with more strength into the green abysses. She was near

the top now, must rescue : and, as she gained the
surface, she was saying to herself, " I told you so,
I told you so."

The grey light was creeping stealthily into the bedroom. It was nearly eight o'clock. Elisa would be here
in a few moments now . . . but there it was again,
the sound of choking that she had heard. Miss Bramley
switched on the light.

   .   .   .   .   .   .

Yes, it was a seizure, Dr. MacRacket said. Of course
she might recover the use of her limbs. We should know
in a day or two. Oh, yes, it was inevitable. He would
send a very good nurse, a nice woman, capable and
cheerful. Miss Bramley must take care of *herself*, too,
he added. Everything would be all right. Leave it to
him. Quite all right. Nothing would be gained by taking
a pessimistic view. One must look on the bright side.
Nothing to be done really, at present, except send round
the nurse. Had she tried to speak at all ? No, not much ?

   .   .   .   .   .   .

The day, like the night that had heralded it, grew
longer and longer. The winter gales could be heard
cracking their knouts at each window, attacking the
hotel as though they were determined to overpower and
sack it, while through all this furious galloping could
yet be detected the more remote sound of the sea battering at rock and cliff. The cold light, which was the very
colour of the sea, penetrated painfully into the hotel
bedroom, where, upon her bed, the old lady lay rigid
and prone as a tree uprooted by the gale. During most
of the day, Miss Bramley thought, she was insensible.
The face had set in tragic lines, and when for a few
seconds each hour or two the spirit was dragged back

through interminable tunnels into the worn-out vessel that had contained it, the eyes flashed again with their brave, accustomed fire. But something, they made it evident, was on the old lady's mind. This occasional life, flickering through the eyes, made still more painful in contrast the surrounding deadness. As a sparking-plug attempts to fire an engine, so the eyes appeared to be engaged in an attempt, as it were, to infuse with life the stricken body. At less frequent intervals it seemed that the eyes were momentarily successful in the task they had undertaken, for from the mouth struggled a few sounds that bore a mimicking relation to human words : thus might an ape, perhaps, essay speech. During these few instants the eyes of the old woman assumed a look of remote but utter sadness, almost of despair ; contained an appeal that came from the distance of another planet. Then, utterly exhausted by the violence of this effort, the darkness of approaching night closed round her again. The nurse could make little of these simian sounds that died on the old woman's blue, cold lips. But she wanted something, of that she was sure. Before the end, very possibly, she would be able to speak. It was often like that : they spoke just before the end came. It couldn't go on for long. She was sinking, the nurse was convinced.

It seemed that these words were comprehended by the felled figure in the bed, for the eyes became insistent, begged and implored help, while for several minutes the meaningless sounds bubbled up and foamed out of the slack lips. The nurse wondered what it could be ?

But Miss Bramley could interpret these strangled utterances ; Miss Bramley knew what the eyes entreated. The old lady, ill as she was, dying perhaps, was still fretting herself about seeing the lawyer. That was what it was. Well, the Companion, for one, was not going to help her. She loved Cecilia in her shrunken and dwarfish heart, but would not aid her, in this matter, though she would have done anything else in the world for the old woman. After all, it was the Floodgays who were answerable for the terrible punishment inflicted on the gaunt, motionless body, and Miss Bramley would be party to no scheme that would benefit them ; do nothing that could be to their advantage, nothing ! Why even now they were besieging the hotel ; never a half-hour went by, but a card was brought up, and on it—in Mrs. Floodgay's writing, of course—" How is Aunt Cecilia ? Can we see her for an instant ? " or " How is Aunt Cecilia ? Does she want anything ? " It was really disgraceful to continue pestering and scheming at a time like this. They were responsible, entirely and absolutely responsible, for the old lady's plight, and Miss Bramley was not going to stretch out her little finger to help them.

The stiff figure in the bed made a renewed effort, struggled again with her words : more fiercely she fought with them. The sombre eyes, gazing from so far away, took on a more tragic glow ; for she was now aware that her Companion had grasped the meaning which she was attempting so painfully to frame. She felt no anger with her, knowing that it was affection, and no mere material greed, that prompted Miss Bramley's refusal to interpret what she understood. No, it was anguish, intolerable sorrow, that burnt from under these deep sockets. If only she could make " Tibbits " understand, give way, in time : for she realized that little time was left. But once more her enemy, the night, carried her off in his powerful, black arms, and the swollen tongue was still.

She lay quite quiet now, the bony ridges and furrows of her face very clearly marked. " No, tell Mrs. Floodgay that I can't see her," Miss Bramley was saying outside the door to John the porter. Every moment they were coming round to the hotel—that is, if they ever quitted it ! So inconsiderate. And it stirred the old lady up again. Evidently they did not mind what happened. How different was the tone of Mrs. Floodgay's note from that of Mrs. Shrubfield's.

" *Ma chère Teresa, Povera ragazza*, I have come round to see if there is anything I can do for you ? Miss Waddington is with me. You have only to say the word. Yr. sincere old friend, L. S.

P.S.—Mrs. Floodgay is here in the hall. That queer, red-haired girl of hers is crying, extraordinarily upset. It is, surely, hardly the time to make scenes of that sort. We have taken no notice of either of them."

What dear old creatures they were ! But how had they heard, Miss Bramley wondered ? However, that was like them. They were ever on the watch to help ; to try, in their quiet way, to do good.

And, indeed, it was surprising how the news of Miss Collier-Floodgaye's illness had spread. In every room facing South the news of the end of it (for such invalid veterans were not deceived by Dr. MacRacket's optimism) was awaited with interest, though with equanimity. (Another name, then, was to be struck off the list !) The sight of Mrs. Shrubfield's carriage, displaying in its open shell the two aged but indomitable leaders, kindled emotion in the ranks, and caused a thrill of loyalty and

enthusiasm to course through their knotted veins.
If it had been correct on such an occasion, if, indeed,
their asthmatic lungs had permitted of it, they would,
from their upper windows, have greeted the dauntless
Marshals with a hearty and united shout of encouragement and loyal approval.

.   .   .   .   .   .

When Dr. MacRacket called again in the evening,
Miss Collier-Floodgaye was unconscious, did not stir.
Night had imprisoned her. The doctor advised Miss
Bramley to wait up with the old lady. The nurse, too,
must stay in the room.

Miss Bramley, meanwhile, dismissed the last appeal
of the Floodgays. No, she could not see them : and they
could not see " Aunt Cecilia." Miss Collier-Floodgaye
could see no one, she added. The night passed tardily
to the watchers.

CHAPTER XXV

LAST POST
" Music, when soft voices die,
Vibrates in the memory."

THERE was no sound, no movement. The dying woman lay there unmoving, apparently unthinking. But who is to know what processes were taking place in that remote mind, buried deep in the night, what memories of childhood were reviving with a strange, if flickering, intensity on that dark screen ? There was present, undoubtedly, the ever strengthening motif of religion. The rainbow-winged butterflies hovered and danced again over the stone walls, through the warm, droning air. The voices pursued them yet more swiftly, trying to secure the fragile, beating sails in their nets, while the host of cherubs that swept after them through the upper dimness clapped their golden wings in leaping, swallow-like flight.

Toward six o'clock in the morning, the expected change set in. The old woman opened her eyes and tried to speak : her brain was alive once more. Perhaps the inanimation of the rest of her body served to give the eyes a more than normal share of life, enabled them to flame with a concentrated intensity. In their dark, cavernous recesses they smouldered fiercely, and the fear in them had deepened into terror. During these few moments, the look of appeal, of entreaty, became doubly vehement ; they spoke, indeed, with infinitely more ease than the tongue, which, in its piteous struggle was tapping

out idiot-tunes against the palate. Not for an instant
did these terrible eyes leave Miss Bramley. As she
moved, they followed her, within the limits imposed
upon them by the immobility of the neck, trunk and limbs.
The Companion, it may be, felt a little inclined to move
out of their range, to busy herself with the trivial para-
phernalia of illness, of pillows, eau-de-cologne and medi-
cine : but they met her anew as she moved within their
orbit. Yet they exercised a fascination over her. She
could not for long look away. Now with the final,
supreme effort of a mighty frame and a strong will, the
old woman contrived to utter a deep, warning moan—
a sound which, though it lacked words, possessed the
old authentic and authoritative note, the personal music
of her voice—and with a shuddering of the entire form,
moved her right hand in the gesture of signing a paper.

The nurse wondered what the patient wanted, as the
old woman relapsed into night. It must be the last
return of vigour, she thought. So often they do something like that. But, just as the old woman was travelling
away from the light, dragged down those endless black
tunnels and corridors, something again touched in her
a chord of memory. Her hearing, possibly, had become
more acute, as the fire in the eyes had burnt more brightly,
from this same restriction of energy. Except for the
tumult of the invading army of winds, and the distant
clamour of the turning tide, the darkness was very silent ;
but, now, a bell could be heard clacking out, high up
under the dome. She opened her eyes. How she longed
to speak with that same iron voice, loud and strong
enough to make any meaning understood, any command
obeyed : and, because time had long since ceased to
have any significance for her, the metallic music occupied

an indefinite period, a stretch that rivalled the whole length of her lifetime. Still the bell racketed on. If only she could make herself heard as clearly; but the words stuck, stuck far down and would not creep out from the guttural hiding-places, while the iron voice upstairs was distinct and determined. Gradually this persistent music draped itself in her mind with a new beauty. She found herself back again in the long tunnel, and now there shone at the end of it, that for the first time she could see, an immense glory. The music, ever deeper and more magnificent, reached her, it seemed, from this burning majesty which she was so tirelessly approaching. As she strode on, for her lameness had left her, the gorgeous butterflies flew in front of her, the pursuing choir of angels rode the air level with her. The iron voice, which betrayed itself through their singing, at the end of the tunnel, was the voice of the Great Judge. She was going toward it. Now they were trying to drag her back, and she would then find herself once more lying there unable to move. They were trying to pull her back down that immeasurable corridor, but she would not turn. She must go on toward the Voice, march forward to the music; meet the Glory. She had left them; and silence and darkness received her.

    .   .   .   .   .   .

But the bell shrilled on. It had only been ringing for a second or two. The tin-tongue rattled through the silence of the empty building; so loudly it racketed that, surely, it must have pierced through the layers of cloud, at this season stretched like blankets, one over another endlessly, and must now echo through the ultimate blue imbecility above. But this lining was in the winter a thing utterly incredible ; while the grey blankets above and beneath yet invited slumber, warm deep slumber. But on and on it cackled, this idiot tongue, trying to inform the sleeper of its monotonous, invariable message, slave to a slave, machine to a machine. It seemed fearful, though, of betraying its trust. Six o'clock, six o'clock, six o'clock, it hammered and ranted. The sleeper could calculate precisely, through long experience, the last moment of this alarum. She swung back swiftly from her wanderings in the pine-forests of Germany, lumbered out of bed into the frozen air, switched on the light, tumbled into her tousled, rumpled clothes, and reset (as later she must reset her clock) her features into their daily, customary perspective. It grew colder and colder. Angrily she shook her body, turned out the light, and creaked blunderingly out of the room.

Now she was wading through the familiar stillness, a silence infringed by a thousand crepuscular crepitations of the hotel corridors. As she advanced, these minute, crackling vibrations were lost in the cascades of sound which her clumsy feet unloosed to dash up against tiled walls. Soon it would be light, she supposed. But before dawn came, there were the grates and the fires to do, and the boilers and the stoves, and the floors and the stairs ; and the grates and the fires and the boilers, the stoves and the floors, the stairs and the grates and the fires ; and her mind wandered without ceasing on this Housemaid's Miserere. It brought a sense of comfort, this recital of hardships. She would feel better by and by. She must light the fires.

First the flames were born in a faint blue flicker, and then, swiftly growing lusty, purred and coquetted at her from their iron cages. The rhythm of their lithe and feline movements woke the reflections that had been slumbering in their nests, high among the overwhelming gold frondage of cornice and capital, which had been overgrown in a breath by the bronze forest of the darkness. Directly the light was turned off, the jungle overgrew all this splendour ; but now all the richness was revealed, and the fire woke all these little reflections up in the branches, making them stir and preen themselves, and peep out of their dark, high nests as a wild creature, moving through a forest at night, would wake all the young birds, set them quivering and twittering.

Now it would grow warmer, she thought. But, as she drew aside the heavy plush curtains, and threw the shutters back, immediately the cold twilight poked and scratched at the window-panes with its sharp black claws, then moaned like a hunted animal that craves shelter. Blue frost flowers could be seen expanding and contracting on the glass, and the cruel wind squeezed through every crevice and conducted a paper chase high up into the grey air of the open space outside, above the Cannon and Anchor, whirling its quarry over and round them, while within the grates the flames for a moment shrank back, became sensitive plants that closed, opened and closed, their red petals. The floors next ; and, after that, would they want tea, she wondered ? The old lady was ill (oh, she'd seen it coming on, of course she had. Why she'd said as much to Miss Thompson a fortnight ago), too ill for tea, she expected. Only one cup of tea, that would mean, to make : but there was as much trouble in making one cup as two.

CHAPTER XXVI

SITUATION REQUIRED

" But why drives on that ship so fast
Without or wave or wind ? "

IT was a few days after the funeral. Miss Bramley had
been caught so fast in all the intricacies of business,
with which the recently dead yet contrive to entangle
the living, that, fortunately, she had been given little
time for reflection. Really, if the whole day was occupied, there was no time in which to think about oneself,
and by nightfall one was so fatigued (it could only be
called *dead-tired*) that sleep hurled itself down on one
like a boulder, knocked one senseless till the morning.
Still, she felt it : it was a break. And she had such a
headache (neuralgia, probably) that she felt inclined to
cry. Into the passage outside, through the half-open
door, was wafted that combined odour of old leather,
dead railway journeys, scented soap and camphor,
which denotes invariably that packing is in progress
somewhere in the vicinity. Indeed the shiny black trunk
revealed its canvas lining, with only a few, precious
things carefully stowed away at the bottom. There !
the chasuble was neatly folded up, wrapped in tissue-
paper, and placed within. It tired one's back, though,
leaning down, and lifting things. Now there were
the two scent-bottles (one had to be careful with glass)
and the piece of 1870 bread in its casket : better put that
at the bottom, too, she thought. It was wiser, perhaps,
to wrap up each photograph separately in tissue-paper,

and then they could not get spoiled. After all it was no use having nice things unless one looked after them properly. The frame was so fragile, wonderful work! The silver-backed brushes must be put in their wash-leather covers : but what was the best way of packing the silver boxes, the filigree box ? Porters were so rough, bumped things about without giving a thought to their value. All they considered was how to get the thing done quickly (she was so tired that, really, she felt she could drop !). There ! that was folded up nicely, too . . . of course she did not mind, but nevertheless it had been a blow—not that it had been Poor Cecilia's fault . . . no, it was the Floodgays that were responsible. The only comfort she could find was the fact that, at any rate, it had not benefited them. . . .

Miss Bramley had been authorized to arrange the service—Archdeacon Haddocriss had officiated—for a funeral was no place for Acting and Affectation. She had seen the solicitor afterwards—a typical lawyer with gold pince-nez and a special, official black-banded top hat for the funerals of his clients—and he had spoken to her very nicely, a cultivated man. " It is dreadful to talk, so soon after the dear old lady's death of such things as testamentary depositions," he had said, " but I should like to assure you that you have not been forgotten."

" Quite so."

" I ought not, perhaps, properly speaking, to tell you any more, but," he added, " I think it may be of comfort, as showing my client's fondness for you, to know that there was an unsigned will in your favour. She was very forgetful, and omitted to sign it. But you may rest assured that you will be treated with due gener-osity. In fact the next-of-kin, to whom the property passes, has already empowered me to give you any one piece of jewellery which you may choose as a memento of the deceased lady."

Miss Bramley said " Quite," again, for it was difficult for her to find another answer. So that was why Cecilia was always asking to be reminded about seeing the lawyer : that was why the dying woman had striven to talk, why she had looked at her in that intent, imploring way.

.   .   .   .   .   .

Miss Bramley had chosen a gold ring, with a curious design of two intercoiled serpents with ruby eyes. It reminded her of Cecilia, who had always worn it, and was very pretty in itself, she thought. She hoped it was not too " showy " for a Companion. The worst of it was that she was no longer as young as she had been (there was no use in disguising it, that was why she was so tired) and, though it seemed silly that it should do so, for, of course, one had much more experience, this undoubtedly made it more difficult to find a situation. She must not forget to buy the *Times*, when she went to the station. It was far and away the best paper in which to look.

It was odd, too, she thought, that she had not heard again from Mrs. Shrubfield or dear old Miss Waddington, very strange : for they had been so kind before the funeral ; both of them had asked her to stay for as long as she liked, placed their houses, practically, at her disposal. But when she had called two days after the funeral, Miss Waddington had been unwell. She must write to them, as there was not time in which to see them : they might know of something that would suit her. They had so many friends.

Here we may say that, as a matter of fact, on the afternoon on which Miss Bramley had called, the two Marshals were having tea at St. Saviour's Vicarage with Mrs. Floodgay. They had not spoken to that lady for two years, but after hearing that Miss Collier-Floodgaye's estate had passed to an unknown, distant cousin, they had felt that she was adequately punished for her offences against them. They had chanced to meet her in the street, the day after the funeral, and there had ensued (for the two old ladies were so impulsive) a lightning reconciliation. "Really," Miss Waddington observed to Mrs. Floodgay, "that little daughter of yours is getting so pretty . . . such lovely hair." At tea, the next day, they had confessed that they had found Miss Bramley's singing "attractive" (they were so *devoted* to music) but she had seemed to them rather . . . well . . . you know . . . rather materially-minded. . . .

.   .   .   .   .   .

Miss Bramley was ready to leave. The vast, black-canvas trunk was already placed on the top of a cab, of which it might have been the very bud or offspring, so much did it resemble its parent in shape and colouring. Just as she was passing through the hall on her way to the door, an elderly military-looking man stepped up to speak to her. It was Colonel Fansharpe. What an extraordinary coincidence: for she had been dreaming of him only the other night—just before Cecilia's death—and she had not seen him, or thought about him, for years! In fact she had not seen him since that snowy day on which she had driven away from Llandriftlog. He was most kind and affable. There was a lot of good in him really.

Colonel Fansharpe had been much struck by the coincidence of seeing her, too. " Fancy seeing her here !" he remarked to Mrs. Fansharpe (Ivy) afterwards. " She must be damned well off, that woman, to stay in an hotel like this ! *I* can't afford it for long . . . she's feathered her nest pretty well, that's evident. A scheming sort of woman, I'm afraid, my dear."

Elisa saw Miss Bramley into her cab. She was quite sorry to see her go. And soon Miss Bramley was slowly jolting past the green plot, with its Cannon and Anchor, past the bow-windowed seaside houses, past the terraces and crescents. The sea flicked a white arm above the walls at her for the last time, and she was in the station, buying the *Times*. " Situations Vacant," she read, " Gentlewoman wishes young Companion, artistic and refined. . . .

.   .   .   .   ,   .

EPILOGUE

" The paths of glory lead but to the grave."

THE Cannon was once more to assert its supremacy over the Anchor, which had held power for a century. During that period the triumph of this latter symbol had appeared, to most people, absolute and eternal. For a hundred years sudden misfortunes, violent death or dispersal of property, had been considered as things irregular, almost indecent, over which it was better modestly to draw a veil. Thus the subsequent adventures of various persons in this narrative are of interest to others, because so utterly unforeseen by themselves. Viewed from the crow's-nest of any of the ten previous decades, the events which were soon to overwhelm the inhabitants of this calm, rather stagnant town were so startling, that their sensations can only have been comparable to those experienced by the Roman Legion which, secure in the knowledge that the subterranean fires of their mountain were extinct, happened to be caught encamped in the crater of Vesuvius at the moment of its first historic eruption. To the people of Newborough, History had seemed dead as the flames of the volcano to the Legionaries. Indeed the corpse of the Dear Departed, who in her life-time had shown so many kindnesses to this country, had long been interred, her memory kept alive only by such ageing and recurrent

ritual as that with which children, here and there, still
celebrate Guy Fawkes Day, or, at intervals, by the
rarer, more dignified observance of Jubilee or Coronation.
But now the old harridan was to rush out of her prim,
neatly-kept grave, and sweep down without reason on
this unoffending place.   Further, she intended to insist
that those who had mourned her should now play the
principal part in a fresh funeral, that the audience should
become participant in the performance—a nightmare
drama that, for all we know, may not yet have been
brought to its culminative, last act, and of which the
present time may serve merely as a more or less quiet
ten minutes interval.

Some six years after our story ends, the "Great"
War broke out.   To this occurrence no one in Newborough was at first inclined to pay much attention.
For a few days it was feared by those retired Majors
of the Auxiliary Forces, to whom war always remains
an interesting possibility, that, as a Liberal Government
was in power, we might not be able to "join in the fun."
This conceivable restraint on our part would, they
agreed, damage fearfully our reputation for good sense
and sportsmanship.   One could always depend on the
Conservatives, if there was a war in progress in any part
of the world—or even if there was not—to plunge
into it, or, at any rate, to become entangled.   For
a day or two suspense hung like a purple thunder-cloud
over the Gentlemen's Club, where flushed and fuming,
sat ex-military officers and superannuated captains in
Yeomanry and Volunteers, in front of gargantuan
whiskies-and-sodas, swelling visible as they made known
their intention, by facial expression as much as vocally,
their intense determination to "do their bit," "keep a

stiff upper lip," and " see it through." Fortunately
there were no tragedies, for the Liberal Government
soon proved that in the hour of need it was everything
Conservative could wish.

The War began everywhere rather quietly. The
Regular Army, though by nature pacific, as are all regular
forces had long been prepared for *a* war—but, as usual,
not for the one that substantiated. This ideal European
conflict, which the military authorities, with their accustomed foresight, had seen coming, and to which, in spite
of all the evidence tending to disprove its identity, they
remained loyal during the opening months of the campaign, was one built on the model of the Boer War,
but larger and shorter ; it was only to last three weeks,
and was, in fact, to be a sort of prolonged Gentlemen v.
Players cricket match. The author, if he may be allowed
a personal confession, joined the army two years before
the War broke out ; and well remembers the talk of war
which was prevalent during 1913 and the first few months
of 1914 ; his memory retains the private prophecies of
Generals that a European War was coming (Everyone
must be ready for it. The shape of the men's toecaps
must be improved, and the right-hand man in the last left-
hand rank but one had the last button but one on his tunic
slightly loose), and their expressions of gratitude, to the
Providence which guarded Britain, that we should have
been vouchsafed the experience of a victorious Boer War
some years earlier as a training, a full-dress military
exercise, a transcendent rehearsal of the coming conflict.
The German army, meanwhile, had been for forty years
ploddingly preparing for the war of 1870, while the Russian Command was feverishly completing its lack of
arrangements for the Crimean Campaign ; for all armies,

unless directed by a genius, foresee and prepare for a war that is over—and never for the one that is on its way.

The embarkation and departure of the First Expeditionary Force from England caused little emotion in Newborough, where the passage by night, in specially constructed shuttered trains, of a mythical host of heavily bearded Cossacks, was much more eagerly discussed. Mrs. Shrubfield, who knew a little Russian, had distinctly heard a dark, bearded figure pitifully demanding vodka in the night, in his native tongue : one of Mrs. Toomany's favourite divorcees had met them at King's Cross when they arrived, and Mrs. Sibmarshe's sister had seen them at Ebur Station. Perhaps more attention would have been paid to the departure of the English troops, had the news of it not been so carefully censored and hidden. It was hardly until fighting began, that the English understood that their troops were in France.

And, by that time, a kindly Government had provided the country with the cry, which would have moved Napoleon to despair : " Business as Usual " ; and a great peace descended on all the people of Newborough —upon all except those few who had relatives fighting across the water. It was feared that the lodging-house keepers would suffer, for the town was rather empty of visitors. Otherwise life remained at present unaffected. The only alteration noticeable was the increased excitement of reading the newspapers. On the other hand, several leading persons answered the call for economy by giving up newspapers for the duration of the War. To these, life became increasingly halcyon. In the local sheets which Miss Waddington was in the habit of perusing, the list of names, with the rhythm of which

she lulled her nerves, was no longer that of stallholders
at charity bazaar or hospital ball, but of their young
male relatives lying dead in France or Flanders. Otherwise life was normal, there had been wars before, and
this one would not—could not—last for long.

.   .   .   .   .   .

It was a dull morning in the first December of the
" Great War," and Miss Waddington, then in her
eighty-seventh year was sitting propped up in bed at
8.30, before a creditable breakfast of tea, toast, poached
eggs and marmalade. The local newspaper was by
her side. So Mrs. Sibmarshe's son had been killed !
Well, one could never have foreseen that. But here
her attention was drawn away by the intruding damp
coldness of the morning—a rather unusual morning
for the time of year, it seemed to her ; though foggy and
cold, there was for once no sound of embattled wind and
wave. It was chilly, the old lady observed, distinctly
chilly in spite of the fire, and she was just asking for an
extra shawl (the light blue one in shell-stitch) when,
quite without warning, death darted at her from the sea,
and Miss Waddington, and her bedroom with her, was
pulverized, fading with a swift, raucous whistling and
crashing into the murky air. It was as though she had
never existed. But so loud was the raging steel voice
that Mr. Paul Bradbourne, right at the other end of the
town, heard a sound for the first time in forty-four years.
He was certain that he had heard something, while in
guarantee of it, he had felt an accompanying tremor,
the stamping of an angry metal giant. His jaw fell
open ; he was puzzled. He rushed to question his
housekeeper . . . but he was never to reach a sure
conclusion as to whether his senses had deceived him,

for the next moment he, too, was disintegrated, and the passing of Miss Waddington from life was most surely the last sound that ever reached him.

Within a few seconds the Superb Hotel stood like a gigantic honeycombed rock, full of gaping caves formerly the dwelling, it was obvious, of some race of splendour-loving troglodytes, for these caverns blazed with the most extraordinary relics of past grandeur, gold and scarlet and solid bronze. As one watched, fresh caves were opened up, each one with a deep roar, as though a ferocious, titanic guardian within were about to spring out and avenge the insult. The four domes puffed lightly into the air like bubbles. Shattered wood cracked and sagged at terrible angles. Next, the attacking ogre snatched away the bow-window of the Gentlemen's Club, but the telescope could still be seen pointing out of the wreckage as if it were a dis-mantled machine-gun. The hour was so early that fortunately no one was in the room to be injured. In all this desolation, only the Cannon and Anchor remained placid and undisturbed on their green cushion. Almost simultaneously the Cricket Pavilion melted into dust and greyness, and the Cemetery was out-raged by those ghoulish, giant hands. Elisa's friend, the Sexton, was killed—a fantastic death, for he was just given time enough to see the tombstones, eternal "Aberdeen" as much as plain ivy-bordered stone, hurled tumbling and whirling through the air, while white marble angels fluttered up into the mist to vanish, allowing the skulls of the lean skeletons beneath to leer hungrily from rusty coffins. The Cemetery happened to shield the Power-Station, and that no doubt was the objective.

The worst was now over : but meanwhile many of the

squares, crescents and terraces that faced South had been transformed into the likeness of excavated cities, and many were those shaken survivors who wished that, in defiance of both custom and medical advice, they had faced North. The inland trains were crowded for several days. And Mr. St. Rollo Ramsden, calm and cherry-lipped as ever, was surprised on arriving at St. Saviour's Vicarage in order to enquire after the safety of Mrs. Floodgay, to observe in the hall mirror that he was wearing a tie, without its usual appendage, the collar! He hurried back through the stricken streets, nervously clutching his neck; for even, in adversity, Newborough eyes were sharp in their scrutiny, and when one was a public man, one had to be careful . . . these stories do so much harm.

. . . . . .

Now it may appear from the account above that Destiny had finished with Miss Waddington. But such was most certainly not the case. Her end did not constitute the annihilation that might have been imagined, indeed it was only after her forcible and unexpected end that the frail form of Miss Waddington impinged upon History, and then upon Art. Her doom was not confined to herself, but, in this comparable to an octopus, after the preliminary fog of ink discharged by the journalists, had enveloped it, was to fasten its tentacles on to thousands of young men, sucking and dragging them down to the depths where they would be devoured. For some reason or other the fate of this particular old woman was seized on as an aid to recruiting. The country blazed with placards, on which was printed in staring, red letters:

REMEMBER NEWBOROUGH AND HESTER WADDINGTON

Her age was the chief attraction emphasized, but, in addition she was described as " a rare and gracious presence, and an inspiration to the poor and needy." Little stories, illustrative of her dauntless courage and indomitable patriotism were related in every newspaper. Her niece, it was written, had on one occasion tried to hide from her a paper containing a Roll of Honour, in which was announced the slaughter of a cousin ; but the aged lady, like the Spartans of old, had insisted on reading it through, indeed over and over again, merely remarking, " He is not the first Waddington to pay the penalty "—a comment with which the niece may have agreed. Then there was the yet more moving tale related by a friend who had begun to read aloud to her —for her eyesight was failing—an account of the Retreat from Mons. The dear old lady had proudly interrupted— interrupted in words, which, though she knew it not, were afterwards destined to become famous. " Do not read it to me," she said, " it is painful and unnecessary *I* am content to know that our lads are doing their duty." But later she was found, with her old eyes glued close to the journal, draining in privacy the last dregs of a bitter cup.

Bishops preached sermons on her fidelity, and a cabinet minister made a touching reference to her in his famous oration at a Guildhall Banquet.

" The Allies," he said, " are not fighting for trade, territory, or an indemnity. They do not demand an inch of enemy ground, they will refuse to receive, when the time comes—as come it must—even one bar of gold ; but, speaking as an old servant, however unworthy, of my country (hrump, hrump ; and after coughing, he surveyed the rosy faces round him), I say, I say again, and I reiterate, that we will not replace the sabre in its holster, nor the musket in its scabbard—until Russia has been requited, France rewarded, and Belgium and Servia avenged and recompensed—and more than recompensed—for the outrages committed upon them; or our reputation for justice will be forfeit, and the name of Hester Waddington will be indelibly inscribed upon the shield of a Nation's Shame—nay, more—of an Empire's Infamy."

The propaganda was effective. Thousands of young men, out of horror at the atrocious death inflicted upon this defenceless old woman, as she sat up in bed before a typically English breakfast, besieged the recruiting-stations, subsequently to be dealt out a variant of her own fate, but on the more remote fields of France and Flanders, Mesopotamia and Turkey. Thus at the moment of her cruelly sudden atomization, Miss Waddington entered the sphere of History, and remained as she had always been, a leader. Now it was that she was to make her first curtsy in the world of Art.

By this time the interest in Miss Waddington, instead of being merely a thing foisted on the public by the journalists and recruiting-authorities in league, had become genuine. The public had become attached to this new heroine, and raised, quite on its own initiative, a considerable sum of money to celebrate her likeness in marble. After having made so much use of the missing corpse of the old lady, it was impossible for the Government to refuse to support any effort for her further glorification. Consequently, her statue (erected in a style of which, had she been alive, she would have disapproved so vehemently as to raise unfounded suspicions in the mind as to its possible merits) now stands as a centre of provincial pilgrimage in Trafalgar Square. As a matter of fact this representation, if such it can be called, of the old lady, is not the work as might at first be imagined, of a young Servian sculptor demented by the horrors of the invasion, and subsequently interned for the duration of the War in a Berlin studio, but of an almost crippled Academician, several years senior in age to Miss Waddington. How this little, old bent man achieved such an energetic group remains a miracle! He had, however, manifestly decided " to keep up with the times," and in spite of a vicious hatred for everything good in the modern movement (while, for example, he always lends the prestige of his name to the periodic demands for the removal or mutilation of any new Work of Art, such as Epstein's " Rima," which happens, by some mischance, to find itself jostled among the vile mob of London statues) had, with true academic eclecticism, adopted all the tricks of the advance-guards, and added them to all the laid-aside tricks of every other move-ment in history. The whole conception, however, is simple and affected, and bears no resemblance to the old lady in figure or countenance. It is also extremely allegorical, for allegory is very remunerative to the sculptor, if costly to those subscribing. It is impossible to ask much for " a plain likeness," but throw in a figure or two of Liberty and Justice, and you can at once sex-tuple your demand by an artistic process of compound multiplication.

The group shows Miss Waddington, a rather unrobed, muscular giantess of ample bosom and straining neck, holding up a large male baby of doubtful symbolism in one hand, and a Bible, or bank-book, or something, in the other. Behind her the lachrymose figures of Justice and Liberty proffer a shawl, like a fishing net; while the octogenarian maiden lady's naked feet are entangled with crosses, cupids, anchors, lifebuoys, shell-cases and banners. The pedestal is quite plain save for the inscription:

HESTER WADDINGTON
PRO PATRIA
"I AM CONTENT TO KNOW THAT OUR LADS
ARE DOING THEIR DUTY."

Her niece, Ella, survives her, but is in a home, suffering from shock. She does not realize that Aunt Hester is dead, and is for ever answering her imaginary calls, and looking for her in corners.

Mrs. Shrubfield barely tided over the War. She came through the actual experience with colours flying, and had left Newborough, for ever, two days after the sea had once more quickened it with history, to take up residence in London. She was immensely interested in the fate and renown which the War had brought her old ally, and was often to be seen in front of the Waddington Memorial with a pensive tear suspended in the corner of her jet twinkling eye. Herself indulged in an orgy of sock-knitting, gave up the use of all German words and the consumption of all non-alcoholic liquors for the period of the conflict: further she did canteen work, and stood for hours behind a bar, serving out drinks to others, in spite of her own need, after the example of Sir Philip Sidney. Alas, while participating largely in the celebrations that inaugurated the Great Peace, when finally it came as a fitting reward for the " Great " War, she expired suddenly from Spanish Influenza—or " La Grippe," as, even in her last moments, she preferred to call it—a suitably cosmopolitan illness, but one which was the direct result of the conflict : so that she perished as much a victim of the hostilities as any man who fell in battle.

Elisa was arrested and interned in the latter part of August, 1914. But, after the calamity at Newborough, she rested under the most grave suspicion. Not only had she been employed for many years in the Superb Hotel, which had been so devastated, but it was now recalled that she had often been detected mooning about, in an apparently quite purposeless way (as it was then thought, by the inhabitants in their good-natured folly) or trying to enter into conversation with the Sexton. And, before she had been arrested, she had been caught turning on the light after dark in one of the hotel rooms which faced the ocean : what was more, the window was uncurtained. At the time, she said her action was due to force of habit, but it was easy, now, to understand to whom she had been signalling across the grey wastes. Nothing, however, could be proved against her, and she was therefore allowed to remain, though, naturally, under special surveillance, in one of those civilian concentration camps, where, since prisoners were so indulgently treated, she was doubtless happy.

Though Mr. St. Rollo Ramsden came through the Bombardment personally unscathed, he was to know sorrow. He gave his white-haired and aged mother to the cause. After the ordeal at Newborough, though uninjured, she felt that it was fairer on her children to move to London, and went on a prolonged visit to a niece living at Hampstead. There, one dark night, a bomb fell, and poor old Mrs. Ramsden paid the Supreme Sacrifice. His mother's tragic end must have acted as an incitement to renewed patriotic effort, for the energy of Mr. St. Rollo Ramsden during those dreadful years acknowledged no limitations. In the inland town, to which as Headmaster, as guardian of his pupils, he had thought it wiser temporarily to remove his boys, he achieved endless useful work for his country. His gift of eloquence made him in demand at every local recruiting meeting. He sat on a Tribunal, and was tireless in ferreting-out conscientious objectors. Generally speaking, he set an example. This was no moment for self-indulgence, and in a true spirit of sacrifice, he unhesitatingly cut down by half the rations of the boys under his care. In addition, meat was allowed only once a week, and himself gave up more sugar, and believed more spy-stories, than anyone in the neighbourhood. He was deservedly popular in his new abode, and it was with great regret that the townspeople saw him leave them, when the Great Peace came, to move his school back to its original, salubrious habitat. Many of his former pupils, though, lay dead in Europe and Asia ; and he caused two beautiful tablets to be erected in the School Chapel—one to his mother, the other to the Old Boys. Indeed it may be said that the Headmaster's Valediction to the Fallen, at the unveiling of these Memorials, will long be remembered by those present at the ceremony. His reputation as an orator was still further enhanced, and it is understood that he nurses new ambitions— that, in fact, he would be willing to seek election to Parliament in order to help ward off the Red Menace. But the town is not so Conservative as it was before the War. The Ghoolingham influence, for example, is no longer there to help the candidate. Up till 1914, in spite of the predatory budgets which were so often denounced, that influence was still paramount, as it had been for three centuries : but Lord Ghoolingham died in 1915, and both his sons were killed serving their country, which, in grateful recognition of their services, mulcted each corpse in enormous death duties, and completed the ruin of the family. The title is extinct, the land and houses have been sold.

Mrs. Toomany, on the other hand, gained rather than lost by her war experience. She contrived to attach herself to a rather disreputable woman of good family, who ran a canteen in France. She vastly enjoyed the work, and later reaped the golden harvest which she had helped to sow—that great crop of gilded divorce cases which is the one clear result of the War.

Cécile Floodgay married a young officer in the Artillery, who was stationed at Newborough Barracks, a year or two before hostilities broke out. They had very little money but were extremely happy . . . he was buried alive by the fall of a shell when with his battery near Ypres, and his widow survives him solely because of her love for her young son, and her belief in spiritualism. The child is said to bear the strongest resemblance to his maternal grandfather, the present Bishop of Gothland, and is already an accomplished mimic.

Sir Timothy Tidmarshe died shortly after King Edward's death. His august relict, recovered from her surprise at the discovery of that ruby and diamond tiara which was found under some clothes, at the bottom of a chest of drawers, continued to live in Newborough. But the bombardment brought her growing invisibility to an unlooked-for climax. Her sons, however, though all good, indeed distinguished soldiers, by the strange fortunes of war, outlived her, and still quarrel fiercely among themselves to this day.

It is better to omit the full recital of these things, of how, as an indirect consequence of the War, little Miss Penelope Finnis was forced to starve herself to a genteel death—for all the rich tradesmen of the town had moved inland, so that there were no girls to instruct in the arts of young ladyhood—while Miss Pansy, left alone, was driven into an asylum; of how Dr. Mac-Racket died of smallpox in Mesopotamia, and poor Mr. de Flouncey's only son was burnt to death in a falling aeroplane. About these things there is such a lack of proportion. The penalties are too severe to be credited. That such things, too, should happen to the descendants of fallen angels is undignified: indeed the position is somewhat improved if, instead, the view is adopted that this is a forged genealogy, and that the genuine pedigree of man is an ascent from the chattering, swarming tribes of simians, ever inquisitive, ever examining and inventing, whose only fall was from a tree-top, in the course of a voyage of perilous but splendid discovery; and that the only bad ape is the stagnant, incurious ape.

OXFORD

MORE TWENTIETH-CENTURY CLASSICS

Details of a selection of Twentieth-Century Classics follow. A complete list of Oxford Paperbacks, including The World's Classics, OPUS, Past Masters, Oxford Authors, Oxford Shakespeare, and Oxford Paperback Reference, as well as Twentieth-Century Classics, is available in the UK from the General Publicity Department, Oxford University Press, Walton Street, Oxford OX2 6DP.

In the USA, complete lists are available from the Paperbacks Marketing Manager, Oxford University Press, 200 Madison Avenue, New York, NY 10016.

THE ROOT AND THE FLOWER

L. H. Myers

Introduced by Penelope Fitzgerald

Myers's great trilogy is set in exotic sixteenth-century India and records a succession of dynastic struggles during the ruinous reign of Akbar the Great Mogul. It is an absorbing story of war, betrayal, intrigue, and political power, but Myers's ultimate interests lie with the spiritual strengths and weaknesses of his major characters. The book explores a multitude of discrepancies—for example the difference between the vastness of the Indian plains and the intricacy of an ants' nest—and yet attempts subtly to balance them. Throughout the trilogy Myers persists in his aim to reconcile the near and the far. *The Root and the Flower* demonstrates both his determination and his elegance in doing so, and, it has been said, 'brought back the aspect of eternity to the English novel'.

BIRD ALONE

Sean O'Faoláin

Introduced by Benedict Kiely

In late nineteenth-century Ireland Corney Crone grows up in a family marked by poverty, pride, and spoiled aspirations. The recurring theme in his own life is the Faustian one of solitude, present in the private dreams of his boyhood and the insistent independence of his manhood. In old age the note of loneliness is more dominant: he is the 'bird alone', reliving the experiences of his youth, above all the secret love for his childhood sweetheart, which began in innocence and happiness, and ended in tragedy and shame.

Everywhere the book shows a poetic mastery of its material and a deep understanding of human nature. Corney Crone's private joys and sufferings belong to a common humanity, and as we read, his experiences become ours.

THE SMALL BACK ROOM

Nigel Balchin

Introduced by Benny Green

Sammy Rice is one of the 'back-room boys' of the Second World War. The small back room of the title may also be Sammy's own living quarters, where he tries to control a drinking habit, and lives with a woman he loves but won't marry for fear of imprisoning her in a life he sees being slowly eroded by the unreality of war.

As an account of the war experience, the book is realistic and unsettling, and as a study of a personality under stress, it reveals perennial truths. As Benny Green says, 'to the battle which Sammy Rice wages against himself no precise date can be attached. The struggle goes on'.

'His theme is of intense and irresistible interest.' *New Statesman*

THE NOTEBOOK OF MALTE LAURIDS BRIGGE

Rainer Maria Rilke

Translated by John Linton

Introduced by Stephen Spender

The Notebook of Malte Laurids Brigge, first published in 1910, is one of Rilke's few prose works. It has at its eponymous hero a young Danish poet, living in poverty in Paris, and is closely based on Rilke's bohemian years in the city at the turn of the century. In Malte's *Notebook* present and past intertwine. He is fascinated by squalor and observes the poor and sick of Paris, victims of fate like himself. Sickness intensifies his imagination, and he recreates the horrors of childhood, probing the many faces of death. It was in this novel that Rilke developed the precise, visual style which is largely associated with his writing.

THE VIOLINS OF SAINT-JACQUES

Patrick Leigh Fermor

Epilogue by Simon Winchester

The Violins of Saint-Jacques, originally published in 1953, is set in the Caribbean on an island of tropical luxury, European decadence, and romantic passion, the story captures both the delicacy of high society entanglements and the unforeseen drama of forces beyond human control. Throughout, the writing is as beautiful and haunting as the sound of the violins which rises from the water and conceals the story's mystery.

'Beautiful is the adjective which comes uppermost . . . outstanding descriptive powers' John Betjeman

TURBOTT WOLFE

William Plomer

Introduced by Laurens van der Post

When this novel first appeared in 1925 the wide critical appreciation it attracted in England was matched by the political controversy it caused in South Africa. It remains acutely relevant, and if, as Turbott Wolfe declares, 'Character is the determination to get one's own way', then history bears the mark of this book and testifies to the depth of its perception.

Plomer records the struggle of a few against the forces of prejudice and fear. The book is full of images of exploitation and atrocity. Yet it is also the love story of a man who finds beauty where others have seen only ugliness. The narrative, which never shrinks from witnessing the unforgivable, is also characterized by sensitivity and self-control, and in the end manages perhaps the most we are capable of: continuing bravery, the voice of individual affirmation.

DEAD MAN LEADING

V. S. Pritchett

Introduced by Paul Theroux

An expedition to rescue a man missing in the Brazilian jungle becomes a journey of self-discovery for his son. Conradian in conception, the treatment in the novel of obsession, verging on madness, is strikingly original.

'a rich, original and satisfying book' *Spectator*

'The events of the story are dramatic and often frightening, but more important is the skill with which the author uses the tensions within and between the explorers to comment on the complexity of human aspiration.' *The Times*

SEVEN DAYS IN NEW CRETE

Robert Graves

Introduced by Martin Seymour-Smith

A funny, disconcerting, and uncannily prophetic novel about Edward Venn-Thomas, a cynical poet, who finds himself transported to a civilisation in the far future. He discovers that his own world ended long ago, and that the inhabitants of the new civilisation have developed a neo-archaic social system. Magic rather than science forms the basis of their free and stable society; yet, despite its near perfection, Edward finds New Cretan life insipid. He realizes that what is missing is a necessary element of evil, which he feels is his duty to restore.

'Robert Graves' cynical stab at creating a Utopia is a poetic *Brave New World* filled with much more colour and dreaming than the original *Brave New World* of Aldous Huxley.' Maeve Binchy

THE ROCK POOL

Cyril Connolly

Introduced by Peter Quennell

'A snobbish and mediocre young literary man from Oxford, with a comfortable regular income, spends the summer on the Riviera with an artists' and writers' colony. His first attitude is interested but patronizing: he tells himself that he has come as an observer and will study the community like a rock pool. But the denizens of the pool drag him down into it. . . The story, which owes something to *South Wind* and Compton Mackenzie's novels of Capri, differs from them through its acceleration, which, as in the wildly speeded-up burlesque, has something demoniacal about it.' Edmund Wilson